The Duke and The Enchantress

THE ENCHANTRESSES BOOK TWO

PAULLETT GOLDEN

This book contains an excerpt from the forthcoming novel *The Baron and The Enchantress* by Paullett Golden. This excerpt has been set for this edition only and may not reflect final content of the forthcoming edition.

Also by Paullett Golden

The Enchantresses Series
The Earl and The Enchantress
The Duke and The Enchantress
The Baron and The Enchantress
The Colonel and The Enchantress
The Heir and The Enchantress

The Sirens Series
A Counterfeit Wife

Romantic Encounters
A Dash of Romance
A Touch of Romance

Romantic Flights of Fancy
Hourglass Romance

Praise for The Enchantresses

"Readers who enjoy a character driven romance will find this a story well worth reading. Paullett Golden is an author I will be following."

— *Roses R Blue Reviews*

"I would say this is a very well-written novel with engaging characters, a compelling story, a satisfactory resolution, and I am eagerly anticipating more from Ms. Golden."

— *Davis Editorials*

"With complex characters and a backstory with amazing depth, the story… is fantastic from start to finish."

— *Rebirth* author Ravin Tija Maurice

"I thoroughly enjoyed meeting and getting to know all of the characters. Each character was fully developed, robust and very relatable."

— *Flippin' Pages Book Reviews*

"What I loved about the author was her knowledge of the era! Her descriptions are fresh and rich. Her writing is strong and emotionally driven. An author to follow."

— *The Forfeit* author Shannon Gallagher

"It is a story that just keeps giving and giving to the reader and I, for one, found it enchanting!"

— The Genre Minx Book Reviews

"The minor King Arthur plot was also a lovely touch, and the descriptions of the library fulfilled my book-loving dream."

— Rosie Amber Reviews

"The author adds a few extra ingredients to the romantic formula, with pleasing results. An engaging and unconventional love story."

— Kirkus Reviews

"This novel highlights how love can cast away the darkness of soul and mind."

—Author Esquire Reviews

THE ENCHANTRESS FAMILY TREE

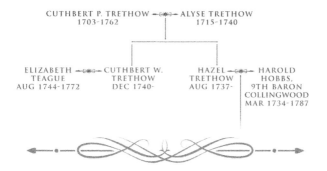

CUTHBERT P. TRETHOW ⟢✶⟣ ALYSE TRETHOW
1703-1762   1715-1740

ELIZABETH ⟢✶⟣ CUTHBERT W.   HAZEL ⟢✶⟣ HAROLD
TEAGUE   TRETHOW   TRETHOW   HOBBS,
AUG 1744-1772   DEC 1740-   AUG 1737-   9TH BARON
                                                  COLLINGWOOD
                                                  MAR 1734-1787

Visit www.paullettgolden.com/the-enchantresses
to view the complete Enchantress Family Tree

*This book is dedicated to my parents
for their love and encouragement.*

A special thanks to Mercury for her patience and support during the long nights of writing.

Newly Revised Edition

This book is a clean historical romance. There are references to kissing and innuendos to marital intimacy, but this is a closed-door romance.

The Duke and The Enchantress was originally published in 2018 as a steamy historical romance but has been fully revised in this new edition as a clean read.

While the original version is still available in audiobook format and by request to the author, all digital and print versions available for purchase have been replaced by this new, clean edition.

If you enjoy reading this book and wish to share it with friends and family, refer with confidence that the version they purchase will be the clean edition. If in doubt, ensure this revision note appears before Chapter 1. I hope you'll enjoy reading the new edition, as this edit has been a labor of love and one I'm proud to share with all readers!

Chapter 1

July 1790

Miss Charlotte Trethow married the Duke of Annick, and all her dreams came true.

Happy ever after started with the chime of the wedding bells, did it not? Charlotte should be laughing with delight as the ducal state coach swayed towards her future in a land far, far away.

Instead, she frowned, eyeing warily her sleeping bridegroom. The nuptials had been conferred only hours prior.

She didn't feel like a duchess.

All she could think as the carriage rolled in the opposite direction of civilization was what happened *after* marriage to duke charming. Not for a moment during their courtship had she considered what happened after the wedding. She had been too distracted by her attraction to him to care.

Dazzled, really. It had been her first time to London and her come-out Season to boot. Nothing could have prepared her for the glitz, glamor, and charm of the Season, much less for *him*. His half-lidded eyes, whispered compliments, and charismatic smile had swept her off her feet at their first meeting. His lips had done the rest.

Even now, her cheeks flushed at the sight of him, her memories of their stolen kisses.

He had wedged himself in the corner of the carriage bench, at ease in the well-sprung vehicle. Long limbs stretched across the floor. Fingers laced over his waistcoat. His breathing punctuated by soft snores. Even in sleep, he was somehow devilishly attractive. She found him irresistible with his lithe physique, the build of a sabreur. Only with him sleeping did she feel confident in admiring him so openly — duchesses should never so boldly eye their husband.

His was the porcelain complexion of a nobleman, accentuated by his ebony hair, fashionably brushed forward, heavy on top and cropped short on the sides and back. Blue eyes, a deep sapphire, although now lidded, never failed to flutter her heart at every glance. His aristocratic nose was well-proportioned to his narrow face. And then those lips. Soft, red, and pouty; she loved his lips.

Dazzled wasn't a strong enough word for the attraction she had felt during their month-long acquaintance. Mesmerized? So mesmerized by his attention to her, and yes, even his title, so enraptured to be the envy of her friends and choice of the most eligible bachelor of the Season, she hadn't stopped to think of life after marriage.

As the thrill of the ceremony dissipated, she knew dread. It began as a small twinge at the base of her spine, but the further the carriage traveled, the stronger the sensation, now nearly consuming her. It was one thing to be the envy of one's peers, but it was *she* who must leave all she knew behind to live as the wife of a perfect stranger.

Not only had she married a man she didn't know the first thing about aside from his ability to find every dark corner at a ball, she had married into a title she couldn't possibly uphold.

Oh, Charlotte from before the wedding would think her a silly ninny for fretting. She was a *duchess* for crying in a teacup! Who wouldn't want to be a duchess? And who wouldn't want to be married to the Duke of Annick? It wasn't so much that her current self didn't want these things as she wasn't certain what to *do* with them.

A lengthy week's journey lay ahead, after which point, she would meet her mother-in-law, sister-in-law, and new home. The idea of being a duchess had seemed dreamy, as had snagging the most eligible bachelor of the Season, but as reality set in, so crept the dread.

She feared above all things the humiliation of failure.

How did one be a duchess? And then there was the new role of wife with which to contend. Could she satisfy her worldly husband? He had been her first kiss, but she wasn't naïve enough to think she had been his. After all, her sister had warned her of his rakish reputation before the courtship began. At the time, it had intrigued her. Now, she was intimidated, if not a tad frightened. Would her inexperience disappoint him? Would he reform himself of his flirtatious tendencies now that he was wed? *Could* a rake be reformed? Her sister thought not, but Charlotte believed if she could be perfect for him, he would want only her, if she could prove herself the perfect duchess.

Charlotte could only hope the journey north would provide opportunities to accustom herself to the changes in life and to her husband. Perhaps, upon better acquaintance with him, she wouldn't feel so low in station, experience, or beauty. As of now, she felt distinctly inferior. Although the finery of wealth and status surrounded her in the plush velvet padding of the carriage, she worried what would happen next.

A cough disturbed her train of thought.

Her gaze shifted from her husband — Drake Mowbrah, the Duke of Annick — to the man seated next to him — his cousin, Sebastian Lancaster, the Earl of Roddam.

The beast of a cousin glowered out the window, making no effort to engage his new cousin-in-law in polite conversation. Charlotte would never get to know her husband with this brooder present. She didn't want him in the carriage, least of all when she was meditating on Drake's lips and discomposed about the wedding night and life beyond, but what was the alternative? He certainly couldn't ride with the servants in the four-carriage caravan heading north, and he expressed no interest in riding alongside their carriage with the outriders.

The two men shared attributes, with their matching profiles and black hair, except the cousin looked more like a common laborer than a gentleman. His skin was tanned, eyes black as coals, hair unfashionably long, and shoulders broad with the sinewy build of a worker. He spoke only when spoken to, and even then, did little more than grunt. This wild animal trapped in their honeymoon carriage gave her chills.

The carriage slumped to one side, hitting a rut in the road, then jolted forward. Drake's head bounced against his chest, waking him.

Alert and alarmed, he braced himself against the side of the carriage. "Is it highwaymen? Are we under attack?" Drake peered out the window to see placid countryside.

The brute spoke for the first time. "Your snoring startled the horses."

The duke rumbled a laugh. "Too right, old man. Too right." Turning to Charlotte, his eyelids lowered sleepily in what she had learned was his flirty expression, he asked, "How is my wife enjoying the view?"

Flustered by those suggestive eyes, she replied primly, "The meadow flowers are lovely."

"I didn't mean the view outside." He leaned forward and rubbed her knee with his slender fingers. "I meant the view of me."

Taken aback by the physical contact in view of his cousin and the boldness of his words, she swatted at his hand, tutting. "I haven't the faintest what you mean."

"Do you like what you see?" He swept his hands over his torso, inviting her admiration.

Before she could respond, scold, or otherwise, Drake turned to his cousin with a mischievous grin and winked.

How — oh! She bristled and sat straighter. How dare he be so crude? And in front of the cousin! His implication that she had been ogling him in his sleep, however true, was beyond the pale. And that wink! Oh!

Of all his flirting in London, he'd only ever spoken sweetness to her, never words laced with insinuation, his flirtation enough to charm the birds from the trees.

Never had he flirted so openly before another person, either, only innocent teasing, typically at someone else's expense, not hers.

Charlotte smoothed her traveling dress with trembling hands. Humiliated, outraged, and flustered, she avoided eye contact. Perhaps she was overreacting. Her cheeks flamed, nonetheless. Flicking her eyes to the door handle, she had the impulse to leap out and run back to London, join her sister and father for the trip home. She was out of her element and knew not how to behave.

Drake clearly didn't require a response, as he leaned back in his seat with a leer, folding his hands behind his head before closing his eyes again.

With the heat of her cheeks singeing her skin, Charlotte crossed her arms and pressed herself against the cushioned bench, wishing she could disappear into the velvet. Her happily-ever-after wedding to duke charming might have been a mistake.

There were two types of women in the world: those who fawned over Drake for his fashionable good looks, the power behind his name, and his easy flirtation, and those who thought him an arrogant rake. Thankfully, his new bride was the former.

His bride. Charlotte Mowbrah, Duchess of Annick. Even her name tasted sweet.

She would make a perfect duchess and a perfect wife. She may not have the training for nobility as did many of the ladies who had sought his affections in London, but for that he found her all the sweeter. The daughter of a Member of Parliament, wealthy, eager to please, and as accomplished as anyone would wish a wife to be, especially when it came to kissing him.

Of course, she could play the pianoforte, sing, dance, embroider, and all necessary skills, but her lips won him over above all other possible mates. He felt a fire behind her lips, the fire of desire and love. Nothing would please him more than a spouse who matched his own needs and wants.

Desire first, followed by love. Priorities, of course.

He regretted not staying in London for the evening so they might share their first evening together in his own residence rather than an inn along the way, but no matter. Arrangements had been made to rent the entire inn, fashioning it with the ducal linens and finery before their caravan arrived.

Drake didn't need a noble London house to woo his bride. All he should need was a glass of wine and words of endearment. She had, after all, married him because she was infatuated, not for anything as distasteful as the title. So infatuated with him, he would not have been surprised if she proposed they stop in one of those flower meadows she kept eyeing so they could celebrate their nuptials early. Alas, his cousin shared the drive. That must give her pause.

Anticipation would have to build before they could exchange those words of endearment. Admittedly, it'd been far too long since he had enjoyed an evening with a woman, far longer than he would admit to any living soul, even his cousin. A man had a reputation to keep, after all. Far be it for Drake to negatively tarnish his own reputation as a lover by night and, well, a lover by day.

The journey would break soon for tea, a change of horses, and carriage maintenance. He wondered if she'd be eager to find one of those dark corners during the next stop.

One look at her clenched jaw told him she would have none of that, at least not yet. No, she would want a private suite before he could accomplish anything more than a chaste kiss. Judging from the whiteness of her knuckles as her fingers tightened around the edges of her pelisse, she might insist even chaste kisses could wait until the evening.

He certainly hoped not. It had taken him far too long to find someone genuinely interested in more than his name, and he refused to waste a single moment by denying his feelings. Drake wanted to express his affection and feel it returned. He needed it as a gambler needed a win, as a bell ringer needed a drink at the inn. Amour. Sweet amour. The elixir of life.

Clearing his throat to ease the growing warmth beneath his starched shirt points, he asked Charlotte, "What's the first thing you'll do as lady of the manor?" Willing her to say *kiss him* would accomplish nothing good, he presumed.

She looked away from the window, eyes wide with uncertainty. Her expression showed a flicker of apprehension mixed with annoyance, as if he had teased her about skipping across the front lawn in wrapping gowns. Not that he'd be opposed to such frivolity.

"Are you quizzing me?" she questioned.

Uncertain what she meant, he said nothing, merely raised his eyebrows.

After biting her bottom lip in thought, she asked, "What is it you wish for me to do?"

What did he—well, aside from express her love for him, he had no expectations. Did she expect him to be a tyrannical husband? He hoped he'd never given that impression.

Perhaps he'd married too young of a woman. Youth seemed to give way to self-consciousness rather than impulsiveness. He wanted impulsiveness and spontaneity. He wanted her to throw caution to the wind, to assert herself. He had thought by marrying her, a lady only eighteen making her come-out into Society, she would be full of excitement and energy, ready to give his mother the boot to the dower house, and, naturally, spend her days loving him uninhibited. Perhaps he had misjudged.

No, he shouldn't doubt his decision, not when she lit a fire in his breast as no other woman had.

Studying her heart-shaped face, her chestnut hair, and her copper eyes, he felt himself sliding into a dream, one in which she would reach across the carriage, grab him by his waistcoat, and plant a kiss for all the world to see—or at least for Sebastian to see, and perhaps any outriders looking this direction. It was not the kiss he wanted—well, that too—so much as her affection, her open declaration to the world that he was her choice above all others, *him*. Not even in his hazed dream could he describe what exactly it was he wanted other than to think of it as desire, affection, attraction, that *something* she felt for him and no one else. Marriage was not enough. He needed... wait, what had she asked? Deuce take it. He couldn't recall the conversation.

Playing it off, he dashed her a naughty grin and waited for her to speak again.

"What do you do as lord of the manor?" she finally asked.

"What do *I* do? I don't do anything." As way of explanation, he added, "I'm a duke."

His cousin snorted.

"You can't do nothing all day," she insisted.

"Why not?" He let his gaze drop to the slender arch of her neck.

"Well, because, um, well, you're a *duke*, practically royalty, really, and so you have responsibilities and estate business and…." She drifted off, at a loss for exactly what dukes did other than sit in carriages across from beautiful brides.

"That's the benefit of being a duke, is it not? To do absolutely nothing except enjoy the spoils of estate managers' labors."

Only a half lie. Drake's mother had served as head of the household since his father's death ten years ago, giving him a chance to attend Oxford, enjoy his Grand Tour, and attend every social function he desired before returning home to rule the roost. Even before that, he was positive his mother ran the household. Drake's father had been far too old to lead the dukedom himself and had ensured his much younger wife would be happy doing exactly what she enjoyed — running everyone else's life.

Drake knew he really should take more of an interest, especially with a new wife, but then, that was the point: he hoped his wife would be the one to take an interest and usurp his mother. It was yet another reason he had chosen Charlotte as his bride. He was certain she would take to being the matriarch of their little family. His role would be to lavish her with affection.

"What do you do with your time, then?" she asked.

"All manner of amusements. Admire beautiful women named Charlotte, fence with Winston, play at truth-saying and peacemaking among the Northumberland rabble, enjoy a billiard game after supping, spend copious amounts of time with Sebastian, and sleep until noon. Oh, did I mention admire beautiful women named Charlotte?" He punctuated his question with a wink.

"I see." She didn't look impressed. Her luscious lips set in a grim line.

What did she expect life would be like? All work and no play? Perhaps for the tenantry, but not for the nobility, not for him.

"I'm convinced you're teasing me." The grim line twitched into a feigned smile. "Now, be serious. I would like to spend the drive discovering what interests we share. Do you, by chance, enjoy music?"

"There are any number of things I enjoy."

"Oh?" Her eyebrows arched. "Like what?"

"Kissing you." He took a moment to openly admire her with a long and appreciative gaze.

"Of all the inappropriate — *oof*!" The grim line of those heavenly lips pursed until the lips disappeared altogether. Pity.

"I don't see why it would be inappropriate. We're married." Drake tried to dazzle her with a smile, but she had none of it.

She was seriously testing his mood.

Their courtship had been such a whirlwind, they hadn't got to know each other all that well, if he were being quite honest with himself. Be that as it may, he noted her behavior had shifted since the wedding.

The Charlotte during courtship had giggled at his flirtations and kissed him in dark corners, leading him to believe she favored him, no artifice to trick him, only genuine attraction. This woman, however, did none of those things, not since the exchange of vows, not since entering the carriage.

Now, she fidgeted, avoided eye contact, and found his humor crass. Where had his minx gone? Who was this woman he'd married?

Nothing of her behavior in London had led him to believe her a title huntress. He never would have married a title huntress. Never. She certainly was giving him the cold shoulder now. Either she was nervous, or….

She had only wanted his title.

Had it all been a show? All the flirtation. All the attraction. Feigned? Had he been duped?

For now, he would chalk up her behavior to nerves. He refused to follow the thought that he'd been tricked into marriage for his title. He had always thought rejection was the worst blow, not to be desired at all or not to be preferred above all others, but being used, being tricked, that was far worse.

With a straight face, an expression he rarely used, he answered her question forthright, his voice pitched from flirty to somber. "Yes, Charlotte, I enjoy music. Are you familiar with William Shield or Johann Franz Xaver Sterkel? I'm rather fond of them. If you'll permit me to be honest, I would love nothing more than to hear you play Sterkel."

She blushed, revealing a glimpse of the minx he'd so admired.

"If you would," she said, "but I don't know Sterkel's work. I could play Mozart or Piccinni, instead, if that would please you. I'm not familiar with Shield, either. Isn't he affiliated with the opera? I can't recall he's written for pianoforte."

"Comic opera, actually," Drake said. "I highly esteem him as a composer. It would please me far more to hear you play one of his pieces over Mozart. I'll ensure you're acquainted with him."

She wrinkled her nose. "I can't say I'm familiar with musical *comedy*. It sounds vulgar."

He tried again with his seductive smile, always a favorite with the ladies. "Steaming with vulgarity. I count down the minutes until I can—"

She held up a staying hand, as though to shield herself from whatever *vulgar* thing he might have been about to say. Her nostrils flared, and her eyes narrowed. Turning to look at the window, she ended the conversation.

Did it matter that all he was about to say was he wanted to hear her play? Dash his sultry looks and teasing if this was how she would react. She was his *bride*. This was their *wedding* day.

With so many mixed signals, he fretted. She had been all affectionate blushes and demure smiles in London, but now she was grim expressions, scolding words, and offended hauteur. He didn't care for the change, not for a second.

Deuce take it.

After all their flirting in London, he had the distinct impression he'd been duped into marrying a title huntress.

Chapter 2

The carriage came to a halt in time to break for a midday meal. A footman in ducal livery helped the Duchess of Annick descend the steps, for when Drake held out his hand for her, she declined. Without looking back to see if her husband followed, Charlotte marched towards the open door of the second carriage.

She remained mortified at his crudeness. *Steaming with vulgarity. Kissing you. Do you like what you see.* The audacity. The sheer impropriety!

Not once in London had he spoken to her in so sordid a manner. He had flirted, yes, but never so, so, well, *so.* Married intimacy was a far cry from kisses in the shadows. And yet that seemed to be all that was on his mind. She didn't care to have the subject flaunted unabashedly, much less in front of someone else. Was Drake determined to humiliate her? Or was it something more—did he treat her with impropriety because she wasn't from an aristocratic family? Surely not…

It was bad enough she worried about humiliating herself, but to have him openly embarrassing her was too much. Was he such an arrogant rake that he wished to mock her innocence? So many possible motives, none of them good. She didn't often admit her sister was right, but she began to suspect her sister was right about him.

If he hadn't been so dashing, she might have made a different choice. Not that she regretted her choice. At least not yet. But she certainly was having second thoughts.

As Charlotte approached the servant's carriage, her lady's maid, Beatrice, stepped out to greet her mistress.

"How is Captain Henry?" Charlotte enquired.

"Oh, he's well. He sang for an hour before drifting to sleep. I was that glad he did. His Grace's valet was none too pleased by the serenade." Beatrice ushered Charlotte into the coach before taking her leave so her mistress could be alone with Captain Henry.

Charlotte climbed onto the bench to coddle her cockatoo. White plumage inside a gilded travel cage took up half the space of the carriage. The bird welcomed her with a squawk, laugh, and incessant bowing, his white and yellow crest rising to attention, the feathers so tall they tickled the top of the carriage.

"Good afternoon, handsome fellow." Opening the cage door, she reached in to scratch his neck.

The soft down of his feathers offered a reassuring reminder of family. She needed him more than she expected, this symbol of home and normality, a reminder that before today, she hadn't been a duchess. She had been plain Charlotte Trethow, a Cornish girl who loved to play the pianoforte and dance, not necessarily at the same time, of course.

Captain Henry arched his neck and puffed his chest so she could scratch his belly. Scooting herself closer, she realized only the seats in this carriage were padded. Even with the padded seat, she could feel the hard wood beneath. Poor Beatrice! How dreadful to be a servant. While she didn't know the first thing about being a duchess, she did know there was no need to travel in discomfort regardless of station. Her first order of business became clear — padded cushions and backrests in all carriages. Was this something duchesses considered?

Despite the hard seating, she delayed her return to the merry wedding party. Her stomach protested, growling rudely. Ignoring her hunger pains, she mulled. She may have returned his flirtation in London, but such had been innocent teasing, nothing more. Now, she would have to act on what the flirting had promised. He seemed too expectant, too *rakeish*. She didn't think she could follow through, not if Drake was going to make everything a grand joke. If he could woo her gently, she might feel more confident. She was a proper ninny now.

"How's my favorite bird?" Drake said, breaking her reverie.

So deep in thought, she hadn't heard his approach. She flushed over the direction of her thoughts.

"He's faring well, but I think he missed me." She rubbed Captain Henry's belly as he bowed to Drake, crest rising.

"I meant you, Charlotte." Drake reached up and caressed her cheek with the back of his gloved fingers.

Shying away from his touch and side stepping his comment with a titter, she said, "Ravenous! I'm always punctual about my meals, you know."

"Not quite the answer I was hoping for." Unperturbed, he returned his fingers to her cheek. "I noticed a garden next door. After our meal, would you take a turn in it with me?"

She could do nothing more than nod as he trailed his fingers down her neck, sending a warm thrill along her spine.

His hand didn't linger.

With a flourish, Drake stepped away from her and pulled a gold snuffbox from his coat. He delighted in a pinch. His attention diverted, she composed herself from the direction of her thoughts and his disconcerting touch.

After helping her from the carriage, leaving her cockatoo in the capable hands of the maid, who waited nearby, Drake escorted his bride to the inn.

Grooms and servants bustled to and fro to exchange horses. Charlotte knew she should feel proud. Any woman would give her left foot to be in Charlotte's place. He was a duke and positively stunning in form-fitting buckskin breeches, Hessian boots with gold tassels, embroidered waistcoat and traveling coat, and an impressively knotted cravat—a man of impeccable taste.

She, conversely, felt inadequate.

Too low of station, not pretty enough, not trained to be a duchess, and certainly not trained to be a lover. What had possessed him to marry *her*?

As if sensing her sideways glance, he queried, "Enjoying being my wife?"

"I hardly know. Am I supposed to be a noble duchess, a flirt, an obedient wife, or plain me?" She blanched after the words tumbled out.

"Try worrying less and enjoying the day more," he answered with a light-hearted laugh and pinch to her chin.

Did he take nothing seriously? Drake was so careless with words, she wondered if he had bothered to learn anything about her during their courtship or if he'd married the first girl he met because he needed a wife.

She feared the latter.

Instead of responding, she listened to the gravel crunch beneath their shoes.

The luncheon proved a satisfying albeit quiet meal. Charlotte satiated her grumbling stomach with cold meats and confectionaries before Drake directed her to the garden next door, leaving the cousin to his own devices.

The garden, a quaint patch of wilderness, held wildflowers, clematis and wisteria, and stone benches beneath shaded arbors. She immediately busied herself inspecting the fragrant wisteria blooms.

Not long did she have before Drake's hand pressed the small of her back, smoothing the muslin of her dress as he encircled her waist with a firm arm. She tensed. He couldn't expect much, not in broad daylight, not in a public place, even if it was somewhat secluded, but did rakes care, especially married ones?

He turned her to face him, tucking his free hand under her chin. His height blocked the sun, casting his features in shadow. Before she could protest, he leaned down and closed his mouth over hers.

After the initial shock, she let him. Lips melded, a sultry familiarity in his kiss. She even snaked a hand around his neck. The aroma of his almond scented pomade mingled with the ham and brandy from their meal, an unexpectedly pleasant mixture, headily paired. For a moment, she was back in London, hidden from prying eyes down a dark path at Vauxhall, exploring new sensations with an irresistible man, no expectations to go beyond flirting, no worry of humiliation, no chance of being seen, just the exhilaration of the moment, the taste of the forbidden. How delicious to be kissed for the first time — and by a rake.

His throaty moan startled her. She leaned away. In response, he tightened his embrace and deepened the kiss. She pressed against his chest.

When Drake shifted his weight, as if to bring her closer, she panicked. Pushing against him, Charlotte struggled for freedom.

Raised eyebrows questioned her as she loosened his grip to create distance. "What's wrong? Why are you pulling away?" he implored, trying to resume the embrace.

"With people so near the garden, we could be seen. It isn't proper."

However true, she couldn't tell him her real reason for stopping his kiss. She couldn't say for sure even to herself — was it that they might be seen? Was it her feelings of inadequacy? Was it his reputation? So many possibilities, all true, yet none sounded rational — they were *married*, after all.

"No one would dare interrupt us," he said, misinterpreting her excuse, or rather taking it quite literally. "I'll kiss my wife anywhere I please. Now, come here." He grabbed her roughly and began kissing her neck.

A moment of panic seized her. Loss of control…
Fear of possession…Desperate to be free of the controlling embrace, she pushed against his shoulders,
but his grasp was unyielding. However much she
didn't want to embarrass herself further, she felt suf-
focated, overpowered, vulnerable.

When he nipped at her ear, she kicked his shin. "I
will not be treated like a harlot. Unhand me!"

In an instant, she realized her mistake. An unmis-
takable pain — raw and humanizing — reflected in his
eyes, not from her kick, but from her rejection. He
was her husband Drake, not an assailant. She hadn't
meant to insult him. How could she explain her fears
to a man of such reputed experience?

"I thought you were attracted to me, Charlotte.
You welcomed my affections before we exchanged
vows. Now you spurn them. What's changed?"

"I, I'm, well, we need to be on the road, or we'll
be off schedule. It's important we stay on schedule."

Without a backward glance, she ducked out of the
garden, not daring admit to him her unease at this
new role she didn't know how to play.

Legs stretched across the thread-bare ottoman, Drake
enjoyed a savory pinch of snuff before continuing
his oration.

"I tell you, old chap, you're lovelorn. You've been
in this foul mood since we left London, and I'd rather
you not be Lord Grumpy for the remainder of the
journey. If I had to wager a bet, and I never lose a

bet, I'd say you're heartbroken. You're woebegone, forlorn, morose, dejected — "

Sebastian Lancaster, Earl of Roddam, held up a hand and opened his mouth as if to speak. Drake waited for the heartsick wretch to refute him.

When his cousin said nothing, Drake continued, "We both know you favor Charlotte's sister. The mystery is why you didn't do something about it before leaving London. You'll never find anyone else like her, let alone anyone who'll tolerate your moodiness."

Sebastian snapped, "I have no wish to marry. Never have, never will. Besides, I barely noticed her."

"Your lies stink, old man. I can smell them from here." He read the longing and regret etched in Sebastian's features. "You're besotted."

They were both enchanted by the Trethow sisters. Drake just happened to be the only one willing to act on the affection; although, he likely wouldn't have acted so hastily if his mother hadn't commanded he bring home a bride. Truthfully, he had run out of time. Charlotte had been introduced to him one month before the end of the Season, long enough for a week of flowers and rides in Hyde Park followed by three weeks of banns.

Mother had made it clear that at three and thirty he needed to find a wife and get on with the business of begetting an heir, which humored him to no end since his father had sired Drake's sister at the ripe old age of three and sixty. As far as Drake was concerned, he had all the time in the world.

Nevertheless, Mother's word was law. If she wanted a bride for him, a bride he would have. Had he not chosen one in London, one would have been chosen for him. During the month with Charlotte, his hopes had risen for a good match.

He shook the memories from his head.

Sebastian had no such mandate, and as such, had the freedom to lose his chance at love from pigheadedness. Sheer pigheadedness.

Sebastian rested his forearms on his thighs and stared at the wooden floor of the inn. "Shouldn't you be with your bride, oh wise one in the ways of women?"

"You wound me with your sarcasm, cousin. Wound me to my very core." Drake placed his hand over his heart. "She's with her maid, preparing for my grand entrance into the chamber of love." Draining his remaining brandy, he said, "I don't think I'm foxed enough to face her."

"You? Nervous about a woman?" Sebastian reached for his wine glass, swirling it before setting it back on the table, liquid untouched.

"It's true. For all our flirting in London, she's chiseled ice now. I'm worried she'll freeze off my nose if I try to kiss her again." Making light of the matter didn't help him feel any better, in fact worse, as it put the blame on her. Not being interested in him wasn't her fault. "Since the wedding, she's done nothing except tut me, swat at me, and remind me to behave as a duke. I think I know how a duke behaves."

"Ever think you might have insulted her?"

Drake scoffed. "She went frigid after the wedding. One minute she's responsive, and the next she's repulsed by me." Exhaling, he admitted, "My valet is waiting, but I don't see the point in undressing. I have a sinking feeling I made a mistake. Do you think she married me for the title? Have I been duped?"

"Do you care? You flaunted your title to attract her, then the effort you put into the courtship was laughable. Honestly, I didn't think you cared whom you married, not with your marchioness waiting in the wings."

At the mention of Maggie, a widow fifteen years his senior, he tensed. He hadn't seen her in more than six months and certainly hadn't notified her he was bringing home a wife.

"You wound me yet again, cousin. I want a wife who enjoys *me*. Wouldn't that be a pretty package? A wife and love all in one. I'd much rather that than a title hunting woman who detests me. I want all or nothing. I'll not force my attentions on a wife who doesn't want me. It's Mother who cares about the lineage, not me. I want—well, forget it." Defeated, he took another pinch from his gold box and stood. "Time of reckoning."

Sebastian waved Drake out the door.

Drake truly wanted tonight to be magical. He wanted to adore his wife until dawn. Those long eyelashes, rich brown eyes—Charlotte was by far the most attractive woman he had met, and he wanted nothing more than to spend the rest of his life loving her in every way he could imagine. While she might have been a hasty choice given the tick-tock to the end of the Season, he had been confident of his selection. His attraction to her couldn't be denied. It was far more than physical. It was, well...

Tonight would be a turning point. He could feel it. He would confirm in her responsiveness if she married his title or him. Tonight would set the precedence for their future together.

As his leaden feet brought him up the inn's staircase, Drake hoped beyond words he would open the door to his minx rather than the ice duchess.

Chapter 3

Beatrice combed Charlotte's hair until the short strands shone in silky waves.

"You're so lucky," the maid crooned in her Cornish accent. "Not a woman in England doesn't wish to be you tonight, if you don't mind my saying."

"I do mind." Charlotte's stomach was tied in knots.

Ignoring her mistress' retort, Beatrice laid down the brush and walked to the bed, smoothing the covers and turning down the sheets. "Here, sit on the bed. You'll be his first sight, a vision of loveliness."

Charlotte stared at her reflection in the dressing mirror, not confident she agreed with that assessment. Despite the attention she had garnered during the Season, the face looking back at her was still plain Charlotte, not a vision of loveliness, not an elegant duchess of striking beauty, not even a lovesick wife. Just plain Charlotte, worry lines knitting her brow and a frown creasing the edges of her mouth.

Oh, botheration. Where was her aunt when she needed her? Aunt Hazel had been like a mother to her. Charlotte's sister Lizbeth, seven years older, had helped Papa raise her, but Aunt Hazel had stepped in as a mother figure, hiring dance tutors, music instructors, elocution coaches, and all else a young woman needed. Aunt Hazel had not, however, taught

Charlotte what occurred between a husband and wife. She wanted her aunt more than anyone right now. Was it the wedding night that set her so ill at ease, made her shy away from his touch? It must be.

As though seeing Charlotte's expression for the first time, Beatrice rushed over, taking Charlotte's hands in her own. The patting of her hand did little to still Charlotte's nerves.

"No need to worry, Your Grace. All married women do it. It's natural between a husband and wife, it is. And you're a lucky one with a handsome husband. Smile away your worries, then come sit on the bed so I can arrange your gown all becoming like."

Charlotte obeyed.

Her maid moved Charlotte's limbs until one arm propped her up, her legs tucked to the side. The lace and silk chemise wrapped snugly around her, emphasizing her assets.

She felt ridiculous.

"How long am I supposed to pose like this?"

"Until he arrives, Your Grace. I'll be on my way now. He might stay through the night, you know, but if he leaves, I'll attend you with a bath." She smiled encouragingly, curtsied, and then shut the door behind her.

Ridiculous. Nothing could be more ridiculous than this.

Charlotte could taste her nervousness, bitter and acrid on her tongue. Too much hung in the balance—a perfect duchess, a perfect wife, a perfect lover. What if he found her unsuitable? Facing the loss of dignity was too much.

But then, what if he *did* find her suitable? Would he make a grand joke of it? Tease her in front of his cousin for the length of the journey? How mortifying! Oh, she couldn't go through with this. The two possible outcomes were both undesirable. Humiliate herself by dissatisfying him or be humiliated later by satisfying him.

The room compounded her worries. He'd obviously gone to a great deal of trouble to have the inn prepared for them in advance. The dinner had been nothing short of decedent with the inn's finest dining room decorated with the Annick coat of arms and liveried footmen, the food cooked by the duke's chef. Her bedchamber was decorated with embroidered linens, vases of flowers, and enough candles to light every house in town. However flattered she should feel, it only increased her anxiety. She couldn't possibly meet his expectations.

Charlotte's arm tingled, numb from holding her weight. Flexing her wrist, she cringed at the sudden sensation of blood flow.

It didn't matter that she had married her duke charming, not if she couldn't be perfect for him. If only she could be herself, but that wasn't good enough, not for a man of such renowned experience and prestige. She'd been daft to shoot for the stars, for she could never shine brightly enough.

Tears welled. Never had she felt so alone. Blinking away the tears, she tried to muster courage for what lay ahead.

Couldn't there be a bell she could sound to alert him of her readiness, to initiate this ceremony so she could be done with it? Chewing her bottom lip in anticipation of her husband's arrival, she waited.

A knock. A soft, tentative tap, thrice on the bed-chamber door.

She bit her lip so hard she drew blood.

At the sight of Drake's face when he peeked around the door and the taste of iron, she shrieked and leapt off the bed, running for the dressing screen in the corner.

The screen separated her from him, protecting her from the unknown, from the inevitability of the marriage bed. To control her sudden shivering and shield herself, she crossed her arms, nails biting into flesh as she hugged her shoulders.

His booted steps creaked the wooden floors. Then came the sound of scraping, weak bedposts protesting from added weight.

The thought of him sitting on the bed made her stomach cramp. She flushed with shame and wondered why she couldn't behave as a normal bride. He would think her mad. No dutiful bride acted like this. Her hands trembled.

"Charlotte?"

He wanted his wedding night. Quivering arms clung to her remaining reserve of dignity.

"I'm not coming out!" Her response resonated more confidently than she felt.

His weight shifted on the bed, scraping post against wood again. "I know you're nervous, but it's only me." After a pause, he added, "What if we just talked?"

"Talk?" She knew better than to assume marriage was consummated with talking. "About what?"

"Anything. Everything. I miss your babbling brook of conversation."

Another cramp. Another tremble. Another blush. She stared at the floor.

If she waited him out, maybe he would leave, then she could sleep in peace without having proven to him he had chosen the wrong bride, a dull, inexperienced girl. In the lengthening silence, a few divots in the floorboards distracted her. She tried to fit her big toe into the holes, anything to occupy her mind.

"What's your favorite piece of music?" he asked, his voice a deep rumble in the silent room.

"Are you angry with me?"

"I'm not angry. Let's talk about music."

He didn't sound angry, rather conversational, as though they weren't sharing a bedroom with her hiding behind a screen and wearing nothing but a thin chemise.

"I, um, I like Mozart," she said, "although it's difficult to get his sheet music in Cornwall. Sonata in C is my new favorite. Why are you asking me about music when you know perfectly well I'm hiding from you?"

She heard him chuckle, a throaty reverberation.

"I confess," Drake replied, "I'm not a fan of Mozart, but I respect him. Would be difficult not to respect genius. Tell me, Charlotte, what do you like about the sonata?"

She felt even more ridiculous standing behind a screen than she had posing on the bed. Couldn't she drum up the courage to leave the safety of the screen? They were, after all, only talking about music.

"I feel skilled when I play it, because of the agility required, though I'm not skilled. Not really. But I like to *feel* skilled. If that makes sense." The conversation emboldened her, a bit of normality in these foreign circumstances. "Sonata no. 18 is a favorite, as well," she continued, taking a single step towards the edge of the screen.

"May I pour you a drink? You could come out and sit with me, tell me more."

She bit her swollen lip, wincing. "Only if you promise you're not angry."

"I promise. I wish only to spend the evening with a beautiful woman, talking about music. Will you make my wish come true?"

Undecided how best to proceed but knowing she couldn't stand behind a screen all night, she stepped out.

Drake sat at the edge of the bed, fully dressed. Why hadn't he changed clothes? Had he truly come to talk without intending for more? Somehow that seemed more insulting than reassuring. When she hesitated, he smiled, a soft and reassuring lilt to his lips, and walked across the room to retrieve the bottle of wine.

The balls of her feet padded across the floor, taking her to the most undignified location in the room—the bed. The mattress sank as her weight met tired stuffing. Watching him pour the wine, she noticed the stiffness of his spine, the tight rigidity of his shoulders. He only acted at ease, she mused. He was as tense as she.

Returning, he handed her a glass before perching on the edge, drawing a leg onto the bed to face her comfortably. "You're beautiful, Charlotte." His eyes reflected the candlelight, blue wicks dancing. In this moment, he was as dazzling as he'd been in London.

"Thank you. You are, as well," she admitted in a hoarse whisper.

He sniggered. "Just what every man wants to hear."

She stared into her wine glass and swirled the liquid. Fruity overtones wafted, a burst of bright aroma, earthy. A sip rewarded a fine texture, a strong core of raspberry, and soft, almost velvety tannins. Nursing the glass, she sipped until there was no more to sip.

Without warning, he reached up and touched her hair, wrapping a strand around his finger before letting it unravel. She watched him watching her.

"Have you played Sonata in D for four hands?" he asked.

It took her a moment to track their conversation back to Mozart, as lost as she had been in his eyes, the proximity of his hand, and the wine.

She giggled. "Of course I haven't played it. I don't have four hands. Silly!"

In hushed tones that tickled her ears, he said, "I meant with someone by your side." He took her empty glass and set it on the floor. "We could, if you'd like, play it together some time."

He reached out to her again, tracing her jaw with his fingertips. The last time, he had worn gloves. This time, his hands were bare. Rough fingertips scratched against her skin. Surprised, and a tad unnerved, she took his hand in hers and rolled his fingers over to study them. Calluses etched the tips of his fingers. Deep, rough calluses. Gentlemen didn't have calluses.

"Violin," he muttered.

"You play the violin?" Charlotte questioned, incredulous not to know this about him. "Is that something dukes do?"

"It's something *I* do. Father thought it would improve my discipline, curb my reckless, youthful tendencies, he used to say. Mother hated it. She insisted I play on the far side of the house so she wouldn't hear it. I doubt she knows I still play. May I kiss you?"

His question startled her, especially after such a confession. His hand still cradled in hers, she nodded.

The mattress sloped between them as he leaned forward. His lips brushed hers, her bottom lip stinging at the contact. Chastely, his mouth rested against hers, a tender kiss, so unlike what she had expected.

Her cheeks warmed the longer he held himself to her mouth, the heat spreading down her neck and through her chest. He tasted of raspberries. This was the Drake she'd known in London, not the crude rogue who made light of intimacy and embarrassed her in front of others, but the gentle lover who made her feel beautiful.

Drake took her hands into his as he retreated, stirring her from the bliss of the kiss. Never had she been so aware of *him*. She wanted more of this, more of the kissing. She leaned ever so slightly closer, hoping he would take the hint and resume.

"Why did you marry me?" he asked instead.

Confused, she shook her head.

"Do you *want* to be married to me?"

She stared, dazed, lightheaded, not following his line of questioning. "Yes, of course, I do. I don't understand."

"Is it that you want to be with me in name, but not physically, not as man and woman? Are you not attracted to me?"

His eyes showed the same hurt as when she'd rejected him in the garden. She'd caused this. She hadn't meant to, but how could she explain that being his wife frightened her, all aspects of the role?

"I *do* want to be married to you, Drake. But I — I would prefer to wait to do the other until we're at the manor. I would feel more comfortable."

"I'm certain we wouldn't be the first couple not to consummate a marriage, but that's not what I want to happen. I want to be with you."

Her lip pulsed painfully as she chewed on it. "I'm not ready. I need time. I know men like you are used to having their way and that it's your right, as well as my duty, but I don't want to be forced. Please, don't force me."

He dropped her hands, his expression darkening.

"Is that what you think of me? You think I would force you? Regardless of what you might have heard, I'm neither a ravisher nor a rake." His eyes darted from her to the door. "This isn't how I envisioned our marriage."

Her heart raced. She hadn't meant to imply he would force her into the act, just force her to decide now rather than later. Perhaps she had used the wrong word. Was it too late to pose on the bed and go through with it? She was bungling this horribly. Maybe he could kiss her more. If he kissed her, she would feel less self-conscious. Or perhaps another glass of wine. Both might help.

She swallowed against the lump in her throat, her mouth dry. Frantic to be desired and not disappoint him, and desperate for him not to be angry, she grabbed for his arm but met air. He was halfway to the door before she realized he'd moved from the bed.

"Goodnight, Charlotte," he said without turning to look at her.

With a soft click, he shut the door behind him.

Chapter 4

Drake crammed himself into the corner of the carriage, eyes firmly shut. However absurd it might be for a grown man to feign sleep, especially over rough terrain, it proved a necessary evil. Anything to avoid conversation or equally awkward silence.

With eyes closed, he could hear the creaks and groans of the wood, the drum of the hoofbeats, and the rustle of Charlotte's dress. No matter how much he wanted to avoid all thought of her, she inundated his senses. The faint scent of her lemon soap teased his nostrils. If he thought hard enough about it, he could still taste the wine from their kiss and feel her softness beneath his fingertips, never mind it had been three days since he last touched her.

This wouldn't do. He couldn't spend the rest of the journey berating himself for not seeing through her ploy. She wasn't interested in him. She had never been interested in him, had only ever wanted the title. The sooner he accepted this, the sooner he could move forward with his life.

Three nights had passed since the disastrous wedding night. Three nights of torturing himself into self-pitying melancholy. The first night, he had got so foxed he nearly missed their departure the following morning and had spent most of the next day stopping the carriage to retch on the side of the road. Not his most endearing moment.

The second night, he had passed out early with a migraine. The third night, he distracted himself with a card game on the other side of town from the inn.

He had only himself to blame, but that didn't stop him from partially blaming her for making him feel so dejected. His mother rejected him. Maggie rejected him. And now his wife rejected him. There was only so much rejection a man could stomach before taking it personally.

Part of him wanted to try again in hopes of winning over Charlotte, showing her there was more to him than a title, but that felt too desperate, too groveling, too pitiful. He refused to prance about pleading *look at me* to a woman who had never been interested in him. It should be his bride who aimed to get to know him, not him trying to convince her he was more than the sum of his parts.

Still feigning sleep, offering a snore here and there for affect, he was surprised to hear the tinkle of Charlotte's voice questioning Sebastian. This marked her first social acknowledgment of his cousin since leaving London.

Harrumph. Even his cousin received more attention from Charlotte than he did.

"How are you and Drake related?" she enquired.

"We're cousins." Sebastian grunted. "Obviously."

"Well, yes. I'm not thick," she said. "I meant by which parent are you cousins? Are you related to his mother or his father?"

"His mother. I only met his father twice," Sebastian answered. "His mother and my father were siblings."

"Tell me about her?"

The cushion of the bench gave as Sebastian shifted position, either from discomfort or to face her better. Judging from the pregnant silence and the tangible tension prickling Drake's skin, he suspected from discomfort.

He couldn't imagine Sebastian having much of anything nice to say about Mother, for Sebastian held grudges deeper and longer than any person Drake had ever met. Sebastian would never forgive her for reporting his whereabouts to his father during one of his rebellious escapes from the Roddam estate, never mind that it had happened more than fifteen years ago.

"She takes her position seriously," Sebastian mumbled.

"I hope she'll like me," Charlotte said faintly.

"You're the new duchess. Should be enough to garner favorable opinion," he grumbled.

Charlotte tutted but made no further attempts at conversation.

Who cared what Mother thought? Drake would laugh if he hadn't heard the tremor in Charlotte's voice. What she needed to do was march into Lyonn Manor and tell Mother to move to the dower house before sunset. And make it snappy. This had been one of his motivations for choosing Charlotte. During their brief courtship, Charlotte had never hesitated to share her opinion and been, truthfully, quite bossy, a trait he found favorable if she were to take over as matriarch of the family and run the dukedom as his mother had for all these years.

Should Charlotte ask him, he could tell her exactly what Mother would think of her. Mother would be dismayed Charlotte wasn't from blue lineage, which in his opinion made Charlotte all the more attractive. At the very least, it gave a silent stab at his mother's prejudices. At most, it gave Charlotte potential as a loving wife, something that would have been scrubbed out of a lady from an early age.

Once Mother resigned herself to that pesky detail of bloodline, she would relish in training Charlotte. His new wife enjoyed socializing, had a head for planning, was admirably beautiful, and acquainted enough with common folk to do her due diligence in the duchy. Yes, Mother would adore Charlotte.

Rather than addressing Charlotte's concern, he remained wedged in the corner, listening to the hoofbeats while inhaling the scent of lemon soap.

The carriage lurched forward, then, and halted, jarring Drake from his faux slumber. From the window, he saw only dales of heather. They were still miles from their next stop.

Shaking his head at his wife's questioning stare, he banged against the top of the carriage.

"Pardon, Your Grace," called down the coachman. "One of the horses is jibbing."

"Isn't it your job to ensure that doesn't happen?" he called back in irritation.

"Yes, Your Grace."

Drake leaned back, crossing his arms in vexation. However lovely the scenery, both in terms of his wife's milky complexion in her lavender traveling dress and the darker purple landscape outside, he resented the delay. He'd had enough of this journey and longed for home. His violin had been left behind for the entire Season, and he loathed having to wait another week to play.

How had this journey gone so wrong? First his wife and now the cursed horse. All his forethought for nothing. He had seen to a flawless trip to and from London by arranging his own horses along the way for the exchanges, his own staff and finery posted at the inns, even his own carriage maintenance needs and equipment at the ready at each stop, all to ensure problems like jibbing and skittish horses wouldn't interfere with the drive.

Sebastian reached for the door.

"I say, old chap, where are you going?" Drake asked, not enthused by the idea of being left alone with his wife, or should he say, the prudish trickster.

"Assuming the problem is the horse, not the coachman, I can resolve it quickly so we may be on our way. That is your desire, is it not?" Sebastian arched a brow.

"What do you know of horses?"

"Enough. We had a jibbing horse in the field not too long ago. Needless to say, he jibs no more and is a fine specimen of working horseflesh."

Before Drake could rib him, Sebastian slipped out of sight. Outside, Drake could hear the shuffling of feet and quiet dialogue of grooms, coachman, and Sebastian, along with the rumble of horses blowing and neighing.

He stared at his wife. She, in turn, stared at him.

Her lips invited a kiss. Her cheek begged to be touched. Her eyes narrowed to warn him to do neither.

With a smirk, he lunged across the space between them, ignoring his better judgement. Taking the seat next to her, his leg pressing against hers, he drew her into his arms before she could raise the alarm. Their lips met in fevered greeting. She feebly pushed against his chest, but her kiss welcomed him, the embodiment of contradiction. He seized the moment before she froze them both.

Lemon soap mingled curiously with the scent of cinnamon. He savored the spice, a starved animal greedy and possessive. The longer they embraced, the more her resolve dissolved. An arm wound about his waist, the other snaking up his shoulder. He moved to her cheek, peppering playful kisses, then down to her jaw, and around to her earlobe.

In this moment, he doubted the prior evidence. Perhaps she did want him and not the title. Perhaps she had been nervous. What did he know of innocent maidens? In this moment, he believed she wanted him as much as he wanted her, a marriage built on more than duty. Hope blossomed.

Nipping at her lobe, he whispered, "You're perfect, Charlotte. Beautifully, wonderfully, deliciously perfect."

She sighed aloud, a smoky tone that accelerated his heart.

The horse would be well rewarded with all the carrots Drake could afford if it would continue its refusal to move, giving him more time with this illusive vixen. If only this moment could last, because in this moment, she was the minx from London. Her neck caressed his lips with a satin touch as he kissed his way back to her mouth. With one hand, he pulled her closer to him. With his other hand, he cupped the back of her head.

Oh, how wonderful it felt to be desired!

Feeling brazen, he promised, "I'll come to you again tonight so we can finish this. You're more than my duchess. You're my perfect wife. I long to make you mine."

And that did it.

Her body stiffened. Her lips clamped shut. Her eyes widened.

Well blast. Curse it. Foul it. Bedevil it. Holy fire and devilish brimstone. Drake cursed to himself every foul word he could think of, dropping his hold on her.

Her head shaking, she pushed against him, her lips parting to speak then closing again. She looked like a fish. A cold fish. An icy fish with a duchess title. The moment passed. He saw no desire in her eyes. Why she had bothered to return his kiss was anyone's guess. She didn't want him, not physically anyway, certainly not emotionally. Had she only responded out of a sense of duty, because she felt *forced* to placate her husband?

Shoulders slouched in defeat, he returned to his bench, crossed his arms, and glowered out the window. He ignored how becoming she looked with her hair was disheveled where his fingers had threaded her locks, with the blush upon her cheeks, a radiant beauty who abhorred the thought of him in any form of intimacy.

Ill-tempered, he thumped his back against the padded seat hoping to supplant his momentary pleasure with discomfort. Anything to distract himself from another rejection. Humiliated. That's how he felt. He knew she'd push him away, but that hadn't stopped him from hoping she wouldn't, hoping she would assent to his invitation, to admit her own desire for him. The first night could be attributed to nerves, but it was day four of their marriage! Nerves should have settled by this point.

It was time he came to terms with his fate. His marriage would never be anything more than a convenient arrangement to keep out from under his mother's tyranny. If only he could stop thinking of how close he had come to having the wife of his dreams.

Chapter 5

C harlotte fell in love. How could she not fall for so handsome a visage, noble countenance, or refined elegance? She sighed, contented with the new direction of her life, the hope it held now that she felt such adoration, such love.

Yes, Charlotte fell in love.

Not with her husband, although she could easily fall in love with his kiss, his mischievous eyes, even his physique. She couldn't, however, fall in love with a man she barely knew, a man more interested in begetting heirs than showing genuine inquisitiveness of her, a man who punished her with silence because she was skittish about her duties, a man who made a joke of everything, especially intimacy.

No, she didn't fall for her husband.

Today, she fell in love with her new home, Lyonn Manor. Love at first sight. The moment she spied the gothic spires through a crop of cedar trees, she knew she was home. From the manicured landscape with its teasing glimpses and enticing vistas to the three-story, seventeen-bay home, she knew this was home.

Teghyjy Hall, her childhood estate, had never felt like home with its quaint and rustic design, the landscape rural with smelly sheep, muddy country roads, and the forever damp sea air. At night, the wind howled. During the day, the salt air assaulted her, abrasive to her sensitive skin. Her sister Lizbeth loved their home, for she was just like it, wild and unkempt. Charlotte, however, never felt at home there, being neither wild nor unkempt.

Here, at this massive manor with a menagerie of servants waiting in the circle drive, she felt she had come home at last. If she had any doubts about marrying Drake, she could set them aside. Clearly, he was a means for her to come *home*.

The caravan of carriages halted in front of the line of staff, a line so long it wrapped around the circle, past the fountain, and down the drive. From the carriage window, she admired the flat façade of the manor, its only curves the half-moon tower staircase next to the entry and two rounded towers at either end, partially obscured by ornamental trees. The home, poised regally, plucked at Charlotte's heartstrings. After the monotony of neoclassical country homes, this manor spoke to her with its reminiscence of Renaissance French château and nod to gothic architecture.

"Do you like it?" Drake asked.

"Oh, Drake, it's magnificent." She smiled, forgetting for a moment the tension of the journey.

He took her hand in his with a reassuring squeeze. "Your sacrifice in marrying me hasn't been in vain. All of this is now yours. Seventeen thousand acres of estate, not including the duchy's one hundred and twenty thousand acres. Pleased to be duchess of all of this?"

Feeling a surge of strength, fueled by the majesty of Lyonn Manor, Charlotte nodded. Yes, she wanted to be duchess of all of this. Emphatically.

"This does come at a price. You must meet Mother," he challenged. "Are you ready?"

"I am. I've never been more ready."

Lyonn Manor imbued her with the confidence she had felt waning each day of the drive. If she were to be mistress of this, then she could meet her new family with unwavering esteem. While the enormity of the estate and awaiting responsibilities weighed heavily, to be mistress of *this*, she could brave anything.

They stepped out of the carriage to be greeted by the dowager duchess, a handsome but austere woman who showed little signs of age except silver strands lacing raven hair, a crease between her brows and around her mouth, and a gold-handled cane in her right hand.

The graceful elegance of the duchess awed Charlotte. The woman stood ramrod straight, as tall as Drake, but with an air that towered above them in condescension and superiority. Charlotte wondered if *this* was to be her future, if this was what a duchess looked like, acted like. Was she what Charlotte was supposed to become?

The woman's eyes bore into Charlotte's, black and piercing, sending an icy shiver down her spine. The handsomest woman Charlotte had ever met, yet not a solitary sign of emotion showed behind the granite face, no pleasure at seeing her son return, no curiosity to meet her new daughter, no recognition of her nephew.

Charlotte flicked her gaze back to the manor to renew confidence. The gabled windows along the roofline, of all things, encouraged her to continue towards Drake's mother, emboldening her to best the beast so she could reign supreme as the Duchess of Annick. Never in her wildest dreams could she see herself filling the shoes of this woman, but by Jove, she would try.

Drake touched Charlotte's elbow, urging her forward to face the guardian of Lyonn Manor. Sebastian ambled behind them at a respectable distance.

"Mother, may I introduce my wife, Charlotte Mowbrah, Duchess of Annick?"

Charlotte curtsied and was in turn awarded a nearly imperceptible inclination of the woman's head along with a thorough appraisal from the bridge of her mother-in-law's aquiline nose.

"Charlotte, this is my mother, Catherine Mowbrah, Dowager Duchess of Annick."

With a throaty tone, the dowager duchess spoke, her welcoming words and stone expression incongruous. "You must call me Mama Catherine. You are now my daughter."

Drake tugged Charlotte's elbow in the direction of a young girl no older than sixteen, the image of her brother with dark hair, height, and aristocratic bearing.

"Charlotte, may I introduce my sister, Lady Mary? Mary, this is your new sister, my wife and duchess."

Lady Mary clasped her hands over her heart and said with timid animation, "I hope we will be the best of friends, Your Grace. I have awaited your arrival since I first received word of the engagement."

Charlotte instantly liked Mary. Lacking the reserved demeanor of her mother, Mary's eyes sparkled, her cheeks rosy with life. She genuinely appeared delighted to have a new sister, and no wonder, if the only other woman of consequence in the house was a gargoyle.

"Please, call me Charlotte. We are sisters now." Charlotte squeezed the girl's hands with friendly affection.

"Enough dawdling," interrupted Drake's mother. "You must meet the head staff."

Two stern figures stepped forward, a tight-lipped, elderly man and a scowling, grey-haired woman. He bowed, and she curtsied, both stiff as sticks.

"This is Lyonn Manor's butler Mr. Taylor. He has been with me since I first married the duke. And this," Mama Catherine inclined her head to the perpetually frowning woman, "is Mrs. Fisk, the housekeeper."

Mrs. Fisk stepped forward, and with all the courtesy her glower could muster, said to Charlotte, "Welcome to Lyonn Manor."

In a moment that had time standing still for Charlotte, Mrs. Fisk turned to the dowager duchess and said, as though Charlotte were not standing there, "If you'll permit me, Your Grace, I request an audience with your daughter-in-law to acquaint her with the domestic affairs of the household. She will also need to consult with Cook regarding the weekly menus."

Charlotte opened her mouth to reply, but Mama Catherine spoke on her behalf. "Her Grace will meet with you tomorrow morning, two hours before tea. You will bring to me the menu after Her Grace's consult so that I may review the changes for approval."

Uncertain how to respond to this slight, Charlotte stood silently, teeth gnashing.

Did they think her incapable of speaking for herself? Why must her decision need supervision?

She hadn't yet stepped foot into her new home, and already *Mama* Catherine established her authority as the irreplaceable lady of the manor. The servants would never take Charlotte seriously now.

While Charlotte didn't have the first clue about choosing menu selections or domestic affairs, she didn't appreciate being talked about as if she weren't present, her authority undermined by someone answering for her. She was made to feel like an unwanted guest in her own home.

One glance at Drake to see if he would give his mother a firm set down for speaking on Charlotte's behalf, not to mention a word to the housekeeper for blatantly cutting her from conversation, affirmed he was too busy playing with his snuff box to notice the exchange.

Catherine dismissed the remaining staff. Looking down her hooked nose, she said to Charlotte, "It takes but one look to ascertain your ignorance of such matters. Nothing will be done without my approval."

Charlotte bristled.

Dismissing her daughter-in-law, Catherine turned to her nephew, only then bothering to acknowledge him. He stood, hands clasped behind his back, feet shoulder width apart, nonplussed to be forgotten in the background. His reward for being a paragon of patience was a stiff nod.

Not that Charlotte had given Sebastian much thought, but she had wondered if the woman would give the cut direct to her own nephew in front of the household staff. Seeing the gargoyle's behavior towards him was disconcerting. Such coldness to her own family!

When Mama Catherine led the way to the front of the house, Charlotte signaled to Drake. More than anything she wanted a moment alone to recover from the abrasive meeting.

He raised an eyebrow, still fiddling with his snuff box.

"I need to instruct Beatrice where to take Captain Henry." She glanced at the servant coach.

Beatrice and Drake's valet were struggling to pull out the cockatoo's massive travel cage, white wings spread inside to balance the bird as the cage heaved to and fro, tilting through the coach door.

"The Gray Parlor will do for now." Drake eyed his mother's back as he spoke. "We mustn't keep Mother waiting. Mr. Taylor will show them the way in your stead."

"I can tell Beatrice myself. I will only be a moment."

As she turned towards the carriages, Drake's hand encircled her arm, stilling her. He shook his head, then nodded to the grim butler. The butler bowed and retreated to the carriage.

"We mustn't delay. You may visit Captain Henry later, but delaying will anger Mother. Come." His hand, still clutching her arm, guided her to the manor's double doors.

With a regretful glance to her bird, she trudged forward.

Never had she felt so powerless. Her confidence drained. Even the arched windows on the ground floor frowned with her, as if the house sympathized.

They entered an oval hall, galleries lined with ornate double doors extending to either side. Of all the balls Charlotte had attended, none of the homes had been this grand. Untouchably high ceilings and hallways the width of ballrooms were only the beginning of the grandeur. She gaped, enamored with the border friezes and coffered ceiling, miniature murals painted in each square.

Not until she'd completed a circle, giddy once more that this was her new home, did she notice Mama Catherine's glare. Charlotte stopped mid turn, feeling three feet tall under the scrutiny.

"A duchess does not ogle," said the gargoyle. "I can see you are going to be a trial." With a glance at the housekeeper, Catherine instructed, "Take her to her room. See she rests before dinner. I give you leave to show her upstairs after dinner. The remainder of the house will wait for the morrow."

Without another word to the family, Mama Catherine about-faced and left, her cane thumping down the east gallery. Mary curtsied and followed behind her mother, leaving Charlotte with Sebastian and Drake, but not for long, it would seem.

Drake patted her arm. "Mrs. Fisk will show you to your quarters. I will see you at dinner."

What Charlotte assumed was meant to be a reassuring endearment made her feel childlike. She didn't want to be *patted*. She was not a child. She was not a pet. She was not a trial.

He and Sebastian left her alone with the housekeeper. Mrs. Fisk stood behind her, unsmiling. Charlotte followed the steely servant down the west gallery and up the rounded tower stairs. Disheartened would be an understatement. Somehow, she had to rise above this. This was her home now. She'd made the choice to marry a stranger because he was handsome, charming, and titled, and now she had to live with that choice.

Somehow, she had to make this work.

I will be your mistress, Lyonn Manor. Somehow. She spoke to the home through her heart, willing her future to be as uplifting as the grand staircase.

Chapter 6

Charlotte rested for several hours, emotionally exhausted.

When she awoke, she didn't ring for her maid, not right away. There was ample time before dinner for her to gather strength and explore her new room, a room she hadn't yet looked about given Mrs. Fisk's hovering. The woman had refused to retire until Charlotte was changed and in bed.

She was, again, treated like a child.

One peek around the lady's chamber made her cringe. Peach wallpaper, peach furniture coverings, peach bedding, peach curtains, everything a pale, nauseating peach. While a spacious and luxurious room, to be certain, the peach did nothing to welcome Charlotte. The peach had to go. A darker shade would do, perhaps a warmer color, or a complementary combination rather than *everything* being peach. If nowhere else in this house could she be mistress, she could assert authority over her own bedchamber.

She began a mental list of necessary changes. After her tour in the morning, she'd need to put quill to paper to list her daily tasks, the household affairs, goals, and anything else that might need her attention, not forgetting her wish to pad all carriages. If she were to be duchess of all this, she needed a plan. Failure was not an option.

It would all begin with this room, her sanctuary. Charlotte sat on the offensively peach settee at the foot of the bed and visualized the redecoration. Even the rug was peach, a plush peach that brushed between her fingers when she pressed her palm to the lush threads, soft and enveloping.

The paintings should go first, she decided. The eyes of women in stately dress stared at her in judgement. She assumed these were the former duchesses of Annick, one generation after another. Who would want these women watching the lady of the manor sleep? The very idea made Charlotte shudder. These stuffy women needed to be removed to the dower house, along with the dowager duchess. Landscapes would be a perfect replacement. If paintings of the home and gardens had not yet been commissioned, she would see to it, for a view of the estate from her bed would be just the thing. At least she now had something to look forward to.

An inspection of the windows revealed an attractive view of the rolling grounds at the back of the manor. She could just make out a columned rotunda on a hill in the distance and the edge of a rose garden below, beyond what she thought might be a grotto.

How dull to arrive and be rushed into the peach terror without a tour of the house. As fatigued as she had been, she would have liked a tour before dinner, specifically from Drake. Such would have given them an opportunity to get to know each other better and possibly a way for them to share a common interest, namely the house and grounds. Did he love it as

much as she already did? She wanted him to show
her all his favorite places and accompany each room
with a narrative of what it had been like to grow up
in what seemed like a palace to her.

A tour from the humorless housekeeper was a
dreadful prospect. Better than a tour from her mother-in-law, Charlotte supposed. There, she needed to
look on the bright side of all situations. Her marriage
may be in shambles, her husband a pompous rake,
and her mother-in-law a granite statue, but by Jove
there was something positive about every situation.

Continuing to explore, she opened the side door,
which led to a lovely sitting room. She assumed the
adjoining room would be the lord's chamber. The
thought of Drake's bedchamber being so close to her
own tied her stomach in knots. If she opened his door,
would she find him inside, perhaps abed, resting as
she had done?

More curious than cautious, she parted the door
of the lord's chamber to peek inside.

Empty. Sighing with relief, she stepped inside.

Drake's room was a mixture of golds and browns,
gold crivelli wallpaper, a scrolling leaf motif adorning
the drapes around the four-poster bed and windows,
and wingback chairs gathered around a mahogany
table. The room suited Drake.

Closing his door, she admired for a moment the
sumptuous sitting room with its inviting escritoire,
red and silver settee decorated with silk embroidery,
and enticing views to the back of the house. Oh, she
liked this room very much.

Returning to the peach horror of a lady's chamber,
she rang for her maid to bathe and dress for dinner.

Given her dinner companions, she wanted to look worthy of her new role. With a bit of care, she would look every inch a duchess and hopefully avoid further criticism and embarrassment.

Beatrice chose a noble gown, sleeves reaching to Charlotte's elbows with ribbons lacing through eyelets from sleeve cap to elbow hem. Silver embroidery trimmed the edges of the azure bodice and along the hem, and a wide silver sash nestled under her bosom.

Beatrice spent an hour preparing a coiffure of braids laced with pearls and silver ribbons. Soft curls framed Charlotte's face.

"You look like a duchess, you do," declared the lady's maid as she added the finishing touches to the ensemble.

"I *am* a duchess," Charlotte corrected, the words said more to her reflection than to her maid.

With a final smoothing of the dress and straightening of the sash, Beatrice sent her mistress to brave dinner.

To Charlotte's surprise, a footman stood outside her bedchamber, waiting to escort her. As daunting as the size of the place, she didn't think she needed an escort. He led her through the bedroom corridor, down the rounded tower staircase, through the west gallery, past the entrance hall, through the east gallery, and to the doors of the lesser dining room. On second thought, perhaps she did need an escort. Two footmen standing on either side of the double doors opened them at Charlotte's approach. The footman who accompanied her announced her arrival to the room, the only inhabitant the dowager duchess.

Charlotte curtsied and stepped forward.

"Seating will be arranged for every dinner party you host," her mother-in-law said in greeting. "I will approve all seating charts to ensure you understand rank and civility. There is an art to designing a seating chart, for some guests should not be seated together, regardless of rank, lest the dinner turn to war."

Catherine tapped the seat next to the head of the table. "You sit here, next to His Grace." Walking to the foot of the table, she tapped the seat opposite the host. "I sit here."

Brows furrowed, Charlotte said, "Pardon me, Your Grace, but shouldn't I sit —"

The dowager duchess raised a hand. "I told you to call me Mama Catherine. As to the seating arrangement, I have always sat here. I expect that to be understood." She moved to the adjacent chair without waiting for a response. "This seat is for Lady Mary. Lord Roddam will sit across from you."

A footman opened the double doors and announced the arrival of Lady Mary. Sebastian and Drake followed shortly behind her, also announced. Charlotte thought it ridiculous to be announced to a room of five family members who all knew each other.

Whatever relief Charlotte might have felt not to play hostess at her first dinner was overshadowed by frustration. She resented her mother-in-law's condescension but hadn't the courage to protest. Any expectation of Drake feeling outraged by his mother's usurping Charlotte's rightful place at the table and defending her position as lady of the manor was crushed. Drake didn't blink an eye when she sat next to him rather than at the foot of the table.

Defend me! She cried inside. *Defend your wife's position in her new home!*

Was this punishment for the botched wedding night? Was this his way of showing her she wasn't mistress of the estate until she consummated the marriage? He was oblivious to her inner rage, oblivious to his mother's rudeness. He exchanged small talk with Sebastian as though this were the happiest of days, his eyes laughing, his lips curved into a smile, happy to be home and unaware of his wife's struggle.

Footmen carrying trays bustled into the room. The butler described each of the dishes served. Charlotte paid not a bit of attention, lost in thought.

On deeper reflection, she questioned if she wasn't taking everything too personally. Was the condescension in her imagination? If she considered their perspective, her tantrum did seem silly. Today was only her first day, after all. Could she expect them to change a lifetime of habits so quickly? Her mother-in-law likely didn't mean to be insulting, and it was merely Charlotte's own insecurities that had her misinterpreting the woman's intentions.

Instead of resenting her mother-in-law, Charlotte should thank Catherine, for this gave her time to accustom herself to her role and learn by example. The seating arrangement also offered a perfect opportunity to talk with her husband, something they'd done little of, which was much of the problem, Charlotte believed.

Yes, she should thank Mama Catherine.

Mama Catherine. The woman certainly did not seem like a Mama Catherine. She-Demon Catherine, more like. Oh, botheration! All the optimistic thinking gone to mush in a single, vile thought. How inappropriate of her. How tactless. Charlotte scolded herself. For all she knew, this was the way of the world, the passing of the torch in ruled measure. She summoned patience to trust the dowager duchess' decisions. This might all be part of some sort of training.

As if the woman could hear Charlotte's thoughts, Catherine turned her obsidian eyes to her daughter-in-law.

"On the morrow, you will report to me after your meeting with Mrs. Fisk. We will begin your tutelage immediately. Our first lesson will cover the local gentry and nearest peerage. I do hope you are socially inclined, for you are expected to host parties and provide entertainment for all persons of consequence in the north, from peers to gentile tenants. The laborers' families also require entertainment, although of a baser nature. Once per year, you will be hostess to the Royal Family. I will expect you not to embarrass us." When Charlotte didn't immediately respond, Catherine said, "Do you understand, gel, or do they not speak the King's English in the West Country?" Her sharp tongue sliced through Charlotte's esteem.

"Yes, Mama Catherine, I understand. I am eager to learn how I may be the best duchess." From the corner of Charlotte's eye, she saw Drake wink at her.

"Nonsense. *I* am the best. In time, we can hope you'll become tolerable enough to assume my mantle after I die."

Judging from the lady's surprisingly young age, Charlotte doubted such an event would occur any time soon. The bat probably had another forty years in her. That realization settled in the pit of her stomach, percolated, and left a bitter aftertaste. Forty more years living with this woman when Charlotte hadn't made it through a single day?

Give me strength, Lord.

"Mary." Catherine turned to her daughter. "You will have three callers this week. Lord Ashford on the morrow, followed by Lord Stroud, and then Lord Pickering."

Mary slouched in her chair. "I want to see Arabella tomorrow, and I most certainly do not want to see *them*," Mary whined.

The snap of her mother's fingers remedied Mary's posture. Even Charlotte sat up a little straighter.

"I will not have you disgrace yourself in front of your new sister. You are already sixteen and need to find a husband before you lose your bloom. Of the three, I have my eye on Lord Pickering. He's a marquess from a reputable family. The estate is not far, and I have it on good authority he's in dire need of money. The match would be amenable to both parties."

"But everyone knows he has a horrid reputation for gambling. And he spends all his time in London."

"All the more reason he's a good match. You'll be left behind to rule the estate as you please. You couldn't ask for better circumstances."

"I *might* consider him, but only because he's more amenable than Lord Ashford. Lord Ashford's eldest daughter is older than I am!" Mary protested with a pout. "And so you know, Mother, I will never marry someone like him. He's too old and froths at the mouth. I could never kiss someone who froths."

"What does kissing have to do with marriage?" Catherine asked. "No respectable woman kisses her husband. Preposterous."

"Why won't you allow me a proper come-out? Why can't I have a Season in London?"

"I will not parade you in front of all and sundry when alliances worth making are done between families of good breeding, not in ghastly ballrooms. Nothing good comes from visits to London, certainly not marriages. Only desperate gels go to London." Catherine stared down her sulking daughter. "I have invited three suitors for this week, and you will entertain them. Do you understand, or are all the women at this table feebleminded?"

"It's not fair," Mary muttered.

"Marriage has nothing to do with fairness and all to do with security and advancement. I was sixteen when I wed, and so shall you be. You will learn your place, Mary, and stop this petulance."

Mary nodded in acquiescence, but her lower lip protruded in silent defiance.

Charlotte smiled reassuringly at Mary before frowning at her own husband, who was deep in conversation with his cousin. Not only had he not heard a word of the exchange, but he clearly had no intentions of taking advantage of the seating arrangement to share conversation. Nothing could be more uncomfortable than spending her first dinner in silence.

Catherine and Mary talked.

Drake and Sebastian talked.

Charlotte ate.

Did Drake's own thoughts of marriage echo those of his mother's? Was this nothing more than a form of security and advancement?

After the announcement of their betrothal, countless ladies had congratulated Charlotte on securing a catch well above her station. Some meant it a sincere compliment, others a vindictive slight, but they all repeated the same sentiment.

Was this how Drake saw their marriage, how he saw her? Did he think her a desperate gel wanting nothing but security and advancement?

Looking around the dining room and at her companions made Charlotte feel like a desperate gel in search of advancement. As much as this had been a dream come true, a place she could finally feel at home, it was far grander than she'd expected. She felt like an imposter. The room was opulent, to say the least. It was difficult to believe this was the *lesser* dining room and that there was a much larger and grander dining room for guests. Footmen stood at the ready around the room, enough footmen for a noble dinner party, all assembled under the watchful eyes of Mr. Taylor. Was such extravagance necessary?

The dinner service was porcelain with exquisite blue and white artistry. The décor was mostly marble and mirrors, everything in the room veined or gilded. Three fireplaces lined the walls, all with marble surround and cherub statues.

Charlotte's mother-in-law matched the room well—cold marble etched with gold. The woman's dress was fit for a queen. Did she always dress this impressively for dinner, or was it to honor the new duchess? As glamorous as Charlotte found the gem-encrusted coiffure and silk with lace dinner dress, she hoped this wasn't the expectation for dinner attire. Even Drake and Mary were dressed in garments of stunning quality. There was a striking smartness to Drake that made her both breathless and nervous.

Had she set her sights too high? Seeing him in his element made her question his decision to marry her — why choose *her* when there were ample daughters of peers raised for a marriage such as this, for a duke such as him? She offered him no alliances, no land to expand his holdings, no extensive lineage, nothing except money for her dowry, which he could not possibly need. Why her?

In a curious way, she related more to Sebastian this evening — now there was a humbling thought. Only Charlotte and Sebastian were, from this perspective, underdressed for the occasion. Sebastian's attire lacked the gusto of everyone else's, tailored yet unadorned. Charlotte wore her best dinner dress, but compared to the ladies in the room, she looked simple, plain, and wholly inadequate. As desirous of this lifestyle as she'd always been, she wasn't convinced how well she fit. She could not have been more out of place had she been a chimney sweep, nothing more than a country girl in a fairy tale palace. How could someone who had lived his whole life in this grandeur choose *her*?

The more she thought about it, the more nervous she became. All the training and practice was for nought, as she fumbled with cutlery, almost tipped her wine, and ate less daintily than did Mary or Catherine. Never in her life had anyone accused her of being clumsy. She'd always outshone others at parties and dinners, but those others had never been nobles. She likened herself to a paste jewel.

Feeling alone and conspicuous, she turned to her husband, interrupting whatever Sebastian was saying by remarking, "I am pleased we're arranged so cozily. Aren't you?"

Both men turned to her simultaneously, two sets of brows arching in surprise.

"Did you need something, my dear?" Drake stared quizzically.

"Yes, actually. I want to be included in your conversation. What are the two of you conversing about?"

Drake and Sebastian exchanged glances before Drake replied, "Horses."

"Oh, I see. I don't know the first thing about horses. What were you saying? Do continue."

"We were discussing how best to breed them," Drake said, his lips twitching.

"Oh." The heat of her blush spread up her neck and into her cheeks. "I believe the two of you may continue your conversation without me."

"No, no, I won't have it," her husband said, leaning back to study her. "You want to be included, so included you shall be. Sebastian was telling me he has a mare with a propensity for kicking the stallion. Curious behavior, wouldn't you agree?"

Charlotte shot Sebastian an incredulous look, as though to ask if Drake were being serious or trying to embarrass her. Sebastian's face revealed nothing. He stared back at her with eyes as black as his aunt's, his face expressionless.

Drake suppressed a smirk when he asked, "Do you suppose she's feisty, teasing the stallion? Or is she not interested in him?"

"This is not a conversation for a lady. Please, continue without me. I've no wish to discuss this." If her cheeks did not catch fire, it would be a blessing.

She hoped her in-laws couldn't hear the conversation from their end of the table. How mortifying.

A quick glance in their direction reassured her they were deep in their own argument.

"Don't be coy," Drake chided. "You're the one who nosed in."

"I didn't *nose* in," she defended. "I merely wanted to be included, but not if you're going to discuss horses. I had hoped you both might wish to discuss something more appropriate, carriage seat padding, for example."

"Carriage seat padding?" Drake echoed.

"Yes. I have ideas for improving the carriages."

He folded his arms, frowning. "Ah. Already asserting your authority, I see."

"I hardly consider carriage seat padding asserting authority, but I would like to see to improvements around the house. My room, for instance, could do with some remodeling. Then there's the unnecessary number of footmen—do we need *all* of them for only the few of us? The overly formal announcements when entering a room are silly. And, well, I could continue, as I do have ideas, and I would like to share them with you."

With such a conversation starter, he'd think she didn't like the house or didn't appreciate her new situation. What woman demanded changes on her first day, especially when this could all have been a display for her benefit rather than daily tradition? This wasn't how she intended the conversation to go, but she said the first thing to come to mind to avoid talk of horses.

"As long as you're happy, my dear. This is what you wanted, yes? To be a duchess?" he asked.

"I *am* a duchess," she responded, lifting her chin.

"Yes, yes you are."

If Charlotte hoped for a traditional ending to the evening, she was in for a disappointment. No gathering in the drawing room for music and conversation. No entertainment of any nature to welcome home the duke and his new bride. In fact, everyone made a mad dash for the door.

Drake and Sebastian retired to Drake's study, wherever that was. At least Sebastian had the courtesy to bid her farewell before departing, saying he would leave for home at first light. He may not be her favorite person in the world, but she felt a stab of sadness at his leaving. The only two people in this house she knew were Sebastian and Drake. However forbidding, his presence was a comfort compared to her mother-in-law, which was saying something.

Mary excused herself early, as well, claiming a migraine. Charlotte hoped to do the same. So fatigued from the journey and the emotional strain of the day, she wanted to sleep for a year, or better yet, for forty years.

Her mother-in-law had other plans.

"Follow me. I must show you the conservatory," Catherine said before Charlotte could make her excuse and retreat.

Uncertain how to decline without appearing impolite, Charlotte complied. Saying she was suspicious of Catherine's motives would be an understatement. The woman had already shirked the duty of giving a tour by foisting it onto the housekeeper, so why now show her one room?

With a thump of her cane, Catherine led the way through the east gallery and into a lavish conservatory, equitable in size to the ground floor of Charlotte's childhood home. Awe-struck, she almost missed the duchess' first words.

"This is the only room in the house without ears. What I have to say need not be heard by the entirety of the staff. Consider it a kindness." Catherine pinned Charlotte with a piercing stare. "You have *not* been properly trained, being a daughter of a mere *tin mine* owner. I find it disgraceful my son married so far beneath him. He may defend your father as being a Member of Parliament and of landed gentry, but that does not excuse involvement in industry, *mining* industry no less. I'm disgusted. You are not fit for this title."

Stung from the tongue lashing, Charlotte lifted her chin, willing inner courage to defend herself.

Catherine continued before Charlotte could respond. "Alas, what is done is done. This week, I will arrange for fittings with the modiste to prepare your new wardrobe."

Her eyes roamed over Charlotte's finest dress. With a sneer, she said, "You will dress as a duchess and dispose of those rags. Once you're presentable, I will arrange elocution lessons. Such a barbaric accent."

Charlotte was desperate to poke Catherine with a hairpin, but nothing good could come of stabbing one's mother-in-law.

"You know why he married you?" Catherine continued, waiting only long enough for Charlotte to frown. "He wished to spite me for insisting he marry. My son had *other* interests than marriage. He is a wastrel and a disgrace. I and I alone run this duchy; therefore, I will see to its future. If you have half a brain, I will teach you how to take my place so that you may teach the heir should aught happen to me. I hope I've made myself clear on all points. Off you go. Mrs. Fisk is waiting."

The dismissal was so abrupt after such harsh words, Charlotte missed her cue to leave. Her mother-in-law slithered away, leaving Charlotte alone in the conservatory. At least, she thought she was alone. Not until she heard Mrs. Fisk's none-too-subtle throat clearing did she realize the housekeeper stood but feet away. The nosy old crow had heard every word of the exchange.

Crestfallen and a tad murderous, Charlotte shadowed the housekeeper upstairs. In hindsight, she thought of at least ten witty responses.

The clincher was the dowager duchess was right. Charlotte wasn't fit to be a duchess. She suspected the comments of Drake were accurate, as well, for he showed limited interest in her. Was she nothing more than a pawn between them?

Despite her desire to see the house, Charlotte saw nothing of the upstairs, her eyes too glazed with hurt and confusion. After an eternity wedged within a single hour, the housekeeper showed Charlotte to her room, the tour at an end.

As soon as her chamber door closed, she collapsed against it. If she were offered the chance to go home, she'd take it. Only, this was home now. How had everything gone so terribly wrong? She had met the man of her dreams, married him, and been whisked to his palace, yet everything was terribly, terribly wrong. A beast lived here, breathing fire and raining brimstone, and her duke in shining armor barely noticed she existed, much less slew dragons for her.

Drake was her one remaining hope. Only he could set everything right. If she explained to him what his mother said, he could laugh away her worries and tell her she misunderstood the cruelty. He could reassure her he hadn't married her out of spite, and with a few adoring words, make her feel beautiful again. If consummating the marriage would ally herself with him, then so be it. In this desperate moment, she didn't care if she was awkwardly virtuous as long as she had someone to love her, someone to defend her, someone to notice her. Thus far, all her decisions seemed to be the wrong choices. Something had to change.

She needed him.

Before she could talk herself out of it, she marched across the room to his chamber door. Her knuckles rapped against the wood. She waited. She rapped again, louder and harder. No response.

He couldn't still be with Sebastian in his study, could he? Didn't he know she needed him? She had half a mind to find him, dismiss Sebastian, and demand Drake's attention. If only she knew where the study was. Oh, blast. She didn't know where anything was in this museum.

Opening his bedchamber door for confirmation, she found the room empty. Swallowing against her temptation to ring the bellpull and ask for directions to the study, she returned to her own chamber to surrender.

No, she couldn't surrender. At least, not yet. What she needed was a good, long cry followed by inspiration and a plan. What would Lizbeth do? Her sister had always been her savior in the past. No task was too small for Lizbeth. Whatever ailed them, Liz would come to the rescue by resolving the problem herself or talking through a solution. She was the most level-headed, rational thinker Charlotte knew.

Except her sister wasn't here to advise her. No one was.

If she were here, Charlotte suspected she knew what Liz would say: fight and conquer. There was no sense in moping, and nothing good ever came from self-pity. She would tell Charlotte to accept her choice, and then make it work because Charlotte didn't need Drake if she could save herself.

That was sound advice in theory, but how was she to put it into practice? She hadn't Liz's courage, and she certainly didn't have the gumption. Liz would have given the Dowager Duchess of Annick a piece of her mind at the first insult. Charlotte couldn't. She didn't dare! Unlike her sister, Charlotte cared what others thought of her. She cared far too much, she knew, but there it was.

Well, she might not have a specific plan of action, but she could conjure a fighting spirit.

Tomorrow, she resolved, would be a new day. Tomorrow, she would stand up to the dragon and befriend her husband.

Chapter 7

"I am the Duchess of Annick," Charlotte repeated to her reflection several days later.

The mirror in the Gray Parlor was an avid audience.

"I have authority and condescension. I *am* the Duchess of Annick."

Repeating the affirmation renewed her strength and quailed her doubts, at least for a few minutes.

She was born for this role; she could feel it in her bones. She'd like to think Drake had chosen her above all other women because of her personality, beauty, and potential as a duchess. She couldn't allow anyone to convince her differently, especially not herself.

The morning after her arrival had been trying. She'd spent most of it with the housekeeper, learning the rhythm of the house, meeting the lesser servants, touring the downstairs, and discussing with Cook the daily menu. With every comment, question, and suggestion Charlotte made, Mrs. Fisk responded that she would take it under advisement and consult with Her Grace, the dowager duchess.

It had taken all Charlotte's might not to dismiss Mrs. Fisk on the spot for her insubordination, for treating Charlotte as though she were of no consequence in the household.

The days that followed had been equally as trying. No matter what change she tried to enact, the housekeeper deferred to Her Grace, the dowager duchess. The duchess herself reminded Charlotte with each hour spent together that she was less than expected, a grand disappointment, and must undergo exhaustive training to fulfill her role adequately.

The only time she saw Drake was at supper, when they would exchange polite conversation, nothing more. Something had to change. She'd not been here a week, and already she was miserable.

Short of starting an open rebellion, Charlotte convinced herself to tread lightly. She could try to affect minor changes, insignificant in the eyes of the dowager duchess, to make the home hers, and in doing so find subtle ways to best the woman. At least, that sounded like a good plan when she lacked the courage to do anything else.

What if she put her foot down only to learn her word meant nothing, and her mother-in-law reigned supreme? Or, possibly worse, she found that grain of courage, forced Mama Catherine out of the way, and then failed at running the estate?

No, she would learn from Catherine while planning a sneak attack. Charlotte needed to gain the support of those around her, test her limits, and discover the chinks in Catherine's armor.

"I am the Duchess of Annick," she repeated.

Turning from the mirror, she laughed to find Captain Henry hanging upside down from his tree, trying to unbraid the frayed end of a rope with his beak. At least *he* was loyal to her.

Moving to the escritoire, she took the opportunity to write letters to Lizbeth and Aunt Hazel. She had already changed for tea and still had about an hour before Catherine would meet her for their daily training. Pulling out parchment from a drawer and preparing the quill, Charlotte pondered what to write. Should she confess to Lizbeth these feelings of inadequacy, or should she profess happiness so no one would be the wiser?

The less said, the better, she decided.

Dearest Lizzie,

I hope you and Papa arrived home safely. I know you will be happier at home, not being a lover of parties or crowds. Send word when you have a moment. The journey to Northumberland was long, but I've arrived to my new home. Lyonn Manor is heavenly, perfect for me in all ways. I want you to visit within the year, or at the latest next spring. The marriage is splendid, better than I could have dreamed. Send my best to all. I will write again soon, but until then, I am

Your loving sister,
Charlotte

None of what she wrote was a lie, exactly; however, the ever-perceptive Lizbeth might read between the hastily penned lines to see the omissions. Charlotte didn't want her sister to worry, and besides, what else could she say about her predicament? That her mother-in-law breathed fire, and her husband ignored her? No, she wouldn't admit defeat and have Liz feeling justified in her assessment of Drake. Let Liz think Charlotte had made the perfect choice, and Drake was redeemed by marriage despite Liz's harsh criticisms to his character. Confessing was a last resort, for that would be too humiliating by half.

After sanding the wet ink, she folded the letter and sealed it with red wax, stamping it with the Annick insignia. There. Written and done. Setting aside Liz's letter, she began a similar one to Aunt Hazel.

Quill in hand, Charlotte hesitated. Should she ask for advice? Such personal questions as, "What do I do if I have yet to consummate my marriage?" seemed wholly inappropriate for a letter, as did, "How does one consummate a marriage? A step-by-step instructional guide, if you please, so that I might not embarrass myself with my worldly husband."

No, that wouldn't do. As much as she would want the answers, she would never dare write the questions. It did seem a shame not to say *something* to her aunt when she needed guidance regarding intimacy. She could, perhaps, hint at needing help, but she wasn't altogether convinced Auntie was as keen as Liz when it came to reading words unspoken.

Chewing her lip, she finally penned the letter.

Auntie,

I have arrived to Lyonn Manor, not a bump or bruise to be had – the carriage is so well-sprung and padded, it was like traveling on a cloud. I miss you desperately and wish I could ask your guidance. Being mistress of a manor and being a dutiful wife are foreign to me. I find myself at a loss. I aim to be the best of both, but I do long for your wise advice and insight. I wish you were here and hope we may visit together soon. By the by, you would love the conservatory. I have in mind to turn it into an aviary for Captain Henry. Imagine his delight! Send my best to Cousin Walter. I will always be

Your favorite niece,
Charlotte

With both letters sealed and addressed, she pulled out a fresh sheet to begin her duty list. She labeled it Daily Schedule and jotted in a left-hand column each hour of the day. In a middle column, she wrote the task to be completed. In a right-hand column, she made comments and reminders.

In Charlotte's former life, before she met Drake, she preferred things orderly, structured. Dress at a certain time, tea at a certain time, smile at a certain time. She scheduled her life to perfection. Some might find her attention to detail silly, but she was happier when she knew what to expect and how to act.

This new life was disjointed. Although today was only mid-week of her first week, already her schedule was not her own with the dowager duchess having scheduled her days for her. Housekeeper meetings in the mornings, tea with the dragon, callers in the afternoon, all scheduled by her mother-in-law. She suspected every day would follow suit with her mother-in-law setting the schedule.

Ruefully, she added one hour per day for "dragon slaying."

With a deep breath, Charlotte studied the Daily Schedule and knew if she didn't start with the most important task on the list, she'd lose her nerve.

She walked to the bellpull and rang for assistance. Within moments, a fresh-faced parlor maid stepped inside with a curtsy.

"Your name is Stella, yes?" Charlotte asked.

The maid looked up momentarily, clearly surprised to be remembered and directly addressed by a duchess.

"Yes, Your Grace," said the maid, her eyes returning to the floor. "Shall I bring a tray?"

"No, but thank you. I wish to make a request." Charlotte inched towards the maid so her voice wouldn't carry beyond the parlor doors.

"A request, Your Grace?"

"Yes. I would like all the portraits in my bedchamber removed. I would also like to arrange a meeting with a local artist, someone skilled in landscapes. I wish to commission paintings of the home and gardens for my bedchamber." Her voice might sound confident and authoritative to the maid, but Charlotte's pulse raced. The dowager duchess could overrule her request in a single breath, thus declaring war.

"I'm only a parlor maid, Your Grace. I'll need to ask Mrs. Fisk, and she'll need to—" She stopped when Charlotte interrupted with a tut.

"You do not need to consult anyone. I trust you, Stella, and I leave this task to you, as well as the select staff of your choosing. I know you can do this,

Stella. I *can* trust you, yes?" Charlotte raised a slender eyebrow.

The maid glanced up, blushing. Charlotte could see the girl's wheels turning. If the maid could please the duchess, this could mean a promotion in the future and more personal requests.

"I will see to both tasks, Your Grace. Is there anything else I may do?"

"No, you're excused. Oh, and Stella," Charlotte placed a hand on the maid's shoulder, transferring confidence to her helper. "Discretion is appreciated." With a smile, she sent the maid on her way.

Returning to the Daily Schedule, she placed a tick mark next to the day's "dragon slaying" task.

Charlotte waited in the chaise longue overlooking the walled rose garden. Her mother-in-law would arrive shortly for their tea. As with every day since her arrival, she'd not seen Drake since the previous evening. He was becoming a stranger to her, not that he wasn't already, but now even more so. She could hardly believe only three days ago she had shared a carriage with him and had done so every day for a week's journey, trapped in close quarters. Why had she not made better use of the time? Yes, Sebastian had been present, which had given her pause, and yes, Drake had been crass and mocking, as well as overly flirtatious, but why had she not tried harder to make conversation?

As much as his indecorous behavior had ruffled her feathers, she'd give her left foot to be trapped in a carriage with him again. Unconvinced she'd act any differently than before, she did prefer his amorous attention to his silence. His silence only confirmed what his mother had said was the reason he married her.

Did he intentionally avoid her, or did he have work to do on the estate? No, of course he didn't work, not according to his own admission and certainly not according to his mother. So, what did he do all day?

Knowing so little about the man and his interests was proving an impediment.

And to think, she'd worried during the drive north about how she'd live with him. She had imagined him accosting her in hallways and making vulgar jests during dinner. As much as she had expected that behavior to embarrass her, she'd prefer it to being ignored. Was this the life she was to expect? How disheartening. Once again, her sister had been right. In addition to her philosophy of once a rake, always a rake, Liz had shared unfavorable opinions of marriage, aristocratic marriages in particular, all to do with women as trophies, set on a shelf to be displayed, otherwise ignored by their husbands. Charlotte had found Liz's criticisms unnecessarily harsh. Now, they rang with truth. Charlotte considered herself naïve not to have taken her sister's wisdom to heart.

Mama Catherine entered the room with a thump of her cane, disrupting all thoughts of Drake. Charlotte rose from the chaise and curtsied, a lump forming in her throat.

"Stand straight," Catherine instructed. "We curtsy to no one except royalty. You need to learn how to incline your head, to whom to incline your head, and to whom not to incline your head. Come."

Charlotte noted with disdain that the duchess had shifted from addressing her as a child to a lapdog. In less than a week, she had been demoted. Should she yip in response? No, her dragon slaying task for the morning had been completed. Breathe, relax, and observe.

Obeying the command, Charlotte stepped forward, holding her head high.

"Let us begin with the acknowledgement of peers, then gentry. We do not acknowledge anyone beneath landed gentry, and even then, it depends on the family. Is that understood?"

Charlotte nodded.

"No!" Catherine snapped.

Black eyes skewered Charlotte. A bead of perspiration trickled down her spine.

"What was that movement—a *nod*? Where did you learn that? Don't answer. Follow my lead."

The next hour involved the most absurd lesson of Charlotte's life—the art of inclining one's head. Catherine thumped her cane to command and shush protests. Charlotte's neck ached at the end of the lesson. Of all the duties she had expected to learn, this was not one.

Only when Stella arrived, bringing a tea tray with cheese, fruit, and cold meats, did Charlotte relax. A familiar face was difficult to come by. Preparing the tea with a baluster-straight spine, she tried to catch the eye of the parlor maid before the girl ducked out of the room. No luck. Stella shuffled off without raising her eyes.

Charlotte wasn't so ignorant that she didn't know how to behave with staff, but she found the whole of it silly. At home, back at Teghyjy Hall, staff were practically part of the family. Many of her happiest childhood memories involved sneaking into the kitchen to steal food in hopes Cook would catch her, as the punishment was always a fresh slice of pie and gossip.

Part of being a duchess, she realized, was behaving like one, for the image she portrayed reflected on the entire family, not to mention the reputation of the title, which would last beyond her and on into future generations, just as she was now affected by the reputation of those before her, never mind she knew nothing of them, at least not yet—she was certain that would be a forthcoming lesson, another snoozer by the dowager duchess. Any daughter of a peer would have already studied the lineages of the great families and known all there was to know about the Annick title and line. Alas, she was not the daughter of a peer. Wholly ignorant in all matters, yet her success or failure as the Duchess of Annick would affect current and future generations. She needed not to befriend parlor maids.

"Friday morning," Catherine said, "you will pose for your portrait between nine and noon in the Gray Parlor. I have commissioned portraits for both you and Drake. From one until four, you will receive particularly special callers in the Red Drawing Room. Lord and Lady Montborough will call, as will Lady Wortham and her sister Mrs. Johansen, then finally, after consulting with the duke about Parliamentary matters, Lord Tidwell will join us. I've taken the liberty to answer the correspondences on your behalf. The remainder of this week's afternoons are booked with invited callers."

Catherine had answered Charlotte's correspondences? The woman had already arranged the next three days' schedule on Charlotte's behalf? Fury coursed through her veins. Charlotte strangled her hands, clenching and twisting them. The nerve! Yet again, she wanted to march to Drake and demand he do something, demand he tell his mother who was mistress of the manor now.

Only after deep breaths did she trust herself not to unleash a tempest.

Unperturbed by Charlotte's silence, Catherine continued, "Over the course of this week, we will discuss your social duties, which will include visiting the poor and hosting charity balls and agricultural fêtes. Are you accustomed to calling on villagers?"

"Yes, of course," said Charlotte, proud she could claim experience of something at last. "My sister and I have delivered food to the miners since I was a child. When the children know we're coming, they'll run from their houses to see us. My sister knows their names better than I do. I have a terrible memory for such things. But, yes, I'm accustomed to such a task."

Catherine recoiled. "That is not how it is done. How disgraceful to give them ideas above their station, to mingle with—no, no, no. You will visit the poor, but you must not engage in conversation. *Never* leave the carriage. The maid will bring the basket to the door on your behalf. It is enough of a kindness for them to see the ducal crest and receive the basket. Do you understand?"

The woman couldn't be serious. Lizbeth was more interested in visiting the miners than Charlotte, but that didn't mean she didn't have a fondness for them. The people were kind and always greeted the sisters with affection. Such visits lifted Charlotte's spirits. She liked the attention every bit as much as the miners did. Of course, she never socialized personally with them, not like Lizbeth, but she would never snub them.

Mr. Taylor opened the door, surprising both women. "The modiste has arrived, Your Graces. I showed him to the Blue Drawing Room."

Catherine's eyes narrowed. "I wasn't expecting him for another half hour." She waved a dismissive hand to the butler. "Let him wait."

With the door shut, she turned back to Charlotte.

"I will attend the fitting and choose the appropriate selections. There will be no country fashion in this house." She eyed Charlotte's dress with displeasure. "I expect you to appreciate all I'm undertaking. You had better be worth the time and money I'm expending."

Head held high, Charlotte responded with, "I am the Duchess of Annick. I will make you proud, Mama Catherine."

Chapter 8

Not until dinner did Charlotte see Drake.

He winked at her in greeting, then spent the entire dinner whinging with his mother about a neighbor Charlotte didn't know. Though it had only been a few days since their arrival, to Charlotte he felt like a stranger. He was standoffish, so unlike the ballroom charmer and Vauxhall rogue she knew him to be. This wasn't how she had envisioned life with him.

Mary ate her meal silently, glum from her call from another suitor. As much as Charlotte wanted to ask her about the gentleman, whose name escaped her, she daren't do so in the hearing of Her Grace.

And so, Charlotte also ate silently, feeling tiny as an insect. The least Drake could do was look at her.

It was all too clear his mother was right. He'd married her out of spite. All his flirtation had been for show. He had his own life with countless, experienced mistresses, and no interest in her. Their wedding night made sense, as well. He had arrived to her suite fully dressed with no indication of *wanting* to be with her. At the time, she had thought she'd pushed him away with her inexperience, but it would seem he never had intended them to have a real marriage. Her sister had been right about him all along.

Charlotte was morbidly depressed.

The only brightness in her day had been returning to her suite to change for the evening and finding the portraits removed from the wall. The sweet taste of success lingered until dinner.

As they finished their last course, Drake turned to Charlotte and shocked her by asking, "Would you join me for cards after dinner, my dear?"

Her heart skipped a beat. His sapphire eyes danced with their usual mischief, but his expression was politeness itself, a far cry from the wolfish grin with which she was acquainted.

"I would love to," she said with a flirtatious smile that hid her increasing despondency.

Throughout dessert, she schemed. This could be her chance. She could finally speak to him about his mother, scold him for ignoring her, and question him about his marital intentions. Setting things straight would be the best course of action.

On second thought, perhaps not.

That might put him on the defense, and the last thing she needed was to lose her only possible ally. No, she needed his friendship. She hadn't the faintest how to seduce a man, let alone one with his reputation, but she had to try. On further reflection, this was the better course of action.

Should she skip the card game and invite him to her chamber? Whatever reservations she still had about sharing a bed were overshadowed by the benefits of intimacy. It could bring them closer, bond them. She had hoped to share an interest over the estate, but she would take what she could get. He wouldn't ignore her if she gave herself to him, and he would feel obligated to defend her against the dragon. Better yet, he could send his mother to the dower house once and for all.

"Drake," intercepted the dragon. "I must speak with you after dinner."

"Of course, Mother. Could it wait until after a game of cards with my wife? You have her all day, every day. It's only fair I have time with her after dinner."

"Very well. I will come for you in one hour."

Charlotte ground her teeth.

After dinner, Catherine and Mary retired to the parlor, leaving the newlyweds alone in the lesser dining room.

Drake nodded in the opposite direction towards the Blue Drawing Room. "Shall we?"

Oh, we shall! She wanted to exclaim. *With all my heart! Be my savior and whisk me away from all this suffocating condescension.*

Instead, she wordlessly followed him into the obnoxiously blue room, as blue as her chamber was peach, and joined him at a table near the hearth. Before sitting, he rang the bellpull to request wine, and then grabbed a card deck from a mahogany bureau on his way back to the table.

Before either spoke, two footmen entered the room, one carrying a bottle and two glasses, the other dashing about to close the drapes against the setting sun, casting the room into a candle-lit darkness, flickering flames dancing shadows on the walls.

Memories of the last time they drank wine together warmed her cheeks. Only a week and a half since their disastrous wedding night, but it felt like a lifetime. Was there a subtle way to invite him to her room? She wouldn't protest, not this time, not after the way Catherine made her feel, not after the way the housekeeper made her feel. She wanted to feel important, desired, and beautiful. Drake could make her feel those things.

Drake poured wine into bell-shaped bowls perched on slender, multispiral, airtwist stems, his movements languid, shoulders at ease. In contrast, Charlotte clenched her hands in her lap. They had only an hour before the dragon would descend. Only an hour for her to find a way to reconnect with him without seeming desperate.

Drake took a moment to run one hand through his hair, tussling it into dishevelment, while the other hand reached into his pocket for his snuff box. After a quick pinch, he brought the glasses to the card table.

A low hum buzzed in her ears at the sight of his lithe frame, her pulse quickening. His long legs showed to advantage in the silk-satin breeches. She imagined what he must look like when fencing, shuffling back and forth across the floor, all speed and strength, his arm moving lightning quick with the sabre.

How had she managed to avoid his affections for the entire journey north when all she wanted to do now was run her hands through his hair? But then, did she? She certainly had in London, but now she could not be sure it wasn't that desperate need to be noticed, to gain an ally, to have a modicum of control over something in her life, rather than a genuine desire for intimacy with her husband. She must be going mad. It was this place. It was his mother. It was the feeling of powerlessness. What she wanted was to know him as a person and he to know her, for the two of them to share a marriage, perhaps even fall in love, but that wasn't how this worked, at least not at this point. Desperate measures were needed.

"I thought we might play piquet," Drake offered.

When she took her glass from him, she grazed his fingers with hers, delaying her capture of the stem long enough to run the tips of her fingers over his knuckles.

She looked up through her eyelashes to see how he would respond to her touch. He gave no indication of having noticed. Instead, he set down his glass and began shuffling the cards without looking at her. Right. Flirtation, apparently, wasn't one of her skills. So help her, she would succeed at this if it was the last thing she did. Wine would help.

The first sip prickled her senses, tingling down to her toes, a pleasant heat settling in her limbs. The second sip flushed her cheeks and tickled her stomach. By the third sip, she knew only how much she needed her husband to come to her tonight.

Drake held out the pack of cards in invitation to draw. They each pulled a card.

His smile was smug. "Looks like I deal." He glanced at her empty glass of wine, his untouched. "Thirsty, Charlotte?" One eyebrow raised, cards poised.

Without waiting for a reply, he retrieved the bottle and refilled her glass. She hadn't meant to drink so much so soon. Yes, she wanted to loosen her nerve, but she did need control of her senses, or this seduction would be for nought.

The game began with minimal conversation. This wasn't turning out how she wanted. Blast. Why wasn't he flirting? With each passing minute, she was reminded of Her Grace's words. He married her to antagonize his mother. He thought her desperate and in search of advancement. He wasn't attracted to her. What other explanation was there for his change in behavior?

Yes, yes, so she had brushed off his affections during the drive north, but it had been a stressful ride, and she'd been nervous, so what did he expect? There was no other explanation for his change in behavior from flirty to frosty. He simply didn't want her. The only solution was to improve her game.

"Point of five," she declared, studying him over her cards.

"Not good," he replied.

"Trio of aces."

"Good." He frowned.

"Want to play for stakes?" She sipped her second glass.

His eyes drifted over the top of his cards. The corner of his mouth twitched.

"It'll be fun." She tittered. "What if…the winner gets to kiss the loser?"

He leaned back in his chair, tongue in cheek, lips curling. "Just how is that fair if both parties are rewarded? If I win, then I get to kiss you, but since you would be getting kissed, wouldn't that make you the winner, or more aptly, both of us the winner?"

Ah, now he was getting into the spirit.

"I amend the prize, then. The winner gets to kiss the other person wherever he or she wants. The loser isn't allowed to protest." Not that she could think of anywhere remotely creative to kiss him besides his lips, which looked deliciously soft this evening.

Drake's *oh ho ho* of a laugh was far heartier and saucier than she expected. It excited her to have captured his attention but renewed the nervous knot in her stomach. Apparently, he liked the wager.

Reaching for his glass, he said, "May the best man — or woman — win." He raised his glass in salute before tipping it between his lips.

Charlotte leaned forward, determined to win so she could shock him by kissing him somewhere unexpected. Or, wait, maybe she should want him to win. No, as curious as she was to find out where he might choose to kiss her — hopefully not on her forehead, as she was tired of being treated like a child — she wanted the upper hand this evening. She was exhausted of being dominated in this house and wanted to assert herself. Yes, she must win. This was *her* planned seduction, after all. She needed to convince him to want her.

"So, Charlotte," he drawled, trying to distract her, she suspected, "enjoying being a duchess?"

She played a card before replying, "Not especially. I feel like a dress-up doll for your mother. What have you done all day?"

"Point of 6, Sixième for 16," he declared, leading a card. "I'm not surprised. My mother is like that. I'm positive the two of you will be bosom friends before autumn, seeing as how you're both likeminded."

After she declared and played a card, Drake played two more, then added, "I spent the day in my study. Responded to letters mostly, and then invited Winston to call. Tedious compared to your dress-up day."

Her cards were a blur. More wine should help focus her attention. Yes, a third glass would do the trick. Motioning for more wine, she declared and played another card. Before her next move, she fortified with a fresh sip.

Sliding her foot across the floor until it nudged his shoe, she ever so casually glided her slipper over the tip, then peered from beneath her eyelashes to see if he noticed.

The only tell-tale sign was the twitching corner of his mouth as he cashed five of his cards.

Continuing her foot's trek over his shoe, she slid further up his shin until she could rest her sole on the edge of his chair. Curling her toes against the inside of his thigh, she enquired, "Where's your study? The tour I received didn't reveal this oh-so mysterious room of yours."

"No mystery. Any footman would show you if asked. It's in the west hall past the stairs." His eyes twinkled when he looked at her.

Was it the warmth of the wine she saw in his eyes or attraction? She felt so lightheaded she couldn't tell what she saw, but she hoped it to be the latter.

"The rounded tower?" she queried.

"One and the same." After laying down a card, he paused, grinning. "Would you like to see it?"

"After the game."

"Bollocks to the game. Our hour is fleeting. Let's go now." He tossed aside his cards and drained his glass with a fluid movement.

"I believe by forfeiting the game, I'm declared the winner."

"By Jove, I hope so. You can collect your winnings in the study." He grabbed her hand and pulled her up with a tug.

Charlotte swayed, the room tilting ever so slightly to the left. She hadn't remembered swirls adorning the blue rug when she came in, but there it swirled, right before her eyes.

"Woah there, my dearest," Drake said.

She felt strong arms steady her and heard a throaty chuckle next to her ear. All she could do was giggle and lean against his chest as he guided her out of the drawing room with one arm at her waist.

Mmm. She won the game, even if by default. She giggled again thinking of kissing him. Oh, wait, she was supposed to be concentrating on the location of his study. Squinting kept the gallery from blurring, but it strained her eyes, causing a slight headache. The wine, in hindsight, might have been a poor choice.

Past the staircase, they came to a small oval hall with a single door. With one hand still on her waist, he directed her inside, closing the door behind them.

The study was smaller than she expected. An imposing floor to ceiling bookshelf stood behind a nondescript desk. Windows faced the front of the house on one side, a lit fireplace with a sitting area on the opposite side. The rounded tower had seemed so much larger from the outside. The room wasn't even rounded. She wanted to ask, try to make sense of the space, but the room spun too rapidly for her to think straight.

She leaned against him for support, his arms snaking around her.

He turned her towards him and waited, his hands holding her steady. "Where's my kiss?" His whisper rumbled, raising gooseflesh on her skin.

Placing her hand on his waistcoat to fiddle with embroidered buttons, she asked, "And I may kiss you anywhere?"

Drake purred as he leaned against the door. "This is your game, my dear."

She felt the muscles of his chest flex beneath her hand as she inched her fingers upwards, over his cravat and starched shirt points. Combing his scalp with her fingernails, she gripped a handful of his hair and pulled him to her.

Her cheek chafed against bristly skin until her lips found his earlobe. She tightened her grasp, holding him in place, and traced the ridge of his ear with her lips.

He moaned in response. Emboldened, she retraced her kisses until she returned to his earlobe, taking it lightly between her teeth for a nibble.

Someone pounded on the door.

Startled, Charlotte pressed her finger to his lips and shook her head.

The pounding repeated, louder, more insistent. "Open the door," the dowager duchess commanded from the other side. "You are late for our appointment."

Charlotte mouthed a simple *no*.

The beast rapped the door with her cane. "I do not tolerate tardiness. We have things to discuss."

To Charlotte's dismay, Drake mouthed *I'm sorry* and dropped his hands to his side. For a moment, she thought she would lose her balance, her head swimming from the wine.

He opened the door to a looming, darkened figure. Although she couldn't see those obsidian eyes, she felt them lancing. And then she almost vomited on the woman's shoes.

"Excuse me. I must retire," Charlotte murmured as she slipped past her husband and mother-in-law, stumbling her way to the staircase.

She worried she wouldn't find her bedchamber, not from dizziness, but from the tears.

"I hate her. I hate her. I hate her," she said to the bare walls of her bedchamber once she flung herself onto the bed.

She cried into her pillow until the tears were spent, until her throat scratched when she swallowed. In a small way, she hated him, too. She hated him for not defending her. She hated him for avoiding her for days, leaving her with that woman. She hated him for choosing his mother over her.

Tonight, she needed him and his reassurance, and he had chosen his mother instead, giving into the woman's commands and snarls rather than ignoring her or telling her to shuffle off while he enjoyed the company of his wife. Did he dislike Charlotte so much? Had he wished for the escape? Why had he even bothered to invite her for a game of cards?

She hated them both.

Tucking her knees under her chin, she tried to rationalize through the haze of wine. Maybe he would still come to her tonight. Maybe his discussion with his mother would only take a few minutes, and then he would race up the stairs two at a time to make it up to her. Maybe she was throwing a tantrum because she had been treated like a child for days, thus relenting to the impulse to act like one. What she needed to do was calm herself and have confidence he would come.

She buried her face in her hands and inhaled the essence of almonds from his pomade, fragrant and intoxicating. Yes, he would come to her as soon as that woman finished whatever set down she had for him.

Chapter 9

The strings cut into Drake's fingertips, bruising already callused skin. His bow sawed rather than glided. His fingers hammered across the fingerboard rather than danced. Furious rather than graceful. He pivoted his palm to stretch from the index to pinky, a multi-octave jump that plagued him despite relentless trials. The transition lacked fluidity.

Setting the violin and bow on the lid of the harpsichord, he snatched the music from the stand and returned to his writing desk. How could he affect this transition without overburdening the phrase?

The worn cushion sank beneath him. With tired eyes, he concentrated on the measure in question. The transition needed to be smoother. *Portamento*, perhaps? Tapping his finger against his chin, he stared until the notes blurred.

He had needed a release after dealing with his mother, especially since he couldn't go to Charlotte until he had purged his anger. With the evening going so well between them, he daren't go to her in anger. Music provided the perfect outlet on this occasion.

Make that every occasion. Music always provided an outlet. He funneled his emotions into his work, crafting pieces, both raw and dynamic, that would shake the musical world if ever played for the public.

Mozart would have an apoplexy if he heard the chaos on this page.

Emotion over technique with a full range of dynamics, Drake's own passions charged the phrases in each movement. His growing stack of compositions mostly consisted of violin quartets with pianoforte accompaniment, but he had composed a handful of short works for solo pianoforte, solo violin, and an opera he may never finish beyond one scene.

He composed music for lovers, music that could stir even the blackest of hearts. In some small way, he saw himself as a revolutionary in the music world, but given society's distaste of emotion, he doubted the *beau monde* would appreciate how such music might move them. He would never find out, for as far as he was concerned, no one would hear his compositions, at least not while he lived. Not quite by choice, rather by necessity. If he could find a way for the music to be performed anonymously, he might brave it, but only for the right crowd, and only if his mother never found out. She abhorred music of any kind and especially loathed his interest in it, calling him effeminate and common.

Her words shouldn't rankle him, not after years of proving through reputation he was neither effeminate nor common, yet her words stung, nonetheless. As far as he was concerned, he would die before the world had a chance to agree with her, as they well might.

This evening's exercise in finger dexterity adequately purged him from Mother's little chat, he decided. The fact his hand ached finalized his decision. Circling his wrist and flexing his fingers, he winced.

It was time to seek out his wife. With any luck, Charlotte would pick up where she had left off. He'd only been delayed an hour, two at the most.

Lord in Heaven, what time was it?

He hauled himself to his feet and snuffed the candles in the room, taking only one candlestick with him. Opening the heavily paneled door revealed a bookshelf behind it. He gave the shelving a hearty push. The double-sided bookshelf yawned into his study on the other side of the music room, serving its purpose well as a hidden door in the wall.

Outside, rain beat against the panes, tree branches tapping and scratching in rhythm with the wind. He hadn't realized it was raining, not with the sound-proofing he had spent a fortune on for the music room, experimental noise dampening he had been told was impossible, yet his room proved otherwise. With enough cob and stone, any room could be silenced. The trick had been to use a combination of dense barrier to reduce sound, absorbent material to stop sound, and gaps to scatter sound.

The room was his sanctuary, cut off from sound, sight, and time. He refused to have time dictate his actions while he composed, so he kept the clock where it would perform a more noble duty — tic-toc to the darkness of the desk drawer.

Shutting both music door and study bookshelf firmly behind him, he set the candlestick on the desk and collapsed into a chair. Hopefully, Charlotte wouldn't mind him coming to her sweaty. He ran his hands through wet hair, grimacing. Better sweaty than angry. A bath would be ideal, but too much time had already passed to make her wait for water to be fetched, heated, and brought upstairs. A quick trip to his washstand would have to do.

Charlotte should still be awake, and with any luck, waiting for him. Anticipation thrummed his heart at the memory of her kiss.

He tugged at his cravat, his throat raw from the linen. Beneath the irritation, his skin tingled at the recollection of her hand at the back of his neck, never mind his enjoyment had been hampered by the cravat itself. He had never seen this side of Charlotte, this dominating side, but he liked it, for this was what he had *hoped* for in London with those glimpses of bossiness. It was this attitude that would have her sending his mother packing to the dower house and taking up the mantle as duchess. Her courage thrilled him personally, as well, not just as a duke but as a husband, as a man. She had *wanted* him, not the title, not the money or power, but *him*. No feigned affection, no prim or chaste kiss, only genuine attraction. There was nothing in their shared moment that made him feel rejected, effeminate, used, or common.

If only they hadn't been interrupted. How far would she have taken their interlude? Would *she* have led the dance? Would they have exchanged those words of endearment he longed to hear, exchanged confessions and laughs, two hearts made one?

More to the point, what had got into her? After all her prickly behavior, she had been a little minx this evening. He loved it. He wanted more of it. His firm belief she'd married him for the title was back in question if she was flirting so determinedly. If she'd already got what she wanted, why bother with him now? He questioned if he had misread the signs this whole time, mistaking her behavior.

Perhaps a quick wash would be the best choice before going to her. He could refresh, put his best face forward, and all that, especially for their first evening of intimacy. If he'd only been an hour, he had time for a wet cloth and change.

Yanking at the desk drawer, he pulled out the timekeeper. Dear Lord in Heaven! One glance at the clock sent all his hopes plummeting to his feet. Three in the morning. How had he been in the music room so long? He swore he had only been an hour, two at the most.

Charlotte would be asleep by now.

He was tempted to go to her regardless. If he knew her better, he wouldn't let a little thing like three in the morning stop him. The fact remained, he didn't know how she would react. He didn't know her at all, really. For all he knew, she would scream for help, bringing half the servants to witness the duke trying to seduce his wife in the wee hours.

Tonight was out of the question. What a fool he had been to allow his mother to rile him to the point of losing his opportunity to rekindle romance with Charlotte. Had she sincerely wanted him, or had her behavior been wine induced? What a depressing thought if she only wanted him because she was foxed. Or…surely his mother hadn't instructed her to do her duty as the wife of a duke. His spirits found a new low at that thought. It was not out of the realm of possibility.

Drake wanted nothing more than to love and be loved. Was that too much to ask? That's all he'd ever wanted and the one thing he could never seem to have. Bollocks to views of *convenient* marriage. Bollocks to the lot of society. His arms were made to hold a woman, his heart made to beat against her breast, his lips made to kiss, caress, and whisper endearments.

Nothing would make him happier than to connect with his wife, really connect with her, and not just physical coupling. Truthfully, he wanted a reason to enjoy his home, his entire home. After years of being cooped inside a private room hidden behind a double-sided bookshelf and cobbed walls, soundproofed from the world, he wanted his home to be his own. Years of a musicless house. Years of the grand ballroom used as a drawing room. Years of silence. He hated having his passions suppressed.

Above all else, he hated being alone.

He fantasized playing side-by-side at the pianoforte with his wife, imagined her playing *his* music. Charlotte played the piano quite well, as he'd learned in London. It was, truth told, what convinced him to pursue her. Yes, time had not been on his side. Yes, she had been beautiful, stunning, really. Yes, she had seemed interested in *him*. But it was all so much more than that. It was hearing her play that sealed their fate. His heart had wept at the thought of connecting with someone so deeply, of ripping out the bookshelf to his music room, of turning the drawing room into a performance hall, of finishing his opera and sharing it with the world, of not hiding himself any longer.

At one time in his life, he believed he'd made such a connection with a woman. He'd been mistaken.

He couldn't say with any confidence Charlotte was his second chance. Times like tonight, she revealed a suppressed passion, not unlike his own, that he was dying to ignite. Had he been mistaken when he assumed she wanted him for his title, or was his mistake seeing a passion that wasn't there? He'd be cursed if he was going to repeat the same error in judgement and give his love away to someone who didn't want it.

He slammed the desk drawer closed with a *thwack.* Why was he destined to this life of rejection and isolation, hiding behind bookshelves?

Mother's beady eyes flashed into his mind, chilling his blood and plunging him back into their conversation.

After Charlotte left the room, Mother had thumped her way past him into the study, and before he could shut the door behind Charlotte, the diatribe had begun.

"You are intentionally avoiding me. Don't deny it." Her cane thudded against the Parisian rug, leading her to the middle of the room where she about-faced and glowered.

Only after the door clicked closed did he reply. "My wife wanted to see my study. I fully intended to seek you out after the tour."

After a nervous twist of his pinky signet ring, he reached into his pocket for the snuff box. There wasn't enough snuff in the world for this evening. Better make it two pinches. Feeling calmer, he swaggered to one of the chairs in front of the hearth and fell into the cushion, box still in hand, ready for the next moment he needed to calm his nerves.

"Nonsense." Mother remained standing, staring down at him from the bridge of her nose. "You've been avoiding me since you returned home. I've had enough. This evening, I told you one hour. You knew I would come for you, so you hid yourself, determined to avoid me yet again. I resent your behavior."

"You caught me, Mother. I confess. I've been purposely hiding from you, engaging my wife as a co-conspirator, never mind that you're the one who monopolizes her time. Snuff?" He held out the peace offering, the contents of which held his mother's one sinful pleasure, a solitary reminder she was human.

Without a glance to the box, she narrowed her eyes and punctuated each word with a thud of her cane. "Don't mock me."

To antagonize her, he hooked a leg over the arm of the chair and slouched sideways. With the box perched on his chest and hands crossed over his waistcoat, he flashed her a sardonic smile.

"Willful, arrogant, and lest we forget, spoiled." She scoffed. "You're too much like your father."

"I'll take that as a compliment." He knew the answer to his next question but didn't dare deny her the pleasure of speaking her mind. "No need to mince your words, as I've little doubt why you summoned me. Out with it. What do you think of her?"

"I assume you chose her to spite me?" She didn't wait for an answer. "I had candidates at the ready, each of beneficial familial alliances, each with dowered properties, prosperous for our coffers, but I agreed to your scheme of choosing your own bride on the condition you would choose wisely. I instructed you to select someone trained since birth, someone of a noble family raised to marry a duke. You know very well I was trained from birth to be the wife of a nobleman. Training her now is fatiguing. She's common and knows nothing of our ways."

"Don't tell me you aren't enjoying yourself. You like her. I can tell." To maintain an air of cool confidence, he laced his fingers behind his head.

"The girl is insolent."

"Mmm. Threatened by her? Worried she's not been trained to obey you without question? Afraid she'll usurp you, possibly be a better duchess than you?" He winked though he knew he was treading dangerous waters.

"Don't be absurd. I'll grant you this; she's pretty and promisingly social. Both will be to her advantage since her purpose is to breed your heir. With any luck, she's already with child."

Drake coughed, almost dropping his snuffbox, before sputtering, "Mother! We've not yet been married two weeks."

"No sense in wasting time. Produce an heir and a spare while she's ripe."

Dragging a hand over his face, he muttered, "Your hounding is more likely to cause impotence, you know."

"I beg your pardon." After a pause, she said, "Your wife has one purpose and one purpose only — to produce your heir. *I* run the estate. *You* hold the title. And now she will continue the line. I'm disappointed by your choice, but she will serve her role adequately enough."

Feeling the stab, he defended, "Don't talk about her that way. She's not a possession. She's a person, and she's my wife."

"You're being sentimental, as usual. I should have known not to expect anything more than sentimentality from you. Allow me to help you think like a man, to think like a duke. Women are nothing more than breeders, a man's property to produce future generations. I should know. You must fulfill your duty while she's young," she commanded.

"Ever think I might be able to do that better if you weren't training her during the day and harassing me during the evening? I've had her to myself for *one* hour since we arrived from London. Bit difficult to perform marital duties with you in the room."

"Don't be vulgar."

"That's what she tells me," he mumbled.

"The fact remains you need an heir. Your age is my concern, as is hers." Catherine leaned against her cane, sighing with aggravation. "She's already eighteen and you're three and thirty, both far older than is customary. You cannot take chances. I speak from experience, as you well know." Lines around her mouth deepened as she frowned. "Seven children, four boys, yet here I stand the mother of a wastrel and a useless girl. While I have never begrudged you the title, you should have been the third son. Even married at sixteen, it took me years to conceive. Then the stillbirths. Learn from my trials. You cannot delay. The longer you wait, the more difficult, the greater the risks. The line cannot end with you."

"It's always a pleasure sharing memories with you, Mother. We should do this more often." He needed another pinch. The room had grown uncomfortably warm.

Her eyes burrowed into his, digging for something. "Are you fulfilling your duties?"

He fiddled with the lid on the snuff box, letting the *click-snap* answer for him.

Click-snap.

Click-snap.

He focused his attention on the lid, willing it to fly off its hinges and whack his mother in the nose.

Click-snap.

"I suspected not. You're wasting your time with that doxy, aren't you? That widow. Spilling your seed where it does you no good. You're disgraceful." After a moment of silence, she amended, "Or is it something else? A *someone* else? What of that, that *Winston*? I've never trusted the time you spend with Mr. Everleigh."

Drake's hands stilled.

"Or is it the music? Are you forsaking your duty for that filth, pecking and plucking on women's instruments?"

He curled his hand into a fist. The ink stains would give him away. She eyed his stained fingers and snarled. Too late.

Her cane poked the sole of his shoe. "Stop wasting time with servant work, and stop calling on that woman, a mere trollop. Don't think I don't know what goes on in her house or that Mr. Everleigh accompanies you. You're wicked and sinful. You shame and disgust me. I'll not have my son known as some effeminate heathen."

His words strained between clenched teeth, he said, "I'm neither sinful nor effeminate. Mr. Everleigh has been my friend for decades. Lady Waller is not a trollop. The harpsichord and violin are not *only* for women. *And* I'm a composer, not a heathen.

I compose music, music that needs to be heard, and by more than peers in drawing rooms. I have a talent, rather you recognize it or not, and I aim to do something with it."

"Talent? Bah! No such thing. There is only money and power. Have you no respect for yourself? Only commoners in need of money compose. If you have no respect for yourself, then what of me, what of the life I've lived? Have you no idea what all I've done for you? You're an ungrateful sloth. I've done everything in my power to ensure you never suffered a heavy hand, or worse, turned out like your father. I've sacrificed and toiled so you may know only freedom. I've indulged you for too long, allowing you to traipse the countryside with your lovers and debase yourself like a commoner. Both habits must end here."

"Indulge me? Allow me?" Drake laughed a single *ha*. "I hardly consider burning my compositions or blocking me from all estate business as *indulging*. You've controlled my life at every turn. Are you so afraid I'm like my father? From the way you treat me, one might think you wish me to be just like him."

Turning her back to him, she walked to the door. "I'll not stand for this abuse. You've no idea what sacrifices I've made for you or how well I've treated you. Not everyone lives a pampered life. Now, go to your wife. If you're a *man*, you'll go to her and fulfill your duty. Consider that an order."

Sitting up, his words heavy with sarcasm, he shouted to her retreating back, "Quick! Get my wife! Your orders have made me positively randy."

Chapter 10

"I believe I should rearrange this room. Don't you agree, Mary?"

Saturday afternoon, a full week after arriving to Lyonn Manor, and two weeks into her marriage, Charlotte and Mary sat in the Gray Parlor, enjoying tea and conversation.

"I thought you liked this room," said Mary.

"I do. It's my favorite room, honestly. But I *need* to rearrange it." Her palm pressed against her chest. "Do you ever feel here in your breast the beating desire to change something?"

Inelegantly, Mary shrugged.

"Well, I do. I feel a keen desire to make changes. Drastic changes, you understand. I've been making lists, and I think it should all start in this parlor."

Mary's response was less than enthusiastic. She shifted in her chair, looking sheepish and uncomfortable. Fidgeting with the ribbons on her dress, Lady Mary asked, "Are you positive it's a good idea? Making changes, I mean. Mother prefers things a certain way, and I don't think she'd appreciate you making changes without her approval. Have you spoken with her about rearranging furniture?"

"Oh, Mary, where's your sense of adventure? It will be great fun! And why should I need her permission? *I* am the Duchess of Annick, after all," Charlotte said.

The week had been so disappointing, she needed to do something to feel she belonged, some way to take control of her new life. Given Charlotte's success with removing the portraits in her bedchamber, she felt empowered to do more.

The Gray Parlor was where she anticipated spending most of her time, given Captain Henry called this room home. She fully intended to turn this into the receiving room, assuming she could convince the butler. The wallpaper was Roman silver with an attractive damask motif. The marble fireplace was topped with a mantel-to-ceiling mirror that reflected a row of candelabras. Three large windows took up the far wall, looking out onto the walled rose garden, admirable blooms spilling over the side of the stone.

The parlor was cozy and personable, unlike the imposing Red Drawing Room preferred by Catherine for receiving callers. That room was as disgustingly red as the bedchamber was peach and the Blue Drawing Room was blue. The room bled red from the draperies to the Moroccan leather chair coverings. And, oh, how Charlotte hated the paintings in the drawing room, looming over the sitting area, faces of scowling strangers. The paintings were of the late duke's family, including two larger-than-life portraits of Catherine and her late husband. Nothing against Mama Catherine or Drake's ancestors, but must the portraits be displayed in the room the family received callers, overlooking the primary seating?

If Charlotte weren't mistaken, the Red Drawing Room, with its hideous décor and nonsensical furniture arrangement, including a pianoforte shoved on the opposite side of the room far and away from all seating, had once been a ballroom. It was massive with astonishing acoustics. If Charlotte had her way, there'd be a ball in that room before winter.

"I don't see why you would want to rearrange the parlor." Tugging absently at her bosom bow, Mary asked, "What would you do?"

"I'm so glad you asked." Charlotte stood, grinning, and sashayed to one side of the room. "Imagine if we moved the settee *here*. And then, wait for it, moved the chairs *here*. You could really see the garden from this vantage point! Come. Stand by me and imagine you're seated at the settee. Is it not a divine view?"

Mary complied, albeit hesitantly. As soon as she stood by Charlotte, though, her expression brightened. "Yes, you're quite right. No one could object to this view of the garden, not even Mother, so long as you don't move her favorite chair." Mary pointed to a lone chair in front of the hearth. The legs were sunk so deeply into the rug, Charlotte suspected it hadn't been moved for decades. "Mother sits there every evening. She won't thank you if you move her chair."

Charlotte ignored that her favorite room was also Mama Catherine's room. It was not as though she was going to steal the room from her mother-in-law, merely adapt it for them both to enjoy.

With a courageous heart, Charlotte stepped over to the bellpull. "I'll ring for Stella."

"Who?"

"Stella." Surprised, Charlotte clarified, "The parlor maid." How long had Mary lived here not to know the name of the parlor maid?

"Oh. I didn't realize she had a name."

Uncertain how else to respond, Charlotte laughed.

Both the maid and her sister-in-law might be reluctant, but she was determined.

One rearranged parlor and two hours later, Charlotte looted boxes, pulling out clothes to throw over chairs, ottomans, and tables. Mary squealed as she twirled with a ball gown in her arms.

Scattered about the room were twelve dresses, one ball gown, and three riding habits, along with several bonnets, one pair of shoes per dress, stockings, gloves, handkerchiefs, and several fans. Oh, it was wonderful to be a duchess! Morning dresses, tea dresses, walking dresses, dinner dresses, and carriage dresses littered the chair arms and the back of the settee.

"I never expected them to arrive so soon. I was only fitted on Tuesday! How is this possible?"

"What Mother wants, she gets. I'm convinced every seamstress in Annick has been working since your fitting to ensure a week's worth arrived immediately. These are only the start. Mother is seeing to a new wardrobe." Still holding the yellow ball gown to her bosom, Mary bowed. "May I have the next dance, Your Grace?"

Charlotte snatched up a periwinkle dress, draped it over her shoulder, and curtsied. "I saved the next dance for you, my lady," Charlotte replied.

Their giggles of delight were accompanied by Captain Henry's singing interspersed with squawks. They danced about the room. Charlotte was too excited to worry about looking silly, and besides, no one was there to see her acting childish except Mary. A short time ago, the butler had interrupted their rearrangement to bring in a flurry of footmen with boxes, all courtesy of the modiste.

Charlotte and Mary collapsed into an empty chair together and buried themselves under bonnets.

"Is it always this exciting to receive new clothes?" Charlotte asked.

"Yes, always!" Mary declared, then rethought her answer. "No, not always. Not when the new clothes are purchased for lecherous suitors who foam at the mouth."

"I don't envy you. Tell me you did your best to discourage the frother's affections." Charlotte donned a bonnet and grabbed an ivory handled fan.

"I tried every trick in my arsenal, but I don't think he was deterred. I even professed to keeping pet toads hoping he'd find me odd, but he didn't listen to a word I said." Mary tried on a pair of half boots while she whinged. "Speaking of not hearing a word, one suitor Mother invited was so old he needed an earhorn to hear me! Lord Collumby. Should have been Lord *Horn*by. The only temptation is he lives in Shropshire, far from Mother. She says he's a wealthy earl who won't live long enough for me to care."

"She does have a point, you know." Charlotte flicked the fan flirtatiously.

Mary wrinkled her nose before they fell into another bout of laughter.

"I knew we would be the best of friends," Mary said. "I'm so happy you're here. Life can be tedious with Mother. I worried Drake wouldn't marry, and then she would have forced on him someone just like her."

Charlotte had to agree that one Mama Catherine was enough for any family, but she didn't care for another reminder that Drake had felt forced into marriage, especially not after sharing with Mary the happiest hours she'd spent since London. The new dresses and parlor rearrangement had her feeling encouraged about the future, so much so, she almost didn't mind the forthcoming evening with her mother-in-law. Catherine had informed her they would be writing invitations for the annual shooting party in October. Another day scheduled by the dragon. Another day not her own.

"I will need an entire room for my new wardrobe, Mary."

"And more is to come." Mary traced the embroidered flowers on one of the dresses. "I'm envious. If this is what it is like to marry a duke, then I want to marry a duke, too. You are so fortunate, Charlotte." After a thoughtful pause, she asked, "Are you happy you married my brother? Do you love him?"

Startled, Charlotte set the fan aside and unlaced the bonnet. In London, she thought love might come naturally over time, but she supposed she had been mistaken. She hardly knew Drake and felt little more than a pawn between him and his mother. Such sentiments couldn't be shared with his sister.

"I admit, I'm dazzled by Drake. I adored him from our first meeting." Hopefully, that was a satisfactory yet noncommittal answer.

Mary nodded. "I understand. Mother says marriage has nothing to do with love. Only commoners marry for love, she reminds me with every call from a suitor. I've oft wondered if she's lying. The way my brother looks at you makes me think Mother is full of fluff."

"The way he looks at me?" Charlotte sat up.

"Oh, you know, like you're the prettiest girl in the world. Starry eyed. He watches you at dinner when you're not looking."

"Well, you must be mistaken. He doesn't look at me like that. *I* would notice," Charlotte protested.

Mary, obviously bored by a conversation about her brother, pulled out a box of ribbons to exclaim over.

Chapter 11

Drake lunged past his attacker, narrowly missing the tip of the sword.

No time for anything more than a swift intake of breath. Without an escape, he would be skewered, a decorative tassel at the end of his assailant's blade.

After a prompt riposte, he shuffled backwards.

His opponent advanced.

The metal of their sabres met in a conversation of quick parries and ripostes.

His arm burned. His shoulder blade protested. His mind needed to be sharper for this moment, his body more rested.

One second of relaxing his guard could prove fatal. He pushed himself to concentrate, watching infinitesimal movements to second guess his opponent.

The battle royale ended with a feint attack to Drake's chest, the sword's intention being Drake's head.

Drake's stop cut and circular parry deflected the sabre. With a quick balestra footwork, he leapt airborne into a flunge, his flying lunge ending with a cut to the man's head.

"Touché!" shouted Drake.

"Aye, I noticed." Winston laughed, removing his wire mask before shaking Drake's hand. "Splendid displacement, mate. It's a good thing we weren't dueling, or I'd be missing my left ear."

"You might be a sight better looking without an ear, old fellow." Drake slapped his friend's back as they moved to the edge of the ballroom to sheath sabres and remove padding.

While Drake and Winston hadn't fenced competitively since Eton, they did meet weekly to stay nimble and strong, strength being an easy win given the heftiness of the sabre, the heaviest of fencing swords.

Winston ruffled his close-cropped hair, smoothing the dishevelment caused by the mask. "Try as you might to insult my esteem, I know you're still bitter about that time Miss Frances chose me over you."

"Good Lord, you're still on about that? Has nothing happened in your life since we were teens? As I recall, Frances had horse teeth. Not a prize I would cling to beyond a year."

Winston threw back his head and laughed.

Mr. Winston Everleigh, eldest son of Viscount Rutherford, held the title of Drake's best mate. While Drake had numerous friends during his visits to London, namely a group of fashionable peers, including the Prince of Wales, most of those friends returned to their small part of the world after Parliament recessed. Winston and Sebastian both lived in Northumberland, making an easy year-round friendship possible.

Not many of his acquaintances could boast a close relationship with Drake, however. From their perspective, he was everyone's friend, a well-liked fellow, and the life of the party, but no one knew him beyond a surface association. Winston was the closest friend he had, and even Winston knew little about him above what Drake wanted him to know. As much as he trusted Winston, Drake limited with whom he shared personal confidences. Even Sebastian heard only what Drake was willing to share, not all of it truth, either, given how determined he was to keep his repetition known.

Winston, specifically, was a friend good for two things: fencing and snuff. The man was a connoisseur of all things tobacco related, from snuff to cigars, and brought Drake the most exotic blends. Although Drake considered Winston his most loyal friend and would second him in a duel in a heartbeat, they discussed only things shallow and comical, always aiming for laughs over aught else.

"I admit, I'm surprised you called on me today," Winston said, pulling off his chest pads to pile onto one of the chairs shoved along the perimeter of the room. "I thought as a bridegroom, you would spend at least a month abed with your bride, and knowing your appetite," he pressed, "I was certain you would be homebound for at least two."

"Who's to say she didn't beg for a moment's reprieve? I'm proud to say my wife is well satisfied with her new situation." Drake winked.

"Splendid! I had hoped the two of you would suit. I worried you'd bring home a younger version of your mother, another tyrant to run your life. I even told Mr. Butler to ready a room for you in case you needed a place to hide from the battle-axe."

"I appreciate your vote of confidence," the duke jeered. "Now, if you don't mind, the lady awaits my return."

"Why not stay a touch longer? Join me at Nero's for a game of Faro or Hazard. She can wait for you to finish a quick game, can't she?" Winston waved over a footman to stow the equipment.

"Not much in the mood for losing money, mate, but next week may be a different story." Drake stood still while a footman slipped on his coat.

"At least stay for a drink," Winston implored.

"Love to, but I should head home. Hectic day ahead. Did I tell you about the ridiculously fake Frenchman who sketched my portrait yesterday?"

Winston followed Drake to the entry hall where the butler handed over a hat, riding crop, and cloak.

"No hard feelings, Wins?" Drake asked his friend. "Listen, I'll make it up to you. Why don't I pick you up tonight after supper? It'll be my first opportunity to visit Maggie. What do you say?"

"Oh ho!" Winston laughed hollowly. "I thought you said things were going well between you and your bride. You've only just returned home, yet you're planning to see Maggie? Do I smell trouble in paradise already?"

"Nonsense! We see eye-to-eye on our marital arrangement, and she has encouraged me in her own way to resume my life as I had before the wedding."

Drake took a step outside the door, hoping to discourage further conversation, now embarrassed to have mentioned Maggie. Winston's reaction had not been what he expected.

"Sounds like the perfect wife," Winston said. "You may just convince me to take the leap if I can have my wife's bed when I want it, my mistress' bed when I want it, *and* my gaming. You've married the perfect woman, Drake!"

"So I have. Shall I pick you up for Maggie's then? There's certain to be a party, and you know what that means." The duke slipped on his hat and cloak.

"Thanks, but no thanks. Not my cup of tea these days. Out of curiosity, will Teresa be there?"

"I would think so. She moved in with Maggie last year." He was surprised Winston wouldn't want to see his lady, a once world-renowned opera singer. "Didn't you know?"

Winston shook his head. "I haven't seen Teresa in ages, I'm afraid. I thought you knew. Lost my appetite for their scene to be honest. I confess I'm surprised you're still in it." Winston studied Drake a moment, chewing his upper lip in thought, then said, "Don't take this the wrong way, but between your wife and Maggie, I don't see the contest."

Drake grinned, ready to end an increasingly uncomfortable conversation. "She'll always be my Maggie," he said cryptically. "If you change your mind, send me a missive, and I'll swing 'round to pick you up."

"Taking the ducal coach as usual?" Winston followed Drake to the front drive where his horse waited.

Reaching for the reins from a groom, Drake replied, "Always. No reason to go if I don't ride through town in as much pomp as I can."

Winston shook his head. "I wonder about you sometimes."

"How's that?"

"I wonder if you visit Maggie because you're still in love with her or because you want everyone to *think* you're in love with her. It would be faster and more private riding, yet you always insist all of Annick knows the duke is visiting his mistress." Still shaking his head, Winston held out his hand for a farewell.

By supper, Charlotte convinced herself she'd over-reacted to both Catherine's and Drake's behavior during the week. The day had been a success with new dresses, a new friendship, and a newly arranged parlor to lift her spirits. After a disappointing first week, she needed a day like today to boost her morale.

Her mother-in-law may show her welcome in unusual ways, but given she'd not yet objected to the parlor, Charlotte assumed the silence to be a nod of approval. Charlotte's word and opinion meant something in the household after all. With her bed-chamber and now the parlor bearing her mark, she felt more settled and certainly more respected, which was quite the feat after the set down her mother-in-law had given on more than one occasion. At this rate, Charlotte would be able to enact more changes from her growing list.

As for Drake, he couldn't be entirely to blame regarding the botched seduction. He had promised only an hour from the start, would never have expected Charlotte to want more, and may not have been in the mood to continue their flirtation after contending with his mother.

With this frame of mind, she renewed her spirits once more for a meal with the family.

From the moment Charlotte sat next to her husband, she noticed he was distracted. Was he thinking about her? Perhaps he was upset about her frostiness during the painting session the morning before — oh, she had been an absolute fright.

She'd snubbed him at every dinner since the night of the failed seduction, mostly from her own embarrassment at having tried to seduce him and failed, but also as subtle punishment for his choosing his mother over her. The morning of the painting session, however, she'd been downright wretched. Her behavior might have been comical to an onlooker, but she wondered if she'd gone too far. Well, at the time it felt justified. In hindsight, that might not have been the best approach.

Batting her eyelashes at his furrowed brow, she leaned towards him.

"I see you have no great love for the soup either," she observed, feeling insipid but not knowing how else to start a conversation.

Absently spooning the liquid, he looked up, his gaze distant. "Pardon?"

"The soup. You've barely touched it."

"Oh." He glanced down, frowned, and set the spoon aside. "Not hungry. A lot to do after dinner."

"Yes, I know what you mean. I've spent hours writing invitations to the shooting party. And here I thought dukes and duchesses spent their time frivolously. You've misled me!" She tittered, touching his arm.

Drake's eyes narrowed. "Is this not the life you wanted?"

"Well, I couldn't say. I had no expectations other than what you told me, as you well know," she chided.

"Oh, yes, I suppose once upon a time you did ask what dukes do all day. Yes, well, now you know."

"No, I'm afraid I don't. I know what duchesses do all day, and it's dreadfully boring. What did *you* do today?"

His frown deepened before he shook his head, airing it of whatever had troubled him.

As though starting the conversation anew, he looked up, his eyes twinkling and his lips curving into a casual smile. "Fenced with Winston. Great sport. And now you have the pleasure of imaging me in tight fencing garb. I'll have you know, it leaves nothing to the imagination."

With a gasp, a scowl, and a blush, Charlotte glanced at Mary and Catherine to ensure they were ensconced in conversation of their own.

"I...I..." She swallowed, summoning the courage to say something witty and flirty in return. "I would like to see that." Chewing her bottom lip furiously, she stared down at her soup bowl.

"Truthfully?" His tone revealed his surprise. "After this week, nay, after yesterday morning, I rather thought you didn't want to see me at all."

"Oh, that. Yes, well, I wasn't feeling my best."

"Understatement of the year, Charlotte. You had ice chips forming on your shoulders. I thought the artist would have an apoplexy when he wanted to paint us side-by-side to capture the romance, but you refused to stand within ten feet of me."

Oh, botheration. She really had behaved badly.

"As I said, I wasn't feeling my best. Besides, who could take that man seriously when his Scottish brogue slipped through his faux French accent every time I annoyed him? It encouraged me to annoy him more."

"Ha!" Drake's laugh startled his mother and sister momentarily. Leaning closer to Charlotte, he said, "You have a wicked streak, my dear. Why am I only now realizing it? I like it."

To her surprise, he reached for her hand beneath the table, cradling her knuckles in his fist and kneading her palm with his thumb.

Her first reaction was to pull away. What if someone saw? How dare he take such liberties with her person? How was she to finish her soup? But then she schooled herself. This was what she had been wanting. Not exactly *this*, but his attention at least.

"Tell me more about this side of you," he said, his voice lowering. "Were you a mischievous child?"

"Anything but. I was the perfect pupil. Everything my tutors instructed, I did. I never wanted to disappoint them."

"How frightfully dull." He chuckled.

"Yes, I suppose you would think so. I must seem dull compared to your…your experience. My sister was always the adventurous one. I never did like adventures unless they were well planned. It was only fun if I knew what to expect, you see. Yes, you would see me as dull."

Realizing she was babbling, Charlotte stopped talking and focused her attention on the exchange of plates by a flurry of footmen. Freeing her hand from his grasp, she tried a few bites of fish, embarrassed both by her confessions and by his seeing her as dull. There was no reason he should see her as anything else, but the realization still hurt.

"You're far from dull, Charlotte," he countered, as though reading her mind. "Always wanting perfection sounds dull, but *you're* not dull. Anyone with a love for music has a heart of passion, and passion is never dull." His smile widened, his fish ignored.

Setting down her cutlery, she replied, "I already told you I don't play well."

"First, that's a lie. Second, you've misheard me yet again. I said nothing about playing well, rather having a love for music. You don't have to play well to love music, and I know for a fact you feel the music to the very soles of your shoes. I've watched you play, remember."

"Yes, and so you should know my enjoyment of playing and my ability are two vastly differently things."

"Stop," he commanded gruffly.

"That was rude." She sat up straighter, affronted. "Whatever am I stopping?"

"Stop berating yourself. You are more than accomplished, your doubts be dashed."

Her face warmed, and her stomach fluttered. Returning her attention to the fish, she hoped again her mother-in-law and Mary wouldn't see her flushed cheeks.

To shift the conversation away from herself, she turned the discussion to Winston, asking about the friend who she'd heard little about. However much she enjoyed Drake's compliments, she didn't want to talk about her shortcomings.

"The last person I want to talk about is Winston," he answered. "I want to talk more about you. From precocious child to duchess. Brava. What made you so ambitious?"

"I wouldn't say I was ambitious. I wanted what, I suppose, most girls want — to be praised and admired. I wanted to be perfect at everything I did. I set my sights on perfection and expected nothing less."

"Ah. I mistook your desire for perfection as obsequiousness, but no, I see it for what it is now. You really *are* passionate."

"I most certainly am not." Charlotte huffed. "I am in full control of my emotions."

"Mmm. Yes, you are a hotbed of passion waiting for release."

"I beg you to stop such talk this instant. We were having a perfectly civil conversation. I'll not have you embarrass me in front of your family. What if your mother overhears?"

"If you gave half as much thought to what you want as you do to what other people think, you could accomplish everything your heart desires, Charlotte."

"As you have? You've made it abundantly clear you don't give a fig for what people think, and where has that got you?" Her hand flew to her mouth, ashamed she'd said such a thing, especially when her whole intention of the conversation had been to flirt.

"Touché."

With feathers ruffled, she tried again to turn the conversation to Winston. This time, Drake complied.

After dinner, the family retired to the Blue Drawing Room, all except Drake, who excused himself, no doubt to work in his study. When he didn't invite her to play cards after dinner, she wasn't the least deterred. Despite a lingering self-consciousness, she was more determined than ever to resume her plan of seducing him. This week had proven how much she needed him as an ally and confidant, even if they didn't see eye-to-eye on conversation topics.

If he didn't come to her tonight, she would go to him. There would be no mistaking her intention. And if he lingered in his study too long, she would drag him out by his ear.

Hopeful about the evening and contented by the day's successes, Charlotte stayed up much later than planned, thoroughly enjoying round after round of piquet with Mary. Not until the clock chimed midnight did they stop.

As she rounded the top of the stairs, she plotted how she might surprise Drake.

If he were already abed, and she could wrangle the courage, she could slip into his bed and wake him. And then what? Perhaps, instead, she should wear one of the more provocative chemises and stand in his doorway with the candlestick until the light woke him. Her intention would be clear, and it wouldn't take nearly as much courage as climbing into the bed uninvited.

She certainly liked the idea of going to him and not the other way around. In this way, she would be the one in command of the situation, and there was nothing more empowering to her than that.

Her smile lingered until she opened the door to her bedchamber.

Chapter 12

At least ten pairs of eyes stared at Charlotte when she entered her bedchamber, all peering down from their paintings on the wall.

She suppressed a sob. The horrid portraits had returned.

How had her mother-in-law known they'd been removed? It could mean only two things. Either the woman had been in her room snooping, or she had a spy reporting back to her.

Charlotte collapsed on the settee, defeated. Never had she felt so voiceless, so powerless. Why was the dowager duchess intentionally making Charlotte miserable?

No. This wouldn't do. Charlotte ground her fist into her palm and pursed her lips. This wallowing wouldn't do. She needed to fight. She had made her move, and Catherine countered. Instead of giving up, she needed to fight harder, needed to declare war, show this woman she would not so easily be beaten. If she were ever to have power in this house, ever to become the lady of the manor, she needed to stiffen her backbone.

"I am the Duchess of Annick," Charlotte commanded to the empty room.

With a stomp of her foot, she yanked on the bellpull.

Her lady's maid, Beatrice, staggered in with a curtsy and stifled yawn.

"Shall I ready you for bed, Your Grace?" Beatrice asked, stepping forward to begin undressing Charlotte.

"No, not yet. We have a more important matter to deal with first."

"Do we?"

"I assume you know Stella? Bring her to me," instructed Charlotte.

"The parlor maid? Please, allow me to aid you. There is nought the parlor maid can do that I can't do," Beatrice pleaded, concerned she had failed her mistress somehow.

"I need you both. Look at the walls, Bea! Look!" She flailed her hands at the paintings, fighting back tears. "I asked Stella to remove the paintings, but they're back. Someone put them back. I need her to do whatever she did before to remove them and see that they do not return. I also need to know who put them back, if she knows," Charlotte explained.

"Oh. Oh, I see," Beatrice's eyes widened as she looked around the room. "I will return in a moment, Your Grace."

Charlotte could always count on Beatrice. They had been together for years.

As she waited, she felt a twinge of guilt. So urgent had she been to regain control, she'd sent her maid to wake poor Stella, who no doubt had an early morning ahead of her. How thoughtless of Charlotte. Too late now. She resolved to make it up to the girl.

True to her word, moments later, Beatrice arrived with a startled Stella.

After expressing her humblest of apologies for the late hour and sudden summons, Charlotte launched into the problem, wanting to resolve it quickly to set her nerves at ease and to allow poor Stella and Beatrice both a chance for sleep.

Looking around the room, Stella physically jolted at seeing the walls.

"I'll be dismissed! Oh, please don't let her dismiss me, Your Grace. Mrs. Fisk must have seen us or else seen them missing. I had two footmen help me, and we hid them. Oh, she'll have us all dismissed." The maid began to panic.

"No one is dismissing anyone. I won't allow it. They may want me to feel powerless, but I'm not. If the housekeeper tries, come directly to me."

Charlotte thought about Stella's words.

What would the housekeeper care about portraits? No, it had to be the dowager duchess. The dragon must have come into her room to snoop, or else the housekeeper came, saw, and reported the change of décor. To maintain power over Charlotte, Catherine must have demanded the paintings be returned. Somehow this was all done at the command of her mother-in-law. The woman made no secret of her disdain, after all.

"I want the portraits removed again, but this time, Stella, have them taken to the dower house. If she wants these on the wall so much, she can hang them in *her* house."

Stella glanced at Beatrice before asking, "Is she finally moving to the dower house?"

Charlotte balled her fists and perched them on her hips, determined and proud. "Not yet, but the least we can do is prepare it for her with the portraits she values so much."

She would like to see the woman's response to this move. This showed Charlotte refused to be bullied.

"I need you to do something else for me, Stella. In place of the paintings, hang drapery. That will discourage anyone from placing paintings on the wall again, at least until my landscapes are completed."

"Yes, Your Grace." Stella curtsied and waited for further instruction.

"Thank you, Stella. If possible, do this while I'm with Her Grace tomorrow. I would have you do it tonight while she's abed, but we're all too exhausted, I think. Please, return to your own bed," Charlotte said with a nod.

The maid left, leaving Beatrice and Charlotte alone. Charlotte slumped into the chair at her dressing table, her spirit worn thin. Perceptively, Beatrice rushed to her mistress' side and began pulling out hair pins to ready for bed.

Beatrice dressed her in a plain, cotton nightgown before turning down the bed linen. "Would you like for me to snuff the candles, Your Grace?" she asked.

Charlotte could do no more than nod. As much as she tried not to feel defeated, the bold move by her mother-in-law weighed on her heart.

With a quick candle treatment, Beatrice left Charlotte alone with her thoughts.

Sheets pulled to her chin, she stared at the wooden canopy. Charlotte couldn't sleep. Was she making too big of a deal out of a few paintings? They were only silly paintings. Seemed childish to declare war over portraits of stodgy women.

But that wasn't the point, she reminded herself.

The point was that she had an opinion, and that opinion mattered. If she didn't want something in her own bedchamber, she shouldn't be forced to live with it. And if she had an opinion about the arrangement of furniture, the opinion should at least be considered. This was her house now.

She needed to talk to Drake. Long gone were her plans to use seduction to gain his alliance. A stern talking to was warranted. He needed to choose a side in this war, with or without the consummation of their marriage.

Restless, she threw off the covers and swung her feet to the floor. After a few minutes struggling to light the candlestick at her bedside table, she crossed the room, heading straight for his chamber.

Hand pausing at his door, she wondered if she ought to wait until morning. It had to be two in the morning by now, possibly later. No, she may lose nerve by morning. If she didn't act on the impulse now, she would never do it. With a deep breath, adrenaline fueling her bravery, she knocked once, then pressed the handle to open the door.

The room was black beyond the sphere of her candle. She trekked forward towards the bed.

"Drake?" She voiced, her words shaking. "Could we talk?"

Self-consciousness weakened her knees with each step. Would he think her a silly ninny? How stupid this might all sound to him.

She ought not to have worried, however, because she saw as soon as she reached the edge of the bed that the duke wasn't in the room. His bed sheets were turned down, awaiting their master, but no master graced the bedchamber.

Breathe, she told herself. Just breathe. She needn't get upset. This was only a minor setback.

Back in her room, she wrapped herself in a dressing robe and slipped on stockings and shoes before creeping down the stairs. With every step, she prayed she wouldn't see a footman. The last thing she wanted was servants gossiping that she had prowled the house, hunting for her husband in her wrapping robe. This was not a dignified way for a duchess to behave. A duchess didn't lurk around the house in undress in the middle of the night.

She needed Drake and was perturbed beyond reason he was never where he should be.

With an unsteady hand on the railing, she circled her way down the rounded stairs, preparing her speech in her head. Without knocking, she pushed open the study door. With a frown, she saw it, too, was empty. He had left for the study after dinner, or at least, she had assumed that's where he went. Come to think of it, she hadn't asked his plans. The chime of the hall clock sounded three in the morning. Later than she had thought. If not in his room and not in his study, where would he be at three in the morning?

This helplessness, this sense of abandonment wore on her nerves.

When she returned to her room, she pulled the bellrope again. It took too pulls before Beatrice sluggishly stumbled in, wiping crust from her eyes as she curtsied.

"Yes, Your Grace?"

"Where is my husband?" Charlotte questioned.

"Your husband?" Beatrice's features contorted in confusion.

"Yes, where is the duke?" Her words were sharp, edged with frustration.

"Is he not abed?" asked the maid.

"If he were abed, I wouldn't have sent for you. I should have thought that much would be obvious. If you don't know where he is, find out."

"Find out where His Grace is?" The lady's maid blinked.

"That's what I said. He's not in his bed, and he's not in his study. I refuse to walk into every room of this house in my wrapping gown trying to find him. Would you have me look in the stables while I'm at it? Someone must know where he is. I don't mean to snap at you, but I'm at my wit's end and need to speak to my husband," Charlotte said.

"A moment, if you please." Beatrice ducked out of the room.

Charlotte paced for nearly half an hour, wondering if Beatrice had fallen asleep on her mission. Or, Charlotte stopped pacing, her heart thumping, what if Beatrice had found him and told him to come to her? What if he was on his way to her room now? Self-conscious, she eyed the door.

Her heart nearly leapt out of her chest when the servant door opened behind her, Beatrice shuffling in, head hung low.

"He's from home, Your Grace. He took the carriage after dinner to, um, call on a friend." Beatrice fumbled on her words.

"Call on a friend?" Her heart skipped a beat, pulse racing.

Beatrice nodded, her eyes not meeting Charlotte's.

Charlotte stared at her maid, thinking. At dinner, he mentioned visiting Winston. Could he have called on Winston and got so foxed he stayed for the night? Seemed plausible. All the same, Charlotte sensed a foreboding.

She'd known from courtship onward but not heeded her sister's warnings. She'd married a rake. And how did rakes spend their time?

Her heart splintered at the thought.

"Dress me. I want to see my husband. Dress me and wake a groom to take me to him. If there's an evening party, he'll need me by his side." This could only end in tears, but she didn't care. She had to know.

"That wouldn't be a good idea, Your Grace, not a good idea at all," said Beatrice.

"I don't care what kind of idea it is. I'm going to my husband, and I'm going now. Who is this friend, and where does he live? Hurry up and dress me." Charlotte disrobed and held out her arms so the maid could change her gown.

"Don't make me say it, Your Grace. Please," begged Beatrice.

Tears threatened at the edges of Charlotte's eyes, her throat tightening.

"And what is it you don't want to say, Bea?" She asked, already knowing the answer.

Beatrice's voice dropped to a whisper. "The friend isn't a *him*."

Charlotte waited, mostly because she couldn't feel her limbs or find her voice.

"The friend is his…his ladybird." The maid's neck flushed.

The threatening tears stung Charlotte's eyes, blurring the room, wetting her cheeks.

Drake hadn't even given her a chance. She might have botched her attempts at flirtation, but he hadn't given her a chance. He preferred another woman.

Her heart shattered. As alone as she felt before, nothing compared to this moment.

She was truly alone.

Her voice cracking, Charlotte replied, "Then I will go to them and scratch out their eyes. Dress me."

"Please, Your Grace. You don't want to do this," warned Beatrice.

"Don't tell me what I want. I know what I want. I want my husband. If you won't dress me, then get me a servant who will!" She cried in desperation.

Beatrice didn't move.

The duchess sank to the floor on her knees. He didn't want her. He married because he had to. He didn't want her.

Between sobs, she stammered, "Leave me, Bea. Go."

Beatrice dithered before darting from the room.

Chapter 13

One dismal week later, Drake found himself at Maggie's for a second time.

Never had he intended to return, nor had he wanted to go the first time. Not wanting to blindside her, he'd first gone from a sense of obligation to tell her about his bride before she heard it from one of her staff. A letter would have sufficed, but he decided a personal call would be preferred over angering her, even if it meant opening old wounds. One never knew how Maggie would react, especially if reduced to a correspondent not worth visiting.

The first time had served its purpose.

Why was he here *again*?

Despair brought him to her door again, that was what. Utter despair. He had no one else to turn to. A world of friends, yet he was alone. Maggie was not even a friend. To whom else could he confide, though? She was the only person who knew his secrets. The only person with whom he could be, to some degree, himself, and confess his thoughts and fears. Knowing she did not care and knowing the more he said, the more she could use against him didn't stop him. Loneliness did funny things to a person.

As such, after a dismal week, he returned, not unlike a patient in need of laudanum.

Describing the past week as dismal was being generous. Unbearable would be more appropriate. For reasons unbeknown to him, Charlotte hadn't so much as glanced in his direction for a week. Dinners were the worst. She pretended not to hear him when he spoke and made a point to engage his sister in conversation for the length of the meal. Her behavior was not that of a shy, nervous, or distracted Charlotte, rather an angry Charlotte wanting to punish him. The tilt of her head, the narrowness of her eyes, the tightness of her frown, all spoke of a punishing anger. She wanted him to feel ignored, wanted him to see her displeasure. The trouble was he could not fathom what he had done. Could she not come to his study and reprimand him instead so that at least he would know where he had wronged? He couldn't apologize for or rectify the error of his ways if he hadn't wittingly done wrong.

Predictably, his mother noticed Charlotte's behavior. As if Drake weren't already melancholy about the direction his life had taken, Mother added salt to the wound with accusations and enquiries to his inability — or was it unwillingness — to satisfy his wife.

The old pattern renewed: insult from Mother spurred a romp in the carriage to Maggie's for all the world to see. However dreadfully guilty he felt for letting Winston believe his affair with Maggie was ongoing, the renewed jabs from Mother regarding his being too much like his father had sent him spiraling into old habits. To make matters worse, he dug his hole deeper with Sebastian during the week by not only implying to his cousin but blatantly admitting to the continuation of an affair with Maggie. Drake had always been prone to exaggeration and insinuation, allowing people to assume what they wished from a simple waggle of his eyebrows, but he had never been an outright liar. So deep he'd dug his grave this week, he couldn't see the light of day anymore. His desperation, it would seem, knew no bounds. Even as he used his mother as an excuse to his irrationality, he knew he was the only one to blame. He did not *have* to use Maggie as a shield. But he did.

As it had in the past, he assumed Winston and Sebastian's cheers and jests of his conquests with the fairer sex would boost his spirits and assuage Mother's needling. The thing of it was, they hadn't cheered. They'd looked at him as if he were the worst sort of villain. He knew, then, he'd gone too far to assure his masculinity. As if that wasn't humbling enough, there was the realization that Mother suspected it all a charade, making his efforts futile.

He only hoped Charlotte would never know the foul things he'd said to either Winston or Sebastian to salve his own soul. If she would give him a chance, he'd spend his life making it up to her. A bit difficult when she wouldn't speak to him. He supposed she was happy with her new title and pleased to be rid of him. Why she bothered to flirt on occasion was beyond his understanding. He knew only one thing — she resisted every attempt he made to charm her.

And so, he settled in his grave.

Maggie massaged his scalp with her free hand, her lap serving as his pillow, while she blew cheroot smoke into his face to antagonize him.

"It's hopeless, I tell you. She doesn't want me." Drake fretted, fiddling with the lace on Maggie's dress. "I have frostbite from her icy glares."

"She's young. Give her time." Her voice was ragged from years of smoking cigars.

"She gets frostier by the day, not warmer. Now, she pretends I don't exist. I don't see how time will repair that."

He closed his eyes to savor the feel of fingers in his hair, imagining them Charlotte's fingers instead of Maggie's. The hypocrisy was not lost on him that while desiring Charlotte's love and affection, he was, instead, lying on another woman's lap. But what else could he do?

"Gloominess doesn't become you. Where is the perpetually laughing man I know? Here lies a despondent duke who should be enjoying *my* company, not talking of another woman." Margaret Collins, the Dowager Marchioness of Waller, inhaled before puffing another cloud into Drake's face. "Do you love her?"

Drake coughed and waved his hand to dispel the smoke. "We're nearly strangers." He paused, undecided how to phrase the next words. "I thought when I first met her, we could fall in love. No, I knew we could, knew we would. I can't explain it, but I knew. I believed we might want the same things. She was the promise of a new beginning and seemed equally as interested in me. I was wrong. She only wanted the title, not me."

Maggie laughed, a sound reminiscent of a cat sharpening its claws. "Nonsense. You haven't seduced her. She'll forget the title once you make love to her."

"That's the thing, Maggie. I've tried! As soon as I put on the charm, she goes rigid. I used my best moves. Now, it's hopeless. She won't even look at me. Trying to seduce her will get me nothing but bruised shins."

"You mistake my meaning. You've no experience with maidens, darling. You're trying to seduce your *wife*, a virtuous young girl. This is different than seducing a mature widow. You must make *love* to her, you see, but not with your body. You've mistaken love for the physical, I'm afraid. Instead, show her a side of you no one else sees, a side the two of you can share," the marchioness said sagely.

Drake stole her cheroot for a quick puff before returning it between her fingers. "You assume there's more to me than shallow good looks and magnetism."

With a tut, she said, "We both know there is. Listen to me, and you will have your wife eating out of the palm of your hands. She is young and afraid of the unknown. I was like her once, though my husband wasn't as considerate as you are to her. To win her, you must woo her. Seduce her not with your sensuality, but with gifts, poetry, and compliments. Tell her how much you adore her. Tell her what you told me; she's the promise of a new beginning. If she thinks she's the most import- ant woman in your life, she'll fall madly in love, and there you will be, a happy Drake. Forget her motives for marriage. *She* will forget them as soon as she falls for you."

"Woo my own wife." Drake snorted. "It didn't work for your husband. You hated him."

"He never wooed me. He took what was his. But you're proof enough it works. A few gifts, a few com- pliments, and here you are, after all these years, still lying in my lap like a good pet." She rearranged the locks of hair falling over his forehead, then cringed. "Oh, that makes me feel old."

"You always know just what to say to cheer my sullen spirit. It's not every woman who compares me to a lap dog."

Pushing himself upright, he turned to see her better, the woman who broke his heart.

She was a petite lady, only showed her age in the smoky voice and crinkles around her eyes. They hadn't been lovers for well over a decade, not since the day Drake inherited the dukedom. Humiliatingly, he had proposed to her the day he received his writ of summons and letters patent. He had been young and stupid. She had laughed at him, scorned him, called him a foolish pup. He had fancied them in love. A rude awakening it had been to discover not only was his love unrequited, but she had used him. Their physical affair ended that day, never to be renewed.

Not until some years later did they rekindle their relationship but in name only. Never should he have allowed it to happen, but she convinced him they needed each other, persuaded him they each could save the other's reputation. Drake became her lifeline to social favor, and she became his supposed ladybird, spreading rumors wide and far about his masculine potency. They agreed to maintain the pretense of an affair for this reciprocal benefit.

For Drake, it secured his renown as a desired lover despite his celibacy. His reputation was everything to him. It defined him. It reassured the world, his mother, and himself that he was not what his mother accused him to be. Yes, Maggie was right. He needed her.

For Maggie, a long-term affair with a young duke did wonders for her perceived femininity, bringing attention to her from new suitors every year, all wanting to know how she had garnered the duke's affection. Maggie was in love with being worshipped, specifically by the youthful infatuation of doe-eyed young men. A new favorite each year was her style.

Although he had been persuaded by her to form a beneficial sort of acquaintance, any semblance of friendship came to an end, yet again, before he left for London. He'd grown tired of her games, tired of feeling used, tired of being reminded he wasn't loveable. The moment his mother demanded he find a bride or have one chosen for him, he knew it was time for a change, a new life, a new chance, and perhaps, God willing, a chance at love. He'd wished Maggie adieu, never to return.

Yet here he found himself again. History repeated. Was he such a glutton for abuse? Did he never learn from the past?

Maggie's grey eyes fixed on a point beyond his shoulder. "She's due in December. I should be elated, but I only feel old."

"Who's due in December?" Drake stared, confused. He ran a hand through his hair.

"My daughter-in-law, of course. She's with child. It's humiliating to think I'll be a *grandmama*. At my age! I'm too young for all of that." She tugged at a frayed thread on top of the settee. "I don't want to be a grandmother. Think what it'll do to my reputation."

Her son, now three and twenty, lived in the manor with his wife. Maggie had taken up residence in the dower house a mile from the main house.

"There's a ducal carriage sitting in your front drive, Maggie. As usual, I took the route through town. Your reputation is assured."

"No more of that nonsense about you not returning. You must. You need me. You'll never convince your wife to love you without my help." She smiled ruefully.

"I want my marriage to work, and I want love. Neither of those things you can offer."

"You need me. Without me, who will ensure your mother's fears are held at bay?"

He didn't reply, his thoughts on his mother's conviction that it wasn't Maggie he came to this house to see but Winston. All his work to secure this reputation had turned against him. This no longer served him. Even if it did, he wanted to put his effort into wooing Charlotte, not convincing the world he was an adulterer. Life had changed, and the sooner he came to terms with that, the better. He said none of this aloud, though, for he knew Maggie wasn't the least concerned about him, only her own reputation. Had he really believed her argument that *he* needed *her* for so long?

Putting out the last dregs of the cheroot in a priceless heirloom next to the settee, she asked, "You think you could love her, then? More than you loved me?"

"I was more than half in love with her before we married. Not for a moment did I suspect she'd become a glacial title huntress."

She reached over and tussled his hair. "Let me throw you a party. I'll host a rout. Two Saturdays from now is ample time to invite guests. Invite Lord Stroud's boy — *he'll* make me feel young again — and tell me then you've wooed your wife. We'll all raise a glass to you."

"A public conclusion to this charade seems fitting."

He had no wish to return, but felt he had little choice, not when she knew so much about him, could easily turn against him and spread lies that would reach his mother. This was her way of offering a clean break, advantageous to her, but a release for him, nonetheless. At least for this return he would know he was being used rather than falling for her persuasions as usual. If her silence required him putting on a theatrical of their ending the supposed affair amicably so as not to lose favor with her next conquest, he would do it and never look back.

"As a final farewell, I'll come. We'll toast to the end." Drake eyed her suspiciously. "Promise me it'll be a farewell and nothing more."

Nothing she said could be trusted fully. An offer for a clean break, or was it another manipulation? Blast, he couldn't be certain. However harmless most of her parties, the routs were notorious for being wickedly sordid. When he had been young and infatuated, such parties had been the boon to his reputation. He'd not been to one since their first split, since he inherited, and he had no interest in resuming attendance. This was a necessary evil, but he could not entirely trust her. Rather than the clean break he assumed she was offering, she could have another trick up her sleeve, another way to enslave him.

"A party amongst friends, nothing more." She pinched his cheek. "I promise."

"Right. The second Saturday of August. My attendance will *only* be to publicly end our imaginary liaison. An amicable break, convincing enough for you to maintain favor. After that, I will devote my days to wooing my wife. Know now, I'll not stay beyond an hour." He glanced at the clock on her mantel. "Speaking of leaving, I best be off. My own bed calls."

"Stay. I'll be bored without company." She reached for another cheroot.

Drake stood to leave. "Take up embroidery."

The sound of her gravelly laugh followed him outside where his carriage awaited, the coachman and grooms half asleep. Normally, they would be enjoying the evening with Maggie's staff, but Drake had promised not to be long and requested they wait. To his chagrin, he'd stayed longer than expected. At least the night air was cool.

The tiger, a young boy only recently hired, had fallen asleep against one of the wheels. One look at the boy made Drake shudder involuntarily. The boy, gangly and short, likely around seventeen, if a day, would have been just the sort to tempt Maggie at one time.

What the devil was Drake doing here? He'd be happier with this place to his back.

He never should have agreed to attend the party. It was another manipulation of hers, using him to gain the attention of other men. He cursed his own stupidity. When away from her, he could think clearly, but in her presence, his thoughts tangled, and he found himself acting not unlike a kicked pup, doing her bidding and groveling to be loved, even while she abused him. It was a curious spell she had on him, one that embittered him.

"Oi! On your feet, you lazy bums!" He shouted to his men with a laugh and watched them scurry to their posts.

The tiger rushed to the platform at the back of the carriage, taking his station.

"You there." He pointed at the boy. "What's your name?"

"Philip, Your Grace."

"Well met, Philip." Drake ducked into the carriage, glad to know Philip was safe on the carriage and not inside Maggie's house. "Home, James!" he shouted to the coachman, tapping the roof of the carriage.

The coach rocked and swayed home, lulling Drake into a head-nodding slumber. He had almost fallen asleep when the carriage door opened with a snap. Lyonn Manor stood silent and dark this evening, the occupants already in bed.

It had been a restless week with him spending his nights in the music room, composing his frustrations until the light of dawn when at last he ambled to his room to sleep until noon. Tonight, he would sleep well, not only from the hopefulness of implementing Maggie's advice for wooing his wife, but also from sheer exhaustion. Tomorrow, he would sort out a plan for romancing Charlotte. If there was one thing Maggie knew well, it was the art of seducing innocents. She may be his least favorite person, but her advice was worth gold.

He dragged himself up the stairs and down the bedroom corridor to his chamber. The moon lit up the room when he opened the door. Why hadn't Bartholomew, his valet, closed the draperies? Drake shrugged off the oddness. He needed to summon Bart anyway to bring a brandy and undress him for the evening.

Before he was halfway to the bellpull, chilling words stopped him.

"Who is she?"

Startled by the voice in the darkness, Drake tripped over the rug and stumbled into the back of a chair, catching himself before he fell.

"What the devil?" he exclaimed.

Taking a moment to compose himself, he walked to the fireplace and lit the candelabra on the mantel.

When he turned to face the voice, his eyes widened to find Charlotte sitting in a chair by the hearth, wearing a wrapping robe and a blank expression. Her chestnut hair flowed loose to her shoulders. If it weren't for the void expression and the unusualness of her appearance in his room so late into the evening, he would welcome this angelic vision. Did she know how beautiful she was with unpinned hair?

"What's her name, Drake?"

"Whose name?"

Indeed, he couldn't imagine about whom or what she was asking. What was she doing in his room at this hour and after a week of ignoring him?

"Your mistress," she clarified. "Who is she?"

Oh. Oh dear. All thoughts of angelic visions vanished.

Someone must have told her about Maggie, but who and why? His memory flickered to what he'd said to Winston and Sebastian. Neither of them would have approached Charlotte. Would they?

Maggie wasn't even his mistress! The whole affair was imagined, faked for their mutual gain. While all the dukedom believed he had a kept woman, he most certainly did not.

"I don't have a mistress," he said, enunciating each word.

"Don't lie to me," she replied. "I'm not feeble-minded. I know you have a mistress."

"No, Charlotte. I don't. Let me be clear on this fact. *I have no one.*" He spoke the truth. Even with his wife sitting in arm's reach, he was utterly alone. He had no one.

"You don't have to hide her. You don't have to hide anything anymore. I know all your secrets, including why you married me. Your mother let it slip. You need an heir, and I'm to be your prized cow. Shall we get it over with now, or are you already spent from an evening with your bird? Would it help if we doused the lights and you called me her name?" Her words pierced him with icy daggers.

He squeezed his eyes closed. Never would he have imagined so ugly of words coming from Charlotte's lips. From her vantage point, those words were warranted.

He didn't know what to say.

What could he say that wouldn't sound like empty denial? Drake had never needed to deny his reputation before, and had, in fact, fanned the flames of rumor for years, stoking the fire further with these two recent calls on Maggie. What a fool. What a blasted fool. How could he have allowed his mother to affect him so?

A fish out of water, he floundered.

None of what Charlotte said was true. He most assuredly hadn't married her for an heir, and he didn't have a mistress. It was she who married for the title. Wasn't it? He only wanted his wife, and oh, how he wished she wanted him, for it was only her name he wished to speak.

"Charlotte, I—"

"Don't insult either of us with lies. I was warned against you from the start, but I was too blind to see you weren't interested in *me*. You only needed a breeder." Her voice wavered, but her expression held its stony countenance. "Is it only the one, or are there others? How many women are there?"

"Stop this!" Drake shouted, louder than he had expected, startling them both. "You are mistaken on all accounts. Don't accuse me of what you know nothing about."

Charlotte stood. "I know more than you give me credit for. I know you haven't spent a single night in your room." Stepping behind her chair, she placed a barrier between them.

"Not true." He lowered his voice. "I've not spent a single night away from home since our arrival. I've been in my stu—"

"Stop lying to me!" she cried. "I know you're not here. I have looked in your room every night for a week, but you're never here. I visit your study, as well, and surprise, you're never there. Be honest with me for once." She clenched her fists on the top of the chair, her knuckles white.

"You're unnecessarily upset. Sit down, and we'll talk rationally," he said, waving his hand to the empty chair.

"Don't treat me like a child," she said with a stomp of her foot.

"Then stop acting like one," he snapped back before realizing his mistake. "I'm sorry, Charlotte. I shouldn't have said that. But you're not giving me a chance to —"

"I don't want your excuses or lies." She unfurled her fingers and crossed her arms over her chest.

He took a step towards her.

She took a step back.

Indicating the chair again, he said, "I'm not going to make excuses, and I'm not going to lie. Sit down, and I'll lay bare my soul, so you may tread on it as you wish. Will you, please, allow me to correct the mistake?"

And then she laughed, a single trill. "You can't correct my mistake. My mistake was marrying you. You're nothing more than…than a rake. You're nothing more than a self-absorbed bounder. I wish I'd never met you."

His world fragmented.

She thought their marriage was a mistake. Had she not married him for the title? Had he not been the only one who wanted more from the marriage?

The sound of his pounding heart drowned out his own words. "Don't say that. Don't you dare say that. Our marriage is not a mistake. I'm *not* a rake. Meeting you was the most promising day of my life."

"Lies. You're no better than all the rest of your peers, entitled, thinking they can have everything regardless of whom they destroy along the way to get what they want. I'm proud to be my father's daughter, for at least he earned everything he has. What have you accomplished? Nothing. Your life has only one purpose, to continue a name. Is that why you fill your days with empty affairs? Is your life so meaningless?"

He took another step forward, reaching out for her, but she shied away, withdrawing to the door.

"Please, Charlotte. You don't mean any of this. I don't have a mistress. I didn't marry you to continue the line. I—"

"Confess everything, and then we can move forward. I will not believe lies," she said, her words venomous.

This was hopeless. If she wouldn't let him speak, what was the point? If she assumed everything he said was a lie, what was there to say? She tried and sentenced him, a condemned man who couldn't raise a defense.

He threw his hands in the air. "If you won't listen to the truth, then believe whatever you want. What do you want me to say if not the truth? I don't have a mistress. I've never had a mistress. I'll never have a mistress."

"You're making a fool of us both."

If he couldn't defend himself, then there was no point in bearing witness to false accusations. "Until you're willing to give me a chance to explain, there's no point in continuing."

"I'll prove it. I'll prove you have a mistress, and then what will you have to say for yourself?"

"You can't prove what's not true, Charlotte. No, on second thought, you should try to prove it, because then you'll believe me."

"Then I could annul the marriage," she spat.

The blood drained from his body, leaving him shaking in its wake. "Don't say that."

"Our marriage hasn't been consummated, and you're an adulterer. An annulment should be possible."

"Charlotte. Stop this. An annulment is only granted in cases of proven impotence, not for adultery, failure to consummate, or otherwise. I wouldn't agree to it even if it were possible. You are upset over a misunderstanding and not thinking clearly. You're saying what you don't mean. Please, give me a chance. Give us a chance. We're worth a chance."

He could see the tears now. Gone was the stony visage, gone the hate, now only pain.

"Charlotte. Please. Give me a chance." He walked towards her again, but before he had taken two full steps, she turned from him and fled the room.

After a few silent seconds, he heard her bedchamber door slam beyond the adjoining sitting room.

Chapter 14

The week following Charlotte's confrontation hadn't dulled her pain or brought any resolution. It'd been a downright dreadful week. Each day brought with it a new emotion, each emotion a rocky coast after a storm. The only constants were Charlotte's sore eyes from sleepless nights and her grumbling stomach from loss of appetite.

The first day, she panicked over her confrontation. The staff must be wrong, and she'd humiliated herself by accusing him of something that wasn't true. The second day, she awoke angry that she'd been put in such a situation in the first place—if not true, how dare he ignore her to the point that she believed such rubbish about him; if true, how villainous not to give her a chance and allow her to humiliate herself in such a fashion. By the third day, she'd talked herself into finding ways to make this work for their mutual benefit, which led to a tearful night. The fourth day, she reached a bleak, empty period, wherein she trudged through the hours unfocused, unable to concentrate. By the week's end, she experienced a surge of determination.

Determined to prove his affair real, she'd stooped to snooping.

Charlotte peered over the railing to spy the hall below, swiveling her head left then right. The coast looked clear. As casually as she could muster, in case someone spotted her, she sauntered down the stairs, chin held high. The key was not to look suspicious.

With not too brisk of a pace and not too shifty of eyes, she turned into the alcove and opened Drake's study door, slipping inside, and closing the door behind her with a faint click. She had at least half an hour. Drake and Sebastian were in the billiard room. She knew. She had looked.

Part of her didn't want to find anything, because as long as there was nothing to be found, there might be some grain of truth to his denial. The other part of her wanted to find something to finally dash that last grain of hope in her breast. Only when she knew for certain what to believe could she move forward.

Earlier, while he sat in the parlor with his sister, she'd opened every drawer in his bedchamber, eyed every nook and cranny, including under his bed, but had come up empty handed. His dressing room was still unchecked since her attempt almost foiled the whole plan. She'd backed into the room, keeping her eyes trained on the bedroom door for signs of his return, only to bump into his valet cleaning the razors. Mumbling a quick excuse of having misplaced earrings, she'd backed out of the room, pink as a variegated carnation and just as contrite.

Then, she'd explored the billiard room, one of his most frequented rooms in the afternoons she'd discovered after shadowing him for several days. She didn't always know when Sebastian called since he rarely stayed for dinner, but if not with Drake in the study, they could both be found in the billiard room.

Strangely, she'd learned more about her husband over the past week than she had when they were on speaking terms. In the mornings, if he didn't sleep until noon, he went for a ride or went to Winston's to fence. During the afternoons, he knocked billiard balls or read in the adjoining library, which surprised her since she hadn't known he liked to read.

In the evenings, he shared dinner with the family before slinking off to his study for the remainder of the night. Whatever he did in his study, he did it for a terribly long time, though it was possible he sneaked off on horseback after Charlotte had gone to bed. During the sleepless nights, she lay awake, listening for his return to his chamber, which rarely happened before the wee hours, if at all. Her confidantes among the staff assured her he'd not used the carriage since that fated evening, so either he was in his study or riding.

Standing in his study now, she felt she'd reached a new low in her life. What wife snooped through her husband's belongings for evidence of an affair? This couldn't be normal. This couldn't be proper behavior for a duchess. Weren't wives supposed to look the other way, pretend mistresses didn't exist? Didn't *all* aristocrats have mistresses? Well, she must have missed that day of lady training because she cared far too much to turn a blind eye.

The study, she realized, was home to more cabinets and bookshelves than she'd noticed before. When one wasn't plotting to search everything for stashed evidence, the furniture blended in with the wallpaper.

Now, she counted each piece, for every cabinet and drawer would need to be rifled through, each book tipped. Not knowing what to look for didn't make searching any easier.

It would be too easy, she supposed, to find a miniature painting of his love, snug and safe inside a locket. Oh, that might be too dreadful to bear. If she found a miniature, she'd know what the woman looked like, and she wasn't confident she wanted to compare herself to a striking beauty.

Beginning her search at the bureau, she shuffled through books and papers, not reading, merely scanning for anything that might hint at bills paid or debts incurred for gifts, such as evidence of a purchased necklace perfect for a mistress. She rifled, foraged, and scoured leaflets and books and more, all for nought.

After searching more shelves and cabinets than she cared to consider, she retreated to his desk. It was the least likely place to find something, for no man would be thick enough to leave evidence in such an obvious place, not that any man would suspect his wife of snooping, but Mama Catherine certainly had a nose for it. If the woman wasn't above spying on her daughter-in-law's bedchamber, she wouldn't bat an eye at digging through her son's possessions.

Alas, there was nothing left to search except the desk. Sitting in the worn chair, she launched into her task. The man was an anomaly. She found clocks, pomade, endless supplies of snuff, and more quills and ink pots than anyone should possess.

Fruitless. Complete waste of time. She lowered her forehead to the desk and lightly beat her head against the scattered papers. What was the point?

What was the point of all this? There was nothing to be gained except more heartache.

Grimacing at her aching forehead, she sat back, slumping into the chair.

And there it was. Right on top of the desk. Right under her nose, or forehead rather. A sloppily scribbled letter with strikeouts, arrows, and various other notations. It was unmistakably a letter written for his mistress.

> ~~I write this letter to I want you to know~~ I am *unworthy of your affection. You are, my dear, the most divine creature I've ever met with wit, charm, and talent I could never possess.* ~~When first I saw you, When I first beheld your~~ *You cannot know how my heart leapt when first we met. You cannot know how lonely has been my life, how empty my home, surrounded by* ~~contr manipula~~ *heartless women who seek to* ~~control~~ *manipulate me. My words may fall on deaf ears, but I must be heard. I'm not an eloquent poet and prefer we speak in person, but as* ~~I cannot as we are parted~~ *we are separated by* ~~an insurm a great an~~ *immeasurable distance, this letter is* ~~my means my heart my only way to deuce take it I hate writing I want to be with you and only you. Have I mentioned you're beautiful? Deuce take it.~~

Charlotte stared at the unfinished letter, dazed. He thought her controlling and heartless. She couldn't deny she'd spurned him on more than one occasion, but she wasn't heartless. Reading the words of adoration that could only describe another woman brought fresh tears, all the pain resurfacing.

All too clearly, he felt separated from his mistress, not willing to risk going to her. Had they been writing this whole time, lovers estranged by the controlling and heartless wife, only able to express their affection through missives? If she didn't leave the room, she'd be sick on his desk.

The letter supplied enough evidence to convince Charlotte he was a liar and a cheat, but it wasn't enough to force a confession. There was, after all, no salutation. Knowing Drake, he'd claim he was talking about his horse. No, if she were to confront him again, she needed irrefutable proof. And then what? Would his confession give her peace of mind so she could wash her hands of him once and for all?

A week later, Stella slipped into the parlor with a tea tray, shutting the door behind her.

"He's requested the carriage for this evening, Your Grace, and according to Philip, he's going to *her*," Stella whispered as she set down the tray.

Charlotte could not help noticing the blush when Stella mentioned Philip's name. "Thank you, Stella. Is everything prepared? No second thoughts?"

"If you insist, we will oblige. James, the coachman, is most upset about it, if you'll pardon my candor. He doesn't know which will get him dismissed, following your orders or not following your orders."

"No one will be dismissed. His Grace wouldn't dare. Besides, this was my idea. I will take full blame for the consequences. What time should we meet?" Charlotte poured the tea as though they were friends conversing about the weather rather than conspirators. The task steadied her restless hands.

"Seven. The shift change is a quarter 'til, so I'll have the hall to myself for a half hour," the maid answered. "Third door on the left."

With an inclination of the duchess' head, Stella took her leave.

Charlotte savored her tea and watched Captain Henry climb to the top of his tree and back down, then once more for the tenth time.

So, Drake would be going to his mistress at last. He'd waited two weeks since Charlotte's confrontation. Should she feel betrayed or triumphant? After stewing over the letter for nearly a week, it was about time something happened.

The plan for the evening was risky and wholly scandalous. Charlotte didn't care. Her determination to prove him a cheat overpowered all sense of propriety. It wasn't as though the plan weren't well thought-out enough to work, but if one aspect failed, she would be left in a far worse situation than she was in now.

What else was she to do? Allow him to humiliate her further? No. No longer would she be made a fool by this family. It was time she took charge. It all started with this daft plan.

The new tiger Philip, who was smitten with Stella, devised the plan himself after Charlotte suggested she follow Drake's carriage on horseback to catch him with the woman. Philip had pointed out every flaw in her idea and crafted his own in its place.

All the parts were now set into motion. No one would find out until she burst in on Drake and his mistress, catching them together. He couldn't deny his affair then! It would destroy every hope she ever had of love, fairy tale romance, and a dazzling hero, but she couldn't sit around being made a fool of by him. Drake's wrath in the aftermath wasn't a concern since she would find him in a wholly compromising position, making anything he said in response hypocritical.

An hour later, dressed for dinner, she was assured Beatrice would guard her room. Should anyone call on her, the lady's maid would say her mistress suffered from a migraine and should not be disturbed.

When Charlotte entered the lesser dining room, she stopped dead at the sight of Drake.

Sparkling diamonds encrusted his cravat and each of his fingers were ringed with jewels and gold bands. His silk-satin breeches, waistcoat, and matching coat were a royal blue with elegant, silver embroidery, tailored to perfection to fit his striking form like a second skin. He took her breath away.

She'd not seen him dressed this stunningly since their wedding. Under different circumstances, she might have swooned. She recalled wistfully when he first called on her in London, arriving at her aunt's terrace with a multi-caped cloak, ringed fingers, a bejeweled cravat and looking marvelously delicious.

She flushed with anger. All his denials of not having a mistress, and here he stood fit for a ball. He couldn't have made his plans more obvious unless he announced it in the newspaper. Was this how it was to be, then? Now that she knew, was he to flaunt when he called on his ladybird?

She took her seat at the table, the tension palpable. Each time she stole a glance at him, he stared back at her, as though in challenge, his gaze inviting her to question him.

When the footmen brought the first course, Charlotte could do nothing more than stare at the plate, unable to eat a bite. Her stomach churned. To avoid drawing attention to her missing appetite, she moved the food around on her plate.

Why did he have to look so dashing for someone else?

"Drake," his mother said after a silent first course. "You are dressed well for dinner this evening. To what do we owe the honor?"

Charlotte nearly choked before he answered. She coughed and sputtered as the family stared at her curiously.

"I'm to attend a rout, Mother," Drake said, eyeing Charlotte with brows raised as if to question her coughing fit. "Small gathering, nothing worth mentioning. I don't wish to be late, so I'm leaving immediately after dinner."

Bother! That wouldn't give her enough time to change. She would have to be swift and hope the coachman could detain him.

"A rout, you say," Catherine replied. "Distastefully disorganized events. Unfashionable." Turning to Charlotte, she said, "I see from your choice of attire, you have the good sense not to attend such rubbish."

Swallowing against the lump in her throat, she said, "No, Mama Catherine, I will be staying in this evening. I fear I will retire early with wishes not to be disturbed. I feel the onset of a headache."

The dowager duchess inclined her head in approval. "Learn a thing or two from your wife, Drake. She knows which parties to attend and which to avoid."

Drake grinned. "I suspect this is not her scene. Although..." He angled towards her, his eyes reflecting the diamonds in his neckcloth. "If you wish to attend, I have no objections. Selfish of me not to invite you sooner. Shall I wait for you to dress?"

Her jaw slackened as she gaped at him. What was this trickery? The entire staff knew he was going to his mistress, yet he dared invite Charlotte to go with him. Was all her scheming for nought? Her head spun with confusion and contradictions. Perhaps this was his way of hiding in plain sight, fabricating this rouse, knowing she'd say no. It certainly made him look innocent.

Before she could reply, Mary whined over her dinner plate. "It's not fair. I never get to go to parties. I want to go to a party."

"I will not stand for your petulance," Catherine scolded.

They bickered for the remainder of the course.

Charlotte could feel Drake's eyes boring into her as he waited for an answer. She couldn't meet his gaze. Wringing her hands in her lap and chewing on her lip, she stressed. If she said yes, where would he take her? If she said no and went through with her plan, would she learn he really was going to an innocent party? This had to be a trick. He must have planned all along to invite her at the last minute to appear innocent. But wouldn't that be too risky — she could, after all, say yes? Oh, botheration!

By the time dessert arrived, she'd still not given an answer.

Drake stood, his dessert unfinished. "I apologize to you all, but I'm afraid I really must take my leave of you, unless, that is, my wife has decided to join me and would like time to change?"

Staring up at him, her eyes wide, her thoughts jumbled, she said, "No, I have a migraine."

Drake bowed and left the room.

Had she made the right decision? The servants must be wrong. He couldn't possibly be going to his mistress if he had invited her to go with him.

There was only one way to find out. Knowing how unusual it must look, but not wanting her plans to go awry, she stood moments after his departure.

"I, too, apologize, but my headache is so severe I must retire immediately." Without waiting for a response, she fled.

She raced to the servant's hall, hoping Stella would be there and the coachman would find a reason to delay departure long enough for her to take her place unseen.

It wasn't too late to back out. Did she really want to see him in the arms of another woman? Why not accept his word and live happily in denial, excusing his absences and nights away as being evenings with friends, nothing more?

Her feet wouldn't obey. They marched her towards certain doom, straight through the servant wing and into Stella's quarters. The maid sat waiting, looking as anxious as Charlotte felt.

"Oh, no, you're too early!" Stella shrieked. "We can't let them see you leaving my room dressed as a tiger! They'll think Philip has been in my room, and Mrs. Fisk will dismiss me as soon as rumor spreads."

"It's not my fault. He left in the middle of dessert. Are you positive he's going to her?"

"Yes, I'm positive, Your Grace. Having doubts?"

"Yes. No. Not enough to stop me."

Stella nodded. "If you still want to go through with it, follow me. I have an idea."

The maid tucked the tiger livery into a blanket, then directed Charlotte down the hallway. They headed to the side door that would lead them out to the waiting carriage and stopped in the hall. Opening a cupboard, Stella ushered Charlotte inside.

"You must be joking, Stella. I'm not going into a wardrobe," Charlotte said with a laugh.

"But you must! You can't dress in my room until the shift change, and by then he'll have left. James can only delay departure for so long. Go in! I'll stand guard outside the door."

"You can't shove me in a wardrobe alone, Stella!" Charlotte stammered, short of breath. Nothing was turning out as planned. "I've no way to undress myself without help."

With an exasperated exhale, Stella said, "I'll help you, but we must hurry. Will you get into the cupboard before someone sees us?"

They crammed inside, Charlotte feeling like a prized idiot. Only a few weeks ago, she'd been a proud bride with the most eligible of men on her arm. Now, she was an insanely jealous woman hiding in a closet with a parlor maid, a broom continuously falling on her. Her sister wouldn't believe her if Charlotte told her. Her aunt would faint from vapors. Her cousin would deny her as a relation. The dowager duchess would have heart failure. Her father would be the only one to laugh and say she was a chip of the same block.

Stella struggled with the ties of Charlotte's dinner dress, fumbling in the dark with unfamiliar finery. With a concentrated effort, she succeeded in undressing Charlotte and then dressing her in Philip's livery, a coat with orange and black stripes, earning the horseman's name of tiger.

The breeches were much too tight in the hip, and the layers of coats made Charlotte distinctly uncomfortable, as did the heavy fabric knotted taut around her bosom to hide her femininity. Her own stays were useless since they accentuated her bosom rather than hid it. Stella was to be credited for the fabric idea, though the compression against her breasts was almost painful. Stella pinned Charlotte's hair under the cap, pulling the brim low over her forehead.

This was the only way. She couldn't very well climb up next to the coachman in her dinner dress.

"Keep your head low, and all he'll see is the cap," Stella said, adding a few more hairpins to trap Charlotte's curls. "No one notices the groom, much less the tiger, so he will have no cause to look at you closely. If you keep your head down, you'll go unnoticed. James will assure your safety. This whole plan makes him ever so nervous."

Charlotte felt guilty for involving them in this harebrained scheme. She shouldn't have put them in this position, but this was the only way.

Stella poked her head out of the closet, spying if the coast was clear, and waved Charlotte forward.

Together, they walked outside to the waiting carriage. With each step, her heart rate accelerated. This was madness! What was she doing?

A frenzy of grooms worked at the back of the carriage, tightening one of the wheels at the direction of the coachman. Everyone who would be on the carriage with her was already in attendance, all except Philip, of course, since Charlotte was to take his place, posing as him for the journey.

She spotted Drake standing by the carriage, tapping an impatient foot. Her heart skipped a beat, and her breath caught. Immediately, she bowed her head, training her eyes to the ground, and widened her gait to appear manlier. All she could do was pray he wouldn't find a reason to get too close to her. At a distance, in the dark, there should be no reason for recognition, but if he stepped too close….

As soon as the coachman saw Stella and the disguised tiger approach, he shouted to the duke, "The wheel is ready, Your Grace! We'll be on the road now. I'm only glad I spotted the problem in time."

"You try my patience," Drake grumbled, climbing into the carriage. He leaned out of the window and added, "I'm eager to be on the road. The sooner we leave, the sooner we return. Get on with it, man!"

Beneath her cap, she saw Stella making a break for it back to the house, leaving Charlotte alone with the grooms. She stood in the gravel yard, lost and uncertain. Nothing about this plan was logical. It wasn't too late to back out. He was probably going to a boring rout with Winston and his friends. This was a complete waste of time.

The coachman made a wide arc in his walk from the back of the carriage to the front, catching her attention and flicking his head towards the back of the carriage. When she glanced back, she saw the platform on which she was to stand for the entirety of the ride, supposedly ready to help with any horse problems that might arise. Should anyone see the carriage, they wouldn't question her as the tiger, as such a position was prized for youthfulness, short stature, and slenderness. It was the perfect disguise in the dark.

As she approached the platform, a groom caught himself just as he began to bow and help her ascend. They all knew of the rouse, of course. Oh, what must they think of their new duchess to be engaging in such antics? With a reassuring smile to the poor chap, whose name she believed to be Algie, if memory served, she steadied herself on the platform and held on for dear life as the carriage sprang to action.

Chapter 15

S he had gone mad. Her mind had taken a turn around the bend and launched her into full blown insanity. How else could she explain standing on the back of a carriage, wearing a male servant's livery, hoping to catch a man in an intimate pose with a woman? Madness. Sheer madness.

Clinging to the leather straps attached to the coach for balance, she wondered how to proceed. She could only catch him if she were *in* the house, but why would the groom assigned to tend to the horses be traipsing around a person's house? The only possibility was to peek through windows until she saw them together.

Unless they were upstairs. Blast. She hadn't thought about them going upstairs. *Of course*, they would go upstairs given there could be only one reason for him to call on his mistress in the evening hours. A footman would stop her if she tried to enter and walk up the stairs. *Please don't let them go upstairs.* This whole plan survived on her wit alone, with her thinking on her feet, a trait at which she did not excel. Her sister was good at thinking on her feet, but not Charlotte. Charlotte had to plan things meticulously in advance. Impulse and spontaneity were not her strong suits.

Yet this night depended on her ability to think fast, or she would fail in her mission. Her being seen by Drake was inevitable, but by then it wouldn't matter, because she would have caught him in *that woman's* arms, thus proving her case. Being seen before he assumed a compromising position would be disastrous.

By the time the carriage reached a stately cottage about the size of Charlotte's childhood home in Cornwall, her legs quivered like jelly. The ride had taken an hour. An hour in which she stood on the back of a bouncing carriage, clinging to a strap of leather and praying she wouldn't fall to her death. She had a newfound respect for her servants. As soon as she could arrange a private word with the steward, she'd give them all a raise. Then, did Lyonn Manor have a steward? This seemed something she should know, but when Mama Catherine ran the estate and beyond, little had been shared with Charlotte aside from social aspects of her role and trivial points like the weekly menu. All things to think about later. For now, there was a mistress to catch.

Charlotte stepped off her platform and ran to the front of the carriage to steady the horses, as was her job as the tiger. She only hoped she didn't inadvertently spook the animals. Algie, the groom, hopped off the carriage once she settled the horses and ran to the side of the coach to open the door for Drake.

She kept her eyes on the ground, listening to Drake's boots meet gravel. After two steps, the sound ceased. Her heart raced. Had he seen her? She strained to listen to every movement. A click, followed by a sniff. Ah, his snuff box. She exhaled in relief.

"Right," said Drake, the gravel beneath his feet shifting and crunching to the cadence of his footsteps. "Don't fall asleep, boys. I won't be long. Long enough to take care of business, nothing more. I have a theatrical to perform, you see. As distasteful as it may be, the show must go on."

She listened to the receding steps.

Not long after did a low voice ask her, "Are you well, Your Grace?" The coachman stood next to her.

Charlotte looked up into James's anxious face and nodded. The coachman must already know her to be mad. Why else would a new wife, never mind a duchess, demand this of her staff? Hopefully, the beds in Bedlam were comfortable.

Looking towards the front door of the house, she wondered what Drake had meant by taking care of business. She couldn't quite wrap her mind around his meaning. And was his mistress really hosting a party this evening, a theatrical by the sound of it? That could complicate the plan. She had anticipated the two of them being intimate with each other, but would they be so bold at a party? And why wouldn't he be long if it were a party, especially knowing how much Drake loved an evening of social frivolity?

A quick feel of her cap and hair assured her all was safely tucked out of sight. And now, to wait. She wanted to allow ample time for Drake to become flirtatious with his mistress. If she could catch them kissing, that would be enough to brand his guilt.

While she waited, she surveyed the house, trying to form a plan. There would be a servant's entrance, but would that grant her access or increase her chances of getting caught? The butler would be guarding the front, so perhaps if she sneaked in through a parlor door, she could avoid detection. From there, she could follow the sound of Drake's voice and wait for her moment to surprise them in an amorous embrace.

After what must have been only half an hour but felt like five, she dashed a nervous nod to the coachman and set off on a gravel path that wound around the house to a terrace. Light and sound flooded the patio. She didn't yet dare step around the corner to see the room from which came said light and sound. Straining, she heard laughter and conversation, but couldn't distinguish Drake's voice. In fact, the tones sounded predominantly female.

Pressing her back against the cold stone of the house, she tried to calm her beating heart. The one element to give her pause was if she could stomach seeing him with another woman. Tears welled but didn't fall. A few swift blinks cleared them away. She had fallen for him in London, or rather, the idea of him. He had been magnificent. Could she live with the vision of him in the arms of another woman?

She must. She must see it for herself as a reminder never to love him, never to trust him.

With renewed confidence, she walked forward. Columns lined the terrace, supporting a balcony above. If she could dart unseen behind one of the columns, she would have a prime view of the room.

With a deep breath, she sprinted through the darkness for the first column. While the terrace was illuminated from the candles in the room, she doubted anyone inside could see outside, but she preferred to err on the side of caution. When she reached the column, she threw herself against it, hiding from view.

She waited, breathless. Her hands trembled. No exclamations sounded from inside, only the laughter and conversation she heard before. It would seem she had succeeded in stealth. Turning cautiously, she pressed her cheek against the column, willing herself to be flat and still. More waiting. More laughter and conversation.

The party would, indeed, be an inconvenience. With other people milling about, how would she ever get inside to find him? To make matters worse, she had yet to hear his voice.

She inched forward to catch a glimpse of the partygoers.

To her delight, the column's position presented an advantageous view, as she could see the entire room. No corner hid from her observation. Double doors to the parlor were open wide, offering the guests an August breeze, and, quite conveniently, allowing Charlotte an easy entrance when she discerned the opportune moment.

The room was a smallish parlor, only two interior doors, presumably one into a hall and the other into something like a study or anteroom. She would need to sneak into the parlor when the guests were distracted and go through one of those two doors to search for Drake. But which door? Could he already be in an adjacent room with his mistress? Or upstairs, for that matter? Was she missing her opportunity?

Surveying the crowd, she saw nothing immediately amiss.

Her eyes roved over the guests, morbidly fascinated by what sort of party his mistress would host and what sort of people she had invited. Her first impression of the scene was of decadence. Lining the walls were buffets of food, dessert sculptures, and more glasses of wine than she'd ever seen. Every inch of the room crawled with people, mostly older women in their early fifties or thereabouts, if she hazarded a guess. Although they conversed, their attention was not engaged on each other rather the entertainment, all eyes facing the same direction. It appeared the hostess had hired a group of young musicians, all of which captivated their audience — Charlotte could not guess why, for they were only there to provide music, not a theatrical, at least from what she could discern. The musicians did not appear anything special, all young men in their teens, perhaps her own age but no older, one at the pianoforte, another turning the pages for the pianist, two on violin, one singing in accompaniment, a splendid soprano, and a few grazing at the sideboard.

As she listened further, she began to realize what must be captivating the women — the music was divine, heaven sent, simply extraordinary talent. She wished she had accepted Drake's impromptu invitation to join, for how magical to enjoy this music as a guest rather than a terrace voyeur. For all her self-deprecation to Drake about not being a skilled musician, she loved the artistry, wanting nothing more than to be as good of a pianist as the young man now at the keyboard. Confessing that to Drake was not something she considered as it made her mediocre talent downright deplorable — a talentless music lover.

So lost in the siren song, Charlotte nearly forgot she was standing on a terrace, attempting to spy on her husband. The music must be the intention of the party, a musical soirée rather than a rout.

She continued to observe, keeping ears trained for Drake's voice.

Her attention perked, but only for a moment, when from one of the two interior doors, two people appeared. An older woman, much like the others in attendance, and one of the musicians. She settled back against the column when she saw it was not Drake. But then, her attention perked once more when she noticed the couple had entered the parlor holding hands, a shocking display of intimacy, made stranger by their age difference, and more peculiar still that he was one of the musicians, not a guest, or so she assumed. The peculiarity did not end there.

Rather than join the guests, they walked to one of the violin players. The young men exchanged words first, and then the violinist traded his instrument for three glasses of wine before following the couple back through the door. Not long had they disappeared before another guest followed them. A card room, then? Charlotte angled for a better view and listened to overhear conversation.

Words garbled beneath the music. No luck.

After a time, the remaining violinist set down his instrument, as well, but rather than heading into what Charlotte still assumed was the card room, he chose to mingle with the guests. In a moment of successive actions, she realized she ought not to be here.

A harmless pat to the young man's cheek by one woman, a kiss to his cheek by another, a whisper and laugh from someone else. Conversation continued, no one turning their attention away from the musicians to witness what Charlotte spied, but right there in the middle of the crowded party, yet another woman sneaked a kiss from the musician. Said kiss turned in three breaths from an unassuming display of chasteness to something quite salacious. Charlotte gasped and covered her eyes. While she had kissed Drake on more than one occasion, she had never *seen* two people kissing. However much she had braced herself to witness it between Drake and his mistress, she never dreamt to see it between two partygoers *in the middle of a parlor*.

What sort of party was this? Why was Drake here? Who were these people?

Peeking between her fingers, she saw someone had relieved the gentleman of his cravat.

She squeezed her eyes shut.

Dismayed, disgusted, panicked.

If she witnessed much more, she might faint. A lascivious public kiss, and now a stolen cravat? Why were they accosting that poor musician?

She decided it was time to make another mad dash back around the path and to the front of the house before she was seen.

Then she heard Drake's voice.

Tearing her eyes from the perversion, she scanned the room again, trying to pinpoint the location of his voice. He was shouting. She couldn't make out the words, but she heard his angry intonation, gruff words barking. It was an unusual sound to associate with Drake, as she'd never heard him angry, never heard him shout, not even when she'd confronted him about keeping a mistress.

Leaning closer, she strained to hear his words.

The second of the two interior doors opened, and Drake stepped out. He took one step into the parlor, then turned to face into the room from which he came.

"I've had quite enough," he said before halting his steps, as if realizing he was standing half in the parlor for all to hear. With a sweep of his gaze, he took in the scene, pausing on the poor musician missing his cravat, then he pivoted to return to the other room, shutting the door behind him.

Though she'd been desperate to discover his whereabouts, she no longer cared. All she wanted was to return home. This scene, whatever it was, held more questions than answers, and clearly she was not going to catch him in a compromising position.

Not until a woman with fiery hair stared directly at Charlotte did she realize she had leaned past the shadow of the column. A woman standing next to the redhead followed her companion's gaze, eyes alighting on Charlotte. Before she knew what was happening, half of the inhabitants of the parlor stared out at her.

The scene in Maggie's parlor gnawed at Drake's memories, a rabid dog tearing at the fabric of his youth.

He remembered his first rout and his first meeting of the marchioness with a mixture of pain and pleasure, a turning point in his life filled with simultaneous heartache and satisfaction.

He had been fifteen and on break from Eton. His father had arranged a soirée to showcase one of Drake's compositions, a point of great contention with his mother, who didn't want anyone outside the family knowing of his musical inclination or want him paraded around his father's friends.

Margaret Collins, the Marchioness of Waller, not yet a widow and the much younger wife to his father's closest friend, had attended, applauded, and approached him, promising to patronize his music if he would come to her home the following evening for a private performance and to discuss his composition plans. He remembered the elation, the sense of accomplishment, even the pride of triumph over his mother's doubts.

The following day, he went to the marchioness. Under one arm was a portfolio of music, in one hand, his violin, and on his sleeve, an eagerness to share his talent with the world. He went under the pretense of being recognized as a composer and musician. A false pretense.

Drake arrived to a scene similar to this evening, different young men, but the same women, albeit twenty years younger at the time. The innocent eyes of a fifteen-year-old boy recognized the party artistically rather than sensually. One young man, a few years older than himself, had been playing a harpsichord, and Drake had erroneously assumed the boy would be accompanying the violin performance. Another boy, this one younger, recited poetry to a group of women. All about the room he'd seen artists, people who would understand him.

All seemed promising when he set his music and violin on the harpsichord lid, flashing a smile at the pianist. Maggie introduced him to everyone one by one, including Teresa, an opera singer who had smoked her way out of stardom, her voice now chalky.

Not until an hour later, after his first sniff of snuff, his first puff of a cheroot, an entire bottle of wine, and his first, second, and third kiss, did he realize none of the people in the room were interested in his music. They were, however, all interested in his innocence. Sycophants. Seductresses. Ravishers. The scene was nothing more than a decadent feast, he and the other male guests to serve as the main course.

Prior, he'd never known affection of any kind, yet that evening, for the first time, he knew love and beauty. He knew the exhilaration of feeling wanted. His music forgotten, the promises of patronage ignored, he explored passion and relished in undivided attention, mistaking the physical for the emotional, mistaking lust for love. The evening had been his first everything, as well as the last time he composed music or played the violin for over a decade. In the end, he wasted his youth in the arms of a manipulative seductress, a predator of young boys, not that anyone could have convinced him of those facts at the time.

As a young lad, he had thought himself in love with Maggie and she with him, such was the perception of youth and gullibility. Hindsight gave him the advantage of seeing she had destroyed many aspects of his life and never once returned his affections. Like a lovelorn youth, he had welcomed that destruction, valuing her as a bedmate more than he valued his own dreams and ambitions. He cared more for what others thought of him and how she made him feel than he did about himself.

At the time, how could he not have become addicted to her? Not once had she accused him of being a molly for playing women's instruments. Not once had she called him uncouth or common for wanting to compose. Not once had she accused him of being like his father. No, she welcomed him with arms wide, with loving caresses, and with compliments. He was hooked from her first kiss.

Tonight was a bitter way to come to terms with his life. Having the actual scene flung in his face changed everything. Certainly, someone could argue it wasn't as bad as that, for how could a willing young man, such as he had been, be a victim? No one had forced him to engage in an affair, after all. He had been in his mid-teens, old enough to make decisions for himself, old enough to say no if he had not truly wanted it. Certainly, someone could argue all of that. Drake begged to differ. It was one thing to make a willing decision based on rational desire and quite another to be manipulated by an authority figure, his own schoolboy innocence used against him. Unless they had been in his shoes, experienced the expertise of manipulation, no one had the right to argue otherwise.

Had he not walked into the parlor tonight, this realization never would have hit him with such force. His memories from youth had not prepared him for what he would see this evening. Guests meeting potential lovers over music and wine? Most likely. Young boys being taken advantage of by lady serpents? No, he had not been prepared.

He had not attended a rout since his early twenties, not since the day of his inheritance, not since he proposed and was laughed out of her house. Even

after later rekindling their acquaintance for reciprocal means, he had never attended a single party, for
the memories of the routs had pained him since they
represented a time when he thought her love was real.

The moment he stepped into the parlor this evening, he saw her for what she was, a predator. To say
he looked at her now with revulsion was an understatement. As willing as the young guests would find
themselves, he knew it for what it was, *ravishment*.
What dreams did these boys hold that the women
would rip from their chests in exchange for pleasure?

Nothing prepared him for the amalgamation of
feelings, the assault of memories. He regretted falling
for her trickery tonight. He regretted it with every
fiber of his being.

While he knew the going-ons of her routs, he
had imagined that as time passed, the male guests
attending would have aged along with Drake. He
had expected not a scene from his past but a scene of
gentlemen of his age enjoying the company of mature
women, nothing more, nothing less, perhaps a familiar face or two from the parties of old, Winston for
instance. To walk into the parlor this evening and see
that the women had aged but the men hadn't, tilted
Drake's world. His breath had shortened, his vision
narrowed, his heart palpitated. He stepped into the
parlor to realize he was not a guest, but a middle-aged
peer witnessing lewdness, witnessing the ruination
of purity, the boys being just as he had been, not for
a moment realizing they were prey, that their lives
were about to be ruined.

The worst part was he felt responsible. He had
continued the charade of their affair to help her attract

new lovers while he maintained his masculine reputation to shunt his mother's fears. The latter he now berated — how could he be so obsessed about what other people thought that he forsook who he truly was? The former, however, nauseated him. By taking part in the charade, *he had helped her attract new lovers*. In his defense, he had no idea the lovers never aged. He had no idea. He thought…but surely Lord Stroud's boy, her most desired conquest this year, was Drake's age….Even as he tried to convince himself, he realized the truth.

Tonight, he hated himself.

He hated everything about his past, everything about his selfishness in worrying so much of what others thought of him that he abetted this woman. It would be a miracle if he escaped this house without being sick on her rug.

All he saw of her now was a she-devil. All this time, he had thought of her as a friend, a confidante, a lost opportunity, a lost love. With the blinders off, he saw the truth. A devil, she was. She would do whatever it took and hurt whomever she needed in order to get what she wanted. He was and always had been her pawn, a way to attract young men who were curious of the duke's long-time mistress. To make matters worse, if that was possible, he had a niggling suspicion he had been a pawn even at fifteen. She had, after all, been amongst his father's friends. Things his mother had said over the years, memories of overheard conversations, swatches of scenes frayed at the edges of his mind. He would think on it later, if he dared, but the young guests of this evening's rout were not the only revelations Drake experienced.

Full of disgust, he stood in Maggie's library off the parlor. The hostess sat on the edge of a chair, smoking a cheroot, as usual. Every cackle from the next room aroused his pity, evoked a sharp shudder, and riled his anger.

"I shouldn't have come," he admitted, not keeping the disgust from his tone.

"You never complained about my parties before." She arched a thin black eyebrow, wrapped her rouged mouth around the end of the cigar, and exhaled a ring before continuing. "Did you expect me to change?"

With a sweep of his hand through his hair, he stared at her, at a loss for words. Hypocritical to criticize her when he served the role of avid participant for years. His disgust turned inward, revulsion at his own behavior.

After a stretch of silence, he said, "I know I promised an hour, but let's call a spade a spade. The charade is over."

"Have you wooed your wife, then? You know you won't succeed without my guidance. Only I know the secrets to seduction."

He suppressed a shudder.

As much as he wanted to rail at her, he thought better of it, forcing himself to remain civil and honest, the goal to take his leave, this time forever. "I believe you've helped enough. The reputation you've built for me has even my own wife convinced I'm unfaithful. I'm going home, Maggie. This will be the last time you'll ever see me."

After two puffs, she replied, smoke exhaling with each word. "You drive an hour to attend my party only to stay half an hour? I'm disappointed."

Maggie's grey eyes studied his before she shrugged and said, "Go. There is nothing for you here." As he turned away, she added, "It's been a pleasure, my pet, but you're easily replaced."

In steady strides, controlling his urge to run, he left the library, drawing the door closed behind him. Drake felt a weight lifted from his shoulders. He was finally free. However much he mourned the fool he had been and mourned the youth he lost, he embraced newfound freedom. Even the situation with Charlotte felt freeing, for he looked at it with the eyes of a free man, a wiser man than he had been not but half an hour ago. All this time he had been pursuing her using the only wiles he knew, those that had been used on him. He had assumed love stemmed from physical seduction, that once they established physical intimacy, they would be bonded. What a blasted fool he had been. It was not, thankfully, too late, for now he knew how to woo Charlotte, and this kind of love making would indeed be the making of love, mutual, earnest, emotional love.

The tinkle of glass and throaty laughs welcomed him when he stepped into the parlor. The women were cajoling their guests, nothing untoward happening yet, but he most decidedly wanted to leave the party before it became any more heated.

Two steps towards the door of the anteroom, he stopped in his tracks. What the devil was his servant doing in Maggie's parlor? His blood curdled.

Standing in a circle of women stood his tiger, the young Philip, head hung low, both hands gripping his cap. The women crooned, eager to put hair on the lad's chest.

Distressed, Drake stepped forward.

As words of anger reached his tongue, he pursed his lips, schooling himself to remain calm and authoritative, for he was not a young man saving another young man from a fate the boy wouldn't know he didn't want, rather a duke indisposed by his servant. He was hard pressed to play the role when his mind and heart screamed to exorcise the she-devils and rescue the unwitting lad from the pit of vipers.

"Pardon me, ladies," Drake said as languidly as he could, affecting the persona of bored nobleman, "but I need my groom. It's time we returned home."

They wrapped protective hands around the boy's arms and pleaded with Drake.

"Let him stay and play," said Teresa, who stood behind Philip, blocking the boy's escape. "One more hour?"

Philip pulled his cap lower and tucked his chin into his livery.

"Come, Philip," Drake drawled, ennui edging on demand.

Assuming the groom would follow, he headed for the anteroom door. His pulse raced, ready to be out of the house, needing his tiger safe, but not wanting to cause a scene. When he reached the door, he realized the groom hadn't moved.

Was the boy going to put up a fuss? If circumstances had been different, Drake would have kept walking, leaving the boy behind as an acceptance of the unspoken resignation, but after his revelations this evening, he would do what it took to save Philip, even if Drake had to perform a theatrical, necessitating his slinging the tiger over his shoulder. That shouldn't be necessary, however, for if he read the boy's body language correctly, Philip didn't want their attention, merely found himself trapped.

Rather than a ducal command, Drake continued his performance, taking a moment to fluff the lace at his wrists, then flash the vultures a sardonic smirk.

"Now, Philip," he said, his tone teasing but testy.

The women around the stableboy chortled, a few pouting, but all backed away, releasing their hold. A couple of ladies hovered, at the ready in case Drake changed his mind and let the boy stay, but most began moving away, their interest returning to the other guests. The tiger, however, remained stock-still.

Drake's temper mounted. Bit difficult to rescue someone who displayed mixed signals about wanting to be rescued.

Rather than allow his ire into his words or his rising panic to show, he pulled out his snuff box. Had he a quizzing glass, he would have given it a swing on its ribbon before raising it to his eye. Without looking at the tiger, his attention on the contents of his snuff box, he poked but didn't pinch.

In a sing-song voice, ever the arrogant and amused duke who could only be mildly annoyed by disobedience, he said, "Philip. If I must drag you away, I promise you will not receive a reference after your dismissal."

Philip shook his head, gaze trained on the floor, then took a step backward, nearly bumping into Teresa. Since the groom was a recent hire, Drake didn't know him aside from a hasty word or two, but nothing about Philip's previous behavior prepared

Drake for insubordination. If anything, the boy always seemed eager to please.

Before Drake could issue another command, Philip tried to push his way through the guests to reach the terrace.

What on earth was happening with his groom?

One of the women said, "He wants to stay. Leave him."

With a click of the box, Drake tucked it into his waistcoat pocket and strode forward, wrapping a hand over Philip's shoulder. In a whisper, he said, "You'll thank me later, lad. Trust me."

When Drake tugged him towards the door, Philip stumbled and fell against Drake's chest. The cap edged sidewise, and a single chestnut curl tumbled down.

Drake halted, his fingers biting into his palm. He examined the curl, his heartbeat erratic. The ringlet spiraled past a shapely ear, golden brown twining to a slender shoulder.

That curl did not belong to a tiger named Philip. That curl and that ear and the trembling form beneath his hand belonged to only one person he knew. Robbed of breath, he glanced around him. No one had noticed. Exhaling through gritted teeth, he reached over to *Philip* and tucked the curl under the cap.

The walk back through the house towards the carriage was a silent one, his grip around *Philip's* upper arm secure but gentle. Should he be angry? Should he feel ashamed? Curious, certainly. The confusion and startling discovery kept him speechless with indecision.

When he stepped into the courtyard, his coachman and footman snapped to attention then froze with matching cringes at the sight of the liveried person escorted alongside the duke.

The footman opened the carriage door, his face flushed. Drake pushed the tiger unceremoniously into the carriage, climbed in after the flailing limbs, took his seat in the front with his back to the horses, and promptly pulled the cap off his wife's head, a tumble of curls flying free of their confinement.

The tears etching her cheeks stopped him from scolding or questioning. She wiped her eyes against the sleeve of the coat, but she needn't have bothered for more tears followed, and before the carriage reached the end of the drive, the silent tears turned to sobs.

He wanted to be angry. He wanted to be furious. He wanted to impress upon her the seriousness of her actions. Her actions, her behavior, her attire, her safety, everything roiled in the pit of his stomach. Had she ridden the whole way here on the back of the carriage, endangering her life, not to mention her reputation, to accompany him? Good Lord. His hands trembled at the thought of her hanging on for dear life. But why? To spy on him? Why not simply accept the invitation he had extended, however short notice?

Her motive struck him, then. *She cared for him.* There was no other explanation. If she only cared about the title, only wanted to be a duchess, she would not have gone to these lengths to follow him. She cared for *him*. She had done this for him, pitting herself against dangers and scandals. His heart swelled. Why had he not recognized this when she confronted him? Too obvious now, he could see she would not have approached him about a mistress had she not wanted more than a title. Daft fool!

So much lost time he had to make up for, time spent first attempting to seduce her, then pouting when she shied from his advances. To think of the times her rejection had angered him enough to ignore her, to leave her in the clutches of his mother, of all people! He could not have been more of a prized horse's arse.

Had he taken the time to welcome her to her new home, to build a life with her, to build a marriage, to *woo* her…oh, the clarity.

Reaching across the space between them, he took her hands in his. "I can't apologize enough for my stupidity, Charlotte. I'll right all the wrongs. From this point forward, you'll know nothing except adoration."

He felt the hot sting before he heard the sound of flesh slapping flesh. The palm of her hand met his cheek with a sharp crack, his face burning in the shape of her handprint.

Her voice shook when she said, "You're a perverse blackguard."

He blinked. Ignoring the branded heat of his cheek, he tried to recall the parlor. What had she witnessed? What had the women said to her? What did she think any of it had to do with him? Bile rose in his throat.

"Is this what you do with your evenings?" Her question was not shouted rather barely above a whisper, her words choked by tears. "Is this where you go? Is this what you enjoy? I expected to find you in the arms of a mistress. I never expected…" She turned to the carriage window. "You're a hedonist and a libertine."

"Whatever you might have heard or witnessed, I had no part. If you'll allow me, I'll explain."

"I don't think I can bear to hear your explanations. Those women. Those boys. I don't want to understand. I don't want to know what you are or what you do behind closed doors."

"Listen to me, please. I have no part in that scene. I used to be one of those boys, a seduced innocent. I've not been part of that since I was their age. I'm not a rogue. I'm not a molly. I don't prefer older women, nor do I prefer young men. I prefer *you* and want to build a life with you. All this time, I thought you only wanted the title. You must understand, no one has ever cared a fig about me. Your coming here tonight proves I was wrong. I should have seen it sooner."

Charlotte hunkered against her bench with a shake of her head.

He pulled at his hair in frustration. "That was the home of a former lover, not present, former, no, not even a lover, my seducer. I haven't been with that woman in over ten years. Are you hearing me? Ten years. My coming here was a mistake. I thought it was a final favor to a friend, but it was a mistake, both the friend part and the favor part. The only thing I want in this world is *you*, but I thought you didn't want me. Are you listening to me, Charlotte? Am I making any sense?"

He realized as she sobbed into her coat that he was rambling, a madman in desperate straits. He leaned back and stared, uncertain what to do.

As desperate as he was for her to understand that all he wanted was to love her and be loved in return by her, he knew nothing he said would penetrate. Nothing he said sounded believable or even coherent. Slumping forward, he cradled his head in his hands.

Not a word was spoken for the length of the drive, a near hour in pained silence, not until they passed the gatehouse of Lyonn Manor, the carriage slowing as it worked down the meandering drive towards home.

Charlotte spoke so softly, Drake almost didn't hear her words. "I want my sister and my aunt."

All he wanted to do was take her into his arms and hold her, tell her she was the only woman in the world he wanted, tell her she didn't need her family because he was her family now. He would do anything she asked of him if she would give him a chance to be a husband instead of a stranger. He wanted to console her, tell her he would resolve everything if she could believe him long enough to trust his confessions.

Instead, he replied, "I'll leave a bank note on the parlor desk, enough to fund their journey north."

Without a word, Charlotte leapt out of the carriage when the footman opened the door.

Chapter 16

Both Charlotte's sister Lizbeth and her aunt Hazel accepted the invitation—said invitations being more akin to desperate cries for help than invitations. In Charlotte's defense, she had been most distraught during her letter writing. The two-week delay for travel would feel like a century, but knowing they would come and knowing they would help did wonders to relieve her tension. That they had only recently returned home from the London trip and would now be on the road again made Charlotte no end of guilty. She would aim to make it up to them when they arrived, lavish them with love and gratitude and prove the trip was worth the effort.

The letters she sent excluded specifics but informed them of Mama Catherine's domination and the misery of living with Drake, emphasizing his ignoring her rather than anything untoward. She had faith in abundance they would know what to do. Lizbeth was the resident problem solver, and Aunt Hazel knew how to deal with people, especially difficult people. If, however, they couldn't help her sort this mess, the least they could do was smuggle her home.

Was it too much to ask for a happy marriage? Instead, she'd suffered the tyranny of her mother-in-law and alienation by a husband who was undoubtedly a wickedly sinful man. Did she dare tell her sister and aunt the truth? Lizbeth had been right about him being a disreputable rake, but she would have never guessed how disreputable.

Charlotte wasn't even certain of the truth. How sinful of a life did the man live? All his denials meant nothing in light of what she'd seen with her own eyes and what she'd experienced, being nearly undressed by those beastly women. That said, she didn't fully understand *what* she had seen. Nowhere in that parlor did Drake seem to fit, as it had been a scene of mature women with young gentlemen. She tried *not* to think about that evening, yet the more she tried not to, the more she wanted to make sense of it. Thinking back to the things Drake said after pulling her into the carriage wasn't terribly illuminating because she had been too upset and too frightened by the ordeal to listen with any understanding. A few snippets resurfaced, such as his mentioning being one of the boys and it being a scene from his past, but those snippets confused her even more. Did she want the answers? Past or present, that he would engage in activities so unsavory disturbed her.

Occasionally, her memories of the man she thought she married surfaced, memories she had to push away, for the man she met and married in London had dazzled her with his smiles and embraces, lavished her with attention, and promised her the world, a far cry from the reality of *this* man. The man of her memory was a flirtatious dandy, yes, but not a hedonist. *This* man was a hedonist.

Following "the incident," as she called it, she tried to come to terms with the reality — as in despair — of her situation. Despite the strides made over the past few weeks, Charlotte reminded herself she had no real voice in the marriage or in the management of the household. She would only serve the family if she dutifully bore a brood of sons, one son right after the other. At least in that, she could raise her voice of descent. Sons could only be born if Drake bedded her, and she would ensure that never happened.

Best to put it out of her mind and move forward, which was exactly what she aimed to do.

Four days after *the incident*, her resolve was tested.

To maintain composure, Charlotte clung to the awareness of his deception. He had deceived her in his true identity. She clung to this knowledge as a lifeline, not to be swayed, not to be distracted, not to be deceived further.

Four days following *the incident*, she found a daisy chain on her pillow and freshly cut daisies scattered across her bed.

The fourth day began with a heavy rain that stormed out Charlotte's planned bazaar for the tenantry and local villagers, forcing her to postpone the festival until the following weekend. The rain blew sideways against the windows, bringing with it howling winds and a grey veil. Outside looked how Charlotte felt inside.

She spent the morning trapped in the parlor feeling sorry for herself, with only Captain Henry's feathery charm and squawking wit to keep her company. She embroidered for most of the morning, played a game with Mary in the afternoon, and then when her mother-in-law visited the conservatory, Charlotte sneaked into the Red Drawing Room to amuse herself with the pianoforte. Not since leaving London had she played, and her fingers itched to give the instrument a try. Nothing could coax her to admit the inspiration had come from hearing the young musicians during the evening of horrors.

The pianoforte was exhilarating. Only at the ducal house in London had she played a pianoforte. Her home instrument, as well as the instrument of choice in London drawing rooms, had been the harpsichord, so it had come as a shock to find a pianoforte at the duke's London house.

Standing in the Red Drawing Room on the fourth day, fingering the instrument, she felt a warm thrill tickle down her spine. A walnut body with iron strings, leather hammers, and dynamic promises. She depressed a key. The voice was soft, mellow. She depressed it again, putting more weight behind her intention. The sound changed. It shouted back at her. With a start, she stepped back and stared, wonderous at its ability to turn a whisper into speech.

Fascinated, she sat and experimented, attempting the softest of murmurs and the loudest of cries, loving especially the breathy tone when she caressed the keys. Though she knew no songs that changed dynamics, she longed to create a conversation with notes.

No one was the wiser for a solid hour until none other than the dowager duchess herself stepped inside to cease the noise. Charlotte knew she wasn't particularly skilled, but she was more accomplished than to have her playing called noise. If the woman hated music so much, why keep a pianoforte in the drawing room?

Charlotte retired to her bedchamber, claiming a headache to avoid dinner and the sideways glances from Drake, who'd been begging for a private word every day since *the incident*.

That was when she saw the daisies. She stepped into her bedchamber to spy her bed decorated in flower petals and a chain of daisies tied together by their own stems serpentining on her pillow, three loops in size. She wanted to press the flowers to her bosom, wear the chain in her hair as a garland, wrap it around her neck as jewelry, dance with it, and admire it for the time and affection that must have gone into making it. To some, it was *only* silly little flowers. To her, it was so much more.

Fortitude and the ever-present memory of *hedonism* helped her resist the flattery, for she knew who had fashioned the chain.

That bounder.

That rogue.

Did he think he could bribe her back into his good graces? Blot out what she witnessed at that house of sin? Forgive him keeping a mistress? Forget his crassness and pawing during the journey north? Ignore his abandoning her to the dragon after their arrival? It would take more than daisies to move her. When Beatrice arrived with a dinner tray, Charlotte requested the flowers be discarded.

Fortitude. She needed more of it, because the daisies were not his only attempt to steal her attention.

On the fifth day, the rain still beating Northumberland into submission, Charlotte found a book of poems topped with a freshly cut rose sitting in the Gray Parlor. With book and rose perched atop her embroidery pattern, she could not dismiss them as belonging to someone else. She wished she could.

Fortitude against the libertine. She must stay strong. Did he think flowers and a few poems would move her?

Curious, she peeked at the book. *Elegiac Sonnets* by Charlotte Smith. Cheeky to find a book of poems by a woman named Charlotte. She'd never been much of a reader, at least not as voracious as her sister, so this book of poems went to show how little Drake knew her. All the same, she was curious what her namesake had written, so she thumbed through it. It wasn't the book's fault for being given by a rogue, after all.

Hours later, a clash of thunder disturbed her reverie. Had she been reading undisturbed for so long?

The words spoke the sentiments of her heart, expressing the sorrow she suffered combined with the hope she kindled. It was quite shocking to see mournful elegies alongside love sonnets, but the combination was startlingly heartening to Charlotte. She couldn't understand how Drake knew to choose poems that reflected her emotions so well, namely her current state of confusion and confliction. How could he know what she felt, he who was self-absorbed and salacious? What did a spoiled duke know of sorrow or yearning?

Proof of hedonism, she decided, for the book was an overwrought display of emotions that had no business being in anyone's library, especially when it so accurately captured her feelings. Her fortitude was stronger than she expected.

She gave both rose and book to Beatrice.

On the sixth day, she thought herself safe from his flowery attempts to gain favor. Although the rain proved only a dull drizzle after several days of storms, she thought it best to remain indoors. And so, Charlotte explored the house. She walked into every room and spoke to every footman and maid who crossed her path. There was no doubt she'd married into wealth, obscene wealth. Each room was decorated into a theme, and most rooms didn't appear to have a purpose other than to look pretty or impressive. A house such as this served one purpose: to entertain. The guest rooms were abundant and begged to be used. A dream would be to host house parties and soirées, really make use of the house, breathe life into it.

Though her time at Lyonn Manor had been dotted with blemishes, she was learning the rhythm of the household and better able to ascertain what needed to be improved and what didn't.

The exorbitant number of footmen, for example, was more to do with the local youth needing employment than to showcase wealth. Charlotte felt guilty for having at first wanting to dismiss them all, thinking them extraneous and unwarranted staff—besides, who would want to stand around all day opening doors? The steward—another little something Charlotte discovered in that yes, the manor had a steward—had worked with the dowager duchess to develop the employment scheme. Since Charlotte could not imagine Mama Catherine doing anything kind for someone else, she assumed it all the steward's doing with Catherine taking undeserved credit.

After a lengthy but satisfying day, Charlotte entered her dressing room to change for dinner. Much to her shock, her dressing table had undergone a dramatic transformation.

Fortitude was slipping.

Get yourself together, Charlotte! How could she possibly be swayed so easily by a handful of flowers three days in a row? He was a sinful rake who had married her to spite his mother. And a few silly flowers were to melt her resolve? She scoffed.

Vases of roses, some pink, some red, some variegated, covered her dressing table. Every inch of the table held a vase, every inch except the middle, where lay a slender box bowed with ribbons.

Her eyes narrowed.

She shouldn't open the box. She should send the roses to the servant quarters.

But it couldn't hurt to peek. Just a flash of a glance to satisfy curiosity. No harm came from looking. She waited until the lady's maid dressed her, the whole time smelling the roses — which, to her disappointment, did not carry a scent — and glancing back at the box. Only after Bea curled and styled Charlotte's hair, did she brave a look.

She unwrapped the box one ribbon at a time, ignoring her maid, who snatched up the ribbons to braid into her mistress' hair. Hopefully, Drake wouldn't notice they were the same ribbons and think she meant to send him a subtle signal of her forgiveness.

She would not forgive so easily.

The last ribbon untied, she lifted the lid.

Bea gasped for them both. "That's some glamorous, Your Grace. You could buy a country with it! Will you wear it tonight?"

An emerald necklace sparkled up at them, winking and teasing, making love to them both with its seductive beauty. Charlotte replaced the lid and stared at Bea wide-eyed in the mirror's reflection. She shook her head before removing the lid for another peek. What would it hurt if she tried it on? Trying it on didn't mean she would wear it, much less accept it.

Bribe? Peace offering? Red herring? Her fingers traced the row of nine emeralds, the green tears dangling from leaf-shaped clusters of diamonds. The touch of the gems chilled her skin as she slipped it around her neck. She could keep this one gift without compromising her pride, couldn't she? Yes, just this one gift she would keep.

On the seventh day, the gardens were sun-washed at last. Charlotte arranged missives for the rescheduled bazaar, her task accompanied by the warbling birds outside the parlor, sounds that excited Captain Henry, as well as her. Unable to resist their call, she took a walk through the gardens. The ground was muddy, but nothing her new boots couldn't handle.

Her first walk was through the kitchen gardens. She found inspiration for new menu items from the orchards, fruits, herbs, and vegetables. When she circled through the formal gardens, she met with the head gardener, who was cleaning muck from the fountain after the rainstorm. As they admired the horses riding a frothy wave atop the fountain, they chatted about the plans for the conservatory, adding aviary delights for the cockatoo and removing anything that could be harmful to him. The gardener was elderly, shambled when he walked, and asked her to repeat herself at least three times after every sentence, but he was notably kind and on her list of most-well-liked people at the manor.

After changing out of her mud-slushed walking dress, she ascertained if Catherine was with Mary in the conservatory, and then sneaked into the drawing room for solitude with the pianoforte. To her surprise, someone had anticipated her.

A hand-penned piece lined the music rack, no title or composer noted. A quick sight read wouldn't hurt, she told herself. Nothing about the style recalled familiarity, the left hand heavily chorded with the right hand fingering an arpeggio-laden melody. The chord progressions were ambitious with more minor chords than major, relying often on all five fingers and overlapping with the right hand in some phrases, the key signature changing frequently.

Unconvinced she was skilled enough for such a piece, she bit her lip, looked around to ascertain she was alone, and gave it her best.

As she played, her heart wrenched. No piece she had ever played resembled this, the passion infused in the notes. Before she had reached the third page, tears blurred her vision and trailed down her cheeks and onto her hands, wetting the keys. The music relied more on rhythm than melody, creating a melody out of the rhythm itself, a rhythm that guided the beat of her heart, much as the beat of drums encouraged the march of soldiers, driving them forward, setting the cadence.

Whoever had composed this knew the rawness of emotion, knew even how she felt when she lay in bed alone at night, wondering if anyone could possibly feel so isolated in a house full of people.

As vulgar as the display of emotion in the music, Charlotte was drawn to it, a butterfly to nectar, her soul aching for the sweetness to sustain her through dark days.

There could be no other person to leave the music for her than Drake. Where had he found this piece? Was there more? Why had he left it for her to play? He couldn't possibly understand the emotion evoked by this music, not when he had so many friends. He could never know what it was like to feel alone.

Knowing she couldn't allow her mother-in-law to hear such music, she stopped playing after only half an hour, clutching the pages to her breast until she reached her bedchamber where she could hide the sheets. She wanted to play this again. She wanted to play it every day and release her emotional turmoil through the music. Accepting this gift was not a slip in her fortitude for it was the music she loved, the soul-deep connection forged by the composer, nothing at all to do with the gift giver.

On the eighth day, she discovered a more practical gift in her dressing room, a new dress with matching parasol and boots. The ensemble would be perfect for the bazaar, too perfect not to wear, even if they did come from *him*. If he was so determined, why shouldn't she take advantage of the gifts? Keeping them didn't mean concession, merely acquiescence, an accepting of gifts but not his apology or attention. After all, it seemed a shame to consign lovely gifts to the dust bin. Yes, this ensemble would be perfect for the bazaar, regardless of the gift giver's intentions.

The eighth day came with even more surprises, though not all from her wayward husband. She met with the steward alone to discuss the family accounts. The discussion was enlightening, to say the least. There was a genius behind the Annick title. What did not come as a surprise was learning the family was proud with a reputation for wealth and condescension, the line held in the highest esteem by the aristocracy and favored by the Royal Family. This she already knew, although the emphasis the steward placed on it all made it that much more intimidating since she couldn't possibly uphold the high standards. What she did not know and was shocked to her toes about was the accounts. The profits from the multitude of subsidiary titles and estates held by the family went to charities, supported local communities, and funded any number of apprenticeships. It was, the steward said, an Annick tradition, not part of the entail, but an expectation of those holding the title, begun when the Mowbrah family first inherited the Annick title.

All was done, however, behind the guise of wealth and condescension. When she asked the steward why these generosities couldn't be done openly, he made a vague remark to say no one wanted to be pitied. Using the footmen as an example, he explained it was far better for the family name, community, and staff esteem for the servants to believe they were honored to be hired to work for so noble a family known than to think a useless and unnecessary job had been created out of pity for their poverty. Knowing they'd been hired for their talent to serve the best, they took that much more pride in their work.

After some thought, Charlotte decided Mama Catherine must oblige the tradition only on the condition the family remained anonymous benefactors, for she could never desire an open show of softness. Mama Catherine was exceedingly proud. All Charlotte's speculation, of course, but she struggled to reconcile the strict matriarch she knew with a generous and charitable noblewoman.

The discussion with the steward left Charlotte both honored to be part of the traditions but also further intimidated. She was now the public face of the family. Their reputation rested on her shoulders. The austerity her mother-in-law portrayed was not something Charlotte wanted to emulate, but it could be required to maintain society's respect. What had her mother-in-law been like when she first became duchess at only sixteen? Had she been prepared for it, or had she felt similarly to Charlotte — an imposter with too big of shoes to fill? Had Catherine always been a cold fish?

With the days going well, all things considered, she did not expect the drama of the ninth day.

The ninth day after the incident, she returned home from hosting her first bazaar, feeling nothing less than victorious. Her first bazaar! A success! While she did not specifically aim to please Mama Catherine, it was the dowager duchess' accolades Charlotte hoped to hear, compliments and approval of a job well done. Victory was in hand.

At least, she felt victorious until she walked into the Gray Parlor to find not a new gift or a pleased dowager duchess, rather Mrs. Fisk ordering footmen to rearrange the room. All the success of her first event drained along with the blood from her cheeks.

The furniture had stayed untouched since she'd rearranged it with the help of Mary and Stella. How appropriate for her mother-in-law to wait until Charlotte's first successful day as a hostess to reassert her authority and dash all Charlotte's hopes.

Raging inside after all she'd suffered, she screeched over the din of footmen. "What are you doing? What is the meaning of this?"

Scowling, Mrs. Fisk said, "The room had been rearranged without Her Grace's approval. I would have rectified the problem sooner, but I do have a house to run."

"Without Her Grace's approval?" Charlotte's fists coiled at her sides. "I *am* 'Her Grace.' What approval do I need in my own home?"

"You're mistaken," scolded the housekeeper. "This is the Dowager Duchess of Annick's home, and I answer to her."

The housekeeper turned back to the two footmen still holding the settee and looking for all the world as though it were not the heaviest of furniture pieces.

"Stop!" Charlotte ordered the footmen. "You take orders from the Duchess of Annick, not the housekeeper."

The footmen carrying the settee stopped midway across the room again.

The door to the parlor swung open, the dragon herself entering the room. Charlotte wanted to crawl into the wallpaper and hide. This was too much to bear. Before the staff, she was about to be undermined and humiliated.

"What's the meaning of this ruckus?" Catherine questioned airily, her tone unaffected.

Mrs. Fisk turned to the dowager duchess with a curtsy. "I am rectifying the problem, Your Grace."

Catherine eyed the footmen, then nodded for them to set down the settee. "What problem would that be, Mrs. Fisk?"

The housekeeper pulled back her shoulders and clasped her hands at her waist. "His Grace's bride ordered a maid to rearrange the parlor without your approval, Your Grace. I will be seeing to the dismissal of the maid, long overdue. I am now returning the furniture to your preferences, as I did with the portraits."

"What portraits?" Catherine's eyes narrowed.

Charlotte's eyes volleyed from Mrs. Fisk to Catherine. If Catherine questioned which portraits, did that mean she hadn't requested their replacement, hadn't been spying on Charlotte this whole time? The housekeeper wouldn't dare make decisions of her own volition.

"The portraits in the lady's chamber, Your Grace. His Grace's wife had them removed without permission, and so I replaced them on your behalf. She has seen fit to remove them again, and as soon as I find where she's hidden them, I will return them once more."

Catherine raised a single black eyebrow, arching it high on her porcelain forehead. "And what makes you think you have the right to disobey the Duchess of Annick?"

"I am loyal to the Duchess of Annick," Mrs. Fisk replied confidently. "I answer only to you, Your Grace."

"In that, you are sorely mistaken."

Charlotte held her breath. Even Captain Henry stood still on his tree.

Mrs. Fisk stiffened but held her proud pose. "Pardon me, Your Grace, but I don't understand."

"I'll not pardon you. I'll dismiss you. I may be the long-standing duchess of this manor, but no one disobeys the Duchess of Annick, regardless which generation. How dare you openly defy Her Grace. When I instructed you to bring her decisions to me, that was a matter of training, not carte blanche permission to disregard her decisions. No one disobeys the Duchess of Annick, least of all a *servant*." With her cane pointing at the door, Mama Catherine instructed, "Meet me in Mr. Taylor's office. You are not to leave until I arrive."

The housekeeper held her head high as she curtsied to the dowager duchess, ignoring Charlotte, then left the room.

"You there." Catherine pointed to the footmen. "Return the settee and any other furniture to how the duchess requested."

The dowager duchess waited in silence for them to complete their task. Only when they left the room did she turn her coal black eyes to Charlotte.

"Do you not care for the house's décor?"

Charlotte stepped forward with a shaky breath. "While I recognize the importance of the portraits, I was unnerved that they watched me sleep. I thought a new location would be more appropriate for them, as well as allow them to be better admired by those who might appreciate their condescension." She swallowed, not ready to admit just where she had sent said portraits. Hesitating, not wanting Mama Catherine to smite her hopes, she added, "I hoped to replace them with landscapes of the estate. As to the parlor, I found it unfortunate the arrangement didn't take best advantage of the garden. In fact, I want to rearrange and redecorate most of the public rooms to be more inviting to guests and allow for better admiration of the gardens." Charlotte hoped she wouldn't be struck down by the gold handled cane.

"And you decided not to consult me?"

"I feared you wouldn't approve."

Catherine snorted in what might have been a laugh if Charlotte knew what the woman's laugh sounded like. "Doubting my approval, you began the redecoration anyway. I'm pleased to find you have a backbone after all, not to mention good taste. The Duchess of Annick cannot be a spineless, simpering simpleton. Do as you wish with the rooms. My only request is that you do not alter the Red Drawing Room until I move to the dower house, which will not be until you're ready to serve without my tutelage."

Charlotte's eyes widened, hardly knowing how to respond.

Continuing, Catherine said, "We'll need to arrange for a new housekeeper. When it comes to so important of a position, we will not post an advertisement rather solicit recommendations from trusted peers. Though you'll choose the person, I will conduct the interviews. In this way, you'll see how it's done and receive the benefit of my recommendations. Understood?" Catherine waited for Charlotte to nod. "I see in you strength and power, but you must first overcome the silliness of youth. I am your mother-in-law, not your enemy. Join me in one hour in the Red

Drawing Room. I wish to discuss the qualifications
required for the position, in addition to your own
preferences for housekeeper."

How was Charlotte to make sense of this
exchange? Neither her mother-in-law nor her husband behaved as they ought. Were they villains? Were
they allies? Were they both selfish liars or generous
benefactors? Mama Catherine's actions and words
gave Charlotte a glimmer of hope that she had misjudged her mother-in-law.

"And you insist she used no coercion?" Drake asked
the line-up of staff, consisting of James the coachman,
Stella the parlor maid, Philip the tiger, and Algernon
the footman. "She didn't threaten to dismiss you if
you didn't comply?"

"No, Your Grace," claimed Philip for the third time
in the past half hour of questioning. "It were my idea."

Stella nodded in agreement and added, "She
needn't force us, Your Grace. I would happily follow
her anywhere. She's the kindest lady I know."

Drake looked to James and Algernon, both staring
at their feet. "And the two of you share this opinion?"

They nodded.

The coachman augmented their story by saying,
"I dinna' like the plan from the start, but Ah'd be
doin' anything for Her Grace. She's been nought but
kind to Stella and the others. I dinna' want her tae
see what she mighta seen neither, but I canna' say
no to her. Ah'd follow Her Grace to Land's End if
she asked."

Drake nodded then waved them all to return to their duties. It would seem they had designed the plan amongst themselves as a means of helping Charlotte rather than Charlotte herself planning a raid of Maggie's house and forcing her staff to comply by penalty of dismissal. Drake's concern had been her safety and that the grooms had allowed her to ride on the back of a carriage without somehow trying to stop her harebrained scheme. He thought perhaps she had threatened them in her distress to catch him with his supposed mistress — what other explanation was there for them to allow her to endanger her life in so careless a fashion? That would not seem the case, though. Any plan to reprimand the staff slipped when he heard of their devotion to her. They had not, by their estimation, put her life in danger, despite it being a risky act, as Algernon had personally seen to her safety during the journey. Drake didn't like any part of what had happened, but after the interview, he was more moved by the staff's devotion to Charlotte than upset with them. Granted, he might have felt differently had his affair been genuine and had he learned in that state of mind that his staff had undermined *him* by encouraging her to follow and spy, but as that was not the case, and after hearing their loyalty to the new duchess, he could not be angry.

The visual they painted of Charlotte had him both stymied and infatuated by his bride, as they described a woman he had not yet seen but had hoped to have married. An encouraging and motivating leader of the staff? A lady so worth their loyalty they would follow to Land's End? They had shared with him how personable she had been since arriving, how conscientious of their needs, all while respecting the duchess and staff relationship.

He had long suspected she possessed the poise and social inclinations of a duchess, but he hadn't imagined her a particularly charismatic person. Even in London she had appeared meek, despite her talk-ativeness, potentially compassionate, but otherwise a follower rather than a leader. Her youthfulness had given way to a perceived selfishness, as well, that he hoped would fade with time. He had relied on his mother to pull out whatever confidence she might possess, and to train her successfully, but it would seem he had misjudged his young wife. After what happened the night of the rout, he knew he'd mis-judged her on a great many things, not the least of which was her motivation for marrying him.

If he could bury his head in the sand, he would. He'd spent days wallowing in mortification that he'd tossed her aside based only on her initial skittish behavior. What did he know of young women? His only experience with women, truthfully, had been with Maggie and her friends, all women of matu-rity and sensuality. The more he tried to justify his actions, the more wretched he felt for how he'd treated her.

All too clearly, he recalled their wedding night. Before entering the room, he'd assumed she didn't want anything to do with him other than the obliga-tory consummation. In his mind at the time, he'd be deviled if he was going to force himself on an unwill-ing girl out of duty, especially when he'd married her under the impression she was as interested in him as he was in her. He recalled asking her why she'd married him and not being satisfied with the answer. Ah, it was all muck.

He'd misread every sign. For years, women threw themselves at him, all making it abundantly clear what they wanted and why they wanted it. If the women in London were to be believed, he'd slept with half the *beau monde*. He never dared call out a woman on such a lie—that wouldn't be gentlemanly, after all—but there were women he'd never met who claimed a liaison with him. With such a life, how was he to read his bride's nervousness and translate it to mean she wanted him? Her rejection had been understood as just that—rejection. All he could associate her dismissal with was when Maggie had laughed him out of the house following his proposal. The more fool he.

Ah, it was all rubbish. He'd made a royal mess of the marriage from start to finish.

All his wallowing fueled his desire to woo her. He *must* right this mess. Believing as he did that she cared for him, there was hope.

From the start, he'd wanted love in his marriage, yet he hadn't given much thought to the hidden qualities of the woman on the other end of that marriage. Charlotte had a personality all her own, dreams and goals, fears and failures. What had he done to learn about these aspects of his wife? Nothing. He'd selfishly thought only of her loving *him*.

He wanted love in his marriage so much, yet what had he done to deserve her affection? How stupid of him not to think of her as a *person*, only as a beautiful woman who might love him. So obsessed with *being* loved, he'd forgotten there were two in that equation. How could they love each other when they knew nothing about each other?

The only love he had ever known was in the arms of a false woman, an unrequited love that grew solely from physical affection, not tenderness of personality or shared interests. Truthfully, he and Maggie had shared no interests whatsoever other than sexual gratification.

He had only expressed love through physical coupling, channeling his ardor into sensual articulation. How does one get to know another through *conversation*? People lie. How does one share affection without bodily contact? Then, all the physical connection he had with Maggie hadn't taught him a single thing about her or her true feelings for him. Curious that. He had thought people lied but bodies didn't. It was time to unlearn what he had been taught.

Charlotte would not be wooed by physical affection, which was just as well since he didn't want to repeat that life again. No, he wanted his wife to know *him* and fall for him just as much as the other way around. It seemed fitting she should know the real him. Best find out sooner rather than later if she even liked the real him.

Chapter 17

The day after the bazaar, Drake sat at a table befitting a king, waiting for Mr. Taylor to bring Charlotte. The autumn air was chilly after the previous week's rain, but the sun was bright, smiling on an extravagant fare. Drake's brilliant idea was an al fresco nuncheon, only he got a tad carried away.

Admittedly, covering nearly every square inch of the grotto with flowers might have been overdoing it.

The tea was hot, his brandy sweet, and the bread warm when the butler announced Charlotte. Drake fumbled his way out of the chair, overly eager to make amends. With a bow and a flourish of his hand, he invited the duchess to join him.

Before she could say something snotty, as he expected her to do—and as would be her right after all he had unintentionally made her suffer—he readied a cup of tea for her and laid cold cuts on a plate with a sizable side of bread. She took her seat, eyeing him askance.

"Did you enjoy the bazaar?" he enquired, hoping to direct the conversation to her right away. His hope was to begin anew, his attention on knowing her better and ensuring she felt seen.

After a sip of tea, she raised her chin and stared out at the landscape, ignoring his question.

"I wager," Drake continued, "you were a superb hostess, and I imagine the attendees were pleased to see you rather than Mother. A far more pleasing sight." He winked at her profile.

She continued to ignore him.

Well, dash it all. Did the flowers put her off? Was it too much? Had he not chosen the right foods? Had she not liked the gifts? He had been certain the gifts would soften her towards forgiveness, each given with her in mind based on what he had learned of her in London. Uncertain what to say to elicit a response, he sat in lingering silence. All he had was his charm, and she was immune to it. Savoring his brandy and the warmth that spread with each taste, he watched her watching the outdoors. *Look at me*, he commanded in his mind. *Talk to me, please.*

A quarter of an hour of silence passed.

At least she had shown up. He had not been certain she would. If that was as much as they achieved today, so be it, for at least his gifts had won him an audience with her.

Not wanting to leave it unsaid, he braved, "Shall we agree to a truce, Charlotte?"

She turned to him, eyes narrowed. "Pardon, but did you say something?"

"I want a truce. To the devil with this tiptoeing around each other. We are long overdue for a candid conversation."

"I'm afraid I can't hear you, Your Grace. I don't speak to libertines." She turned to the table to indulge in the food she'd heretofore ignored, adding item after item to the plate he had already prepared for her.

"A libertine, am I?" He leaned forward in his chair. "Can you be so certain?"

"You're a perversely sinful man, and I do not wish to know you," Charlotte said to her plate, which was so piled with food, Drake was tempted to laugh. He resisted.

"The devil I am," he protested instead.

"Mind your language. I will not be subjected to your vulgarity."

"Not to state the obvious, but I'm your husband whether you wish to know me or not. Now, I offer a truce and want us to talk. A real talk, Charlotte." With a slight hesitation, he added, "I'm not above begging."

"Your being my husband is an inconvenient technicality. I do not see the benefit of a truce, for it is you who have wronged, and I'm undecided if I can forgive you. You've made a joke of my life."

"Charlotte, sheathe the blade, please. I didn't invite you here to quarrel."

"You know perfectly well we have nothing to say to each other," Charlotte countered, taking a bite of bread.

"I'm in earnest. I don't want us to be strangers, or estranged, for that matter. Let's begin with this: list for me my sins. Tell me how I have wronged you, so that I will know everything I must make right. Be specific. Being a man, I may be ignorant of half the ways I've antagonized you. Let's leave no stone unturned. List my sins, and I will endeavor to reverse them all. I'm not above going down on my knees when I beg."

"I don't regard you as quite so ignorant, Your Grace." She took another bite and looked at him only long enough to gouge his eyes with her own.

"Consider me the daftest man in England and explain my sins in five languages."

She heaved a sigh. "How tedious." Another sigh. "Very well, but know I do not appreciate the blatant humiliation you suffer me to endure in listing your sins." Her body rigid, her spine straight, she said, "You've made me miserable, and nothing you say can assuage that sentiment."

"Have you tried to like it here?"

"Don't be absurd," she retorted. "I love the manor and the staff, but the elements are against me. You were horribly rude to me on the trip here, embarrassing me in front of your cousin with crudeness, and then you abandoned me from the first day we arrived, allowing your mother to lord over me. You've never tried to talk to me, and you've certainly never defended me to your mother. And now you've taken a mistress without so much as giving me a chance, preferring to carry on at sordid parties with, with, oh, with those people. How is all of this to be borne? How am I to endure a life where I'm so unwanted?"

Drake leaned back, mulling over her accusations.

"You're not unwanted, Charlotte. And I'm trying to talk to you now," he defended, his voice soft and pleading.

"Yes, well, I've now laid at your feet your sins. What do you have to say for yourself?"

"I don't know where to start." He swallowed against the lump in his throat. "I didn't abandon you. At least I didn't intend to. I was under the impression you only wanted the title, and having got it, you wanted no more to do with me. I left you to my mother because I believed that was what you wanted.

You never came to me. You never indicated wanting to see me. I thought you were happy in your new role."

"No. I didn't want the title." She stared at her hands folded in her lap. "I only wanted you." She chewed on her bottom lip. "But you pushed too hard, too fast. And then you walked away without looking back."

"That's not fair," Drake rebutted. "I saw no evidence that you wanted me. Every advance I made, you pushed me away, to the point of physical violence and accusations of ravishment, might I add. How was I supposed to know you wanted *me* if you did everything to prove you didn't? The few times you were receptive to my attentions, you followed them with days of coldness. Please, don't think I'm accusing you, just defending why I thought you didn't want me around."

Charlotte snapped back at him, "I did not push you away. Countless nights I went to your room, hoping to talk or to…to…well, you weren't there. You were off cavorting. The only times your affections have been unwanted were on the journey here, and even those weren't entirely unwanted, merely too much, too soon. You treated me like one of your mistresses. You may be worldly, but I am not. Instead of talking to me or showing tenderness, you would paw at me and then sulk when I didn't like it. All I've ever wanted is you, but you've been too self-absorbed to notice, wanting only to undress me."

Tirade at an end, she shivered and snatched up the bread. As she chewed the bread, he chewed on her words.

"Charlotte, I'm sorry. I swear to you, I thought you were happier without me. I believed you'd used me for status." He rubbed the back of his neck, deuced uncomfortable by his own short sighted- ness. "I wanted to go to you, but I knew you didn't want me, and so I spent my evenings nursing my wounded pride."

Her gold-flecked eyes studied his as if filtering truth from lies.

Coolly, she said, "And so, to salve your pride, you sought affection from those heathens."

"No. Believe me when I say this. *I have no one.*" He paused, reaching for his brandy to prepare for the inevitability of all he was about to confess.

Drake took a deep breath. "The woman you think is my mistress is most certainly not. I won't deceive you by hiding that I once thought myself in love with her, but it was nothing more than a boyish infatuation that ended over ten years ago. I went to her only to tell her of the marriage because I didn't want to anger her by not doing it personally. I will never see her again."

Charlotte said nothing, her shoulders round- ing ever so slightly. Having finished the bread, she returned to chewing on her bottom lip, waiting for him to say more.

"I'm not as, er, well-traveled as you would think me." He hesitated, shifting in his chair and clearing his throat. "I've only been with one woman. You may choose not to believe me, but I speak the truth and certainly wouldn't admit this otherwise. I've only been with one woman, and I've not been with her for ten years. I am very much celibate. Given my reputation, I suppose you'll think me a fibber, but there it is."

Setting his glass down, he leaned an elbow against his armrest and began to wring his hands, feeling a cold sweat on his brow. He couldn't believe he was saying these words. What would she make of him? One seed of doubt might be enough for her to question him. After all his work to build a secure reputation, he was recklessly abandoning it for the sake of truth to the last person on earth he wanted to question or doubt him. She could mock him if he attempted to explain how Maggie took advantage of him, ravishing his youth, never mind he had thought himself a willing partner. She could, instead, or perhaps as well, think of him as his mother did, that he was like his father. She could...well, for all he knew, she would fling his honesty back at him, use his words against him.

But he had to try if there was to be any peace between them.

Holding her gaze steady, he continued, "I'm not a rake and have no interest in being one. For me, physical affection is as closely tied to emotional attachment as my heart is to my soul. The one person I've been with, I loved dearly, and so I gave her my body and my heart. My body belongs to no one except the woman of my heart. I'd like, if you would give me the opportunity, to offer you my body and my heart."

Charlotte visibly swallowed before reaching for her tea, whetting her palate. She stared into her cup for some time before responding.

"What of the scene I witnessed?" she asked the tea leaves.

He pulled out his snuffbox for a pinch to relax his nerves. The box trembled in his hands. Such confessions were never meant to be spoken, not by a man, not by a duke. Two pinches to be safe. He returned the box to its pocket.

"You witnessed a scene from my past. I have not been party to that madness since I was the age of the boys in attendance."

Charlotte set the cup and saucer on the table. "I don't think I want to understand but proceed with an explanation, if you please. I need to understand."

"Don't pity me when I say I was taken advantage of at a young age, for you must understand I was quite willing. More than willing. What young man wouldn't be?" He chuckled, making light of a grim truth. "You witnessed the precursor to a scene two decades in my past, *not* my present. The hostess of that rout was my first and only lover, and that affair ended when I was nigh three and twenty. While the woman is real, any rumor of an existing affair is fabricated."

He paused, taking a deep breath, not certain how else to explain what she had seen or how much he should explain without doing more damage.

Best be out with it, old man. He exhaled from his cheeks and said, "She was the wife of one of my father's friends, and she invited me to call on her under a false pretense. Being the fifteen-year-old buffoon I was, I went to her. I arrived to just such a scene as you witnessed, only I stayed until its conclusion. What I *thought* would happen and what *did* happen were two different things, I assure you, for I believed I was attending a musical soirée. That was not the case.

I was seduced by a master manipulator. So masterful, I didn't realize it until the other evening. After all these years, I still believed it had been a mutual love affair, despite the age gap, at least until I witnessed it through the eyes of maturity. Think of me what you will, Charlotte, but I was young and naïve, still am, apparently, since I fell for her ruse again and attended that ridiculous rout the other evening thinking to do her a final farewell favor."

He downed the remainder of his brandy. If all this honesty didn't improve the relationship, he was at a loss as to what would.

With an abrupt laugh, he said, "I never expected a carefully crafted reputation of being a womanizer would interfere with my having the woman I want. Oh, that sounded less than eloquent. I'm not a poet, Charlotte. I couldn't even finish the letter I started to write you. And if you don't believe how terrible I am with words, I'll show you the draft."

She gaped at him. "You wrote that letter for me?"

"Well, of course — wait. How do you know about it?"

A flush tinted her cheeks as she looked down at her hands.

"Ah," Drake said, grinning. Apparently, her snooping hadn't been restricted to riding on the backs of carriages.

"I don't understand. Why would you *want* people to think you're a womanizer?"

"Mmm. I'm not at all confident I'm ready for that conversation," he admitted.

"If you want a truce, I need to understand. What am I to think the next time I hear a rumor about you? I need to know everything."

He needed another pinch for this conversation. And another brandy. He sated himself with a fresh glass and a savory pinch before daring to continue.

"One false rumor can ruin a man." He rubbed the back of his neck again, feeling the prickle of sweat despite the chilly autumn air. "It only takes a single seed of doubt to taint an entire family for generations."

She huffed. "If what you've said is true, you've been the source of the false rumor."

"No, that's not at all to what I'm referring."

Circling her hand in the air, she urged him to continue.

"I'm referring to my father, not to me. Ah, where do I begin? His, er, reputation was nearly the undoing of the Annick title and Mowbrah family name. We're a proud family, you must understand. You see, my father was a violinist. His dream was to be recognized for his talent, but he never was, maybe for a lack of talent, maybe because of the reputation." Drake cleared his throat. "How do I explain this? It only takes a single rumor, false or true, to ruin a man and his family. Curse it. I'm bumbling this."

To his surprise, she reached a hand to touch his arm, nodding for him to continue.

"You already know I, too, play the violin," he said.

She nodded.

"From an early age, my father filled my life with music, hiring tutors and the like. It would seem I had the talent he lacked. My mother protested to every lesson and every concert, accusing my father of, shall we say, feminizing me. She wanted me not to follow in my father's footsteps, but to aim for more, er, manly pursuits, something more fitting of a duke's heir."

"Oh. I see," she said, her hand still resting on his arm. "But why care what she thinks? Her opinion hardly matters if you know the truth."

"But it wasn't only her opinion. The entirety of the *beau monde* knew of my father's less than savory company of fellow musicians."

She laughed. "'Less than savory'? What are you talking about? Besides, that has nothing to do with you, and from what I know of you, you've never cared a fig for what anyone thinks."

"Don't I?"

He stared at her, frowning, watching her expression change from incredulous to concerned. A gust of wind rustled through the flowers and across the grotto, cooling the beads of sweat lining his forehead.

Blotting his face with a kerchief, he said, "For all my proselytizing that I don't care what others think, I do. You see, it wasn't that my father's friends were musicians, although that was part of the problem seeing as how the art is associated with trade rather than aristocratic pursuits. The trouble was…" He heaved an exhale, shifting in his chair, the kerchief strangled in his fist. "My father enjoyed musical soirées, not unlike what you witnessed."

He flicked a glance her direction to see if she was catching on. Her brows were drawn together, no signs of recognition. Continuing, he said, "He enjoyed *lively* parties. The guests were almost exclusively…" He cleared his throat. "Men." Drake closed his eyes, steadying his nerves. For all he knew, Charlotte would be on the next carriage to Cornwall, for if she didn't accuse him of being like his father, she may fear the family line was tainted. "My mother blamed the music."

Redirecting his point, he said, "The Annick title is a proud one, and I'll not have anyone question my family or me. My mother has always feared my father's sins would become my own. It only takes one rumor, Charlotte. One. When I was old enough to understand, I began handcrafting my reputation. I may have no interest in the life of a libertine, but the reputation suits me and ensures no one will ever question the Mowbrah line. I value my reputation above all things in life and maintain it meticulously."

He sank lower in his chair and defensively set an ankle over one knee, affecting a casual demeanor, although he desperately wanted to erect a barrier between himself and the words he had spoken so candidly to Charlotte. He only hoped the words wouldn't come back to haunt him. His plan for today's nuncheon had been for *her* to speak, not for him to confess secrets.

Speaking so softly, he almost didn't hear her, Charlotte said, "You value what other people think more than anything, including me. You would have kept all of this from me, living a lie, never letting me know you."

"That's never been my intention."

Removing her hand from his arm, she said, "Yes, it is. It was more important to you to prove to the world you still had a mistress than it was to get to know your wife. I understand your reasons, but I don't understand how you could be so obsessed with your father's reputation that you forsook your wife, your only goal to continue some charade. You've made our marriage foolish."

"That was never my intention. I am ashamed of my choices. I'll do whatever it takes to right my wrongs. Give me a chance to make things right. I'm dreadfully sorry for everything, Charlotte. I've gone about everything terribly, but you must know I want to be a good husband. I'm incredibly attracted to you and want you to feel the same. What can I say that will convince you we deserve a fresh start?"

She chewed on her lip. "Will you defend me to your mother?" she asked out of the blue.

He wanted to laugh. Of all that he had just confessed and all he could do to show he was earnest, her first words were of his mother. Absurd!

"I don't see why I need to defend you. My mother isn't a beast, you know. Aren't the two of you getting along famously?"

"No." Charlotte's spine straightened, her chin rising. "Why hasn't she moved to the dower house?"

"I suppose she wants to ensure you're ready before she leaves you to run an estate."

"Am I of such low birth that I need constant supervision?" she asked. "If you care about me, you'll stand up for me when she demeans me. Tell her not to monopolize every minute of my day."

"This isn't my battle." He raised his hands defensively. "If you're displeased with something, stand up for yourself. Tell her. She won't respect you if *I* do it. Have you ever thought of telling her to sod off?"

"She's *your* mother!" Charlotte stood and made to leave.

"Wait! Please, don't go." Drake stood, as well, and laid his hand on Charlotte's arm to still her. "I'm listening. Be patient with me. She's not an easy woman to live with, but she will respect you more if you stand up to her. If I step in, she'll only be displeased with us both and think you're weak-willed. I'm not being harsh or inattentive or inconsiderate or whatever it seems I'm being, truly."

He tugged at Charlotte to return to her seat.

After some hesitation and more biting of the abused lower lip, she sat. The table took her attention for the next few moments until she decided to try one of the sandwiches.

"*You* must stand up to her," he said. "While we're being candid, allow me to confess it was one of the many reasons why I was initially attracted to you. I felt you were someone who would stand up to her. You were opinionated and bossy—I mean this as a compliment, I swear—perfect for dealing with Mother. Stand up to her, and she'll respect you; otherwise, she'll continue to rule the house. She's not about to relinquish her control to someone who isn't ready."

He waited for her to say something. A vow to stand up to Mother. A denial that men could be seduced. A defense of his father. An accusation against him. Anything. Instead, she focused on the sandwich. Perhaps she needed time to digest all that had been said.

In an attempt to change the subject, he said, "Sebastian is coming for dinner tonight."

She groaned.

Glad to have a response, even if it was a groan, Drake chuckled into his brandy glass. After a swig, he said, "I'll occupy him in the study for the evening. You should try liking him. He'll be your brother-in-law before long, you know."

Charlotte's head jerked up. "He most certainly will not! Don't you dare start rumors. Lizbeth would be horrified."

"I hate to tell you, Charlotte, but they're besotted. Didn't you pay any attention to them in London? Or did you have eyes only for me?"

She grimaced. "They most certainly are not besotted. Lizbeth is a spinster, and it's cruel of you to tease her. Besides, she would never be interested in someone like your cousin. The only reason they were in each other's company in London was for our benefit. They tolerated each other at best."

Drake shook his head. "Your sister may call herself a spinster, but she's still quite a catch." At Charlotte's raised eyebrow, he clarified, "Too bookish for me, of course. But not for my cousin. Did you know they have been corresponding since our marriage?"

"They most certainly have not! My sister would never correspond with a man who isn't her betrothed! It's simply not done. Don't say such things," Charlotte admonished him.

"And since when have either of our relations followed decorum or social expectations?" He tipped back his glass to award his silent victory a drink.

"Be that as it may, I cannot believe my sister would be interested in *him*."

"Shall we place a wager?" Drake suggested.

"Ladies do not make wagers. More to the point, I do not wish you to feel a sore loser when you see that I'm right." She smiled smugly, but at least she smiled.

Wouldn't Charlotte be surprised after Lizbeth's arrival, he thought, endlessly humored that the blossoming love affair between his cousin and her sister had been completely lost on his wife. While he had no doubt her sister would have headed straight for Northumberland at Charlotte's request regardless, he did wonder if a hefty portion of Liz's enthusiastic acceptance to the invitation was due to his cousin's presence. A double win of helping the sister and seeing Sebastian. Or Drake was a hopeless romantic.

Charlotte was the eager one to change the subject this time. "The sonata on the pianoforte — who composed it? I didn't recognize the style."

The glass of brandy paused at his lips. He set the glass on the table. "Did you like it?" he asked tentatively.

"It was coarse."

And there it was, the dagger to the heart. Drake slumped in the chair.

"But I liked it," she amended. "No, I more than liked it. I want to know how the composer melded inside my heart. No one has a right to see any other person so intimately. It was incredibly vulgar, but..." She leaned forward and said *sotto voce*, "I want more. Tell me, who is he? Do you have more of his music?"

His heart pounded. "I do have more. I'll arrange for more sheets. May I hear you play? Nothing would give me greater pleasure than to hear you play this particular collection of music. We could, dare I say, play a duet? The composer in question has written any number of violin pieces with piano accompaniment."

She blushed. "I am hardly skilled enough for an audience, but I won't say no. Tell me — who is the composer?"

Drake drummed his fingers against his leg, eyeing her hand still on the arm of his chair. Did he dare?

Well, if not now, then when? She had not protested to his musical inclinations so far, nor had she run from the house when he indicated his father's own inclinations, such as they had been. Safe so far, with the worst confessions shared, she surely wouldn't now accuse him of being common or otherwise. Yes, it was time. It was, he realized now, the only way for them to have the kind of marriage he desired.

Pushing himself out of the chair, he offered his hand. "Come with me? I have something to show you."

She stared at his proffered hand. "A name would suffice. Or are you planning to show me your collection of the composer's work?" The words mixed curiosity with skepticism.

"Come." He inclined his head towards the door.

Slipping her hand in his, she stood and followed him into the drawing room.

Outside his study, he paused. He needed to gather his wits and be positive he was making the right decision. Once confessed, there was no turning back. Could he bare his soul to a near stranger who didn't entirely trust him?

The music was controversial in theme and style, challenging convention. It reflected him at his rawest, an outpouring of inner turmoil, which was hardly something he would want to share with another person. He may dream of sharing his music with the world, but he never planned to admit it was his own, rather the compositions of someone he patronized. Could he share all of this so easily with Charlotte?

"Tell me. Why did you like the sonata?" he asked, his free hand holding the door handle.

Her eyes brightened as she said, "It was unlike anything I've ever heard. While it tried my abilities, it was neither technical nor memorable, at least not in terms of melody. It was...how do I describe it? Rhythmic and emotional. I wanted to hate it, if I'm being honest. I felt every chord down to the pit of my stomach. I feel improprietous saying this, but the music spoke of my heart's desires, as if the composer knew how I felt. As impossible as it sounds, the composer knew my sorrow." Charlotte pressed her hand to her chest.

"Ever think the composer wasn't writing how *you* felt, but rather how *he* felt?" Drake questioned.

"How absurd. Of course, he wrote how I felt. Why would a composer write about himself? A composer writes for the performer. I don't know how he was able to capture such depth in the notes, but he did. He knew me, Drake. The notes were for me," she insisted.

Drake chuckled. The sonata in question certainly had been for her, but not in the way she thought. He'd envisioned the piece accomplishing what his letter couldn't, to explain how he felt about the misunderstanding and the sorrow that had ripped his heart.

The sonata was his way of communicating to Charlotte how *he* felt. Never in his wildest dreams would he have imagined she felt the same. To his chagrin, he realized instead of recognizing the music as a reflection of each other, they each saw it as a reflection of themselves. A sonata to bond them, yet they were both too self-centered to see it as anything but about themselves. Drake laughed aloud at the irony. The music had touched her in ways he hadn't expected. While she may not understand *him* from the music as he had hoped, he understood *her* better now. If what she said was true, then he knew how she felt. Oh, sweet Charlotte. If he could kiss away her heartache, he would. The trouble was, he was the cause of it.

"We are more alike than either of us anticipated, I declare," Drake said. When she bristled, he added, "Don't take offense. I mean it as a compliment. An observation. Despite our rough start, I believe we are well suited. I hope you'll take to heart my offer of a truce."

He squeezed her hand.

She didn't remove her hand from his, but she did look startled by the gesture. "I'll consider it. Now, are you going to show me the music or not?"

He grinned and opened the door to his study. In quick steps, they stood in front of the back bookshelf. A month's worth of brandy he would have paid to have her expression memorialized on canvas when he opened the shelf and the door behind it to reveal the rounded room beyond.

He led her into his private music room and urged her inside to explore. She stood gaping rather than exploring as he lit the candelabras to flood the windowless room with light.

An old harpsichord stood in the middle of the space, the one that had taken residence in the Red Drawing Room until replaced with the pianoforte. On top of its lid perched his violin. A music stand stood next to it, slender and gold, still holding the latest draft that had been troubling him for weeks. Bookshelves lined the curved walls with music scores and other texts. Towards the back of the room sat his desk, messily arrayed with scores, quills, ink bottles, and sand pots. With a grimace, he noticed one of the scores strewn out on the floor. If he had anticipated a guest, he would have tidied.

"What is this?" Charlotte broke the silence at last.

"This, my wife, is my music room." He stepped forward, pulling the bookshelf closed now that the candles were lit.

Dashing past her to the harpsichord, he lifted his violin and bow to play, hoping to break the tension.

With a quick wink, he fingered a coiled melody, tightly wound at the base of the pegboard, a scurrying little theme before he pushed higher, releasing the coil to an impetuous and intensifying agitation. He glanced at her as his bow sputtered outbursts of brusque rhythms.

She stared at his violin, brows drawn together. With a pizzicato flourish, he lifted his violin from his chin and bowed. He had only played an improvised phrase, but it hopefully demonstrated enough of the same style from the sonata that she would recognize it.

"I don't understand," she said, staring at him from across the room.

Returning the instrument to the lid, he dashed back to her. "What's there not to understand? This is my secret room. I commissioned the construction when Mother forbade me from playing music in the house. She called it a waste of time, noise, the practice of commoners, effeminate, and a few other choice descriptors." He gestured grandly around the room. "This is where I spend most of my nights, tucked away, flitting from one piece to the next. I can never seem to focus on one work at a time, so I move from one to the next and back as inspiration strikes."

Warm breath tickled his face as she exhaled a whoosh of air, as though his words knocked the wind out of her.

"*You're* the composer?" she asked, her question somewhat accusatory.

Drake smiled. "Yes. This room is where I compose. And at least half of these bookshelves are filled with my work. Some finished, most not."

The color drained from her face. Drake's smile wavered. Her reaction wasn't building his confidence. She had admitted to liking the music, hadn't she? He felt exposed, vulnerable, ever so slightly unhinged.

"I need to sit," she said hoarsely.

With the flat of his palm on the small of her back, he led her to the harpsichord, sitting next to her when she took to the bench.

His thumb circled the muslin of her green dress. If he hadn't felt the stiffness of her spine and known from previous experiences that the results would prove disastrous, he would kiss her to restore color to her cheeks. The whole of having her in the music room, of sharing his music, filled him with anticipation, one part fearful, the other part winsome. Did he feel exposed or seen? Was there a difference? She now knew his passion, his hidden self, the part of himself he shared with no one. Terrifying and freeing simultaneously. Here, she sat in his private room, looking lovely with her chestnut curls, her bottom lip rosy from all the chewing it suffered, and her copper eyes. Oh, how he wanted to kiss her.

Reprimanding his own reckless thoughts, he reminded himself not to behave rashly.

"Well? What do you think?" he asked, hoping to change the direction of his thoughts.

Shaking her head, she asked, "Why hide this? Why not tell me?"

"I suppose I worried you might not like my music. Or might not care. You could have mocked me. You could have laughed or belittled me." He shrugged, his smile sliding downwards. "Given the fear of rumors, I've habituated the secrecy. It's my passion, no one else's. The room, also, provides a retreat from the rest of the house, allowing me to vent frustrations when needed."

"You're in *here* at night?" She turned her head to see him, looking almost startled to see him sitting by her.

"Yes. I'm in here, not out at a soirée or with another woman. I'm in here," he said, his words *morendo* in tone.

"Oh," she exhaled the word in another whoosh of air. "But the sonata. Who wrote the sonata?"

"I did." His thumb continued to draw circles on her vertebrae.

"You." She echoed. "You composed the sonata."

Nodding, he indicated the harpsichord behind them. "Would you like to see more of my work? Perhaps play?"

Still looking at him with a touch of wonderment, she gave her curls a shake. He was more than disappointed. All of this and she didn't want to see or play the music? Well, blast.

"No, not now." She took her abused lower lip between her teeth. "No, right now, I'd like to kiss you."

His heart thumped so hard against his ribcage he wondered if she heard it. Before she changed her mind, he leaned towards her, only to find her hand against his chest, stopping him.

"You misunderstand. I don't want you to kiss me," she said.

He raised an eyebrow, horribly confused.

"*I* want to kiss *you*. I want to kiss the composer who spoke to my soul, but only on the condition that you not kiss me back." She slipped her hand over his cravat and around to the back of his neck.

With fingers tightening around his hair, she pulled him forward, brushing her lips against his.

He didn't move. His eyes remained open, watching her as she closed hers and pressed her lips to his. He fought his instinct to return the kiss, to reach out and embrace her. His body and soul caught fire, yet he remained as still as he could, allowing her to lead this dance.

She twirled her fingers around his hair and sighed against him. By God, he was a happy man. A happy man indeed.

That evening, Drake enjoyed a brandy with his cousin, the two men relaxing in the study after dinner. To his chagrin, Charlotte's kiss flashed in his memory at unexpected moments of his conversation with Sebastian, distracting him.

"You promise to send notice as soon as she arrives?" Sebastian asked for the fifth time.

Drake waved his hand, then reached for his glass. "Only if you promise to propose, old man. You very nearly let her get away."

His cousin grunted. "She won't want me. She may not even welcome my advances. Regardless, I don't deserve her, and that's the truth of it."

"You're right, of course. You don't deserve her," Drake agreed, smiling mischievously over his glass. "I needn't bother sending a footman to announce she's arrived if you're not going to take action."

"So help me, I will throttle you if you don't tell me when she's here." Sebastian growled.

"Make up your mind! It's all nonsense anyway. She looks at you as if you were a ripe peach. I say, marry her and be done with it. If you'd rather pout, alone in your misery, at least spend the next month wooing her. A few stolen kisses would do you some good." Drake chuckled.

"You have no shame," Sebastian replied, but Drake saw the twinkle in his cousin's eyes.

No harm came from a little matchmaking, Drake decided. And suddenly an idea formed. Two ideas, actually. The corners of his mouth curved up. The next month should prove most interesting if he had his way. He needed the cooperation of Charlotte's aunt, in some small part the willingness of his mother to grant a favor, and his own cunning. Yes, this month he'd play matchmaker, both for his cousin and for himself. With any luck, both sisters would be wedded, and dare he hope, loved.

Chapter 18

The manor twittered with excitement. Charlotte's anticipation spread like wildfire amongst the staff, all eagerly awaiting a peek at Charlotte's family.

Charlotte's own delight couldn't be solely attributed to her family's arrival, though. Partial credit went to Drake. The day of the nuncheon had been a pivotal day for her. Knowing she couldn't entirely trust words over actions, she planned to watch his behavior to assure herself he had spoken candidly. All the same, his words had meant a great deal. For the first time, at last, he showed a genuine interest in their getting to know each other better.

She wanted to speak to her aunt before she made any moves, said anything more, or even made plans for interactions alone with Drake. Nothing had changed yet between them, but she had hope for the first time, as though she stood on the precipice of change. The air was ripe with possibilities, an almost palpable excitement at the dinner table each evening.

During their talk, she had felt it possible to build a friendship with her husband and from there, a romance. She was helplessly in love with the idea of his composing music, and oh, such music! Drake had always seemed such a shallow person, yet he had composed music of depth that reached into her heart, spoke to her soul. *That* man, The Composer, could have her mind, body, and soul. *That* man was neither shallow nor self-absorbed.

How could she reconcile these two so very different people—the vain Drake with the soulful composer? Drake walked through the world with an air of superiority, knowing all women he encountered would prostrate themselves at his feet in swoons of adoration and all men would envy his fashionable good looks and easy manners, not to mention his title. But the man who composed the sonata experienced the world as a chaos of emotions, at times fearful, even sorrowful, and other times hopeful.

In her present state of mind, she saw Drake and the man who composed as two different people: Drake, a pompous dandy, who was so intimidated by his own mother that he could very well be called a milksop, and The Composer, a passionate and courageous gentleman, who would stop at nothing to show the woman he loved the ends of the earth if she so desired.

The two gentlemen would have to merge for her somehow, but her husband differed so greatly from the other man, she couldn't connect the two with ease. When she looked at her husband, she saw Drake, but when she closed her eyes, she felt The Composer. Whoever The Composer was, he excited her, thrilled her until her toes curled. If a friendship did develop with Drake, perhaps she could more easily see qualities of both men in the single person.

Admittedly, she wanted more time with The Composer. He understood her emotionally and physically.

The sonata had spoken of her inner conflicts and yearning. The person who wrote that piece knew the fear of failure, the intimidation of expectations, the sorrow of solitude, all while desiring love, admiration, and recognition.

He even understood her well enough to be kissed. All the worries of what kissing could lead to and all the anxieties of a demanding kiss that expected too much melted away when she had kissed The Composer. He understood her most basic need and welcomed her affection. If only she could see Drake in this manner. If only he could understand her as The Composer did. Time with Drake, communication with him, and her aunt's advice were the keys to happiness, she was positive.

Three days before Aunt Hazel and Lizbeth arrived, Charlotte found a new sonata on the pianoforte, a piece full of hope and desire, the phrases pausing in anticipation of a climax before plunging into another variation of the theme, always building to a climax that never happened, illustrating the aspiration-filled expectation of pure hope and want.

Two days before they arrived, Charlotte discovered a diamond and emerald hair comb on her dressing table, which she resolved to wear at the end of the week for the dinner party she had arranged for her aunt and sister, along with the emerald necklace. The dinner party would be her first solo prepared event at the manor.

The day before they arrived, her ensemble for the dinner was finalized with a birthday gift of a Kashmir shawl. No longer suspicious of the sudden onset of gifts, she welcomed them with glee. The shawl had been waiting for her in the dressing room, another gift from her husband. Accompanying the gift was a hastily sketched note wishing her a birthday as beautiful as she and filled with abundant happiness. Unable to help herself, she pressed the note to her bosom and twirled about the room.

The day of the arrival, Charlotte thought more of Drake than she did of the impending family reunion. The past several days had been the most pleasant she had spent since coming to the manor. Mama Catherine even encouraged Charlotte to see to all the preparations for the guests and design the dinner party on her own.

Without a housekeeper, Charlotte instructed the maids herself as to which room to ready for which guest. She chose which staff would greet her aunt and sister at the entrance of the manor and even chose the groom who would keep watch on the road to notify them of the approaching coach — a task Philip accepted with pride.

Charlotte waited in the parlor for the announcement. That morning, a postboy from the Black Swan Inn had arrived with a missive from Hazel and Liz with their estimated time of arrival. To say Charlotte waited anxiously would be an understatement. She sat in the parlor feigning embroidering, her hands shaking more than sewing. She threaded, unthreaded, and rethreaded. Every sound, every footfall caused her heart to race. Soon! Soon her aunt and sister would be here with her! Her heart could burst from the excitement.

Despite the familial flaws, she felt proud they would see Lyonn Manor and know she was mistress of such a grand estate, the Duchess of Annick.

Although they would spend the first day or two in the Red Drawing Room as the formal receiving room for all guests, she couldn't wait to show them the Gray Parlor, her special place. The settee was newly positioned against the window looking out to the walled rose garden. The mirror that had once hung above the mantel now hung on the wall facing the back windows, reflecting the garden and bringing more light to the room. Mama Catherine, who also favored this room, had remarked favorably on the change — Charlotte humored herself to imagine her mother-in-law thought the rearrangement *splendid*. The chairs now faced the fireplace with the two mounted paintings of Charlotte and Drake situated where the mirror used to hang.

Charlotte loved the new portraits. The painter had taken so long to finish them that she had begun to lose hope in ever seeing them. For all the artist's faux French flair, and for all the difficulty she gave him during the session, the painter knew his art.

The paintings captured their essence, not only their beauty. Charlotte's own painting reflected her eagerness to reign supreme, the bright-eyed hope of a future at the estate glinting in the painted eyes. Drake's painting wasn't at all of him, but rather of The Composer. Drake's smug, flirty lopsided grin was nowhere to be found in the artwork. Instead, The Composer was in the painting, staring out at Charlotte with such intensity, she felt weak-kneed with attraction. How the painter had captured them both so well when they'd been quarreling the whole time, she could only wonder. And how had he seen The Composer through Drake's façade, a person no one else had ever witnessed?

Oh, yes, she couldn't wait for her family to see the parlor. In this room, she felt most at home. She could admire The Composer, remind herself of the happiness she felt at first seeing Lyonn Manor, bask in the redecoration success, and above all else, spend time with Captain Henry, who often perched on the back of the settee to help her with the embroidery, though he preferred unraveling her thread to any other occupation.

For most of the morning, Charlotte thought what she would say to them. Her letter to each had been written in a desperate panic, a sentiment she no longer harbored, not after the week of gifts, not after the nuncheon.

Of course, she still found Mama Catherine intimidating, and her marriage was far from healed, but she didn't feel the sense of urgency as when first writing the letters two weeks prior. Both Aunt Hazel and Lizbeth would arrive expecting to find her miserable. Far from happy, she did at least now have a grain of hope to which she clung. She had come to somewhat of an understanding with both Drake and Catherine — a truce, as Drake had called it.

Prioritizing her concerns seemed the most sensible approach to discussing her life with Aunt Hazel and Liz. Before taking up her embroidery, she had made a tidy list, organizing what she wanted to say and how she might say it. While Mama Catherine hadn't moved out yet and was still pulling the strings, Charlotte didn't consider her mother-in-law a discussion priority, not now, not after Drake's insight on what his mother valued and Charlotte's need to stand up for herself once she felt comfortable in training.

That knowledge did not make Mama Catherine a pleasant person, nor did it help Charlotte feel any more confident in her role, but it did resolve her concerns for how to deal with her mother-in-law, which was, at one time, to be a discussion point with her family.

Now, however, Drake was the priority. Her marriage was the priority. Without resolving the remaining conflicts, she could never expect him to fall in love with her.

Explaining the problems to her family wasn't so simple. When she had written the plea for their help, she had been ready to admit that she made a poor choice in marrying Drake. Now, she wanted her happy ever after, and so help her, she would get it. But could she relay the concerns and desires to Hazel and Liz, namely when those concerns and desires had changed?

Well, you see, I thought I despised the crass and pompous man I married because I thought he was having an affair, but then I discovered he frequented lascivious routs with young boys and mature widows. Now none of that matters because I'm keen to fall in love with someone else, a man I call The Composer, who leaves me secret messages in the form of sonatas. Oh, and did I mention that the two men are one and the same?

That simply wouldn't do.

I need to find a way to consummate my marriage with The Composer behind my arrogant husband's back.

That would be even worse, not to mention equally as nonsensical and rather scandalous for a discussion.

You see, I dressed in groom's clothing and rode on the back of a carriage to catch my husband with his mistress only to find him in a room full of grape-feeding Roman decadents, after which time I decided I wanted a love affair with a composer hidden inside the body of my husband.

Nothing seemed to do. No matter how she worded it, she sounded half mad.

For all the prioritizing and list writing, she couldn't decide how to describe the problems. Asking how to seduce one's husband wasn't exactly a drawing room conversation she wished to have, and how could she even explain the kind of seduction she wanted — a seduction of the soul, wherein her husband would be so enamored with her that he would want to spend all his time with her, get to know her, compose for her, and perform music with her?

Bit difficult to seduce a man when she didn't know the first thing about seduction, body or soul, and she certainly didn't know how to tantalize him into falling for her. Her country charm had been enough to snare admirers over the years, even catching Drake in the end, but she needed more than fluttering eyelashes to ensure a successful marriage.

The kiss had been something on which to build a foundation. As much as she'd enjoyed his attentions in London, he was always needy and insistent when it came to intimacy. When she kissed him in the music room, she was able to take the lead. It had been an empowering moment for her.

Could Aunt Hazel and Lizbeth guide her in such complex needs, especially when she failed at the words to explain those needs?

The time to plan was at an end, as Drake himself flung open the parlor door to announce the carriage had been spotted crossing the bridge before the gatehouse. Mr. Taylor had shuffled off to fetch Mama Catherine and Mary, as well as assemble the welcome committee of staff.

"Oh, Drake! They're here!" she exclaimed, stating the obvious as she carelessly tossed her embroidery on the side table and rushed to join him.

Captain Henry squawked at the fuss. Wouldn't the cockatoo be delighted to see his Auntie Lizzie!

Drake smiled and offered his arm. "I'll resist the urge to rush to my study and write a note to Sebastian that his ladylove has arrived. He did say I should notify him *the minute* they arrive, not a moment later," he teased, his blue eyes twinkling with mischief.

"Don't you dare leave my side. And no more teasing, especially in front of Lizbeth. She would be mortified! I will not have their arrival ruined by your matchmaking."

Charlotte took his arm so they could walk together towards the manor entrance.

Drake, Charlotte admired, appeared in rare form, as spirited as she remembered him being before the marriage, full of smiles and goodwill. He fairly bounced with each step, as eager for company as she, although she suspected for different reasons. He likely saw this as a perfect opportunity to shamelessly flirt with her aunt and tease his sister-in-law.

Before long, they were all assembled in front of the manor, watching a post-chaise jostle its way down and around the hilly drive. The luggage coach must have been sluggish, as it wasn't immediately following their carriage. Charlotte didn't worry. There would be maids enough to help Hazel and Liz refresh until their own lady's maids arrived with the luggage. Charlotte felt a pang of guilt yet again for their coming in such haste, so much so that rather than riding in comfort, they had hired a chaise.

Unwittingly, she squeezed Drake's arm as the carriage drew closer. If she'd thought about it, she would have found it humorous given he was the reason she requested their visit in the first place.

She eyed her husband as they stood waiting. Despite her emotional struggle the past month, she had to admit he was as handsome as ever, laced and frilled for the occasion, dressed to impress this mid-morning in his blue embroidered waistcoat and coat and satin breeches, also blue, to match the sapphire of his eyes, heeled shoes with silver tassels, an elegantly knotted cravat, and his devilishly tussled hair with almond scented pomade. His attire showcased his long and lean physique to perfection, she observed, warming her cheeks at the memory of the music room kiss.

For a moment, she lost herself in the magic of that memory. The Composer. An intoxicating combination of empathy, compassion, and amour. Oh, how she hoped Hazel and Liz could help her find a way into her husband's heart, to meld the two personalities so all she saw when she looked at Drake was what she felt for The Composer.

As if sensing her gaze, Drake looked down at her and winked. How foolish to be admiring her husband when her family was nearly upon them. She flushed anew.

The post-chaise rolled to a stop. One of the Annick footmen rushed to the carriage door to assist the ladies. Charlotte could see a length of fluttering plumes flapping through the carriage window. Her heart leapt with joy.

Standing next to Charlotte, Mary rocked back and forth on her heels, excited to make their acquaintance. Mama Catherine stood on the other side of Mary, tall and proud, her gold handled cane marking time on the gravel.

The footman held his hand to aid first Aunt Hazel, wearing a wide-brimmed hat with sky-high ostrich feathers and a lively travel gown with lacy sleeves, and then Lizbeth, adorned in a simple country carriage dress but at least in the newest style of the high waist, a smart pelisse, and an amethyst cameo hanging about her neck.

Charlotte waited for no one.

She raced over to her aunt and sister, arms outstretched in welcome. "I'm so happy you've arrived. Please, come meet my mother- and sister-in-law."

Before she could introduce them, Drake strode over, and to everyone's surprise, drew in both ladies with a familial hug. "My two favorite beauties!" Drake took Hazel and Liz on each arm and directed them to his mother and sister.

When the trio stood before Catherine, Charlotte hovered behind them, conflicted, glad that Drake was so welcoming but jealous that he was stealing the show.

Drake introduced everyone. "Mother, this is Hazel, The Lady Collingwood, and this is Miss Trethow." Turning towards Hazel and Liz, he said, "And this is my mother, the Dowager Duchess of Annick, and my sister, Lady Mary."

Catherine inclined her head, while Mary rushed up in greeting, taking both of their hands in her own.

Stepping next to her sister, Charlotte said to both Lizbeth and Aunt Hazel, "You both must be exhausted. Until your lady's maids and additional luggage arrive, I'll arrange for a substitute. I'll have you shown to your rooms for a brief respite and send someone to you shortly. We'll await you in the Red Drawing Room in an hour."

Charlotte waited in the Red Drawing Room with Mary and Drake for her aunt and sister to resurface from their respite. She had scheduled the day to perfection to demonstrate her prowess for hosting and to offer them all the comforts they could imagine while visiting.

In anticipation of their return from upstairs, Stella brought in the tea tray.

Like clockwork, Aunt Hazel joined them. Liz, forever carefree with no sense of time, would undoubtedly arrive to the drawing room late.

Hazel bustled over to the group. "Oh, Charlotte! I am as happy as a mistle thrush! What a beautiful home this is, and you are lovelier than ever." Hazel sat next to Charlotte in one of the chairs facing Mary.

Drake stood in front of the marble fireplace, one arm on the mantel, the other holding his snuffbox as he flipped the lid open and shut with incessant clicks. He beamed at Hazel when she sat, a glow in his expression.

"And you, my dear Hazel," he said, "will steal my heart before the month has ended."

Hazel reached for her ivory handled fan and fanned her face. "You're a dreadful flirt, young man, but I appreciate your attentions to this old lady." Hazel tittered.

Drake stepped over to Charlotte, placing a hand on her shoulder. "But alas, today is for Charlotte. She has been looking forward to your visit for two weeks." He squeezed Charlotte's shoulder. "You'll be most pleased by the strides Charlotte has made in running the manor, Hazel."

Charlotte reached over to take Hazel's hand. "Oh, Auntie, it has been a whirlwind of training! I have so much to tell you. Later today, shall I show you and Liz the manor? The Gray Parlor is a must to see, and Captain Henry will be beside himself in feathery happiness to see you both."

Charlotte paused to breathe, then hurried into excited chatter, feeling more like herself than she had in a month. "I must introduce you to the Hallewells. They are wonderful company. Lady Hallewell has visited every week since I arrived and brings with her all the gossip that country living can offer."

"My goodness, little butterfly, calm your excitement," Hazel teased. "I declare I shall enjoy this visit enormously. I believe Liz is all eagerness to walk the gardens, though. You know how she loves to explore nature." Hazel turned as the drawing room door opened.

Lizbeth entered, then, following a formal announcement of her entry by the butler, and Charlotte readied tea for everyone, adding a healthy helping of milk to her own. After serving refreshments, she watched Drake for the next half hour as he gave her relations a tour of the portraits — all of his father's family. She was eager to show them the new portraits in the Gray Parlor.

She enjoyed Drake's animation and welcomed the delay of having to talk alone with her aunt and sister. Still undecided how to express her needs, she embraced the postponement Drake's talkativeness afforded her.

She wanted them there with her, but she couldn't put into words what she needed from each of them. From her aunt, she needed the intimate guidance only a married woman could give, all questions she'd have to ask without Liz's presence, for an unmarried woman could not be party to such a conversation. From her sister, she needed the comfort and companionship only a sister could give, and there could be no better sister for that than Liz, who was the embodiment of love and understanding.

Both Aunt Hazel and Lizbeth anxiously glanced over at her throughout the half hour, but Charlotte refused to feel guilty for letting Drake talk. She needed this time to gather her wits. Only, by the time she set herself to wit gathering, Drake none-too-subtly dragged Mary out of the room with promises of riding, despite the looming clouds.

At last, the three sat alone in the room. Charlotte studied the threads of the rug.

After silent minutes passed, in answer to the expectant looks Hazel and Liz gave her, she stumbled through descriptions of her duties as a duchess, the bazaar she hosted, and anything she could think of to put off the inevitable.

Only when they asked her directly how life was progressing with Drake did she confess concisely that the honeymooners did not share affection. And in that magic way that Aunt Hazel always possessed, she understood the problem without Charlotte having to say another word. A weight Charlotte hadn't been aware of lifted from her shoulders as soon as Hazel spoke.

"*Make* him love you," commanded Hazel. "He's a young man still wet behind the ears. He doesn't know what he wants only what he thinks he wants, so teach him that you're what he wants. Seduce that man."

As reassuring as Hazel's knowledge in marital arts, Charlotte hadn't anticipated the humiliation of the words said aloud. If Charlotte could have found a hole to crawl into, she would have. Seduction? Love? Charlotte flushed.

Her aunt wasn't finished. "Seduce him well enough, and he will fall in love with you. If you can stomach the embarrassment, I will share my best kept secrets, although not in the presence of Lizbeth."

For that, Charlotte was eternally thankful. With little prompting, Hazel agreed to meet her in her sitting room after dinner. The evening couldn't come soon enough.

After dinner, Charlotte waited in the upstairs sitting room, her palms sweaty. She had barely touched the food from thinking over Hazel's words. Make him love her? If she had the power to do that, he would already be infatuated. *How* could she make Drake love her? Could she even accomplish such a feat as to *make* him love her? While she knew little of love, she doubted anyone could be made to do something they didn't want to do. Would Drake want to love her?

Charlotte jolted when the door opened.

Aunt Hazel, all reassuring smiles, strolled in, shutting the door behind her, and taking the chair across from Charlotte.

Well, this was it. The unveiling of the boudoir secrets. The exchange of knowledge that would make or break her intentions to seduce her husband, body and soul. Her pulse raced as she stared at her aunt, speechless.

"Would you like to start," Hazel asked, "or shall I?"

Charlotte's eyes widened.

"Right," said Hazel. "Am I to assume the marriage bed has not been satisfactory? It rarely is for the woman."

If Charlotte gripped the armrests any tighter, she worried she'd break them. Why was she so nervous? This was only Aunt Hazel, and Charlotte could always tell her anything and everything. But this topic seemed a reflection of her failure as a wife. She was conflicted what to explain first—that she had failed to consummate the marriage or that she needed to know how to make him fall in love with her, *her* not their marriage bed.

"Be assured," Hazel said, "you already possess all you need to make him love you. You don't need my help. All you need is confidence. You've always been strong of mind, so harness that confidence and all will be well." Hazel reached over to pat her niece's white knuckles.

Charlotte studied her aunt, a woman who wore her age well, the only lines on her face those from too much happiness. Hazel's eyes were framed by fan-shaped crinkles from smiling, the edges of her mouth rounded from laughing. Her hair, always worn stylishly, only showed grey at the temples. Not born into the aristocracy, she had married for love a man who so happened to be titled, a baron from Exeter. Although born in the West Country, the daughter of a gentleman, Hazel rose to her position in society with grace and good humor, becoming in short time a pillar of her community, a respected matron whose opinion mattered. For all Charlotte's life, she had envied her aunt and the ease at which she accomplished her goals.

Why did everything seem such a struggle for Charlotte? For all Hazel's guidance, Charlotte couldn't slip into the role as naturally as she wanted, not like her aunt. The hauteur expected by Mama Catherine did not help matters, so at odds with the socialite boisterousness of her aunt.

"I can't, Aunt Hazel," Charlotte said, her voice strained. "I don't know what to do. I don't have any confidence to harness."

"Nonsense. You have always held your head high. Now, don't be embarrassed. It's only us. I gathered from your first letter there was dissatisfaction in intimacy. Let's not mince words. Is he too quick about it? Too rough? He strikes me as someone who would be so arrogant he wouldn't think twice about the woman. I've guessed it, haven't I? Yes, I can see from your expression, that's the problem. He rushes in, a flurry of manly muscle, does his business, and leaves you unfulfilled. Worry not because I have the very secrets you need for fulfilment. Why are you shaking your head? That is the problem, yes?"

Five shades of crimson later, Charlotte shook her head. "Not exactly."

"Out with it! You said in your most recent letter he ignores you and is rarely home. Not to be indelicate, but does he have a mistress?"

"Well, that's closer to the truth." Charlotte swallowed. "You see, there was a bit of confusion when I thought he had a mistress, but he didn't, and then I thought he was ignoring me, but he wasn't, and now, I think he wants to love me, but I thought he didn't, and that was only because I thought I knew him, but I didn't, so I'm in a bit of a sticky wicket. Does that make sense?"

Hazel smiled, then with raised eyebrows, shook her head. "Afraid not, my dear. Not a wit."

Charlotte licked her dry lips and tried again, "How do I make him *love* me?"

Her aunt thought for a moment. "So, this is a problem with love, not marital relations. I see. Yes, that changes our conversation."

Charlotte half smiled, not ready to admit it was a problem with both.

Hazel hmmed in deep thought. "At first, keep him wanting more. Give him glimpses of you but hold the cards to your chest. As far as he knows, you're holding a winning hand, but to be certain, he must keep playing. The further the play, the more privileged he feels to be at your table, a lucky man to be at game with you, always wanting to know the cards in your hand and if he has a chance at winning in the next round. By the time he's seen the whole hand, he's already taken in by you."

"And just *how* do I do that?" Charlotte implored.

"You have more depth, my dear, than you give yourself credit for. Of all the interests and opinions you possess, I'm positive you haven't shared with him half. Share yourself a little at a time. He'll take the bait. I'm surprised, honestly, that you haven't wrapped him around your finger already. He was enthralled with you in London. What happened?"

"I turned him away," Charlotte admitted, staring at her lap.

"Oh, I see. And when was this?" Hazel frowned.

In a whisper, Charlotte answered. "On our wedding night."

"Oh. Oh dear." Her aunt shifted in her chair, settling against the cushion. "Oh my." She looked at Charlotte then at the floor then back to Charlotte. "Am I to understand that you—no, let me ask this differently. When *did* you receive him after turning him away?"

Charlotte felt the heat in her cheeks. "I haven't. That is to say, we haven't. I turned him away, and we never, well, I'm undecided what to do now."

Hazel sat in stunned silence for what felt like a week, or at least a full day. Then, startling Charlotte from her chagrined meditation, Hazel clapped her hands and laughed, throwing her head back in a fit of hilarity. Charlotte looked up and stared blankly at her aunt. What could possibly be so funny about this predicament?

"Oh, my darling! Only you could end up in this situation. Now, now, don't bristle. You are far too

clever to take offense. I would imagine your husband
is on the edge of his seat to see your cards by now.
You have teased that poor man more than I would
have ever dared recommend!" Tears formed at the
corners of Hazel's eyes as she continued to roar with
laughter. "Oh, Charlotte!"

"Well, I don't find it all that funny. What do I *do*?
How do I, you know, seduce him?" Charlotte asked,
annoyed that her aunt found the situation so amusing.
She wished she could see the humor in it.

Hazel stood and hugged Charlotte's neck before
sitting again and retrieving her handkerchief to dab
at the corners of her eyes. "Don't frown. Your smile
is too pretty for all that frowning. However much
trouble you feel you've caused, I think you've done
yourself a service. Your husband is terribly arrogant,
but in your own way, you've made yourself superior by denying him the very thing he wants—*you*.
I mean that both physically and emotionally. He'll
appreciate you when he gets you, and he'll be humbled by the wait."

Charlotte thought about that for a moment before
smiling. And then she too was laughing.

Hazel continued before Charlotte could interrupt,
"The better he knows you, the more he'll see what the
two of you share in common. *That* is the key to your
seduction. He will fall in love with not only you but
the connection between you both. Your seduction of
his mind *is* the seduction of the body, for the two of
you will naturally want to share more once you form
that bond. Go to him when his defenses are down. Flirt
with him with those glimpses of your interests and
passions to whet his appetite for knowing you more."

"I know we share one thing in common. But is it enough?"

"Make it enough, silly goose! Don't give up so easily. The more you share, the stronger the bond. Start with this little something you have in mind, then expand." Hazel's smile encouraged Charlotte.

The music. She had to anchor everything on the music. If it was The Composer she wanted, then of course it had to be the music.

Nodding her understanding and feeling the rise of confidence, Charlotte said, "Let's suppose we connect over this commonality. And then let's suppose I'm feeling brave enough for…more. What do I *do*?"

"Let nature take its course." Hazel continued to smile, then after seeing Charlotte's grimace, she added, "You're the one holding all the cards, remember?" Aunt Hazel lowered her voice, although they were the only ones in the room. "I recommend — don't blush when I say this — you *explore*. However much you'll be embarrassed, your exploration will make it less frightening, and he certainly won't complain. Take control without allowing him to pressure or rush you."

Charlotte indeed blushed at the thought of… exploring, whatever that might involve.

Hazel lowered her voice to a whisper. "Most men, on their wedding nights, go to the lady's chamber wearing their fancy banyan, and without ceremony, take the virtue they think is owed to them. Then without bothering to take their leave of the poor, traumatized bride, they walk out to smoke their pipe. You now have the advantage in that you'll be the one in command, saying when and how, but perhaps don't walk out and smoke a pipe afterwards. Smelly habit and all that." Hazel tittered. "It will all come naturally once the two of you have fallen in love. I wager you'll both find your heart's desire with honest conversation. Mark my words."

And if the evening weren't embarrassing enough as it was, Hazel added a few suggestions that had Charlotte short of breath. Who knew married life could be so titillating?

Chapter 19

Rain pounded against the windows of the Red Drawing Room, trapping the troupe indoors and spoiling all plans for the wilderness walk Drake had conspired in hopes of getting Hazel alone for some quality conversation.

The day was not a complete wash, Drake realized with endless amusement, as Mr. Taylor announced the arrival of the Earl of Roddam. All eyes turned to the drawing room door to stare at Sebastian. The man in question was soaked from head to toe and dripping a dark puddle on the rug.

When Drake wrote his note to Sebastian that morning, the day after Lizbeth and Hazel's arrival, he had a hearty laugh that Sebastian would have to sulk in his castle instead of coming to Lizbeth, for no man would be daft enough to ride across the countryside in this weather. Oh, how wrong Drake was. It would seem nothing could stop his lovelorn cousin, not even sheets of sideways rain.

Drake stepped forward to squeeze Charlotte's shoulder in a silent plea for her to take good note of his cousin's soaked attire. If this didn't convince her that Drake's assertions of the love interest between her sister and his cousin were correct, nothing would, for who else would ride across fifteen miles in hard rain and slick mud to see the relations of a cousin's new wife except a man besotted?

If she realized the significance of the dripping Sebastian, she made no indication. Drake smirked at the top of her head anyway and wished they had made the wager.

"I say, old chap, you're dripping on my rug," Drake said to Sebastian with a hearty laugh.

Aside from a subtle cringe, his cousin ignored him, instead locking eyes with Lizbeth, who, likewise, had eyes only for Sebastian, going so far as to stand at his arrival and lean towards the doorway as though she might burst full speed into an embrace. Did no one else in the room find this a keen source of entertainment? One glance at Hazel told him he wasn't the only one enjoying the show.

However diverting, a perfectly good Persian rug was being ruined.

"Good heavens, man. I'm sure neither of our guests wants to spend the afternoon with a drowned rat. Have my valet see to drying your clothes." When his cousin didn't move, and in fact, seemed deaf to his words, Drake tried a different tactic. "If you stand there one minute longer ruining my rug, I will assume you've not come to see these beauties, but rather have come to rescue me from polite conversation. I will be forced to take you into my study for the remainder of the afternoon. Consider that a threat."

Without hesitation this time, Sebastian bowed to the group and absented himself.

Drake turned to Lizbeth, "Well, well, well. Quite the conquest you've made with my cousin."

All eyes turned his direction.

"I beg your pardon," Lizbeth said, affronted.

She took her seat but kept her spine straight and her chin high. He chuckled at how similar were the reactions of the sisters when faced with a bit of ribbing. A lifetime of this reaction incentivized him to joke more often.

"No, no, you can leave the begging to Sebastian." He laughed. No one laughed with him, though he did spy a glimmer in Hazel's eyes.

"I'm sure I don't know what you mean." Lizbeth remained stoic, but a tell-tale flush had begun its journey from the neckline of her dress to her chin. It continued to rise as Drake's smile widened.

"Oh, I think you do. It's not every man who would ride through a rainstorm to call on his cousin. No, I do believe he's here to see *you*, Miss Trethow. Deny it all you want, but the evidence reveals the truth. Not even my rug would dare refute me."

"Stop antagonizing my sister," Charlotte interrupted with a huff. "We all know your cousin is... peculiar. Perhaps he enjoys riding in the rain."

Drake threw back his head and laughed. "Oh, my dear. I had no idea you could be such wonderful comic relief."

Charlotte turned on him with a death glare. "If you don't behave yourself this minute, I'll have Mr. Taylor remove you."

He sobered, the corners of his mouth twitching. "Oh, no. Anything but Mr. Taylor. I beg your mercy, sweet wife."

She hid a smile.

While Sebastian took his time in returning, Drake, Charlotte, Lizbeth, and Hazel made tedious conversation. Drake would never let him live down this day. Sebastian returned wearing Drake's personally tailored clothes and fidgeting with the too-tight neckerchief. The poor man was nearly bursting out of the coat and breeches, looking much like a wolfhound wearing a prized terrier's shirt.

All Drake's worries that he wouldn't have a chance to speak with Hazel alone were for nought. Sebastian and Lizbeth paired off to the far side of the room to discuss whatever it was lovesick intellectuals talked about, leaving only Hazel and Charlotte with him.

Leaning over his wife's chair, he wrapped an arm about her shoulders and said, "I'm anxious to have an audience with Hazel regarding the upcoming dinner party. Why don't you entertain us at the pianoforte, dear wife? You have such extraordinary skill."

Charlotte looked at him with nothing less than suspicion, but she acquiesced and strode to the opposite side of the room to play. He hadn't thought it would be this easy to get Hazel alone. He congratulated himself on his ingenuity, turned a beaming smile to Hazel, and sat in the chair Charlotte vacated, the cushion still warm.

"Ah, Hazel, even on this rainy day, the sun shines through you," he began. "May I beseech you for two small favors while I have your ear?" His smile never wavered.

"Anything, my boy. You need only ask. Of course, the flattery helps." Her eyes twinkled as she fanned herself, though the room was autumn cool.

"I would delight in nothing greater than to see my sullen cousin down on one knee before your niece.

Will you help me make that happen?" he put to her bluntly.

"Why, you're quite the matchmaker!" She tittered and glanced at Sebastian and Lizbeth, both deep in conversation. "I don't think they need our help, do you?"

"You don't know my cousin. He's as stubborn as he is thick when it comes to matters of the heart. Leave it to him, and he'll let her leave Northumberland at the end of the month. Then I'll have to listen to him sulk for another year," he said.

Hazel held her fan over her mouth conspiratorially. "What do you propose?"

"Nothing too obvious. You could, perhaps, escort them for a walk at the dinner party?" Drake suggested. "He'll want to invite us all for outings as an excuse to see her, so for my part, I'll decline all such invitations. That will diminish the size of the group and give you more opportunities to distract Charlotte so our besotted pair may have time together. Between the two of us, I'm positive we can craft ways to throw them together unchaperoned."

"Oh, ho ho! You are shameful, young man!" Hazel laughed. "Unchaperoned my left foot. Lucky for you, we are of the same mind. I'll see what I can do. Now, you said you had *two* favors?"

He didn't answer immediately. Instead, he watched his wife at the pianoforte, admiring her. There was an elegance about her frame. Her hair was curled in ringlets that framed her heart-shaped face. Her eyes closed as her hands danced over the keys, making love to the keyboard, her cheeks rosy from the exertion. She made even a stuffy capriccio beautiful.

Looking back to Lady Collingwood, he toyed with the tassel on his shoe, unsure of himself.

"Hazel, I—" He hesitated. "You and I saw a good bit of each other in London, and we've always got along well. May I be honest with you without censure?" He paused, looking back to his wife.

"Continue, my boy." Hazel folded her fan and set it in her lap.

He rested his forearms on his thighs. "I need your help. A matter of some delicacy. I need, rather, I want, no, I wish, ah, how do I say this without sounding crass or mad? I'll just come out with it, and you can make of it what you will. How do I make my wife love me? You know her better than anyone. I'm confident she has told you that I have made some monumentally poor decisions since bringing her here, and I wish to make amends, but I'll be deviled if I know how to win her over. How do I make Charlotte love me?"

Hazel's eyes laughed, although she remained thoughtfully silent. When she didn't immediately reply, he jumped in with more explanation.

"I've been surprising her with dresses, jewelry, and poetry. I think I'm softening the hard edges, but it's not enough. Is there a kind of gift you know she'd like? I'll buy it, whatever it is. A small country, perhaps?"

He paused to tug at the tassel again.

As he opened his mouth to expound again, Hazel lifted her fan and covered his lips with it. She said, "You would do well to listen."

His hand paused mid tassel-tug, and he waited, listening.

And he waited.

He waited still longer.

They sat in silence, the fan pressed against his lips. Was he missing something?

He pushed the fan aside and said, "I'm listening. What's your advice?"

"Just that. Listen. You're so busy talking, you don't listen. Charlotte will tell you how she wants to be loved, but you must listen. Let her take the lead. Listen with more than your ears and talk with more than your mouth. Even now, are you listening to her play?" Hazel flicked her fan towards Charlotte. "She's expressing herself, and instead of listening to her with your heart, you're talking to her aunt about buying jewelry. Go give your wife the attention she craves, and show her she's the most important person in your world. Can you do that?"

Drake nodded, feeling foolish, as well as grateful. A quick glance at Sebastian and Lizbeth made him feel even more of a half-wit. Sebastian was leaning against the wall, listening intently as Lizbeth talked. Listen wasn't even the right word. He was enraptured by whatever it was she was saying. Well, drat. How'd his cousin know more about how to love a woman than he did?

With a flash of a smile to Hazel, he swaggered to the opposite side of the room to join his wife at the pianoforte.

"The Argot sisters, Mother," Drake instructed several days later while the rest of the family enjoyed a picnic hosted by Sebastian.

"And why is it I'm inviting them to the dinner party? I'm not fond of their mother, as you well know," his mother replied from her chair in the study.

Drake tucked the box of cheroots in his desk drawer, lit the one he was holding, and joined her, hooking one leg over his chair and sliding into the cushion to lounge languidly.

He inhaled the strong, earthy flavor of the tobacco before replying. "You're inviting them because I wish them to be invited. Isn't that reason enough?"

While his mother had always seen to the invitations and party plans, and such had been preferable for them both since he had no wish to waste time with such tedium, he now felt a pang of irritation.

This was *his* house, after all, yet he was having to request invitations from his mother. He shouldn't feel resentful since he never meddled before, but it irked him now.

His mother treated all events at Lyonn Manor as though she were hosting at *her* house, and he never thought before how unsettling that felt. It had once been her house, but it became *his* house when his father died, so why did they still carry on as though it were hers? The plan, to his mind, had always been his wife would replace his mother as the matriarch of the family, taking over his mother's role in household duties, especially. Now, he rather thought this should be something they ought to do together, he and Charlotte.

He really ought to shift the direction of his previous plan to them working in tandem. They were, after all, the Duke and Duchess of Annick, both head of the household and both duty bound to uphold the title in all its complexities. He was annoyed his mother had never included him in estate business but that had never been an expectation on either of their parts, so he could not really blame her. It was *he* who annoyed him most, for he had never shown an interest in the estate or anything beyond the necessity of sitting in the House of Lords every Parliamentary Season. With the new direction of his life, he was interested now.

His mother reproached him. "Sending an invitation this late is ill-mannered. They're not likely to come on short notice."

"While you're at it, see to it one or even two of the three sisters are seated next to Sebastian."

His mother narrowed her eyes. "Am I to presume you wish my nephew to take to one of these empty-headed gels?"

Drake choked on a puff of smoke as he guffawed at the idea of Sebastian being tempted by one of the snotty chits. "On the contrary, they're a perfect contrast to Charlotte's sister and will thus show her to advantage. He'll have eyes only for Miss Trethow with even one of those yappy brats at his side. I should feel guilty for using the girls so abominably, but I don't. They are title huntresses of the worst sort. Will you adjust the seating chart?"

"I will see that it happens, but I would prefer you choose a more suitable bride to throw at my nephew than Miss Trethow. Training Charlotte has been tiresome, and she was at least educated in the art of hospitality and aristocratic decorum, no matter how gauchely. Miss Trethow is far from qualified. She's wild, countrified, without style or manners. I like her spirit and conversation, but she's uncultured." She poked Drake's leg with her cane.

"And you'd consider Sebastian cultured, well-mannered, and stylish?" He arched a brow. "Not everyone marries for title and duty, Mother. Ever think the two of them are hopelessly in love?"

Catherine snorted. "Only commoners marry for love. Regardless of their reasons for romantic interest, the title requires duty. One cannot avoid duty. It is Sebastian's responsibility and that of his future wife to fulfill the requirements of his title. Love or not, his wife would need to learn at haste how to be a countess. He can only hope she is a quick study."

Three short puffs later, Drake shrugged and said, "Whatever you say, Mother."

Nothing his mother said surprised him, but it all made him grumpy.

He shouldn't have to explain himself to her, explain his cousin to her, or seek her approval. He was a grown man, and this was *his* house. But how, after all these years of allowing her to run the household in his stead, could he demand she move to the dower house and let him be the lord of the manor? The whole of it made his head ache. All his talk to Charlotte that she ought to give his mother the boot, and now he realized he should have taken care of this ages ago, first with the interest in the estate business, and then with the booting of his mother.

She leaned on her cane to leave, but then settled back to add, "While we're discussing guests, I have invited the Marquess of Colquhoun to dine with us. He may be Scottish, but the estate is not far north and is exceedingly profitable. He is well connected, and the alliance would be wise. I believe him a good catch for Mary. Have a word with her, Drake. She was unforgivably rude to the previous suitors, much to my mortification. See to it she is polite to the marquess. You have a way with the girl. I intend to invite him again if he likes the look of her."

He grunted.

Leaning his head against the chair back, he gnawed at the end of the cheroot. He hesitated to bring up this request given his mother's most recent accusations, but the more he hesitated, the stronger he heard his conversation with Charlotte echoing in his mind. It was time to stop worrying about the opinions of others, especially his mother's.

Clearing his throat, he said, "If we're exchanging desired guests, I'll add one. Another last-minute invitation, as it were. I'd like to invite Winston. I mentioned the dinner to him during today's fencing match, not realizing he hadn't received an invitation."

Her eyes narrowed. "I don't like that boy and do not want him in my house. He is a gamester and associates with rabble. I will invite the Argots, but I will not invite that boy." She thumped her cane. "I assume there's an ulterior motive to your wanting him here?"

And there it was. The insinuation. Likewise the reference to *her* house. His own best mate couldn't come to dinner because his mother didn't want Winston in *her* house.

"I want Winston at the party, Mother. It's been nearly two months, and he has yet to meet Charlotte."

"He is a rogue. I don't care how wealthy his father is. He is a rogue, and I will not soil the dinner with his presence. Invite him to go riding if you desire his company so ardently." She stood to leave, daring him to have the last word.

He let her win.

The days rolled by, days in which Drake tried Hazel's advice. He couldn't help but notice Charlotte seemed more at ease with her family present. He was sure it had nothing to do with his listening and all to do with her family.

Most days Charlotte practically pirouetted through the manor in such high spirits. She spent her mornings in the Gray Parlor with her sister and Mary while Hazel broke her fast with his mother. Most afternoons, she received callers in the Red Drawing Room with Lizbeth and Hazel by her side. The afternoons, he suspected, were especially rewarding because Charlotte had the opportunity to show off her hosting skills, a role she relished.

Personally, the evenings were Drake's favorite time of the day. Naturally, he enjoyed his mornings of sleeping until noon, as well as the weekly fencing match with Winston, his afternoon chats with Sebastian or whatever diversion he could invent, and his late evenings in the music room, but it was the early evenings when he had time with Charlotte. Not exactly private. Not exactly intimate. But she sat by his side every evening, nonetheless.

He counted down the hours to dinner. With each passing evening, their discussions relaxed until she spent most of the time laughing with him. Her eyes twinkled. Her laugh chimed. His heart pounded.

Drake drank her in with his eyes, inhaled her lemony freshness, and sensed her warmth with every pore of his skin. The conversations varied, but he focused each on her thoughts and interests, discovering in her answers just how much he genuinely enjoyed her company and deeply enjoyed *her.*

She carried on about her garden walks. He listened. She shared ideas for improvements to the house. He listened. She described her visits to the neighboring village. He listened. She talked about her childhood and how her father had spoiled her. He listened.

He did everything in his power to follow Hazel's advice and not dominate the conversation as he was prone to do, but it was more than following her advice. By Jove, he *liked* listening to Charlotte. When she wasn't offended by his jokes or denying a compliment from insecurity, she bubbled with conversation. He'd never shared such unalloyed conversations in his life in which he could be himself without reservation or machinations.

A revelation that startled him for at least a day, was that he didn't feel the need to joke inappropriately around her. He always had been a jokester, but the more he talked with her, the more he came to realize he made jests to deflect his own insecurities. Not that he didn't continue to enjoy a dirty joke, but he didn't feel the need for crass humor. Most of his jokes had been part of his reputation, something he no longer needed. He was perfectly content sharing plans for the future and listening to her ideas and stories.

The evening before the dinner party went especially well, at least from his perspective. The more she spoke, the more he realized how many interests they shared. Their conversation was simple, nothing earth shattering, but he enjoyed it immensely.

That evening, as with most dinners during the week, Sebastian joined them and monopolized Lizbeth's attention while Hazel enjoyed his mother's conversation alongside a bored Mary.

Drake had Charlotte all to himself.

"And what of the Red Drawing Room?" he asked in response to her discussion of redecorating rooms.

"I've wondered since I first saw the room. Did it used to be a ballroom?"

"It did, but not during my time. My father used to regale me with stories of the grand balls he'd host. No one can say he couldn't organize a squeeze."

"Oh, how disappointing that it was transformed into the gaudiest of all drawing rooms." Charlotte took a moment to enjoy a few bites of her dinner.

"Am I to assume this is a prelude to you wanting to turn it back into a ballroom?"

She thought for a moment then shook her head. "I won't deny I long to host a ball, but I'd much prefer we turn it into a performance hall. Imagine the concerts we could host!"

Drake's heart soared to hear such a declaration. Not only did she refer to them as collaborators with her use of *we*, but he'd wished to do the same for years. Even if he wouldn't showcase his own compositions or perform the music himself, he'd still enjoy bringing music back into the house, filling his world with that which he held dearest. His greatest dream, which he'd told no one, was to bring the music to the people, not for drawing room entertainment to wealthy peers, but music for the people who genuinely enjoyed music, regardless of their status.

It had always been nothing more than a dream. He would have never risked his reputation to realize such a dream. But if she wanted to host concerts....

Drake smirked. "Are you saying this because you know I compose, and are trying to win favor?"

"No, I'm saying this because it's what I've wanted since the first day I arrived." She eyed him askance, as though to test if he believed her. "The acoustics in the room are exceptional!"

"Mmm. Then I suppose I should never kiss you senseless in that room. All in the house would hear," he goaded, hoping his teasing didn't result in a kick to his shim.

"Oh, how gauche you are." She swatted at his arm but rather than take offense, she hid a grin.

Progress.

"It's only a dream, of course," he said. "We could never do it. Mother would never approve. She abhors music and the whole scene." However true, he desperately wanted the two of them to find a way to make this shared vision possible.

"This is *our* home. If we want a performance hall, then we shall have a performance hall."

"Look who suddenly has a will of iron. And you're going to stand up to her, then? Tell her to sod off?" He eyed the other end of the table to ensure his mother wasn't listening. She was deep in conversation with Hazel, looking livelier than he'd ever seen her. Hazel was a good influence.

Charlotte deflected with, "She is *your* mother. I still have training to complete. *You* need to stand up to her as much as I do."

Tutting, he reached under the table to squeeze her hand. "Tell me more about the conservatory."

Her eyes lit up, and she launched into an explanation of her grand plan for an included aviary, work already underway but far from complete. The conversation circled back to music before dinner concluded. He wanted to know, specifically, which pieces she favored and which techniques she found challenging. As she spoke, he began composing a piece for her in his head, a piece that would be written in his style but for her talent, evidencing her skills to advantage.

Such conversations, however brief, however casual, filled his heart with a warmth he'd never known, for he realized he'd chosen the perfect wife, even if she still needed convincing.

With each passing day, he became more enthralled with her vivaciousness, captivated by her vibrancy. An unexpected benefit of encouraging her to do all the talking was his ability to admire her while she talked. He could esteem her smile, regard her countenance, appreciate her rosy cheeks, delight in the slope of her neck, and in general take the greatest of pleasure in her beauty.

How had he ever thought her an ice duchess?

Drake suspected he might see the ice duchess return and ruin their newfound friendship if he tried something as imprudent as kissing her in a dark corner. Drake hoped it wasn't too much to ask that one day he be able to kiss her whenever and wherever he'd like without risking their relationship, being called a libertine, or being slapped or kicked. Better yet, for *her* to kiss *him* whenever and wherever. They'd made such progress. Was it enough for life-long happiness?

Drake had never enjoyed his mother's events at the manor and generally made himself scarce, for she always invited the same droll people. For the first time, Drake enjoyed a dinner party held at Lyonn Manor, and he owed it all to his wife.

She had arranged the party herself, except for a few minor details his mother saw to correct, including the invitation of additional guests, such as the Argot sisters and the Marquess of Colquhoun.

As the family stood in the receiving line to greet the guests, he watched Charlotte. While his mother had taught her the art of condescension, Charlotte donned it with a warm grace his mother did not possess, making the guests feel as though it were not an honor to be invited but Charlotte's honor to receive them. His mother had only ever conveyed the stern message that the guests should feel fortunate to be invited to the noble home of the Duke and Duchess of Annick. Drake hoped Charlotte didn't allow his mother to dampen her compassion, replacing it with steely hauteur.

Despite the two weeks of intermittent rain, the weather held steady long enough for the ground to dry, enabling the guests to take wilderness walks and drink madeira on the grotto outside the Red Drawing Room.

The only disappointment was the absence of Winston. Drake had no one with whom to commiserate about the stuffy guests since Sebastian had absconded with Lizbeth and Hazel for a walk in the park, and since Charlotte was playing the dutiful hostess, flitting from group to group.

Mother had cornered Mary and the marquess. His heart did go out to Mary, for the man wouldn't suit no matter how noble his brow. Mary grimaced every time he spoke, his long, grey beard bouncing against his belly with each laugh.

Drake enjoyed the evening as best he could, finding a few acquaintances with whom to whinge. He talked about the upcoming shooting party with some of the men, complimented some of the ladies into blushing, and eventually settled next to Colonel Starrett. Always fond of the pensioner, he had spent some of his youth learning to hunt from the old man, although Drake proved a terrible shot no matter how many times he tried. May he never need to draw a pistol at dawn.

"How's Duncan?" he asked the colonel between sips of wine.

"Following in my footsteps, the good lad. I've purchased him a commission. He is too overeager for my liking, what with the trouble brewing in France, but he has a good heart and a desire to serve Crown and Country. I'm proud of the boy. I only worry what will come of him if we go to war." The colonel's bushy brows met on a wrinkled forehead.

"I'm glad to hear he's made a decision. The service is a good choice. Does he hope to see action or avoid it?" Drake didn't know the first thing about playing soldier, but he liked the Starrett family and would hate to see anything happen to Duncan.

"I'd like to see him avoid it. He wants otherwise. He wants to make a name for himself with decorations and accolades. I keep telling him war isn't what he thinks. He'd do better in the reserves, hold rank from a safe position and take on a wife while he's young and un-maimed." Colonel Starrett huffed.

"I take it he doesn't see the sense in marrying? Twenty is a perfectly respectable age for a young man to wed." Drake couldn't imagine marrying at twenty. He shuddered at the thought.

"That's what I tell him, but Duncan's a headstrong boy with ideas of grandeur and a romantic notion of war. A few bullets whizzing past his head will remedy that view. I only wish he'd see reason in leaving a son behind before becoming a hero. Ah, is it time for dinner?"

Drake looked up to see everyone filing back into the drawing room. He shook the colonel's hand, set his glass on a footman's tray, and headed across the room to find Charlotte.

She stood next to his mother, smiling at him in greeting as he approached. She radiated happiness, her newfound confidence glowing about her as a halo. This confidence became her.

They led the guests into the formal dining room, a room rarely used, grand enough for royalty.

Not until he took his seat did he see with satisfaction that Lady Margot Argot, the eldest of the Argot sisters, sat next to Sebastian. His cousin cast the poor girl a notably menacing scowl. Unperturbed, she continued to flirt. Lizbeth sat adjacent to Sebastian and in full view of him but not close enough for conversation. Perfect. Before the month was out, Sebastian was certain to propose to Lizbeth. Posting her just outside his reach would drive the man batty, not to mention the contrast between Lizbeth and Lady Margot was too perfect not to goad Sebastian into a needed reminder that he would never find anyone quite like the eldest Trethow. One dinner wouldn't do the trick, but it was one more success in the matchmaking scheme.

His mother sat at the head of the table. The seating suited Drake well enough, because it allowed Charlotte to sit next to him at the foot of the table. She looked stunning in a silver and green gown adorned with the diamond and emerald necklace and matching hair comb he had given to her.

At last, after a tedious evening, he could finally relax and speak with his wife. Admittedly, he had been waiting all day for a chance to put to her more questions.

Removing his gloves, he turned to Charlotte to initiate conversation, but she was already in conversation with someone else. Well then.

How silly of him to assume they'd talk as usual at a dinner party when the whole of the evening was meant to entertain others, not themselves. He turned to Lady Hallewell on his other side, ready to play host. The rub was, she was already speaking to the person to her left.

Drake grunted. Begrudgingly, he sat in silence through the first course, admiring the back of his wife's head.

The room filled with a cacophony of clinking cutlery and voices, but above all he heard the contralto sound of Charlotte. The smells of food wafted to his nostrils, but he focused on her feminine scent, allowing her to invade his olfactory with the usual lemon mixed with a hint of jasmine. She smelled heavenly.

He meditated on her while trying not to pout.

As he sipped his soup, his knee itched. No, that wasn't quite right. It tickled.

Something was touching his knee. It was a queer sensation that worked up from his kneecap to mid-thigh. Just as he set down his soup spoon and reached a hand to his lap, the tickle became a squeeze. In reflex, his knee jerked up and banged against the table. A hush fell at his end of the table, all eyes turning to him. He smiled broadly until they turned back to their conversation.

Charlotte paused her own conversation long enough to turn to him. "Are you well, Your Grace?" she enquired.

"Yes, perfectly well," he answered with an inquisitive stare.

Wearing a sly smile, she returned to her conversation.

Two spoons of his soup later, and he felt the pinch again. With a subtle glance down at his lap, he nearly laughed aloud in surprise. Charlotte's hand rested on his thigh, long fingers stretching across the silk breeches. The devil! She was flirting. Nothing terribly naughty, only teasing, but given it was the first time she had extended a hand—literally and figuratively—he couldn't help but grin ear to ear. He turned back to his soup, while she conversed animatedly, no one the wiser.

Lady Hallewell turned to acknowledge him. "It is so good to enjoy a party hosted by your lovely wife. I daresay she's making quite the impression," she said.

"I concur wholeheartedly, my lady," he said, sampling his wine.

As the liquid warmed his pallet, Charlotte's foot joined the under-the-table flirtation by slipping behind his calf with a toe-curling caress.

So startled, he choked on his wine, all heads near him turning to stare. He waved a hand and feigned a grin while gasping for air.

After regaining his composure, Lady Hallewell gave him a squinting look before turning back to the person on her other side. Drake sat still, too concerned about chocking to eat.

Before long, both hand and foot retreated. As delightful as the teasing, he was relieved. He did not desire embarrassing himself, and besides, how cruel that she would tease him with tender caresses when she knew he could not respond.

Ah! The minx! That was her game, was it? Well, he would see about that.

Not long did he have to wait for Charlotte's hand to return for another pinch to his knee. This time, he was ready, coiled to strike. He captured her hand, lacing their fingers. Only after a sidelong glance did it dawn he had offered his dominate hand, requiring he either not eat for the remainder of the meal, or use his non-dominate hand. Then, he could also free her and deal instead with whatever further flirtation she had in store.

Footmen arrived to exchange dishes, bringing the meat to replace the soup. As he watched the dance of plates, Charlotte's foot returned, tickling his ankle with her toes.

He squeezed her hand.

The venison with its garnishes and rich aroma sent his stomach into a deep rumble, but Charlotte's teasing took precedence. He couldn't relinquish his hold on her hand. The food competed for attention, his stomach begging for sustenance. Venison was his favorite dish. Blast. He closed his eyes and swallowed. Of all the times to flirt with him, she chose a crowded room with venison for offer. Cruel, bewitching enchantress!

A battle of feet ensued, as she attempted to rub his calf again, and he tried to shoo her foot to her side of the table. At least he had control of her hand. For the entirety of the next course, he tugged at his cravat, half starved, half infatuated. Her leg rubbed against his, stocking to stocking. The voices in the room funneled into a low hum, the only two prominent sounds being the rumble of his stomach and her dulcet tones, a veritable symphony.

What did Charlotte think she was doing? Madness was the only explanation. Did she want him to humiliate himself? Choke on his food? Spew his wine? When had the room become so unbearably hot? He had half a mind to excuse himself from the dinner, pick up his wife, and carry her to one of those dark corners he had teased her about. Only a firm kiss would do.

Instead, he gave up on food altogether and, with her fingers still laced in his, he inched his hand to touch her thigh. Two could play at this game. Without so much as pausing in her dialogue, she freed herself from his grasp and slapped away his hand.

Right then.

At least he was safe to eat dinner at last. He didn't suppose one of the footmen could return with the venison. Deep sigh.

There wouldn't be an opportunity to get Charlotte alone again for at least a day since some of the guests would be staying the night, but he eagerly awaited that moment. Vengeance would taste sweeter than any dessert. The flirty little devil!

Chapter 20

T he next morning, Charlotte floated through the manor on a cloud of contentment. The guests had showered her with compliments regarding the party — her first successfully hosted dinner party!

Looking back to when she arrived at the manor, she was amazed at how worried she'd been about embarrassing herself. Nothing scandalous had occurred and no one complained or looked bored. She could be confident no one would leave her party with stories of how rottenly she hosted or how ill-behaved her husband had been, which, if she were being quite honest, had been one of her concerns.

After wishing farewell to the few remaining guests who stayed the night, she spent time with Lizbeth, one of the many sisterly moments she'd been able to share since their arrival. She suspected her sister thought her a silly ninny, but she looked up to Lizbeth. Liz had always been the courageous and carefree one, the one full of unbridled passion. They didn't always get along, namely because of their seven-year age difference, but also because they were wholly different people with often opposing tastes and beliefs. That didn't stop Charlotte from wanting her sister nearby.

She'd spent the past few days trying to talk Liz into moving in. Lyonn Manor had more than enough space; the library would keep Liz busy given her love for books; and it wasn't fair for her to be a burden to Papa when Charlotte could support her. It would be silly for Lizbeth to seek employment when Charlotte's new family was so wealthy, not that she'd ever understood Liz's interest in keeping busy and feeling useful.

They strolled through the formal gardens, arms linked.

"I'm proud of you," Lizbeth said. "You've made the best of your decision to marry, and I couldn't ask more of you than that. I expected you would beg me to hide you in the luggage on the way home, but no, you've made a home for yourself despite the troubles. I couldn't be prouder."

Charlotte directed them through the crab apple hedges to better admire the autumn flowering with vibrant yellows and reds.

"There isn't much to be proud of, at least not yet," Charlotte rebutted. "I've stumbled my way to this point. One fumble, and I'm positive they'll realize I'm an impostor."

"Nonsense. You were born for this role. When I wanted to romp in the fields, you wanted to host tea parties with your dolls. This is your calling, Charlotte."

Unsure what to say, Charlotte smiled bashfully and steered them to a bench. Her sister may enjoy walking, but Charlotte much preferred to sit and admire the scenery. The air was chill, but not cold. This was just the sort of coze Charlotte needed.

"Was Aunt Hazel able to advise you on your marital troubles?" Lizbeth asked.

With an awkward, stuttering laugh, Charlotte said, "Oh, you know Aunt Hazel."

"Is there any way I may help? Anything I can do or advise?"

"Lizzie, you're always trying to save everyone. I mean that kindly because that is precisely why I sent for you. I wanted you to save me. As it turns out, I don't think I need saving after all. Isn't that funny? Though I wouldn't turn down an offer of you telling my mother-in-law on my behalf to pack herself off to the dower house. I've had quite enough of her bossiness."

"Catherine? Goodness. I rather like her. A bit frosty, a tad forbidding, but she's soft on the inside if you get her talking. We had quite the whinge the other day. I ran into her at the folly on the wilderness walk."

Charlotte was stunned. Lizzie was already on a first name basis with the Dowager Duchess of Annick? And she *rather liked her*? Never would Charlotte consider her mother-in-law a *bit* frosty or a *tad* forbidding, and never for a moment *soft*. The woman was a she-devil!

"Whose side are you on?" Charlotte accused.

Lizbeth laughed softly. "I'm not on anyone's side. I can see why you might not like her, but have you tried chatting with her? Informally, I mean, not as part of your training. She loves to walk and takes great pride in the park. If you start with a topic she enjoys, I think she will open to you."

"I have no intention of any such thing. The last thing I want to do is talk about follies with her. She has done nothing but insult me since the moment I arrived. She has it in her head this is *her* house, and she intends to defend it to the death." Charlotte shivered at the crisp breeze.

"All I did is speak to her as though we were equals. Don't let her bully you. I would imagine she is a lonely woman who would treasure companionship. Speak your mind, Charlotte."

"Ha! And be struck down by the cane? No, thank you." Resting her head on her sister's shoulder, she added, "I do envy you, Lizzie. You have courage I could never have."

They sat in silence for a time, listening to the wind rustle the leaves until Lizzie expressed a desire to walk alone in the garden. Charlotte kissed her cheek and returned to the manor.

When Charlotte returned, she discovered everyone was busy with their own plans. Hazel was enjoying refreshments with the dowager duchess. Mary was visiting her friend, Arabella. And Drake was nowhere to be found, though the butler assured her he was home.

She tingled at the memory of her bold flirtations during dinner. She wasn't certain what had come over her, but she had been fueled by confidence. Perhaps it was knowing he couldn't react. More important than a physical seduction was her desire for them to establish a shared interest. Could her teasing not serve as an olive branch to open conversation, though? She hoped so.

That he had been undeniably handsome in his dinner attire had helped her feel flirty. He'd dressed in the height of fashion, tailored, silk knee breeches and form fitting coat accentuating his physique, and clocked stockings to emphasize his long, muscular legs. His cravat had been accented with lace and emeralds, and his waistcoat had been embroidered with a floral and greenery motif, all in an effort to match her own gown and jewelry.

He'd been breathtaking. It hadn't been lost on her that most of the girls in attendance had ogled him, namely those dreadful Argot sisters.

With the evening going so well and the thoughts of marital happiness foremost in her mind, she hadn't been able to resist temptation. Granted, the aftermath of her braveness had left her feeling abashed, but also the teensiest wicked.

Olive branch extended, she'd spent the evening thinking of ways to prompt more musical conversation, the anchor to what she believed would be their shared interest. Curiously, knowing he wasn't a rake made everything less intimidating, from conversing to flirting. He wasn't so worldly to find her inadequate or inept. She no longer feared he would laugh at her childish attempts to be coquettish.

Today, now even, she was primed to connect with him. Having disappeared after showing out the guests, he most likely hid himself in his music room. Knowing where to find him awarded her a sense of security she hadn't expected, a kind of affinity between them. After all, who else knew he'd be in the music room or that such a room existed? No fears of affairs, no worries of secrets, no insults of avoidance, only a shared knowledge—he was at this moment creating music.

Swiveling the bookshelf in his study, the door on the other side already open, she stepped inside the candle-lit room. As expected, he sat behind his desk, quill in hand, looking quite startled to see her.

She was giddy at the sight of him. His coat and waistcoat were slung over the harpsichord lid, leaving him only in his ruffled shirt, breeches, and stockings. His sleeves were rolled up, and a sprinkling of ebony hair peeked from the vee of the shirt. Never in her wildest dreams had she imagined finding him in a state of undress. Her pulse quickened to see his bare forearms.

"Charlotte? What are you doing here?" Drake wheezed a single laugh. "I mean, come in! You're the first person to turn the bookshelf aside from me. You'll pardon my state of shock."

He returned the quill to its stand, then stood and stepped around the desk, his lips curved in a welcoming smile. He walked to her and held out his hand. She didn't move, arrested by the sight of his bare, cravatless throat.

"Come. Sit. I can't tell you how pleased I am you're here. And perfect timing because I have a surprise for you," he said, as she slipped her hand into his and let him lead her to the harpsichord.

"A surprise?"

Settling her at the bench, he darted back to the desk. "Pardon the mess. It's unfinished. I'll pen a clean sheet when I finish." Taking sheets from his desk, he made his way back to the harpsichord, then set the music along the rack. "I'd be honored if you'd tell me what you think."

She hesitated to turn around, not because she didn't want to see the music, although she was nervous he would ask her to play for him, but more specifically because she could not help but to admire him. Without the waistcoat and coat, his form displayed to advantage, his shoulders wide and his waist tapering to his breeches. He most certainly didn't wear padding, as did most men. She hadn't noticed before just how strong was his physique. Clearly muscular from fencing, his arms and torso were long, lean, and agile. She took a deep breath and turned to the music.

Before her sat a piece for four hands. A scan showed a simple enough theme with a more complex recapitulation. The music looked enjoyable to play with some of her favorite elements included, the very elements she had mentioned to him at dinner the previous week. Had he written this for her only since then? Flattered didn't do her feelings justice. Honored came closer. Flabbergasted, more like. Whatever she felt, it filled her with joy beyond words.

She looked up at him, seeing before her The Composer rather than Drake. No wonder she had allowed herself to admire him physically — this was her dear friend The Composer! Yes, she recognized him now, the only man she trusted, the only man who held her heart. He smiled differently, but she couldn't put her finger on what was different about this smile. Before she could study the smile further, he sat next to her.

"I wrote it for four hands so we could play together." The Composer rolled his sleeves one more fold until the fabric rested above his elbows, his forearms flexing with the movement. "Want to give it a go?"

Nodding, she smiled, one part shy, one part encouraged.

He had composed something for them to play *together*. Of course, he did. The Composer understood her and must share the same goal — to bond over music. She was lightheaded with exhilaration.

With a grin, she readied her hands on the keys and her eyes on the music. He counted them off, and then they played.

The music began with a warm, sinuous melody, then established a dominating theme from that melody, building and complicating it with bold and feisty phrases. Repeated and recapitulated themes reigned. Although this was her first time seeing the music, she played it with graceful ease, confirming he had indeed written the piece for her skills and her pleasure. It was written precisely for her abilities and preferences.

Another surprising discovery was how well they played together. They felt each other's style almost intuitively. Although unmarked on the sheet, she sensed when he wanted a *ritardando*, just as he sensed when she preferred a phrase in *larghetto*. The music was far from finished, yet she felt how it ought to be played, anticipating what should come next, she and The Composer working in tandem.

She laughed aloud when their hands crossed in one phrase, her right hand shifting up two octaves while his left moved down two and then back over. When their hands joined for an entire line to play overlapping chords, she laughed so heartily she nearly had to stop playing. The heat of his palm held only an inch from the top of her hand, their fingers moving together in perfect unison through the chord progressions.

The music ended in the middle of a dramatic phrase. Ah, yes, unfinished.

She sighed both from the pleasure of the experience and disappointment that the piece wasn't complete. She wanted to know how it ended.

"Do you like it?" he asked, his eyes searching hers for approval.

"I do! Oh, I like it very much! And what fun for us to play together. Will you promise to finish it?" She pleaded.

He smiled deeply. "Anything for you."

And then she realized the difference between Drake's smile and The Composer's smile. Drake's smile was a playful, sardonic grin, lopsided with coyness. The Composer's smile, however, reached his eyes, a genuine, wide smile that lit up his face and revealed dimples in his cheeks.

He had dimples! All this time, and she never knew he had dimples. She had known him since May, been married since June, and here it was mid-September, and she only now discovered dimples.

Without thinking first, she pivoted on the bench and reached a hand to touch one of the dimples. Drake flinched in surprise, his smile faltering. She looked into his sea blue eyes and smiled until his dimples returned, then she reached up her other hand to touch the opposite cheek.

"You have dimples." She stated the obvious.

"Do I?" He raised his eyebrows with surprise.

She traced the divots with her fingertips.

Urged by the shared moment, Charlotte leaned in and kissed him. His bare forearm slid up hers to grasp her hand, interlacing their fingers. Did he feel what she felt—how natural was the kiss, as though they had been meant for each other? Never had kissing

Drake been like this, not with his needy and dominating affections, but sharing a kiss with The Composer felt completely natural.

She leaned back, ending the kiss as quickly as it had begun, albeit reluctantly. His eyes were such a deep blue they almost looked black in the candlelight. Her composer.

This had been perfect. Before either ruined the moment, she thought it best to leave, then they could both reflect on the perfection for the remainder of the day.

Pushing back the bench, she stood to leave.

He reached for her hand. Rather than stop her, he merely kissed her knuckles, still smiling that deep, genuine, dimpled smile. She could feel the redness of her cheeks and neck like a branding iron against her skin.

"Thank you for the music," she said before leaving. "I'd very much like to play the finished piece with you."

Drake watched her depart, feeling the *thunk* of the bookshelf more than hearing it.

Perfection. However brief her visit, everything about it had been perfect.

Had she felt it too?

He returned to his desk, setting down the last page of the composition so he could work on it more. If the moment had not been so perfect, he would go after her, for he felt bereft of her company, the room empty and cold without her. The hesitancy stemmed from fear of puncturing that perfection. If he went to her, outside the music room, perhaps it wouldn't be the same. Perhaps she would be annoyed he pressed his attentions further. Perhaps…

The bookshelf opened again, flooding the room with temporary sunlight from his study.

He blinked.

Charlotte stood in the doorway, haloed by the light.

He questioned her with an eyebrow until she pulled the bookshelf firmly closed, shutting them both in the room once more.

She walked halfway into the room before stopping. Chin raised, shoulders back, she said, "I want more."

When she hesitated, he opened his mouth to reply.

She held up a staying hand and continued, "I want more of this. The music, the companionship, *you*, but you as the composer, not the rogue. For the first time in our marriage, I felt we were of the same mind. I don't want to rush anything, though. I simply want more of *this*."

Nodding, he patted the bench next to him, afraid to speak but ready to play another piece, any piece, whatever she wanted that would constitute "more of this."

Charlotte shook her head. "Lizbeth is likely to return from her walk soon, so I want to be in the parlor when she arrives."

"You're leaving?" Drake stood, his hand over his heart.

"I only wanted you to know that I thought this moment perfect. It seemed a disservice not to tell you, for I know you put your heart and soul into the fragment we played, and I know you wrote it for me, for us." Her voice hitched. "I think the more we confess to each other, the more open we are, the better.

I stepped out of this room and realized how silly to leave you wondering how I felt, especially since it was *your* music that made me feel the way I did, the way I do. Was I right to return?"

He nodded again, still standing hand to heart.

She smiled, not coyly, not shyly, but radiantly.

Uncertain how much he could get away with while she was still feeling courageous, he took a risk. Covering the space between them, he swept her into his arms, linking his hands behind her back and kissing her, albeit gently, chastely, smiling as he did so, a laugh on his lips.

She didn't tense as he expected, instead wrapping her arms around the sweaty nape of his neck. With a sigh, she returned his kiss.

When he released her, he clasped her hands, linking their fingers and drawing them to his chest. He fell into her golden-brown eyes. "You're beautiful, Charlotte."

Giggling, she drew free of his grasp and twirled towards the door.

"Wait!" he begged. "Give this to Lizbeth?" He crossed to one of the bookshelves lining the room and grabbed a book from the topmost shelf. "She's welcome to explore the library, but since it's in the bachelor wing, she may not have discovered it yet."

Charlotte took it from him, eyeing him inquisitively, as if to determine what ulterior motive he may have to give his sister a book. *Further matchmaking with the cousin?* Her gaze seemed to ask.

He shrugged and winked.

"I will see she gets it," she said before tiptoeing to kiss his cheek.

Chapter 21

D rake's horse trotted home, leading the way while Drake woolgathered, reflecting on the past two weeks since Charlotte's bold visit to the music room.

He should have been analyzing his morning's loss to Winston during their sabre practice. He should have been examining how he missed Winston's obvious feint so he wouldn't make the same mistake again. Such a feint in a real duel would have left Drake maimed or worse, not that he ever found himself in real duels, but such errors in judgment were worth reflective study.

What he should have been thinking and what he was thinking were quite different. His thoughts remained steady on Charlotte.

For some peculiar reason, he had thought their bourgeoning relationship would be restricted to the music room, almost as though she was confident within the room, connected to him in the room, but did not see him the same way outside the room, however illogical. She took him quite by surprise, though. Every day since her first blessed visit to the music room, she had surprised him with at least one stolen kiss outside his private domain. During two afternoons in a row, she had even gone so far as to pull him into a corridor for the kiss — the vixen had been lying in wait for him!

Needless to say, he whistled throughout the day, and best make that throughout the day *every day*.

And that wasn't even the best part of the past two weeks. The best part was that Charlotte visited the music room every afternoon when Lizbeth and Hazel were elsewhere engaged. The visits consisted of mostly harpsichord playing, a few times her accompanying while he played violin, and a handful of moments spent talking about the compositions.

Their only point of contention was her desire for him to debut his work. He was less inclined to have that discussion and skirted the topic. It wasn't from shyness so much as a fear of censure.

What would people think of the music? What would people think of him? Would the similarities between father and son be forefront in people's minds? He knew it was cowardice, but after a lifetime of shielding himself with a false reputation, he couldn't sacrifice it all with a single moment that would lead to a lifetime of doubt. Now, he had even more reason to protect the family name, for he wouldn't have Charlotte subjected to ridicule. Charlotte insisted he was being silly and hounded him about it all the same.

And that proved their only point of contention.

The significance of her visiting the room superseded his desire for more physical contact, for nothing could make him happier than spending time doing what he loved with someone he loved. Well, that wasn't quite accurate, was it? Did he love Charlotte? He was undecided how he would know if he loved her or not, for he had little on which to base such an emotion. His only experience was loving Maggie. Now that he knew what it felt like to have Charlotte by his side, he knew without doubt he had never truly loved Maggie, only the attention, the adoration, the sensuality, all of which he had mistaken for love, something he had never experienced in his life in any form, be it parental love or otherwise.

Based on his limited previous experience, he decided it safe to say he was falling in love.

No matter how many times he saw her in a day, his heart skipped a beat at the sound of her voice or a glimpse of her dress whisking around a corner. He smiled more often with her than he ever had at any other point in his life, a deep smile that reached his heart, not the surface smirk. She even instilled confidence in his compositions. For the first time, he held hope in the palm of his hand.

When Drake first met her, he saw her inner passion and was drawn to it, desiring more from his marriage than duty, but for the first month of their marriage, he feared he had been mistaken and she wanted nothing from the marriage, leaving him to the same empty life he had already been living for far too long, only this time trapped in a loveless marriage with no hope of redemption or a second chance; yet, now, oh, now, he held hope. He could see ahead a marriage of love and happiness, of passion and sensuality. With Charlotte, he thought it possible to be the man he had always wanted to be, a lover and composer.

Could she ever fall in love with him?

Her sister Lizbeth certainly disapproved of him, of that he had little doubt. He tried to surprise

Lizbeth with another book only to be thanked with chilly politeness. Given their interactions in London, he assumed she thought him objectionably shallow, especially in contrast to his cousin, but perhaps she would grow to like him as a brother given time. He did suspect some of her prejudice was due to her believing him an unredeemable rake.

What no one knew aside from Lizbeth and himself, or at least he didn't think anyone else knew, was he'd flirted with Liz when they first met at a masquerade. This was before he'd met Charlotte, of course, when he'd become slightly frantic about finding a bride. There had been no attraction between them, and he knew after one conversation they would never suit. Such an encounter shouldn't be held against him. Lizbeth held it against him, though, thinking him reprehensible.

If Lizbeth could bring happiness to his reclusive cousin, he would do all in his power to welcome her to the family and make her stay comfortable. Unfortunately, he doubted she would be in his camp for winning over Charlotte's heart. Hazel, on the other hand, would support his pursuit of Charlotte's love. He was confident of it.

So deep in thought was he that he almost collided with Mary.

"Watch it!" His sister scolded, tugging at her horse's reins. "Didn't you see me? I've been waving to you, Drake."

Indeed, he hadn't. All he had seen since leaving Winston's estate was Charlotte—a vision of loveliness.

"Sorry, sis. Tad distracted. Where are you going?"

She wore one of her nicest riding habits, her hair styled too impeccably for a horse ride, the long black curls pinned behind her head and flowing down her back, all topped with a fashionable bonnet.

"I'm off to see Arabella, of course. Where else would I be going?" she asked defensively, her words clipped, too brusque not to rouse his suspicion.

"Hmm. Seems to me you're heading in the wrong direction to see Arabella."

"She's meeting me by the lake. Is that a crime?" Her horse pranced impatiently, sensing the tension of her mistress.

He tutted. "Let me guess. You're off for a tryst with the Marquess of Colquhoun. I knew you'd find his beard irresistible."

She wrinkled her nose. "Horrid man. You should have seen his teeth! I don't know where Mother finds these men. Please, talk to her for me. Make her stop throwing me at them," she pleaded, expertly veering him away from the original topic of her destination.

"That's between you and Mother. Leave me out of it. But you know, she does speak from experience on the wisdom of marrying an older gentleman," he said, then with a waggle of his brows added, "Widowhood has its advantages."

Mary snorted. Looking away, she eyed the horizon, lost in thought for a moment, then enquired, "And what if I've already found someone?"

Ah, so Mary was stepping out with someone, was she? Either this was a new development or all her complaints to Mother about being only sixteen and not ready for marriage were for show. The little sneak!

"I assume the mystery man is meeting you at the lake, not Arabella. I also assume he is someone Mother wouldn't approve. If I'm right, then I most heartedly do not approve of you meeting him unchaperoned. Regardless of his intentions, it would compromise you to be discovered alone with him. That may very well be his plan if he's a fortune hunter. Before you defend the blackguard, know they can be persuasive when it moves them and convince you of their deepest love."

Drake turned his horse around and shimmied next to her, deciding to change his plans for the day and follow her instead. He did not trust her groom for a second, for while the groom hovered in protective watch, Mary was a skilled horsewoman and would give the man the slip in the blink of an eye.

No matter how exhausted from fencing or how anticipatory to see Charlotte, he refused to allow Mary to compromise herself because she fancied some rogue.

"You needn't worry. I won't be meeting him alone. His father will be there, too," she replied.

"Oh ho! Is he really? And I'm to take your word for it? Not likely." Drake thought for a moment, swatting at an onslaught of midges and wishing her words to be true so he could head home and relax. "If you'll tell me who he is and agree not to meet him alone, I'll arrange it so the two of you can meet safely without sneaking around. And I won't tell Mother, at least not until I've had a chance to get to know the boy and decide if he's suitable or not. Agreed?"

"Would you really?" Mary's eyes lit with excitement. "I promise! May I go to him now and tell him?"

"Cheeky, but no. I'm not as cavalier as you take me, at least not with your safety. You can send the groom to tell him. Now, who's the lucky fellow?"

"Duncan. His father's purchased him a commission. Isn't that grand?" She beamed.

"Duncan Starrett, eh? A finer lad you couldn't have chosen. Mother would never approve, of course, but I like him well enough." True words, but Drake felt unnerved, nonetheless.

He didn't care for Duncan's disrespect to meet with Mary in private. The boy should have come to Drake first to ask permission to court Mary, not gallivant with her behind his back. The greater concern was the boy's father. Drake had little doubt Colonel Starrett would be waiting by the lake with his son, but that didn't fill Drake with the confidence it should. The colonel had confessed his desire for Duncan to beget a son before heading to the Army. Drake could only imagine the colonel *wanting* to compromise the two rather than chaperone. Not that he thought poorly of the colonel, but wealth and ducal connections did funny things to people. If that was his game, Colonel Starrett had underestimated the Dowager Duchess of Annick, for even if Mary found herself in a delicate way, Mother would force a marriage with one of the peers she had already chosen. Deceit beget deceit, and Mother would not stand to be deceived. He could see it now — the Earl of Collumby would be the likely winner since the earl was desperate for an heir but rumored beyond the ability to produce. A win-win.

Drake shook his head to himself. He could not imagine any of this of the Starretts, but again, wealth and connection did funny things.

Rather than vocalize any of his concerns, he said, "When you send word to young Starrett, tell him I'll arrange for the two of you to meet under my ever-watchful eyes. Take heed, Mary. If I learn you've met with him alone, you'll never again think Mother is the wrathful member of the family. And if he tries so much as a stolen kiss, he will find himself at the bottom of the lake, and you the marquess' blushing bride—gift wrapped."

"You're my favorite brother!" With that, she clucked her horse to move past him to the manor.

"I'm your only brother, cheeky monkey!" he shouted after her before spurring his own horse to follow her, eager to get away from the outdoors and the hoard of midges.

He thought about Mary and Duncan, but mostly he thought about his mother for the remainder of the ride to the stables. Mary was the second woman in a month to ask him to stand up to his mother. He'd left Mary's matchmaking to his mother, but he realized now the importance of taking a greater part. Should Mary not find a suitable husband, she would remain at the manor for life, completely supported by him, not that he minded, but he doubted she would want to live at Lyonn Manor forever.

The crux was that Mother would settle for no less than an earl for Mary, while he would approve her marriage to someone like Duncan Starrett—should the boy prove honest—hardly a fitting match for a duke's daughter. All the same, Drake had no qualms with the boy or his family and would prefer his sister marry for love. Duncan had an uphill battle to prove himself, but he *did* have a chance with Drake at the helm of matchmaking. Mary's happiness was at stake; yet another reason he needed to steel himself against a coming battle with his mother. This would take far more armor than he possessed.

When he arrived home, he left his horse to a groom and headed inside, sweaty, fatigued, and ready for a bath. The fencing workout had been good but exhausting, and the thought of facing his mother took its toll on his remaining stamina. Drake shambled through the gallery to the stairs.

With a hand on the railing, he paused. He wasn't entirely confident of the household's plans for the day, but it was about time for Lizbeth's afternoon constitutional and Hazel's tea with Mother, which would leave Charlotte alone for another hour or thereabouts.

Renewed with purpose, he decided to snag the newest sonata he had sketched for her, still largely unfinished, and slip it onto the pianoforte in the drawing room for Charlotte to find. That would delight her for the free hour while he bathed. Turning from the stairs, he stepped into his study, hesitated to dig out his snuffbox for an invigorating pinch, and then continued to the bookshelf.

The study filled with the sound of music when he cracked the bookshelf ajar. He held the door partially gaped, hoping to remain unnoticed. Charlotte was there. Alone. Playing the very sonata he had intended to retrieve.

The bath forgotten, he leaned his shoulder against the study wall and listened. The sonata in question turned the montage of sensual moments with Charlotte into musical form, capturing the newness with which he now saw her, a confident woman who enchanted him. He didn't know if she would recognize the piece as written about her and for her, but as long as she enjoyed it, that was all that mattered.

Listening to her play brought pure elation. His wife. His music. The two loves of his life together in one sound.

In part, the music had been written to show her skill to advantage, as he composed the piece with not only her preferences included but also what he knew she could play skillfully. He might challenge her skill in the future, but now was the time to tailor the pieces to her assured abilities. In addition, the music had been written to express himself with what he couldn't capture in words. Her interpretation of what had been written was her way of expressing herself in return, a conversation between the two of them.

And so, he listened. He had spoken through the music, and she was replying through the keyboard.

He was overcome with love after hearing her reply. As she reached the recapitulation, he swept the bookshelf over the rug and entered. A surprised Charlotte gasped at the intrusion, her fingers landing on discordant keys, the sound dissonant but no less beautiful, conveying their own expression.

Charlotte looked up, startled, her fingers interrupted mid chord. Drake swaggered into the room, drenching the space into momentary sunlight from the study before he closed the door. Her smile faltered when he headed towards her, a frisson of masculinity.

With each encounter over the past two weeks, her embarrassment had dissolved, gradually empowering her. She had controlled their liaisons, determining when, where, and how they would meet. She ensured each time they interacted would be when she was most apt to see The Composer. Catching him off guard had a similar affect to visiting him in his music room, she had learned, for when she lay in wait in the corridors, he was so startled, he had no time to shield himself with the Drake-mask. The Composer had proven himself to be a patient and understanding man, not to mention a ready receiver of her affection.

His expression now, however, alarmed her. In the short space between the door and harpsichord bench, she saw *Drake* approaching rather than The Composer—she had never seen *Drake* in her composer's room before! Her breath caught. His blue eyes were the color of the deepest chasm in the ocean, and he exuded masculine desire.

Anxious, she remained still on the bench, watching wide eyed as he swung around the harpsichord and wrapped his arms around her shoulders in a bear hug.

"You're perfect, Charlotte. Positively perfect."

She reached up to clasp his forearm, uncertain as to if she were dealing with Drake or The Composer, as he seemed a curious combination of both. What a silly contradiction! He was only one man, after all, and yet...

"Don't be absurd," she said. "No one is perfect."

She bit her bottom lip as she realized how many times she wished to be perfect. The perfect duchess.

The perfect wife. The perfect lover. Did he know how much her heart ached to embody perfection?

He sat on the bench next to her to face her, deepening his dimples with a broad smile. She almost sighed aloud in relief to see The Composer's smile. Almost.

"How long until you need to return to the parlor?" he asked.

"We have all day. We're alone in the manor."

He arched a brow. "All alone?"

"Lizbeth and Hazel have gone for a tour of Sebastian's castle. Mary left to visit Arabella. Mama Catherine is paying a call to—"

Her words cut short as he cupped her cheek in his palm.

She wanted him to kiss her. It was that simple, yet it was that complicated. He had arrived not as she had expected. He had arrived as an amalgamation of her husband and her love, garnished with an intoxicating masculinity she was unsure if she could resist.

Here she was trying to know him better, hoping they would fall in love first, when all she wanted in this moment was...*him*.

His hair was wet with sweat, his hands strong but gentle, the calluses on his left hand tickling her skin as he stroked his thumb across her cheek, and his scent—oh, his scent.

She had never smelled anything so masculine. His usual almond aroma was replaced with a strong fragrance of sweat, horse, and *him*. It was a musky bouquet that ought to be repellent, but it was quite the opposite. The musky cologne of *him* tantalized her. She couldn't even distinguish The Composer from Drake in this moment. She simply wanted to be a proper wife to her husband, a wife in all ways. Was it too soon?

"Charlotte," he said, innocent of her desires, "Will you spend the day with me? Here, the two of us, making music together? I would love nothing more than to spend time with you."

She leaned closer, hearing him but not processing his words, wanting only for him to kiss her.

His thumb swept over her bottom lip, but his eyes didn't shift from hers. "I want to love you. Will you let me love you?"

Charlotte gazed into the eyes of the composer — yes, there he was, her love — trembling at his words of love. What did he mean by them?

When she didn't respond, he said, "We can play a duet, if you'd like. Tell me what you want. I'll do anything for you."

"Love me," she said.

Without hesitation, he pulled her to him and captured her mouth in a kiss so full of ardor, her toes curled in her slippers.

She was breathless when he leaned back to admire her with a dimply smile. Oh, his smile. She had begun to catalogue his smiles, and this one was her favorite.

She reached up to touch a dimple. "Is it always like this?"

She hadn't expected him to know what she meant, yet he chuckled and kissed the tip of her nose. His eyes were so full of humor and happiness, she thought her heart would burst.

"Love me," she commanded again.

Dipping closer, his eyelids fluttered closed, and he covered her mouth with his once more.

Drake wanted to confess every thought he'd ever had to her. From the cradle onward, he wanted to share everything, and in return, he wanted to hear all her thoughts, be they fears, dreams, admissions, embarrassments, whatever. Everything.

They lay together on the floor of the music room, the rug burning a rash against his forearm. He had propped himself to see her better, to gaze into the copper eyes of the most beautiful woman he had ever known.

Between laughs and stories, he leaned in to kiss her cheek and down her jawline in syncopated staccato. Then the other cheek. Then her forehead. Then — well, there was only so much a husband could do before being swatted away with a laughing plea to *stop, you silly man.*

The day had not gone as he had planned, but it was a day he would not soon forget. Charlotte taught him a new meaning to love making. Instead of two bodies joined in carnal pleasure, he felt connected to her by a string from his heart to hers, the two being of one body, one person, one soul. He had never known it could be this way.

It was curious the direction life took, especially when plans went awry. Oh, not his plans for the day, although he supposed that, as well, but his plans in life. One plan after another had always failed, be it his music, his first proposal, his first attempt to love someone, his reputation, his mother, his opera, his agreement to marry out of duty, his wedding night....

The list continued. All his plans had failed, one after another, enough to give a man a complex, really. Yet here he lay with the love of his life, surrounded by music. It was as though all his plans failed for a reason, this reason.

If he could freeze this moment, he would, not because he feared the moment after, rather because this moment was too beautiful not to savor.

Charlotte's fingers laced with his free hand. She snuggled closer as she shared a story from her childhood. He listened. Enraptured. Sliding his rug-burned forearm forward, he captured one of her curls, free of their hairpins, and twined the silk about his finger, relishing in its perfection.

"What would you have done?" she asked at the end of her story, one of the many she had shared.

"I would have picked her up and tipped her unceremoniously into the ocean for goading you."

"Silly, that's not what I meant, but I appreciate your consideration." She smiled ruefully. "Liz has always been the courageous one, never afraid to take a leap of faith. I must have stood on that rock close to an hour before she convinced me to dive in. Mind, I didn't like it one bit when I did — the water was *freezing*! But the point is, I did it. I felt ever so brave afterwards, even if I shivered all evening. I took the plunge and was fortified for it. Liz knew I would be, of course."

"Mmm hmm." He grinned.

"You're not even listening! Here I am pouring my heart out, and you're not even listening."

He kissed away her pout, then returned to grinning.

"Well?" She eyed him askance. "Are you going to tell me why you're grinning?" As if only now realizing she was bare skinned beneath the blanket they shared, she pulled the cover closer to her chin and inched away from him with a blush. "Never mind," she said. "I don't think I want to know."

His grin broadened. "I just composed a *recitativo* for my opera." Sitting up, he retrieved his shirt from beneath the harpsicord bench. "You're my muse, my darling."

She, too, sat up, tightening the blanket around her.

With a final kiss to the tip of her nose, he added, "My love."

It took little encouragement to entice her to join him at the bench to dance fingers across the keyboard as he shared his vision for the opera he once believed he would never finish. The recitative was only one of the missing pieces, but he knew the others wouldn't be far behind in inspiration. Already playing in his mind was the aria to follow the recitative, and *ooh*, was that a possible duet he could hear, the ensemble incited by the aria? *Slow down, old boy*. First, the recitative. Before leaving their love nest, he fully intended on putting quill to paper, Charlotte by his side.

Chapter 22

One week and a special license later, they all stood on the cliffside of Dunstanburgh Castle, Sebastian's home, celebrating the nuptials of Sebastian and Lizbeth. Drake's chest swelled with pride that with Hazel's help, his matchmaking efforts paid off, and Sebastian had finally proposed to his perfect mate. Now, Charlotte would have her sister living only fifteen miles away, and his cousin could find the happiness he deserved, not to mention Drake would have a lifelong opportunity to befriend his prickly sister-in-law, a challenge he couldn't resist.

The wedding party was small, including only himself, his mother, Mary, Hazel, Charlotte, the bride and bridegroom, and a handful of Sebastian's servants. Drake thought it a heartfelt and beautiful wedding, the love birds ogling each other through the vows and everyone present able to see how deeply in love they were with each other.

Although, he conceded, he didn't know how he had a moment to notice the ceremony when he had eyes only for Charlotte. His attention was trained on her through the speech and the vows, as though today represented his marriage to her, the woman he knew as a confident, passionate, and enchanting soul.

She almost didn't seem the same woman he had married. He remembered their wedding in London at the close of the Season, his bride a blushing girl who giggled and gaped at him, in awe that he had chosen her. The woman standing before him now was a duchess in more than name. She had grown in only four months into a poised lady of elegant refinement, a leader in the household who earned the respect of the staff, a supporter of the downtrodden in the community, and the most sensual muse Drake had ever dreamt possible.

As Sebastian slipped the ring on Lizbeth's finger, Charlotte glanced at Drake, followed by a bashful but coy smile when she realized he was watching her. Truly, the most wonderful woman, and she was his.

The wedding party moved inside the castle after the ceremony, but not for long. Sebastian had arranged a full evening of entertainment since the entire party would be staying at the castle for the night, even Mother, entertainment that included an extravagant meal, games, and fireworks that evening.

The irony was that the celebration wouldn't be attended by the wedding couple. Within moments of relocating inside, Sebastian whisked off his new wife to begin their wedding night in the afternoon hours. Of all the people in the wedding party, Drake appreciated that sentiment the most and gave a silent hoorah to his cousin, eager to rib him about the whole of it after the honeymoon.

As soon as the couple disappeared, undressing each other with their eyes on the way out the door, Drake stepped over to Charlotte and offered his arm.

"Walk with me?" he asked.

She took his arm and chided, "I've only just escaped the wind, and now you want me to brave it all over again?"

"I'll block the wind for you." He winked, directing her back outside and towards the gazebo at the edge of the cliff, leaving behind a trio of bewildered ladies who had been abandoned by the only two couples present.

Dunstanburgh was as different from Lyonn Manor as the two cousins were from each other, the homes a reflection of their masters. The castle, which his cousin had painstakingly rebuilt into a comfortable home, sat on a cliff overlooking the North Sea, the stone walls formidable, the land wild and unkempt, surrounded by marshlands and rock covered beaches, and the weather unpredictable, all so unlike Lyonn Manor with its rolling hills, manicured landscape, and serenity.

The cliffside was a noisy affair, Drake thought. Kittiwakes cawed from the marsh. The wind howled and whipped about them. The waves beat against the cliff with a foamy mist that reached all the way to the gazebo.

Charlotte turned to him, clutching her bonnet. "The gazebo is almost large enough to be a pavilion. I wonder that he didn't think to enlarge it. It would certainly make an ideal location for a small orchestra during a fête."

"I really don't imagine Sebastian ever planned to host a party. A picnic, perhaps, a place for reflection, but a party? I don't think you realize how reclusive my cousin is."

"Poor Lizbeth. I hope she didn't marry him to stay close to me. I begged her to move here, but I couldn't bear to think I'm the cause of a lifetime with that man." Charlotte tightened the ribbons under her chin to secure the bonnet and sat on one of the benches in the gazebo.

"You underestimate the power of love, my dearest. Didn't you see the way they looked at each other during the ceremony?"

Charlotte ignored him and said, "I asked her just this morning if she was only marrying him because she *must*. Although they've not had any time alone, I worried, perhaps, he found some way to — well, I would hate to think her marrying him because she *must*. There seems no other reason for the rush. A special license? It's insupportable! Why not wait for the banns to be read and do it properly?"

"Ever think they wanted to marry before Aunt Hazel leaves? She leaves in two days, Charlotte. It would delay her an entire month for the banns to be read, pushing too close to the winter months for her travel."

"Nonsense. It's not going to snow in October," Charlotte dismissed.

Drake laughed, looking out onto the rough sea, waves rising in white caps and barreling towards the coast. "I hate to be the bearer of bad news, but life in Northumberland is altogether different than you're used to in the south. In all likelihood it *will* snow in October, the first snow of the year. Certainly, the snow could hold out until November, but by then, Hazel would be in a carriage traveling south, possibly caught in the weather. Are you willing to take that risk? Sebastian and Lizbeth were not so willing."

Drake scooted closer to his wife on the stone bench and slipped his arm around her shoulders. "Personally," Drake continued, "I think she took one look at the castle and decided putting up with Lord Grumpy was worth being mistress of Dunstanburgh."

Charlotte laughed, likely finding his suggestion more absurd than Lizbeth falling in love with Sebastian. He hoped she would be able to spend more time with her sister now, for as much as she loved Lizbeth, she didn't seem to know her own sister well. Even Drake could tell Lizbeth's disposition matched the atmosphere of the castle, and her heart belonged to his cousin.

"Has Mary told you," he asked, "about her new beau? I took them both riding the day before yesterday."

"A new beau? No! Why didn't you tell me? Is it the marquess?" Charlotte turned to him, as beautiful as ever against the backdrop of the ocean.

"Not the marquess. I had hoped she would tell you herself. I hate to ruin the surprise, but it seems I already have, however inadvertently. The beau in question is Duncan Starrett."

She frowned. "The colonel's son? Are you positive that's a good match for her? You don't suppose he's a fortune hunter, do you? And what about all her protests about being too young?"

"She's promised not to do anything rash as long as I agree to let her see him. All his visits will be chaperoned. While I don't think he's made any professions of love, she has agreed to wait until after her eighteenth birthday before accepting him, should he propose. I hope you won't disapprove of the match. I'll already have Mother to contend with, but I can delay that unpleasant conversation for at least two more years. I'm only pleased she'll marry for love and not duty. After all, if I had married for duty alone, I might be sitting here with a stuffy daughter of a duke who has terrible breath and a hatred for music rather than sitting here with you." Drake squeezed her shoulder.

"Are you saying you married for love?" She scoffed in exaggerated disbelief.

"I might have done." He smiled when she blushed at his response. Clearing his throat, he asked, "We are in the guest quarters for the night, separate rooms, of course, but I thought, perhaps, you might consider sneaking into my chamber?"

She tensed beneath his arm, making him feel self-conscious for asking. When she didn't say anything in response for a lengthier bout of silence than he cared to sit through, he tried for a more persuasive tactic.

"Frankly, the rug burn is paying its toll. It's been a full week of the most wondrous time I've ever spent in my music room, but…." He cleared his throat again, unexpectedly nervous about the request. "I'd like to wake up to find you next to me, see you there at first light. If you're not opposed, we could resume the arrangement when we return home. My chamber or yours, I don't care. What do you say?"

He tried to keep his tone lighthearted, on the edge of jovial, but inside he was tense, his pulse racing. The request would move their relationship in a direction far more intimate than most couples ventured, never aristocratic couples, only those commoners too poor to have separate rooms or too in love to care. By Jove, he wanted to share with Charlotte those intimate moments of sleep, her face being his first sight when he awoke. As much of a lark sneaking about in hidden rooms had been this past week, he wanted more.

"I don't know," she said. "I want to, but I'm not altogether decided I'm ready."

His shoulders slumped. Not ready. As in she shared his passion for music and now physical affection, but she wasn't ready for the emotional connection, to love him.

Her cheeks turned rosy, and she hid her face against his shoulder. "You'll think I'm silly if I tell you why."

"Try me," Drake dared.

She sighed, still leaning against him, her bonnet askew, the ribbons tickling Drake's nose.

"I've fallen a little in love with someone else," she confessed.

The world stopped. His heart stopped. He heard nothing except silence, the world frozen in place by her words.

"And I'm not confident," she continued, "how I feel about *you*, Drake."

Even his breathing stopped.

Her words smothered him. Here he sat, hopelessly in love with her, and she loved someone else?

Who?

She was never around anyone other than him, was she? He thought of the times she and her sister had explored the wilderness park on the estate, the time she had gone on a picnic with her family and

Sebastian, all the times he hadn't been around, instead holed up in his music room or fencing with Winston. Had she met someone else, used the family outings for clandestine meetings?

His heart splintered.

After a length of silence in which he didn't respond, she said, "I've fallen a little in love with a man I call The Composer. When he smiles, he has two irresistibly handsome dimples. He listens to me when I talk, understands how I feel, has the most brilliant ideas of his own, and oh, when he kisses me, Drake, I hear the music of the celestial spheres, the choir of heavenly angels. We're one soul joined."

She sighed and nuzzled closer to him.

Exhaling as the earth reset its spin on its axis, Drake pushed her bonnet out of his face and tried to make sense of her words.

"Are you talking about *me*, Charlotte? Or is there another dimpled composer kissing you I should know about?" Oddly, he felt jealous of himself.

"In a way, yes, but in a way, no. *You're* Drake, and *he's* The Composer. I'm falling for one but uncertain about the other. You see, you're altogether a different person outside the music room. I know it sounds silly, but it's true. Inside the room, your smile is genuine, and your eyes are soulful. Outside, you leer. You're sardonic with a wolfish smile that threatens to make a joke of me or devour me, maybe both. Drake is recklessly impulsive. The Composer is patient. I want to be with the man in the music room, not the lusty wolf. Does that make sense?"

He laughed so heartily he had to remove his arm from around her shoulders to drum an accompaniment on his thighs. When he looked back at her, she was scowling.

"See. You're Drake right now. Mocking me. If I told The Composer, *he* would understand. You do nothing but laugh at me and think I'm silly." She crossed her arms over her chest. "The world is a joke to you, but have you noticed you're the only one laughing?"

The words took a moment to sink in before he sobered. "I'm not laughing at you, my darling. I'm laughing at the strangeness of being considered two people. You do know that I *am* The Composer you claim to adore, don't you? I bury that part of me deep inside because no one would respect me if I weren't what they expect me to be, but The Composer *is* who I am. Don't you see that? Can't you see through the illusion to the real me?"

She picked non-existent lint from her dress.

Ah, she was quite serious, then. It was absurd, but it made sense. The trouble was reconciling one self with the other. It would be better for her to accept him as he was, of two minds, but if she couldn't love all of him unless he changed....

He rested his elbows on his thighs and perched his chin on steepled fingertips. "I want you to understand something. No one, not even Sebastian, has seen my private self. Only you. But you must love all of me, not just the private side. The public face isn't a complete farce. It's me, as well. You can't fall in love with part of me and not all of me. You need to love the whole, even the wolf. While inside I'll be your composer, I will *always* wear the public mask. Can you see your composer and me as the same person, love us as one?"

Never had he thought of himself as being two different people, a façade for the world and his true self with his music, but he knew she was right. What she wanted, he feared, was for him to blight the public mask and be his private self openly, show the world his depth. This was something he would not do, could not do, and he prayed this wouldn't keep her from loving him fully.

Oh, he wished she would say she loved all of him, for this would forever be who he was, a man who kept his soul private while he entertained the world with a mask.

The longer he waited for her answer, the more it sank in that he wouldn't get an admission. She didn't know if she could love all of him. Simple as that. She didn't know. Maybe it was enough for now that she loved the real him, the side he had once feared to show her. In time, maybe, she could learn to love all of him. He could hope, for if she couldn't, it wasn't really love.

He smiled, then, a deep and genuine smile full of all the love he felt for her.

"Ah, there you are." Relief written in her expression, she touched her hand to his face.

He leaned in and kissed her, putting into the kiss his truest self, willing her to see him, all of him, and love him.

When they returned to the castle to join Hazel, his mother, and Mary, the remainder of the afternoon enjoyed a festive atmosphere with a game of charades and a feast fit for a king. Only his mother retired early, leaving the four remaining guests to enjoy the fireworks on the cliffside.

As they stood under the night sky, watching the exploding colors sparkle against the backdrop of stars, Drake wrapped his arms around Charlotte, leaning her against his chest. He knew without a shadow of doubt he loved her more than he would have ever thought possible. She knew his true self and was even a little in love with him.

He whispered for her ears only as the sky filled with rainbows, "Have you decided if you'll stay with me tonight, my love?"

She nodded against his cheek. "I will."

Chapter 23

Several days after Lizbeth's wedding to Sebastian and the departure of Aunt Hazel, Charlotte and Drake arrived in the ducal carriage at Winston's estate.

Drake had arranged for her a surprise, but he hadn't yet given anything away except that it would be held in Winston's grand ballroom and had been arranged, at Drake's request, as a belated wedding gift from the Prince of Wales himself.

Charlotte couldn't imagine what the prince would have helped Drake arrange or why it would need to be held in a ballroom at someone else's estate, but she assumed it must be extravagant. Her excitement, part nerves and part anticipation, bubbled over during the ride to Winston's estate.

When the carriage pulled up and the groom set down the steps and opened the door, Winston approached to greet them with a bow. "At last, I have the pleasure of meeting the Duchess of Annick! Drake has sung your praises. I've been remiss about calling on you."

She inclined her head politely and offered him a gloved hand. Much to Charlotte's surprise, Winston wore casual riding attire, hardly appropriate dress for hosting entertainment.

As if reading her thoughts, Winston said, "I'm only here to greet you both and meet the lady who has stolen my best mate's heart. My home is yours."

He waved his hand towards the house, waiting only for Drake to guide Charlotte to the door before turning away and walking towards what Charlotte assumed were the stables. How odd. What sort of surprise would Drake have arranged to send the host retreating from his own house?

A stout, jovial butler waited for them at the front door, leading the couple to the ballroom before shutting the doors behind him. Charlotte was even more confused when she walked into the room. Two chairs separated by a small table faced a stage. She glanced at Drake, who wore his best nobleman expression for the occasion — the epitome of ennui. She turned back to the stage. It was decorated like a Turkish house with a faux courtyard, complete with carved wood lattice windows, colorfully decorative rugs, matching throw pillows for furniture, and a fig tree.

Drake directed her to the two chairs, offering her to take a seat. When she did, eyeing him with suspicion, he merely raised his eyebrows. All he was missing was a quizzing glass. Antagonizing man!

Unseen and unheard, a footman had poured their glasses of wine. She knew this only when the glasses appeared on the table between them.

"What is this?" she asked, looking from her glass to Drake to the stage, then back to the glass.

"Wine."

She scowled.

Drake raised his glass in salute before turning his eyes to the stage.

She didn't have to wait long before she heard music. Charlotte scanned the room. When shifting in her chair and craning her neck produced nothing except the empty ballroom, she assumed the music came from behind the stage, an orchestra hiding behind the scene.

Oh, the music was gloriously dramatic! Cymbals crashed, triangles chimed, violins played. Charlotte didn't fully understand what was happening, but she looked at Drake with barely contained excitement. With an arch of one brow, he swirled his wine.

The stage remained empty, but the music continued for another five minutes. And then, as Charlotte began to wonder why she was forever staring at an unchanging stage, a young man walked from behind the set, pausing in the faux courtyard to look towards the Turkish house.

Tears stung her eyes as the young man began to sing in German about a woman named Konstanze. The young man sang an aria about his desire to find his beloved, who had been abducted by pirates and sold to the Pasha. Before long, an older man joined the stage, plucking fake figs from an equally fake tree and singing his own aria.

The surprise was an opera. Drake had arranged a private showing of an opera — *for her.*

An entire opera, complete with opera company, orchestra, and set. She saw no difference in the opera performed before her and one performed in London other than they were sitting in chairs in a ballroom in Northumberland rather than in a box at the King's Theatre.

For the entirety of the first act, she looked from the stage back to Drake, still in awe that he had arranged this and done so just for her personal enjoyment. By the second act, her eyes never left the stage, completely enthralled by the lives of the captive Konstanze and her maid Blonde, who were enslaved by their captors, trapped in a Turkish harem and hoping to be rescued by their true loves.

Charlotte held her breath when the hero found his Konstanze, furrowed her brows when the two heroines and two heroes were caught by the guards, laughed at the bits of humorous dialogue, especially between the head guard and Blonde, and fell hopelessly in love with Belmont's desperate attempt to break into the house and rescue his betrothed.

Charlotte wondered….if she were locked inside a house, captive, would Drake find a way inside to rescue her? Would he scale the walls, ascend by a hand-tied rope ladder, appear in disguise, or whatever else it might take to rescue her from the confines of her cage? If he could arrange this show exclusively for her, decidedly, he would stop at nothing for her happiness.

Oh, how she had misjudged him for so long. Her heart soared. Throughout the final act, she cast Drake a few more glances, seeing only beside her the man she had come to love. She wasn't positive when it happened, when she fell in love, maybe on the cliff at Dunstanburgh when he made his case for loving all of him, perhaps in the music room during their duets, maybe right here in this moment. Regardless of when, she loved him.

When the opera concluded, she clapped feverishly for the singers. The small orchestra stepped out from behind the stage, still holding their instruments, and bowed. Drake stood up next to her and applauded.

"Did you enjoy Mozart's *Die Entführung aus dem Serail*?" Drake asked as the singers and musicians departed by the side door of the ballroom.

"*The Abduction from the Seraglio*? Oh, I loved it, Drake! It was humorous and dramatic all at once," she exclaimed.

"I was under the impression you didn't favor comic opera. I seem to remember you telling me that once." He nodded to the footman.

"I don't recall. I'm certain if I did, it was only to irritate you," she admitted.

He held out his hand. "May I have this dance, my love?"

"Dance? Whatever are you talking about? We can't dance by ourselves, and besides, there's no music." She laughed at him remaining seated.

Undaunted, Drake kept his hand held out to her. A quartet of violinists returned to the ballroom, then, and struck up a minuet. As soon as the music began to play, he arched an eyebrow.

"There's still the problem of the dance, Drake. We can't dance with only two people."

He snatched her hand from her lap and said, "Leave that to me. I'm leading, after all."

And sure enough, he worked out the minuet so that they danced it together, promenading and twirling without the advantage of other dancers. The only time Charlotte had laughed quite so much was when they first attempted to play the harpsichord together. As they danced, Charlotte had such a brilliant idea she couldn't believe she hadn't thought of it before. She would host a soirée in honor of a new composer. If she invited the right people, they should come quite far to hear the debut, and certainly they would come if she invited the prince. It would be a testament to her hosting skills and to her love for her husband.

This would be a debut for them both, in a way, hers as a hostess who no longer required the tutelage of her mother-in-law, thus banishing the dragon to the dower house, at last, and his as a talented composer, either anonymous if he wished, or potentially with a grand unveiling that he was the genius behind the music.

Would Drake allow it? Even if the music was to be debuted anonymously? And did she have the courage for such a bold move? The soirée would have to be perfect, for if one aspect went wrong, she'd be a disgrace, not only her but the family name and the Annick title with it. If he could arrange an opera for her private viewing, surely, she could arrange a soirée for him.

The part she wouldn't confess to him was her hope this would help The Composer break free from his mask — no need for impulsivity, vulgarity, jests, or other attributes of his mask, only The Composer for all the world to see.

That evening she nestled next to Drake. They were snuggled before the hearth in his bedchamber.

"Drake?" She ran her fingers through his hair, massaging his scalp with her fingertips.

"Hmm?" he murmured, his cheek resting against her shoulder.

"What would you say to my hosting a soirée with musical entertainment? An evening of music.

We could turn the Red Drawing Room into a performance hall for the event, just like we talked about." Charlotte wasn't at all optimistic this conversation would go as planned. But why should he not want to debut his music?

"Sounds splendid, my love. Mother won't like it, but she can stuff a stocking in it for one evening. Would you be playing the piano by chance? I would love to see you play. You think you don't have skill, but you do, far more than you realize. You're a natural, Charlotte. You could play one of the Mozart sonatas you so enjoy." With his arms already wrapped about her, he hugged her closer, kissing her shoulder.

"I would consider playing, yes, but only if we played a duet. Could we?" She inched lower to face him.

"It will surprise everyone to see me with a violin, but if it'll entice you to play, then I promise to consider it." Drake trailed a finger down her forearm.

"We could play the duet you wrote. You know, the one I like the most." She looked at him from beneath her eyelashes, hoping for a flirty pose.

He frowned and leaned away from her. "No."

"Please, Drake. It's time people hear your music, time they know what a skilled musician and composer you are. I'd like the entire evening's concert to be only your music. I want to invite a soprano to sing the new aria from your opera. I want to invite a quartet to play some of your older works. I, especially, want us to perform the duet *and* the piece for four hands," she pleaded.

"Charlotte, no. My music would be scandalous on its best day, and I don't want all of society seeing me that way. At best, they'll say I'm a talentless milksop. At worst, well, I'll not have them question me or ridicule you, and I certainly don't want my father's name dragged through the mud again. It'll bring all the old gossip back to the surface. I will not have people mock my family. I have worked too hard on my reputation for all to fall apart. I told you already that my private life is private." Drake released her from his embrace and laced his fingers behind his head.

"But we don't have to say you're the composer. I can announce that all works are by an anonymous composer I wish to patronize. No one will know it's you unless the debut is a success, and you feel comfortable sharing the fact. The only thing I'm asking is that you perform with me."

"I'm not as courageous as you, Charlotte. The one and only time I debuted my music it changed the entire course of my life. Looking back on it now, that change was not for the better. Do you know that after that concert, I didn't compose for a decade? You're the only one of us with any real courage. You're not afraid of anything, and I envy you for it," he said, his eyes full of admiration she didn't think she deserved.

"I'm not at all courageous. I tremble every time I am to be seen as a duchess and not plain Charlotte. I'm so afraid of failure that I cried myself to sleep every night when I first moved here. I'm afraid I'll make a fool of myself in front of everyone, and they'll all know I'm an imposter, that I'm nothing more than a country bumpkin, a nobody from nowhere pretending to be nobility." Her voice cracked at the admission. "I'm afraid I'll disappoint everyone. Most of all you."

What compelled her to confess that? She hadn't even admitted that fear to Hazel or Lizbeth when they visited. She had shown them, instead, that she was skilled at her new position, regardless of her worries.

"No more self-deprecation. You could never disappoint me, Charlotte. You're perfection itself." He wrapped his arms around her again. "You would laugh to hear yourself say that if you really knew what the *beau monde* was like. They're all fake, all pretending to be someone or something they aren't. They snub their noses at those below them, then they go home to tup the stableboy — husbands and wives! You can't fear society. They're all already afraid of themselves and afraid of everyone else learning their secrets. I think each of us, ultimately, is shielding ourselves from harm, be it fears of failure, criticism, or even unrequited love. Don't you see? None of those people are superior to you in any way."

She let him hold her, comforting her by stroking her back and feathering kisses across her forehead.

But then she braved saying, "Then what do you have to fear? By your own admission, they're all fake, so what harm would come from a debut?"

He sighed and buried his face against her neck. Mumbles, mutterings, and curses could be heard, followed by a muffled scream, and then he turned back to face her, smiling again.

"You're going to be the death of me, woman. Do whatever makes you happy. But only on one condition," he said.

"What might that be?" She eyed him skeptically.

"You stay here with me tonight," he requested.

Before she could respond yay or nay, he scooped an arm behind her knees, held her tightly to his chest, and stood with her cradled in his arms. She shrieked and paddled her feet as he carried her across the room.

Chapter 24

*C*lick-snap. *Click-snap.*

The lid of the snuffbox clicked open and snapped closed in Drake's fingers.

Nervous was an understatement. Mix anxious with excitable and stir it with a splash of terrified and that might be a more apt emotion.

In the past hour, he had transitioned from a casual pinch of snuff to lining it along the back of his hand. Somehow even that didn't quell his nerves, although a slight lightheadedness had settled.

This evening was Charlotte's soirée. Guests bustled about the Red Drawing Room, enjoying madeira, ratafia, and conversation before the concert began. The rugs had been rolled and removed to enhance the acoustics, mirrors placed around the room to reflect the evening candlelight, and chairs from both the formal dining room and the Blue Drawing Room arranged facing the pianoforte to best view the musicians.

He had to hand it to Charlotte; she selected the guests with skill. The soirée was attended by known patrons of the arts, some all the way from London, and any number of well-to-do individuals with musical appreciations, all who, Drake surmised, would be more open to his musical style than his mother's stuffy traditionalists. Genius, he thought to himself. Charlotte was pure genius.

They weren't the sort of artists and thespians his father favored, nor were they among Maggie's crowd. These guests were well known for their generous patronage to the arts, one lady in particular being known to have given an impressive largesse to write the libretto for a recently debuted opera. Charlotte must have gone to great lengths on his behalf to discover these individuals and persuade them to attend a soirée so close to winter months.

The soirée took nearly a month to arrange, and even that was short notice for the guests who traveled far. One of the saving graces was the artfully scheduled shooting party that had been held the week prior, for those already attending the shooting party merely extended their stay by a week to enjoy the soirée.

Drake was positive Charlotte was a genius. She might still feel insecure, always worrying she'd make the wrong choice or embarrass herself somehow, but he knew she was a natural hostess and party planner, far superior to his mother, though he'd not admit that to the latter.

The *coup de grâce* of this soirée was the attendance of Prinny, complete with liveried royal footmen. The prince may only be eight and twenty, but his word was worth gold. If he favored the music, no matter if everyone else in attendance hated it, the composer's music would soon be played at every performance hall in the country and beyond.

It hadn't taken much persuading for the prince to join the shooting party and then stay a week longer for the concert. When asked, Prinny had remarked how easily bored he became without a good party. Truthfully, the extended stay offered the opportunity to flirt with more ladies.

Now, Prinny stood at the double doors to the grotto, flirting and dressed as a veritable fop, his powdered hair and rouged cheeks humoring Drake beyond words. Prinny marched to the beat of his own drum, despite the changing fashions that no longer favored the old style. Not that Drake would ever laugh at the prince's expense, but patches and powder were simply not the rage now, though that fact was lost on the lad.

Drake needed a laugh. His nerves were drawn taut, ready to snap. Despite the well-planned party in his honor and the impressive guest list, he felt one part flattered and one part violated. As much as he really did want his talent recognized, he didn't feel comfortable having his private world on display. This whole affair left him too vulnerable. His emotions would be presented on a gilded platter for them to skewer. He had never written for an audience, only for himself, the outpouring of his own emotions. Even if the guests didn't know the name of the composer, he would still be able to hear their reactions to it, not to mention shoulder the blame and judgment for having emotionally wrought music in his house — after all, it was considered indecorous to *feel*.

By this token, the styling of the music was unique yet risqué. His playing was unique yet risqué. The family history was unique yet risqué.

The whole of him was coiled, waiting for censure.

His loyalty to Charlotte was divided — he was touched by her thoughtfulness, by all the work she

put into this event for him, to show him how much
she cared for him and his talent; yet, he resented
she so easily gave away his private self to the world
when he thought he had made it clear that the man
behind the mask was for him to choose with whom
he shared, and he had chosen her, the only person
to enjoy his innermost self. Even if he admitted to
the guests that he was the composer, he would *not*
remove his mask. They would, instead, see a bored
noble waving away their criticisms and compliments
with a flick of an embroidered kerchief, stifled yawn,
and possibly a lift of a quizzing glass, accompanied by
a tasteless joke to deflect. *No one* would see his dimples. Drake suspected Charlotte wanted to rip free
his mask and witness his behavior shift so that the
world saw the real him. Perhaps he did her discredit
with this assumption. Alas, his suspicions were raised,
nonetheless. She would be sorely disappointed if this
were the case, for he could not rip away a mask that
was permanent. This *was* him, even if in part, even
if only in public.

Whatever internal conflict he struggled with, he
needed to sort it within the next few minutes, for
there would be no going back once the music began.
Tonight would make or break him; he feared the latter.

Click-snap.

Mother had tucked herself on the opposite side of
the house, promising, or threatening rather, to return
after the performances. She left when she saw the
rugs being rolled, incensed by the rearrangement of
the drawing room into the semblance of its old ballroom designation, even if only for one night, not to
mention incensed by the presence of the guests and by

the choice of entertainment. Not even the presence of the prince could move her. And, in fact, his presence incensed her all the more. She shared choice words about the prince being in her house, as she wasn't a fan of him or his companions.

He knew that this scene, regardless of the differences in guests and tone, brought back her worst memories of his father's parties, and for that he was sorry, but this was the beginning of what he hoped would be *his* scene, a tasteful appreciation of music, nothing of the old sort.

Presumably, his mother had figured out by now that the compositions to be debuted were his own. Or not. She was only passively aware he still composed and likely didn't know he had enough compositions to fill an entire calendar's worth of soirées. As far as she was concerned, he only dabbled now and then in penning a piece, never fully committing himself.

He knew the debacle of a debut from his youth was foremost on her mind, as was his father and the whole mess of a scandal. In some small part, he felt as though he were betraying her. While crafting a reputation as a libertine might not seem like something a boy would do for his mother, it had been. He'd been protecting her as much as himself, along with his father's name. After all these years, it seemed he'd come full circle, once again in a house full of music lovers, ready to put himself on display. This time would be different.

Click-snap.

Drake clicked open the snuffbox and pinched another line onto the back of his hand. With a sniff, he snapped the box closed and tucked it into his pocket.

No more. He was irrevocably dizzy from taking too much in such a short period of time. At this rate, he'd never want to take snuff again.

He searched the crowded room for his wife, finding her surrounded by a few of the local ladies, outshining them all in her silken blue evening gown with matching sapphire necklace, one of his more recent gifts to her. Tendrils curled around her face with ringlets tied at the back of her head, peacock feathers rising from the coiffure. A duchess. She looked the part. Her posture straight but graceful, her head inclined condescendingly but with a warm smile, her instinctive actions as hostess sealing her as the most celebrated woman in the north. A natural duchess. Much like the evening of the dinner party, Charlotte glowed, clearly within her element. Since the moment guests entered the room, she had flitted about with invisible angel wings, moving from group to group to honor the guests with sincerity.

He was only disheartened that Lizbeth and Sebastian were still enjoying their honeymoon, otherwise he was convinced they would both attend, if for no other reason than to support Charlotte since neither of them knew he composed.

The time of reckoning arrived when Charlotte stepped over to the pianoforte and requested the guests take their seats. Tapping his front pocket, he reminded himself no more snuff, at least not until he stopped feeling giddy. He may need to tie his hand to a potted plant to keep from the nervous habit, especially since his fingers had started to tremble uncontrollably.

Charlotte welcomed everyone, thanked them for attending, described the musical selections and program for the evening, and said more than was necessary about her ardent support of the anonymous composer. To still his hands from shaking, Drake clenched his fists until his knuckles ached.

The entertainment would begin with a soprano, followed by a violin quartet, and then an assortment of works until he and Charlotte ended the performance with a duet, the final *pièce de résistance* being their sonata for four hands.

When the soprano stepped out, he realized she was the very woman who had sung the aria at Vauxhall during his courtship with Charlotte. For a moment, he forgot his fears as his heart swelled. Charlotte was full of surprises this evening and all of them for him. The soprano had, he was sure, been selected as a nod to their courtship.

Drake remained standing at the back of the room, too anxious to sit. After the soprano's first sultry notes, Charlotte joined him. He affected a pursed-lipped half-grin and half-grimace in reply to her delectably stunning smile of greeting.

When his hand inched towards his pocket once again, he restrained it, pinning it behind him.

Lusty tones swept over the audience, a mounting theme with a convention-challenging rhythm thrumming a tattoo in their ears. Drake closed his eyes. For the first time, he heard his music performed as it had played only in his head. As glorious as this moment, he wished he could blot out the sound and leave the room until time for their duet. The presence of the audience unsettled him. He couldn't stomach seeing their reaction to such sentimental music.

The soprano sang of unrequited love.

He remembered the day he began writing this piece, some ten years ago, the day he realized Maggie never loved him, that his mother never loved him, that his father never loved him, that no one loved him. All the love in the world he could give, and no one wanted him. Could the audience feel the heartbreak in the music? Could they feel the pain? He couldn't watch, for he feared what he would see — shallow individuals with no capacity for emotional depth, insulted to be exposed to feelings. He needed to leave the room and fast.

Opening his eyes, he turned to Charlotte, who watched him with curiosity. With still trembling fingers, he touched her cheek. She reached up and clasped his wrist, nodding to the door.

She knew. She understood. She was perfect.

They slipped out of the room unseen. Their absence wouldn't be noticed until the soprano finished, so they had ample time to escape for a breath of sanity. Still holding his wrist, she led him to his study, pulling the door closed behind her.

When the door handle clicked, she commanded, "Kiss me, Drake."

Without hesitation, Drake closed the space between them in three quick steps, pressing Charlotte against the study door in a needy kiss. Tonight's distraction was well planned, for she knew exactly how many minutes they had before they needed to reappear in the drawing room. When she saw his discomposure at the opening performance, she knew her decision to be good.

As he kissed her, cupping her face in his quivering hands, she covered the back of his hands with her own, then realizing she couldn't feel him through her kidskin gloves, tugged off each, tossed them aside, and once more covered his hands with hers, hoping to warm him, settle him, reassure him.

He murmured against her lips, "I love that you know me so well."

Clinging to her as though she might float away, he nestled his forehead against her neck and whimpered. She had known this evening would be difficult, but she had complete faith he would gain confidence as the night progressed. Hearing his music performed would boost his esteem. Receiving the compliments of the guests would fortify him, even if they only thought him a patron of the anonymous composer. Before the soirée ended, Charlotte knew he would feel safe to remove his mask. In all likelihood, he would not realize when it happened. A natural response to the audience's accolades. The revelation he could be himself. No need for a public face.

She wrapped her arms around his waist, holding him tightly. His current emotional state echoed through the voice of the soprano, filling the manor with heaven's song.

One of the stories he had shared with her had described his debut during his teens as a violinist and novice composer, namely the pride he felt to share his talent, the elation to be recognized, the conviction with which he had played. However much Charlotte wanted *this* debut to recall those feelings, she knew it might take time. Since the result of his original debut had not gone to plan, namely leading to an outraged mother, accusations of effeminacy, exposure to a seedy group, and then the ruination by a master manipulator, he must fear this second attempt could end similarly. Impossible! He was an adult now, a duke, entertaining a crowd of proper patrons of the arts. There were no similarities between then and now.

Reaching up, she ran her fingers through his hair, soothing him. All their talk of not caring what others thought, yet here they were, hiding from the guests. She had known he would need her support. When arranging the program, she had ensured the longest piece came first to allow for this time of fortification.

With an exhale, Drake leaned away from her, kissed the tip of her nose, then turned to sink into one of the chairs by the unlit fireplace.

"Should I light a candle?" he asked, surveying the moonlit room for the first time.

"No. We'll need to return soon." She walked over to him to massage his shoulders.

"I knew it would be difficult, but I didn't think I would feel so discomfited. I can't even enjoy hearing the music from fear," he admitted.

Leaning over the back of the chair, she kissed his cheek. "Tonight, you're the bravest man I know."

"Am I?" he asked rhetorically, feeling his pocket for his snuffbox. "I don't suppose you want to ring for brandy?" He tipped his head back to look up at her, worry lines on his forehead.

"After. We need to return soon. The aria ends in seven minutes, and I must introduce the next musicians and piece."

"I don't need seven minutes to get thoroughly foxed. Seven seconds? Two minutes? I'll make it fast."

As tightly wound as his nerves were, the last thing he needed was inebriation. She wanted him to be himself, the genuine and talented composer, not a stumbling Drake, quick with a joke, a slur, and gruffness. No brandy. There must be something she could do to help, though. She stared at the mantel clock, which she had moved from his desk drawer prior to the guests arriving, knowing when she planned this little interlude, she would need to keep an eye on the time.

Circling around his chair, she raised the hem of her dress and petticoat to perch on his lap before draping her arms around his neck. "Talk to me. What's it like to hear the aria performed?"

There was no escaping the music, even from within the study.

He closed his eyes and rested his head against the chairback. "Heaven. It's how I heard it in my mind." His words began with a *largo* rhythm, slowing and broadening to *larghissimo* as he added, "No, better. I can't describe it. It's...*love*. The language of love, the expression of love, the...I don't know the words, but I feel it *here*." He pressed a fist to his heart.

Opening his eyes, he studied her before drawing her to him with a *lento* embrace, so in contrast to her *veloce* heartbeat. Their lips met in another kiss, this one fueled with a different kind of passion than she was accustomed from him, one of languor amour, of time halting, soul-charging tenderness, of perfect harmony.

Some hours later, the entertainment ended, the final piece played by both Charlotte and Drake on the pianoforte, the sonata for four hands. They stood and bowed to the applauding audience before Charlotte made her final remarks and expressed gratitude to the guests for attending.

The entertainment at an end, the chairs were moved about the perimeter of the room so guests could resume socializing. The doors to the adjoining Blue Drawing Room were opened should anyone wish to play cards, which it seemed quite a few gentlemen did, and the double doors in the Red Drawing Room were opened to the grotto to encourage guests to drift into the chilled autumn night, a welcome coolness after the stuffy heat of the room. Lanterns lit the outdoor space for an enchanting evening. Footmen circled on cue with trays of beverages. In addition, a refreshment table manned by Mr. Taylor lined one wall. Charlotte had considered setting up a refreshment room, but she did not like the idea of guests drifting away when the goal was for them to converse about the music, specifically in Drake's hearing.

Charlotte's first stop was to the refreshment table. She desperately wanted a glass of lemonade. Her mouth was parched, her lips dry, her throat tight. This was the moment. The guests heard a carefully chosen variety of compositions, and now they would talk amongst themselves and to her of their opinions.

While she loved Drake's work, she knew he worried they would find it too coarse, too licentious. Society, especially aristocrats, was not supposed to feel emotion, not supposed to be exposed to feelings. A young lady attending her first ball could not even express her enjoyment without criticism. There was only duty and honor. Emotion trampled on tender sensibilities, gave way to vapors and migraines, and dishonored even the most honorable of men. Simply put, emotion was vulgar.

How would Drake respond if they found the music distasteful, if they insulted him without realizing it was the duke they criticized? Would they blame his new wife for allowing coarse music into his noble home? Would they blame her country roots, accuse her of being common, regardless that she was a gentleman's daughter? Or would they place blame on Drake, thinking he had influenced his wife by way of his father's purported scandals?

Charlotte downed her lemonade with a flick of the wrist, smiling at those around her and grabbing another glass. The Prince of Wales stood in a shadowed corner of the room, talking with Drake. She headed their direction for a quick word before she'd need to circulate amongst the guests — it would not do to circulate before personally thanking the prince, after all; although her motives were more self-inclined, namely the desire to further fortify Drake with a smile and touch of her hand to his arm.

"Lean, dynamic, aggressive," the prince was saying to Drake as she approached. With a slight incline of his head when she approached, he continued, "I found it almost wry, to be honest. Pray, can one say music possesses an attitude? I believe this music did. Do you think this composer would consider attending one of my parties? He could conduct the quartets himself, I daresay."

Before she heard Drake's response, Lord and Lady Hallewell caught her attention. She excused herself and walked over to the Hallewells.

"Wherever did you discover such a composer?" Lady Hallewell asked before Charlotte came to a full stop. "I was telling Lord Hallewell how bold and lusty the violin was in the final duet. And what a beautiful couple you both made on the pianoforte! I had no idea His Grace played. So rare to see a gentleman on the pianoforte — what talent he has. And what music! Tell her what you were saying, Horace." She turned to her husband.

"As I was saying," Lord Hallewell joined in, "the soprano was fiery with a gutsy sound. Did you note how each piece grew bolder, more rugged through each movement? I've not heard the likes. I'd enjoy more from this fellow. I can respect his wish to remain anonymous, but I suspect he'll want the credit when more patrons step up. Or should I say *she*?" His lordship waggled his bushy brows at Charlotte.

Charlotte tittered and said, "The composer is a *he*, and yes, I hope he will tie his name to the works before long. Are you interested in a private performance to hear other pieces, or even having the music you heard today accompany a party or ball you're hosting? I could arrange it if you should desire." She hoped she didn't sound too pushy, but if she didn't advocate, who would?

The couple eyed each other for a moment before Lady Hallewell replied, "I might be interested in having one piece performed at a party. I prefer dancing, and I'm not confident the music is right for dancing, but I would have a giggle to surprise my guests with one of the sonatas."

"Oh, the composer *does* have a collection ripe for dancing. I chose entirely different selections for this evening, but I could bring you a few of the dances to consider," Charlotte dared.

"Yes, do. I'll come to you so you can give me a taste on that magnificent pianoforte. Would it be too soon to say two days from now?" Lady Hallewell asked.

Plans set, Charlotte removed herself to mingle. While everyone she spoke with recognized the style as eccentric, she didn't hear a single negative critique. She assumed Drake had heard the same, for when she eyed him across the room, his countenance was full of satisfied merriment. Already she could see his public mask slipping, The Composer emerging as his confidence increased.

The only person in the room who frowned was the dowager duchess. Frankly, Charlotte was shocked to see Mama Catherine. Her mother-in-law had made a point by not attending the musical performances, and it had been assumed by both Charlotte and Drake she would not attend any portion of the soirée. And yet there stood Mama Catherine. Charlotte's pulse raced. Could this be a good thing? Could, despite the frown, Mama Catherine be ready to recognize her son's talents and abandon the bad memories musical affiliation inspired? Charlotte could only hope. At the very least, her mother-in-law could see what a splendid job Charlotte had done in arranging the event, marking, she hoped, the finale of her tutelage and thus the departure of the dowager duchess to the dower house, ready to relinquish her post to an accomplished new duchess.

After all, Charlotte labeled the soirée a marked success. Nothing could ruin this night, not for her or Drake. Accolades poured in for the composer and hosts.

The soirée would extend into the late hours, all guests who were not already staying from their attendance to the shooting party were invited to remain for the evening. Most were delighted, some bowed their apologies. The prince was among the latter and would not be taking advantage of the State Rooms. He had confessed to evening plans elsewhere, although he admitted his departure could be delayed as long as necessary—Charlotte hoped this didn't mean he would monopolize Drake's attention into the wee hours, not after the strain the event would put on Drake's nerves.

They would both need to relax after this. As much as she enjoyed hosting her first party, she wanted her home to herself again. Thankfully, all guests, shooting partiers included, would leave in the morning. Charlotte was tempted to cartwheel through the long galleries in her morning gown to celebrate their departure once the final carriage was seen on its way.

"A disgrace to the Crown, if you ask me." A solitary voice rang out above the din.

Charlotte followed the sound to see Lord Stroud, one of Mary's former suitors, standing at the refreshment table with several other gentlemen. His quizzing glass was raised but did not reach his eye. He tipped his wine glass to his lips, seemingly unaware he was the sudden center of attention. Foamy white spittle gathered at the corners of his mouth, his balding hairline gleaming in the candlelight.

A hush fell over the room. He spoke only to those around him, but no one could mistake his words, not when he trumpeted them with *forte*, progressing into *forzando*.

"I hear she's so frigid he still visits the Waller estate regularly, and we can all guess what goes on there. Like father, like son, I always say. Everyone knows the old man was a back-gammon player, favoring the old windward passage, as they say. If our evening entertainment isn't proof enough he's a devout sodomite, I'll eat my best hat." The man guffawed over his wine glass before adding, "Next time I know he's visiting the Waller house of sin, I'll pay a call to his ice duchess and thaw her properly."

Charlotte felt the blood drain from her body.

The room remained so silent, she could hear her own heartbeat.

Drake was a laughingstock. She was a laughingstock. The family was a laughingstock.

Her body trembled. These were the words they all thought but only one man voiced. Charlotte had failed everyone. She had caused this. This was her fault. She was party to the realization of Drake's worst fear, of her mother-in-law's worst fear. His father's name was dragged through the mud. His name was dragged through the mud. If she could sink into the floor, she would.

There was only one thing to do: draw her shoulders back, raise her chin, and act with poise and grace to mollify the situation. She paid one last glance to Lord Stroud. He caught her eyes and raised his glass to her.

The best course of action was to pretend he had not spoken. She could smooth over the humiliation with a smile and a laugh. No one would be indecorous enough to acknowledge his words, surely, but if they did, if they all joined in the mockery, she would feign poor hearing and continue to smile.

From her peripheral, she caught sight of Drake moving across the room with determined strides. It was most definitely Drake, not The Composer, all signs of the latter vanquished behind the steel mask of the duke.

Please, don't make this worse, she willed him silently. *Please, don't react. Please, don't be reckless. This isn't you. You're my talented composer, not an impulsive rogue.*

Horror struck, she watched Drake trek across the room, and in one swift motion, without breaking stride, pull back his fist and plant a facer right into the man's tipped wine glass, crushing it against Lord Stroud's face and sending him flying into the refreshment table. While the table broke his lordship's fall, it did not keep the beverages and food from tumbling onto his head when he slid to the floor.

Chapter 25

C haos erupted around her when Lord Stroud removed his hand from his face to reveal a blood drenched mouth.

"My toof! You broke my bloody toof!" he shouted, waving his blood-covered hand.

The Prince of Wales walked over to stand next to Drake, and while staring down at the fallen man, he boomed for all to hear, "I say, you should watch where you're walking. Look what a mess you've made by tripping over the table linen. You must be terribly embarrassed. Here, allow my footmen to help you."

Not but a second later, two of the prince's royal footmen appeared and dragged the man from the room.

Charlotte felt roots growing from her feet, securing her to the floor. Unable to break free or move, she stood and gaped. How was she to smooth over this incident now? It had been her own husband to cause the disturbance, humiliating himself and her with it far more than Lord Stroud's words ever could. He'd made a spectacle of them both.

Without sparing another glance to the ruined table, she did the only thing she knew to do — carry on. To the nearest guests, she said with as much detached hauteur as she could muster, "I do hope that poor man will be well."

The blur of faceless guests around her agreed.

One voice said, "Not a party until Lord Stroud trips over table linen after too many tipples."

Another voice joined in. "By Jupiter, the prince called a spade a spade, did he not?"

And yet another, "How embarrassing to be so taken by drink one makes a spectacle of himself in front of royalty. He'll never live this down."

Voices joined in agreement. By the time Charlotte made her way around the room, the story seemed confirmed — Lord Stroud had been so foxed he tripped over his own feet and fell into the table. Witnesses attested to it. No one made mention of Drake's behavior or of Stroud's words.

Charlotte hardly knew what to make of the development. All was not ruined? Drake's reputation was not harmed? The rumors of old would not circulate after all? It seemed too good to be true. Had no one seen what happened, or were they all being polite for her sake, eager to gossip the truth once they left? Despite the good fortune, Lord Stroud's words and his bloodied face imprinted on her so that she heard little else for the remainder of the party. Her fear was that he had spoken what everyone believed. And it was her fault for convincing Drake to bring music into the house and open himself to possible censure. It had been that censure that caused him to react violently, nothing like her tender composer.

She could not quite meet his or Mama Catherine's eyes after the soirée resumed, so afraid to see in their gazes the repercussions, if not with the partygoers than within themselves, their fears realized, and all Charlotte's fault.

After the remaining guests retired, Charlotte returned to the empty drawing room to instruct Mr. Taylor to unroll the rugs and rearrange to its usual state. Drake promised to join her shortly, as he had invited the prince for a drink in the billiard room. When Charlotte walked into the Red Drawing Room, she found Catherine waiting for her rather than Mr. Taylor or any of the staff.

"A disgrace," Catherine said as Charlotte approached. "This was an insult to the Royal Family. The prince will report to the King and Queen of what a shamble has become of this dukedom. A disgrace to the whole family, our line, and the title. All my work these many years has come to nothing. We'll never recover from this scandal."

Charlotte took a deep, calming breath, prepared to defend herself, but unsure what to say when the woman was right. She wanted to defend the debut and Drake's part in it, placing blame only on her not taking better care with the guest list — although, in defense of that, Lord Stroud had been someone else's guest, not someone she had intentionally invited. Be that as it may, she should have seen to it that no one attended unless they were explicitly on the invitation list. Her failing, not that of the soirée or of Drake. And yet, she couldn't defend herself on this point because, in truth, if she hadn't had this harebrained scheme, she wouldn't have needed so exclusive of a guest list. That ought to have given her pause. She should have listened to Drake. This was her fault and a scandal they might not recover from, just as Mama Catherine said.

Before Charlotte could speak in either agreement or defense, her mother-in-law continued with a reverberating thump of her cane. "A duchess should act with poise and grace, considering the Crown in all behaviors and decisions. We represent the Crown in all we do. This whole event rang of self-indulgence and ineptitude. You have spit on my legacy."

Catherine let the words sink in until Charlotte opened her mouth to speak. Cutting her off, Catherine said, "I should have known from the start you were impudent. Do you enjoy lowering yourself? Do you in any way understand your place, your duty as a duchess? Have you considered your position when making any decision related to the household? You are no longer the lowly daughter of a tin mine owner, yet you consistently act like it."

Charlotte saw in the dowager duchess' piercing eyes pure betrayal. Would this be the same betrayal she would find in Drake's eyes once they met in private? Her heart broke at the thought. She had single-handedly seen to their fears being realized. All Mama Catherine's work to undo her husband's reputation...all Drake's work to build the antithesis of his father's reputation...and what had she done? Brought it all back into the house with a single party.

"How dare you expose my son to this, you insolent girl." Her Grace snarled, teeth bared. "This is what music does. Music stirs emotion and confusion when there ought not be any. Music impassions, turning sense into sensibility, sparks violence, makes hedonistic heathens of otherwise good people. I have seen to it my son would not be exposed to this. I have seen to it our name would not be associated with this. Yet you expose us to sin and scandal. All I have done, hoping to pass on my wisdom so Annick would remain prosperous and in good repute, and this is how you repay me, how you repay my son for marrying you. I have led this dukedom since I was sixteen, and I will not see it or my family destroyed by the likes of you."

Charlotte felt sick. If she didn't leave soon, she would be sick in front of Mama Catherine, sick all over the drawing room floor.

Catherine beat her cane against the floor, her usual hauteur slipping. "You slap my rules in my face, turning my drawing room into a den of hedonism, inviting these *artists* into my home and performing that *rubbish*. You have tainted everything."

The dowager duchess' austere veneer cracked and peeled, her eyes red-rimmed and watery. Her shoulders rounded as she leaned heavily on her cane, her breathing labored and punctuated by choked sobs. Charlotte was torn. Part of her wanted to run from Lyonn Manor, a failure, not only to herself but to her family, to her husband. The other part wanted to embrace her mother-in-law; for all the hideous words she shared, all the anger she lashed, it was said out of the pain that Charlotte had caused.

With a voice that cracked and quivered, Catherine continued, "You couldn't even keep your perversity to yourself. Before the guests, you engaged in a vulgar display on stage, your hands and arms entwined with my son's to play sentimental muck on the piano. Distasteful. Disgusting. The music, the perversion, the ungenteel behavior, all ruining what I have devoted my life to building. Our reputation, my reputation, my son's reputation, *ruined*. You have disgraced and shamed this family."

Before she could say more, Charlotte ran from the room. She ran until she reached her own bedchamber, locking behind her both the door to the adjacent sitting room and to the corridor. She never wanted to see Catherine or Drake again, not after bringing such shame to the family.

Chapter 26

The Prince of Wales, for all his talk of having evening plans elsewhere, stayed into the wee hours, knocking balls in the billiard room and depleting Drake's brandy. Not that Drake resented the prince staying overlong or enjoying a friendly evening inebriation, but he was exhausted from the strain of his music being exposed, chagrined about the cause of his bruised and cut knuckles, and eager to go to Charlotte, who would likely have choice words for his impulsive action, which fairly ruined the party she had painstakingly prepared for him. Alas, he did his duty and entertained the prince, along with a few other gentlemen who had joined them after all others had retired.

By the time Drake stumbled his way to his bedchamber, early morning light shone through a part in the curtains. Whatever temptation he felt to join Charlotte in her room was doused by the tilt of the floor, the stench of drink, a pounding headache, and sheer fatigue. His wobbly thoughts before drifting to sleep—fully clothed, he was to discover when he awoke—were how empty his arms felt without her and how heavy his heart not to wish her a good night, thank her, or apologize. Whatever he might have thought past that was lost to incoherence and a resounding snore.

By the time Drake rose for the day, it was well past noon. He grimaced at his mirror. Cruel reflection. Did it not have the courtesy to lie? At the very least it could veil the truth with a solitary compliment, perhaps a reminder of his noble profile, always a favorite. Alas, all it had to say was that Drake's eyes were bloodshot and sunken into shadows and his hair unruly in all the wrong ways as his pomade had reshaped one side to look remarkably like the inverse of his pillow. He smacked parched lips, cringing at the taste of stale drink. He was too old for this. Evenings with twenty-something-year-old princes were simply not his style anymore.

Best ring for the valet, old boy. Bart would make him a new man in no time. He rubbed a hand against the overgrowth of stubble on his cheek. Yes, a shave, a bath, a hearty scrub to the teeth, all would make him right as rain and ready to greet the day, whatever the time. First order of business, once he was presentable, was to seek out Charlotte. Had any of the guests lingered, or did the family have the house to themselves? He hoped the later. With a groan against his pulsing temples, he pulled the bellrope.

Throughout his readying for the day, which included a cup of black coffee and heavily buttered toast, he focused on clearing his head, sobering, and reflecting on the soirée, namely his cringeworthy behavior. Aside from the slip in decorum, which the prince smoothed over—one of the primary reasons Drake felt obligated to entertain him for the better part of the evening—the debut had gone splendidly, more than splendidly. He could laugh aloud to think how nervous he had been. Nothing but compliments and curiosities greeted his ears at the conclusion of the performances, everyone vying to know the identity of the composer, how they might feature the music at their own parties, and how they might go about becoming patrons. This had been a dream come true.

The only upset of the evening had been his reckless reaction to Lord Stroud. It could have ended badly, but, again, thanks to the prince, it had not. That said, he suspected Charlotte would be most aggrieved by his actions. He could hear her now, whining about his being *Drake* rather than *The Composer*. Much to the dismay of his valet, he chuckled during the shave. Was it unusual to look forward to hearing one's wife *whine*? He rather liked it. One smile would hush her heartache, one of his dimpled smiles. Yes, that was the ticket. Not that he wasn't ashamed by his behavior, more in keeping with a green lad born on the wrong side of the blanket than a mature duke, but one ought not to let such unpleasantness weigh about the shoulders—could ruin good posture.

What he was eager to share with Charlotte, after she finished whining and scolding, of course, was his epiphany during the party. Could one call it an epiphany? Well, why not? It was *his* thought, so he could call it whatever he liked. Epiphany would do. Sounded grander that way.

The thing of it was, however much Lord Stroud's words had stung, Drake had realized his greatest fear was utter hogwash. For so long he had feared society's censure, but when the moment came, the world didn't end, the room didn't buzz with gossip, and he wasn't all that bothered. He came face-to-face with

mention of the old scandal, along with new and more
personal accusations, and none of it bothered him.

What upset him into action was how Stroud's
words affected the people he cared about.

For all her stoicism, his mother had been in tat-
ters. He'd never in his life seen her so visibly shaken,
even if he was the only one who would recognize his
mother's change in expression. His only wish would
have been for her to remain on the opposite side of
the house, never to have heard Stroud's silliness. If
it made her feel better, Mother could place blame on
him for hosting the soirée. He could shoulder that
blame for her if it would help. For upsetting Drake's
mother, Lord Stroud deserved a bloodied face. His
regret wasn't punching Stroud rather not going to his
mother afterwards. Instead, he had paid loyalty to
the prince, not leaving his side for the remainder of
the evening. His mother had needed him. She would
have lashed out, but he would have let her, offering
her solace by his silent support. Alas.

His mother wasn't the only reason Stroud was
now missing a tooth. The man had insulted Charlotte.
Drake worried about any upset Charlotte might feel
for being publicly insulted. When he had taken her
measure after the incident, she had shown no signs
of anger or humiliation or otherwise. She had epito-
mized poise. Looks could deceive, though. Knowing
Charlotte, rather than be upset about Stroud's insults,
she would feel responsible for the blemish, from
Stroud's words to Drake's reaction, all because of her
insistence to host the debut. By her logic, she would
feel to blame for resurrecting the old scandal, which
was just as much hogwash as his fears had been. He

couldn't wait to see her so he could tell her just that — after she whined about his bad behavior, of course.

Ah, the scandal. The remembrance of his father was inevitable. If Lord Stroud hadn't said it, someone else would have. And what of it? Drake was a different person than his father, and his music was worth recognition. After a lifetime of fearing those very accusations, he simply didn't care. What he cared about was his family.

A knock at his dressing room door interrupted Drake's thoughts and Bart's shaving.

His grin was lost on the butler. Drat. He had hoped it was Charlotte.

Mr. Taylor bowed. "Someone named Mr. Kingston has requested an audience, Your Grace. Shall I tell him you're from home or see him into the Red Drawing Room?" Mr. Taylor asked.

Drake sighed. So much for a peaceful day. "See him to my study when I ring, Taylor."

The butler bowed and left.

Drake hadn't expected callers today, but on second thought, it seemed foolish not to. Could this be an interested party seeking to learn more about the compositions? The purpose of the soirée, after all, had been to garner interest in the music.

By the time he finished dressing, went to his study, and rang for Mr. Taylor, Drake had worked himself into an excited fervor over the possibility of talking about music.

Should he confess he composed the pieces or remain anonymous until a few more performances had been requested by third parties? Should he name a price for each request or offer the music as a gift?

He certainly didn't need the money, but he did want the recognition — people might be leery about gifts. The purpose of patrons when it came to composing music was for composers to earn a living, something Drake did not need or want, but supplying music *gratis* could prove tricky. Where was Charlotte when he needed her? He couldn't make these decisions without her. He wouldn't make them without her.

Mr. Kingston, an older gent with a wreath of hair around a bare crown, waddled into the room on the butler's introduction, his girth knocking aside one of the chairs in the sitting area. Drake stood to greet him with a dashing smile.

"Welcome to my home, Mr. Kingston. Would you please be seated?" Drake waved a hand at the chair in front of his desk.

He would have to plan this better for the future. Maybe he should talk to potential patrons in the sitting area instead of with a desk separating them. The desk made everything seem so impersonal. Next time, he could have brandy at the ready. Depending on the guest, perhaps an aged Scotch instead, though he didn't care for the flavor. Charlotte would know what to do.

"I'll not mince words, Your Grace. I'm here on official business to request an apology on behalf of Lord Stroud." Mr. Kingston huffed.

Drake's smile froze as he studied Mr. Kingston, and then it broadened into a laugh. "You're quite the jester."

"I am not. Lord Stroud requests a written apology for your ungentlemanly behavior. If you weren't a peer, he would take you to court. As it is, you have two days in which to comply with an apology. I will arrive at this time in two days to collect." Mr. Kingston coughed at Drake's continued laughter.

Straightening to his full height, Drake's smile slipped into a smirk. "Let me get this straight." He fluffed the lace at his wrist, a nobleman who was already bored with the conversation. "*He* wants *me* to apologize, when it was *he* who insulted my family. Shouldn't *he* be the one writing an apology?"

"Lord Stroud demands an apology for your striking him. Such behavior is uncouth and will not be tolerated by a *true* gentleman." Mr. Kingston puffed out his chest. "Issue your apology or be prepared for the consequences," he threatened, clearly not intimidated by Drake's title or lace.

"And what, pray tell, will be those consequences? Is he going to besmirch my name?" He followed the question with his noblest and snidest chortle before eyeing the clock, as though he had far more pressing matters to attend to. "I give you my answer now, an emphatic *no*." Drake enunciated his words, increasingly annoyed that the lout dared to demand an apology when Stroud deserved a far more ruthless thrashing than a single strike.

Mr. Kingston didn't hesitate. "I have been tasked with providing the consequences should your answer be displeasing to his lordship. You, sir, are hereby challenged to a duel. Name your second and your weapon, and I will arrange all details with your second. If you should need time in which to consider those two, I will return at the end of the predetermined two days for the name of your second and the weapon of choice."

Good Lord!

Drake wasn't certain if he should laugh or rage. This was serious business. Lord Stroud hadn't been joking with his request for an apology. Drake resented the churl for blackening an otherwise promising day.

Pulling out a bit of scrap paper, he wet his quill and wrote Winston's information. Not wanting to waste his sanding on this nonsense, he rolled the ink with a blotter to dry it. "Here. The name and address of my second. The weapon will be the sabre. Good day." He tossed the paper for the man to catch and walked out, leaving him to Mr. Taylor.

He shouldn't have been so hasty. Winston hadn't yet agreed to be his second. Drake should have taken the request for an apology more seriously, given it more thought. He stormed to the stables for his horse, determined to beat Mr. Kingston to Winston before his friend disowned him.

Several hours later, he returned to Lyonn Manor, fit to be tied. Winston hadn't hesitated in agreeing to be his second or in working out the details with Mr. Kingston, and even found the whole affair a lark. Two Corinthians against aged, corpulent fools, he'd said. But Drake wasn't laughing. As confident as he felt with a sabre, he never flirted with danger or with situations that might provoke a duel. A churl's lost tooth hardly warranted putting Drake's life on the line, much less the life of his second, for that wasn't a fate Drake wanted on his conscience.

He would have found such circumstances a grand adventure at one point in his life, but now he had a bright future ahead with the woman he loved. He had plans for his music, plans for the estate, plans for his sister's marriage, and plans for children should he be blessed with any. Risking his life wasn't on his task list. With his honor and his family's honor now on the line, he had no choice. One could *not* refuse a duel if challenged.

It had been his own doing. He knew better than to strike another gentleman, especially in front of others, but at the time he had felt justified. He still felt justified. In fact, he would do it again. But a duel? Really? He scoffed to the empty gallery as he made his way back to his study.

When he opened the door, ready to pound out a tune on the defenseless harpsichord, he came face-to-face with his mother. Any thought he might have had to approach and embrace her, apologize for any discomfort she felt over Stroud's words, fled at her expression, at the cane she raised and pointed at him like an accusing finger. So, it was to be like that.

With a curse, he crossed the room, tossing his hat on a chair, which missed and fell to the floor. He didn't care.

He pulled out his desk chair and sat with a grunt, eager to put the desk between the two of them. The last person he wanted to see was Her Grace The Righteous Disciplinarian, not when he had been hoping to seek her out — after talking with Charlotte first — to offer sympathy to His Mother The Misunderstood Matriarch. Hadn't he already decided she could blame him if she wanted? Yes, he had. That was before Mr. Kingston's visit. That was also before she shook her cane at him with narrowed gaze. Deep sigh.

As much as he wanted to let her blame him, anything to help her feel better, he didn't want to hear it now.

"*You*," she began, "are irresponsible and shame me with your behavior. I can only blame your wife for your common behavior. This is her fault. She is to blame. She is a disgrace to all of Annick. If you had married someone of our ilk, none of this would have happened."

Normally, it would have taken more than that to set him off, especially when he knew she was upset and deflecting, but the words about Charlotte struck the wrong chord. Blame *him*, but not his wife.

He raised a staying hand before his mother could say more. Crossing his ankle over the opposite knee, he leaned his chair back onto two legs, rested his elbows on the armrests, and steepled his fingers, locking eyes with hers.

"I am humbly sorry for the hurt I know you feel from last night, but I will not have you blame my wife for *anything*. The hurt you feel should be aimed at the person who made you feel that way—Lord Stroud. Nothing my wife nor I have done has caused your pain. Before you blame the music, know I will not stand for it. For too long I have held my tongue. If you want to discuss Father or if you want to express your hurt, I'm here. If you have come to sling insults at my wife or at me, then our conversation is over before it has begun."

She fumed, gripping her cane until her knuckles turned white.

Drake nodded, understanding she only wanted to play the blame game. "Your place is in the dower house, and you will remove there by the end of the week." He paused only long enough to let the words sink in, and then he continued, "From this point forward, Charlotte is irreproachable, answerable only to me. There is to be only one mistress of Lyonn Manor, and that mistress is my wife. You've done your duty by preparing her for the role. You may continue to do so from the dower house, if it should be her wish; otherwise, I consider her training complete."

He waited for her response. Minutes ticked by while their eyes remained locked. For the first time in his life, his mother was speechless. He only regretted this conversation had not been one of emotional healing.

Dropping the legs of his chair, he stood and leaned his hands against his desk. "For ten years, I have allowed you to continue to rule this house with an iron fist because it suited us both. I then allowed you to continue your reign when I brought home the new Duchess of Annick because I believed it would suit all of us. It no longer suits. I am grateful for all you have done, Mother, but your reproach is unpardonable, regardless of your reasons. Nothing will ever be perfect enough for you because no one is as perfect as you. I will not allow you to hurt my wife so inexcusably, your blame of her as tasteless as Stroud's insults. Please understand that as harsh as my words are now, I mean no disrespect and want you to know that as your son, I'm here to support any pain you must be feeling. I will not, however, have you deflect that pain to Charlotte."

Catherine stared down her son. Without a word, she about-faced and thumped out of the study.

Drake exhaled and slumped into his chair. He'd spoken too harshly. He knew his mother was hurting inside yet he'd kicked her out of the house.

No, no, he needed to stop defending her behavior. Her pain was no cause to lash out at others. No, he'd done the right thing. There may not be a way for him to repair his relationship with his mother when she shut out everyone, especially him, but once she removed to the dower house, he would make it a mission to strengthen their relationship, to wear down her resolve and soften her edges, if it could be done.

Gah. He wanted Charlotte. He wanted to wrap his arms around her waist and rest his head against her bosom. She'd know what to do about the muck of the day. He pulled the bellrope.

Within moments, Mr. Taylor entered the study.

"Bring Her Grace to the study, Taylor," Drake instructed.

On second thought, perhaps he ought to go to her. No, it would be better if they spoke in the music room, a place of comfort and privacy. They had so much to share at this point, he should request a tray, as well. Yes, that would be just the thing.

"Pardon, Your Grace, but Her Grace is from home," answered the butler.

"From home? Where is she?"

"She's moved out, Your Grace." The corners of the butler's lips twitched.

"I beg your pardon." Drake wheezed a single laugh. "I'm afraid I misheard you. For a moment, I thought you said she moved out of Lyonn Manor."

"You did not mishear, Your Grace. Her Grace has moved to the dower house."

"And you didn't see fit to tell me?" Drake thundered.

"Your Grace didn't ask." The butler bowed and waited.

Of all the impertinent...

"Be gone before I dismiss you without a character." Drake punched the desk.

With a wince, he made a mental note to stop punching objects or he wouldn't have any hands left with which to duel. The knuckles on one hand were already bruised and cut from the wine glass and Lord Stroud's teeth. He flexed the stiff fingers and hoped the wounds wouldn't interfere with the agility of his sword hand. At least the wounds looked worse than they felt.

Glum, Drake stared unfocused at his knuckles.

The dower house.

Why the devil would she move to the dower house? The soirée had only been that evening. When had she left? But no, who cared. *Why* was the most pressing matter.

His ungentlemanly and quite public behavior would have certainly embarrassed her, but enough that she would move out? Without even speaking to him about it? Charlotte should have been ripe with a scold for him, not a packed bag. She hadn't even moved out when she thought he had a mistress, although she had been terribly close. Had Lord Stroud's rubbish about her frigidity upset her so much? She should know by now Drake found her to be the most sensual woman in the world, not to mention Drake had already publicly defended her for the slight.

Time for a walk, he decided. A walk should help clear his thoughts, a determined walk to the dower house.

Chapter 27

Two miles west, his feet brought him to the Palladian mansion renovated especially for the grandmother he had never met. He lumbered to the front door and struck the knocker purposefully, the sound echoing into the hall beyond.

While waiting, he envisioned tossing Charlotte over his shoulder and carrying her back to the manor. Or maybe she would fling open the door, embrace him with a kiss.

Impatient to see Charlotte, he struck the knocker again and followed that with a hard pounding against the wood.

"Charlotte?" he questioned the door. "What's happened? Was it me? Was it Stroud? Was it my mother?"

He waited. Silence.

An eternity passed within the few empty minutes. Feeling his front pocket, he cursed at having left his snuffbox on the desk. That morning, he'd decided it was time to tuck the treasured box out of ready reach. It'd been a necessity, really, given his overuse at the soirée and subsequent headache. Now, he anguished of his decision. He wanted a pinch.

Drake stepped back and looked at the windows along the first story. Would he cut a romantic figure by ascending on a rope? Blast. Nothing on which to hang the rope. No rope on hand either. Scale the wall? A serenade, perhaps? Sing for her attention? *Be practical, old boy*. He eyed the windows on the ground floor instead.

With waning hope, he descended the front steps. Dodging the hedges in the flowerbed, he peered into a window, swearing he saw a flash of pink.

"Charlotte?" he questioned the window before tapping on the glass.

He had worried she would be upset with his behavior, but he never thought she'd be *this* upset. Just wait until she learned he'd got himself caught up in a duel. All he'd wanted to do was defend her; was that so bad? The actions were reckless, but the intention was heartfelt. Right?

He trudged back to the portico and perched on the steps, twining his tricorn in his hands. Red and orange leaved oak trees sang a rustling tune next to silent cedars as the crisp autumn wind whipped through the branches.

"Well, Charlotte, I'm not leaving," he said loudly enough to be heard from the front hall, if indeed that was where she sprinted when she caught him peeking through the window. "I'm going to sit here and talk to you through the door and hope my words aren't wasted."

With a shaky breath, he launched into the speech he'd hastily composed during the walk from the manor to the house. "I *think* you think the soirée was a failure, but it wasn't. If you could have seen it through my eyes, you'd feel differently. Heavens, Charlotte, you were perfect. You *are* perfect. The soirée was perfect. You hosted with the charm and dignity my mother has never possessed. You even recovered the party from my blunder. I suppose that's why I'm talking through a door now. My blunder. I know Stroud embarrassed you, and I know I embarrassed you, and I'm sorry on behalf of both, but don't take the events of the evening to heart, for the only person who failed was me. I shouldn't have reacted so hastily."

He leaned his elbows against his thighs, tricorn waving between his knees. "I'm ashamed of my behavior, but I can only say that I did it in defense of your honor and that of my family. I acted out of blind fury and, dare I say, love. I'm sorry I acted rashly, but this is who I am, Charlotte. I need you to understand this. I'm a rash man who acts before I think. Nothing will change that. When I asked you to love all of me, not part of me, I meant it. You can't love the composer but hate the reckless fool, not when they're both me."

Leaning back onto his hands, he scowled at the landscape. The brightness of the day juxtaposed his inner turmoil. He felt downright dismal, yet the sun shone brightly overhead, and the thrushes conspired against him, warbling gaily from the trees.

He shivered from the chill of the wind, the portico pediment blocking the warmth of the sun. Soon, all of Northumberland would be shrouded in a cloud of winter.

With a glance over his shoulder at the sealed door, he continued, "I need you to know that I make terrible decisions. I'm impulsive. I behave solely on emotion. I need *your* logic and attention to detail, your knack for planning to balance my life and help me make the right decisions. While I am sorry I embarrassed you, I can't promise I won't do it again if faced with a similar situation. As sorry as I am, this is me. If you can't love me for all my irrational impulsivity, well, it's not really loving me, is it? I'm a passionate man. I'm arrogant, wretchedly so. I'm spontaneous. But this is who I am. You can't only love the parts of me you like, the tender bits you see when we're alone together. The tenderness is only for you. You must love all of me, even the parts you don't like."

Retrieving his handkerchief from his coat pocket, he shined the tips of his shoes. There. Better. He tucked the dirty kerchief back in place, then rested his chin in his open palm.

"I feel like an actor in a play making my monologue." He laughed dryly. "Although if you're not listening, I suppose it's a soliloquy. Oh, Charlotte, I hope you're listening."

A lone cloud passed overhead, sweeping a frosty breeze through the front columns and chilling him beneath his coat. He shivered.

"I had an epiphany, you know. I've been champing at the bit to tell you, but the day got ahead of me, and now this. In short, I realized I didn't care what people thought as long as I knew the truth. There's no point in trying to impress anyone, you see. All the hiding I've done in my life, all the reputation building, it's all been to avoid the censure of the past, but none of it matters." He rubbed the back of his neck, his knuckles smarting. "The aristocracy is made up of nothing but shallow and conceited people who have done nothing more with their lives than inherit a title. Who cares what they think? I hope you won't take my brashness to heart, Charlotte, or hold it against me too long. If you can get past caring what they think, then I've not really embarrassed you, have I?" His laugh sounded hollow to his own ears. "You outrank all of them anyway. The soirée was perfect even with the blunder, in my opinion. Besides, perfection is a lark. Just look at my mother. She's so obsessed with perfection she's miserable that nothing and no one is ever perfect. Please, don't turn into my mother. Let's enjoy the imperfections of life."

As a last-ditch effort, he tried the knocker again, not that he thought she would open the door.

"Don't you believe in happily ever afters?" Drake pressed his forehead against the cold wood of the door.

Speaking more softly than before, talking more to himself than to the front hall beyond, he said, "I do. I never did before, but I do now. I believe in happily ever afters, but I don't think they turn out how we expect. It's not a single moment that determines life as happy from this moment forward. We must work at the happy part when times are tough, but we know we'll always be together and able to resolve any conflict if we work as a team. You're my happy ever after, Charlotte. My world rises and sets on you. You're my horizon. As long as I'm with you, I'm invincible. I'm desperately sorry that I embarrassed you at the party. Please, forgive me and tell me you believe in us. Tell me our life will be happy no matter the odds because we will face the trials together. Don't you love me, Charlotte? Just a bit? Enough? Even a little?"

Silence answered louder than words. Defeated, the pit of his stomach settling into his shoes, he slumped down the steps to walk back to the manor.

Charlotte's forehead pressed against the inside of the front door, her hand on the handle. Encouraged after a deep breath, she opened the door, dashing out onto the portico.

"Drake!" she cried.

He pivoted to face her, his expression one of wistful surprise.

She opened her mouth to speak, to explain, to apologize, to *something*, but all she could do was stutter a sob before she raced down the steps to throw her arms around his neck. His arms came around her with a breath-stealing tightness. The warmth of his breath against her forehead, just below where he rested his cheek, spilled her brimming tears. What a fool she had been.

Into his neckcloth, she said, "I love you more than a bit. But only the teensiest more."

With the rumble of a chuckle, he urged her to come with him into the dower house, his arms not leaving her shoulders, only loosening enough for her to turn and walk with him. He took her into the front parlor before ringing the bellpull.

What she had learned in her brief hours at the dower house was that it was always staffed with a skeleton crew. She had been relieved at the discovery, to be honest, for her decision had been so hasty, she had half expected to arrive to a dusty and locked house either empty of furniture or with the bare necessities covered by Holland covers. Thankfully, that had not been the case.

Only after a maid — who did not bat an eyelash at the duke and duchess requesting tea in the dower house's parlor quite out of the blue — had brought a tray did Drake release his hold on Charlotte. Even then, he remained close enough for their knees to touch. With a sniffle, Charlotte steeped the tea leaves.

He said not a word. The personification of patience. Fleetingly, she thought of him as The Composer, for *he* was always patient and understanding, but the curious thing was, when she looked at him, she saw neither her composer nor the rogue, rather she saw her duke charming, perfect in his imperfections. How had she ever seen him as two different personas? He was simply *himself.*

She giggled. When she glanced at him from beneath her eyelashes to see him arching a questioning brow, she giggled more. Oh good. The tea was ready. Pouring them each a cup, she added a dab of milk, then handed him the steaming elixir.

"I'm not angry at you," she said at last, toying with the handle of her teacup. "I'm angry at *me*. I convinced myself you would be so distraught over what Lord Stroud said that you would hate me. I thought it better for everyone to remove myself before making things worse. *I* was the cause of all that went wrong. Had I not hosted the soirée in the first place, you wouldn't have needed to defend with fisticuffs. It was me who insisted your music be heard, me who desperately wanted everyone to see your tenderness and sentimentality as well as your talent as a musician, me who wanted to prove to Mama Catherine I was the perfect hostess, me…well, you get the idea. I wanted to go to you, but then feared my presence would upset you more. I made the family a laughingstock, Drake. Your father's name was tarnished, all because of me."

She wanted to shed more tears, but instead she giggled again.

Drake's brow arched higher. "As poetically as you're waxing, my love, I must enquire what's so funny if you're as villainous as you claim."

With another chortle, she said, "You should be ashamed of me."

"Hmm. Yes, I can see why that's a laughing matter."

"I'm laughing because you're *not* ashamed of me. You came here to apologize to me when *I'm* the one at fault. Don't you see? I'm a silly nit because I made all these false assumptions about how I thought you would feel, when none of it was true. When I saw how badly my choices had hurt Mama Catherine, I just knew you would be inconsolable."

"Because I'm so often inconsolable."

She swatted at his arm. "Make light of it now if you will, but I was overcome, I tell you. Mama Catherine was quite undone, and it was my fault to have resurrected the old demons. I believed I had betrayed you both. Just as you once said, one seed of doubt, one rumor could crumble us all with scandal."

He waved his free hand, setting his teacup and saucer on the tray. Only after taking her hands between his did he say with a grimace, "You keep mentioning Mother. I'm afraid to ask."

Charlotte tugged at her bottom lip with her teeth. "She shared with me how much my betrayal hurt her and the family, including the prince."

"I bet she did." Drake sighed, rubbing her hand between his. "Will you believe me when I say you betrayed no one? You are the most courageous woman I know. All my mother and I have done is hide behind façades, hers marble and mine a domino. Then you arrive and do all in your power to help us be ourselves. The only betrayal is us to ourselves, and we are the sole ones to shoulder that blame. As for the prince, well, he was thoroughly entertained and will likely inundate us with countless invitations that we will gracefully decline because I'm too old to stay awake past my bedtime."

Of all the responses Charlotte wanted to make, his jest did the trick of having her laugh instead of saying any of them.

One glance at their hands entwined shook the laughter from her lips. "Your knuckles!"

Drake groaned. "They hurt so terribly, I may not make it back to the manor without assistance. I'm positive I'll need to lie in the rest of the day. If you don't nurse me back to health, I may expire from the pain."

With a squint she said, "They look worse than they feel, I take it? Well, to be safe, since I can't have you expiring *yet*, I suggest we return home. As lovely as the dower house is and as kind as the staff, I miss my bird, my bed, and you. I could hardly sleep last night—a fox screamed every time I drifted to sleep! It was ghastly."

"Never fear, I'll protect you, my fair lady. But first, are you going to eat these biscuits, or shall I?"

Not long into the next day did Charlotte receive a caller. She had been on her way to root out Mama Catherine for a much-needed talk when Mr. Taylor informed her he had seen Lady Hallewell to the Grey Parlor and would have a tray sent directly.

"What a pleasant surprise," Charlotte said, smiling politely as she prepared their tea.

With any luck, her eyes had recovered from their red-rimmed and puffy state from the morning prior. So distracted by Drake, and then with her plans of what to say to Mama Catherine, she had not spared her mirror so much as a glance since returning to Lyonn Manor.

"I should hope it isn't a surprise," Lady Hallewell said with a chortle. "We arranged to meet in two days, didn't we? So that I might hear the dance music you promised. Don't tell me you forgot," she admonished, a hand to her bosom.

"Oh, no, I'm afraid I did," Charlotte confessed, bringing her teacup to her lips. "All has been settled, but I have no qualms in sharing with you, since we have become dear friends, that I was utterly distraught after the soirée, so much so I forgot we were to meet. I do hope you'll forgive me, as it won't interfere with the music I promised."

Despite an age difference, she did consider Lady Hallewell a friend and hoped to deepen the friendship as they got to know each other better.

"Distraught? Whatever for? The soirée was a complete success, and I must commend you for hosting the first and only enjoyable party that has ever been held at Lyonn Manor. Your mother-in-law's parties are always dreadful bores, as anyone will tell you." She tasted her tea, thought for a moment, then said conspiratorially, "I don't suppose you have any sherry? No, no, forget I asked. Let's enjoy the tea."

"I could ring for sherry, if you'd prefer." Charlotte moved from her seat, but Lady Hallewell shook her head. Once settled, Charlotte continued, "If you'll permit me to speak candidly, however indelicate the subject, I'll admit I was distraught over the words said about His Grace's father. The, er, brawl didn't mitigate the situation either. I was afraid the soirée, and especially the music, was sullied beyond repair. You can understand my distress, my lady."

"Edwina. Call me Edwina. I believe we're past formalities, don't you?" She patted Charlotte's hand.

Charlotte said with a smile, "On the bright side, Edwina, my soirée will be the height of discussion."

It was strange to make light of what had felt so tragic not twenty-four hours prior. Drake's perpetual cavalier attitude made peculiar sense in hindsight, for what else was there to do in the face of drama and scandal? Wallow in melancholy? Do as she had and run away? No, best to face it with a laugh.

"There's an understatement!" Edwina tittered. "Your mother-in-law has never hosted anything but bland dinner parties with the same pretentious guests. The *beau monde*, and more to the point the aristocracy, does not waste time with bland parties, especially not with officious hostesses. They thrive on gossip for their entertainment, and I'll be the first to say, your soirée produced enough entertainment to flap lips since Lady Thyme eloped with her father's coachman."

"Had you said that to me yesterday, I would have protested that it was the scandal of the year from which we would never recover," Charlotte admitted.

"They're all convinced Lord Stroud tripped over the linen," Edwina said. "It doesn't matter what they saw or heard. Whatever the truth, once guests leave with tongues wagging, they embellish, always to the detriment of the person they don't favor. It would seem you are well liked, dear Charlotte. All I heard during my calls yesterday was how enjoyable your party was and how foxed Lord Stroud must have been to trip and fall headlong into the table. I couldn't possibly repeat the names they've called him and still attend church on Sunday." Edwina clapped her hands in amusement. "They are counting the days until you host another event, hoping desperately that someone else will make a fool of themselves so they have something new about which to gossip." When Edwina recovered from laughing, she added, "If guests ever leave with nothing to gossip about, they'll claim the event a dreadful bore. We're entertainers more than hostesses, you see."

Charlotte drank in every word, elated by all Edwina shared. It was one thing to hear similar sentiments from Drake, quite another from an acquaintance. "I won't deny I'm relieved Lord Stroud's accusations didn't stir the pot. That was a sizable portion of my distress, worry he would spread lies."

"Fiddle faddle! Everyone knows his offer for Lady Mary was rejected. He'd say anything to save face, the old coot."

"But to go so far as to accuse the previous Duke of Annick of being a sinner? That's beyond the pale!"

"It is, is it not? Tells us more about Lord Stroud than the duke, I'd say." Edwina hesitated, running her forefinger around the rim of her cup. "Since we're sharing confessions as friends, allow me to say I never did believe what they used to say about the duke, your father-in-law, that is, not the present duke. I didn't know him, personally, but I met him briefly when Horace and I were courting. His Grace was a man of some magnetism. I don't see how the rumors could be true, but I'd be the last person to know such things."

Charlotte tilted her head with interest. As much as she wanted to know more, not only about the duke but also the scandal that had so shaken Mama Catherine and guided Drake's decisions in life, she did not pose any questions or make any remarks. After all, this was about family, and she refused to gossip about her own family. That did not stop her from listening to whatever Edwina cared to share.

Edwina eyed the portraits above the mantel, the new ones of Charlotte and Drake. "Everyone's delighted about the new duchess who knows how to entertain. Your husband, you must know, is a local favorite, always the life of the party. If it's not impertinent for me to say, I believe the two of you are a perfect match." She sampled a sandwich from the tray. "Mmm. These are delicious. Now, let's talk music. I'm under strict orders from two of my neighbors to invite the mystery composer to their holiday festivities. The festivities will only be *en famille*, but my neighbors have large families. Tell me, is the composer desirous of fame, fortune, or both?"

For the next half hour, they talked of music, complete with a sampling of dances. Charlotte teased she might be able to convince the composer to visit Edwina himself to finalize the arrangements.

By the time Lady Hallewell left, Charlotte was in good spirits, feeling so confident about herself she was more than ready for her conversation with her mother-in-law.

Never could she have anticipated how vulnerable Mama Catherine was beneath the marble façade, as Drake called it. She hated knowing she had any part in hurting Mama Catherine so abominably, but she could not help how someone else felt. The best she could do was apologize and try to understand. Lizbeth had spoken on friendly terms with Mama Catherine during her visit, which sparked courage that Charlotte could do the same.

Before she made it to the conservatory, where she suspected her mother-in-law might be hiding, Mama Catherine turned into the east gallery, intercepting Charlotte.

The startled expression on Catherine's brow told Charlotte she had not expected to be sought out, least of all by her daughter-in-law. It could have been Charlotte's imagination, but she would swear Catherine's eyes darted for an escape.

"Mama Catherine," Charlotte said in greeting, aiming for a welcoming tone, one that might invite conversation, despite their previous interaction being so heated. She nodded in the direction of the conservatory, her hand outstretched in invitation.

Catherine's eyes narrowed. "Is there something you wish to say to me? I am pressed for time and have no wish for an idle tête-à-tête. Whatever you have to say, say it here and now. Be quick about it."

Providence at work to provide a small enough window for Charlotte to speak without losing heart or a missed opportunity for a more personal exchange?

"I first wish to apologize for any emotions you suffered over the behavior of one of my guests. I had hoped we could speak more intimately, but as it is, I'll get to the point." Charlotte took a deep breath and said the most difficult part before her confidence waned under the penetrating glare of the dowager duchess. "Mama Catherine, there is room for but one duchess, and I want to be that person. Since my arrival at Lyonn Manor, I have believed only in my inability to fill your shoes, yet after the time you've spent preparing me for this role, helping me learn all I never could have learned without you, I *know* I'm ready." Charlotte swallowed against the tremble in her voice.

Her mother-in-law raised her eyebrows so high they nearly touched her hairline, but she remained silent, her black eyes looking deep into Charlotte's soul. For five breaths, Charlotte almost lost her nerve to continue. Never had she known Mama Catherine to hold her peace, allowing someone else to drive the conversation. Charlotte had expected interruptions and impediments.

Best not to press one's luck.

With a shaky breath, Charlotte said, "I never knew my mother. My sister took her place, raising me alongside our father. When I arrived here, I hoped to find a warm and loving mother. Instead, I was met with harsh coldness."

The dowager's brows lowered, furrowing, her lips pursing together into a grim line.

Charlotte continued, "Please do not take offense, for I have come to realize that your behavior *is* love. I know you love me as a daughter and have done all in your power to prepare me for success and protect me from failure, just as you have done all these years for Drake. You love him and have wished to protect him. I realize now that all you do, you do out of love, though it's an unusual way of showing love."

She paused in case Catherine wished to contradict her. The dowager remained silent, leaning heavily against her cane.

"We are more alike than you may realize," Charlotte said, "and I admire you and thank you for all you've done. It's time, however, that your children walk on their own, even if we stumble. You must allow us to fail so that we may learn. You can't protect us forever. It is time, Mama Catherine. It's time you move to the dower house, but I do not wish to lose your guidance as I grow into a duchess you'll be proud of. I would be honored to continue our daily luncheon so we may continue to work together to make the Annick dukedom prosperous."

To Charlotte's surprise, the dowager's lips twitched into a grimace that could have resembled the start of a smile on another face.

At last, Mama Catherine spoke. "I move at the end of the week. You will be pleased to know my son shares your sentiments, as he requested my departure only yesterday."

"He did?" Charlotte was unable to keep the shock from her voice.

"Yes, he made it abundantly clear *you* are the Duchess of Annick." She sneered. "I'm relieved to see one of you still has sense. I will call upon you next Monday for our luncheon. I expect you to arrange our meal in the conservatory," Catherine instructed. "Now, if you'll excuse me."

With a twitch of her head, Catherine turned to carry on with whatever task she was about before Charlotte stumbled into her in the gallery.

While this moment was filled with the elation that she finally stood up to her mother-in-law, it was bittersweet. How different might her marriage have been had she known from the first day her mother-in-law wasn't the enemy? Then, it might not have changed anything, for Charlotte still would have needed to accustom herself to Catherine's harshness and criticisms. She would be a difficult woman to love, but Charlotte was determined to try.

Chapter 28

Before dawn could rouse Charlotte the next morning, incessant knocking at her bedchamber did. By the time she had wrapped her nightdress with a wrapping robe, Mary rushed into the room. Charlotte was relieved to see Drake was not abed, undoubtedly having slipped out some time in the early hours with inspiration ringing in his ears.

"Good gracious, Mary." Charlotte yawned, approaching her sister-in-law. "Whatever is the matter?"

"Oh, Charlotte. It's dreadful! I came as soon as I could dress. My maid woke me but half an hour ago with the news." Mary hopped in place, from one foot to another. "Drake duels at dawn!"

Charlotte braced herself against the bedpost. "Pardon?"

"Lord Stroud challenged him to a duel. Drake should have been given weeks to apologize, but it seems the duel is to be this morning! Oh, Charlotte, what are we to do?" Mary's eyes glistened, her eyelashes wet.

"He can't duel! He just can't," she protested. "Why did he not say something to me? No, we must stop him. He simply can't!"

"Well, he is! My maid said his horse is already gone from the stable." Mary bit her knuckles to stifle a sob.

"We can't do anything unless we know where it's held. What did your maid say?" Charlotte tugged Mary to her dressing room as she spoke.

"She didn't know anything aside from there being a duel."

"We must find out where it's being held. Let me dress. We must question the staff," Charlotte reassured, although she felt as frantic as Mary. "Who would know? More to the point, who would tell us the truth without feigning ignorance?"

"Does it matter? There's nothing we can do. He's already left. And women aren't allowed at duels." Mary covered her face with her hands.

"Hand me that hairpin. Yes, that's the one. I need you to rouse James the coachman while I finish dressing. Can you do that? Or find a servant who can?" Charlotte placed two calming hands on Mary's cheeks, willing herself to be in command of her faculties for both their sakes.

Mary nodded.

They had one hour before dawn to make haste. One hopeless hour. What could they achieve in so short of time? Charlotte had two choices: wallow or act. She could not sit around waiting for an uncertain ending. The least she could do was be there, even if she was too late to stop him from fighting.

Sometime later, James brought the carriage to a stop near a copse of leafless trees. He set down the steps himself and opened the door to hand down the duchess and Lady Mary.

It would have been faster to ride, but the coachman had insisted, just in case something untoward happened. Charlotte understood his meaning but refused to think more on it. Drake would be fine, she told herself. He had to be.

"Just through there, Your Grace. You should have a clear view of the hollow and will be hidden from view." James pointed to the tree line.

"But I told you to bring us directly to him," Charlotte protested, clasping Mary's hand for support.

"As much as I wish I could, I can't do that. You can't be seen, Your Grace," said the coachman.

Charlotte nodded, grim, and hurried with Mary to the edge of a crag. The sky was bright with a pre-dawn glow. They knelt at the ridge, shielded by the steep slope below them.

When they looked to the hollow, they could see the duel already underway. Charlotte gasped in horror. She'd arrived too late to stop them.

A handful of witnesses gathered around the sabreurs. A portly man stood near Winston, both men watching the progress of the sword play. Lord Stroud was no match for Drake's physique, but the man had undeniable skill. She covered her mouth when he parried Drake's attacks.

"Oh, Mary. This is all my fault. I'll be the death of him," said Charlotte.

"No, no, this is all my fault! Lord Stroud is retaliating because of me. I was selfish to think my actions would have no bearing on my family. I stomped on his foot when he proposed, you know," Mary confessed.

However humorous, Charlotte's concentration was on the field.

Lord Stroud possessed more skill with a sabre than Drake expected, but even so, the man struggled with its weight. Clearly, Stroud fenced, but likely with a foil rather than a sabre. Stroud's moves were fluid, his plan of attack concentrated, but Drake felt assured the man's reach was sluggish. Strength and agility were on Drake's side this day.

With these observations, Drake did not worry about the outcome of the duel. From his perspective, the duel was merely a formality in restoring Lord Stroud's honor. Stroud couldn't seriously mean to harm him.

When he and Winston had first arrived to the field, they had found Stroud, his lordship's valet, Mr. Kingston, a surgeon of questionable repute, and a handful of Stroud's pals waiting. Though Stroud's face looked like it'd been mauled by a lion from the damage of the wine glass shards, he didn't deserve sympathy.

Through the new gap in his front teeth, Stroud had lisped, "Here to make arrangements for your wife's thawing? I'll warm her for you."

Drake ignored the baiting.

Bartholomew, Drake's valet, helped the duke out of his riding cloak and readied him for battle. The anticipation of a match normally would have excited him. Today, it annoyed him. He didn't appreciate waking before dawn or leaving his wife's warm bed. Spending the morning reciting sentimental poetry from between the sheets held far more appeal.

Mr. Kingston approached. "Lord Stroud offers you this opportunity to apologize if you should wish to forego the duel. He's willing to accept the apology now."

The cad likely didn't know how to fence and had been hoping for pistols at dawn. Drake's laugh, a solitary *ha*, was loud enough for all to hear.

Neither peer was behaving particularly civil, as dueling etiquette dictated, but considering the company and the cause were equally uncivil, no one complained.

Within moments, they were in position, then in battle.

Lord Stroud lunged.

Drake parried and riposted.

Swords clashed. Feet danced.

Stroud advanced. Drake retreated.

Drake advanced. Stroud retreated.

Stroud's skill startled Drake. He hadn't anticipated the man to be an advanced fencer.

After a lengthy conversation of blades, Drake launched himself into a flunge, his signature move. Stroud stumbled backwards, parrying. That should have ended the duel.

Despite the opportunity to do so, Drake made a split-second decision not to disarm Stroud. Instead, he hesitated, then taunted the oaf, a mongoose against a venomous snake. If Stroud wanted honor restored, he'd have to earn it.

"Fight like a man," Stroud said, feinting a strike that Drake anticipated. "Can't you best me with your own weapon of choice?"

With a balestra, Drake lunged but didn't strike. Instead of threatening his target, he remained in prep. He advanced again, taunting.

Stroud riposted, foaming in anger at Drake's teasing. "Fight me!" Stroud demanded.

Stroud's nostrils flared as he lunged at Drake, his reach underestimated. Drake stepped aside, *inquartata*. Their swords locked.

Deflecting his opponent's sword, Drake spun away from reach.

Each stepping back, they faced each other, sneering.

"When I finish with you," Stroud said with a snarl, "I'll have my way with your wife. Then I'll see to your sister. She's ripe and nubile. I'll take her over your dead body, make a woman of her, blood spilt from two Mowbrahs in the same day."

The words were so cruel and unexpected, they sank fangs into Drake's skin. He advanced, hot with rage. And stepped into Stroud's trap. With a *passata sotto*, Stroud had his moment of victory as blade met flesh.

Stroud's sabre sliced across the duke's chest from sternum to shoulder.

Chapter 29

Drake staggered, surprised to see a red stain widening across his shirt.

Feeling the warm wetness spread across his chest, he growled. "Are you satisfied, Stroud? Is my blood enough for you?"

"I'll not be satisfied until you beg my pardon or disarm me." Stroud flung blood from his sabre onto the grass.

Dizziness swept over Drake as he watched Stroud nod to Mr. Kingston.

The fat fool of a second stepped forward and said, "At this time, I must ask if you will issue his lordship an apology."

Blinking against his reddening vision, Drake coughed a laugh. "I only apologize to gentlemen."

The duel resumed.

Drake wouldn't make the same mistake twice. Humbled by the consequences of his own arrogance, he made short work of the duel.

Drake feinted to invite an attack.

Predictably, Stroud parried and riposted, leaving him open for Drake's second intention.

The duke parried. Launching a counterattack, he caught Stroud's sabre at the guard.

At the twist of his wrist, Stroud cried out. The sabre dropped.

Stroud was disarmed.

Drake stumbled away, ignoring the man and his limp wrist.

Winston caught Drake before he collapsed. He wrapped Drake's arm over his shoulders. They reached the tree stump at the edge of the hollow, the duke protesting he could seat himself.

"Deuced arrogant fool," Winston said. "You could have disarmed him in seconds. What were you trying to accomplish?"

"Playing with my food like a deuced arrogant fool?" Drake mocked, intaking a sharp breath as he moved.

Winston frowned. "Stay still. Losing blood here, mate."

"Nothing a brandy can't cure. Need a clean shirt."

His valet made short but painful work of undressing the duke's torso. The surgeon rushed over to join them.

He knew if he looked down, he'd see sliced flesh and blood. It hurt like the devil.

Woozy, Drake closed his eyes.

Vaguely, he was aware of his valet Bart tipping a flask to his lips and encouraging him to drink. Drake sputtered but swallowed, a fire in his throat that spread into his chest.

He drifted out of consciousness.

An icy cloth swept across his bare flesh, startling him to awareness. Unsure how long he'd been unconscious, he fought for control over the grogginess. His eyelids were heavy, and his head pounded. His chest flamed with an excruciating pain and weight, as though someone stood on him. In his stupor, he questioned if Stroud had poisoned the blade, but no, the sensation had a tug more than a sting.

He almost chuckled — what a fabulous scene for his opera.

When he opened his eyes, he groaned to see the surgeon suturing him, stringing him with catgut just like his violin. Later, he'd need Mr. Taylor to summon his own physician; Lord only knew what this sawbones was doing to him.

The flask returned to his lips from an unseen hand. He greedily drank the liquid fire, feeling better already. Dizziness subsided.

He braved a glance around him. Winston and Bart stood next to him, both looking far more concerned than they should. It was only a little blood loss, after all. Lord Stroud and his cronies huddled not far, watching the show.

Nothing seemed unusual about the scene except the two stableboys running across the field towards them.

Had the surgeon given him laudanum? Was he hallucinating? He couldn't remember bringing grooms. Lord Stroud's men perhaps. Maybe inept assassins sent to finish him off.

He grunted at a menacing tug below his collarbone.

The surgeon cleaned the remaining blood from Drake's chest, then wrapped a long length of cloth around Drake's naked torso.

No sooner did the man step away and Drake attempt to sit up, then the two grooms arrived. One of the boys bull-rushed him.

For a moment, Drake thought he'd need to muster strength to defend himself. Then he saw his wife's face beneath the groom's cap. As the realization dawned on him, she leapt into his arms in a painfully tight embrace. He drew Charlotte to him for a hungry kiss, strength renewed by her presence.

A faint footfall crunching over dead brush sounded not far from him.

Stroud sniggered. "I *knew* you were a buggerer. Like father, like son. I wonder what your wife would say to find you in a tender embrace with a stableboy. Care to pay for my silence?"

Drake relinquished the kiss only long enough to quip, "Who's to say she doesn't encourage a bit of caudle-making? Learn to live a little, Stroud." With a smirk, he resumed his admiration of Charlotte's lips.

Only after he felt his wife had been thoroughly kissed did he get a good look at her, a vision of loveliness. With a dimpled smile, he kissed the tip of her nose.

Winston spoke first. "I never thought I would have an affinity for women in breeches, but these two lovelies have taught me otherwise. Shall we encourage a new fashion trend?"

Drake looked up to see his sister standing next to Winston and Bart, her face flushed under a groom's cap. However annoyed he should be to see his sister at a duel, he was far more relieved he hadn't been seeing double.

Lord Stroud and his men were halfway across the field already, gone and soon forgotten. The surgeon was nowhere to be seen.

Drake tightened his hold on Charlotte despite the throbbing of his chest. He refused to be an invalid. Testing his strength, he tried to sit up, groaning from the effort, a stabbing in his chest giving him pause. Charlotte, perched on his lap, protested, hugging him until he stopped moving.

Drake said to his audience, "I don't suppose the three of you would mind terribly if I had a few moments alone with this fetching stableboy?"

Just then, his carriage rolled towards them, James at the reins.

"Ah, I've never been so relieved to see my coachman. I amend my request. I'd like privacy with my wife inside the carriage. Mary, love, take my horse so Charlotte and I can have the carriage."

Mary's face turned rosier in response. "He's not side-saddled."

"Well, you're a groom, aren't you? Ride like a man."

Mary stared in horror.

James interrupted from the carriage. "Her ladyship may ride with me. No one'll be the wiser."

After Bart helped Drake into his riding cloak to shield from the chill air, and Winston helped situate him into the carriage despite Drake's protests, he settled next to Charlotte against the cushioned seats. Cautiously, he snaked his arm around her shoulders to pull her close, grunting from the pain.

His chest would be a reminder for a long time to come of the consequences of arrogance, consequences that could have been dire.

"What are you doing here, Charlotte? A duel is no place for you." Drake kissed her temple.

"My place is by your side." She nuzzled against him. "I only wish I had the opportunity to convince you that nothing was worth risking your life, especially not a silly insult from a nobody—hadn't we already decided we didn't care what others thought?"

"Ah, Charlotte," he murmured into her hair. "Not worth it, no, but there are unwritten rules for gentlemen. One can't decline a challenge. I wish you had stayed abed, waiting for my return. There was no need to expose yourself to this violence."

"I had to! I couldn't let you die over something so silly. I rushed here to stop the duel. I arrived too late, though, and I think I've made things worse."

"Worse? How could you ever make anything worse?" He asked.

"I kissed you wearing groom's clothing! That man and all his friends saw."

"The joke is on him, my love. No one could mistake you for a boy. Your, er, assets aren't disguised this time."

He waited for her to realize her bosom was attractively accentuated by the snug groom's coat. She hid her face against his shoulder.

"Know this," he said, lifting her chin to lock eyes, "I couldn't care less what Stroud or anyone else thinks. No one's opinion matters but yours. Are you disappointed to find Drake fought a duel rather than your composer apologizing to avoid it?"

"But you *are* my composer. One and the same. I love you, all of you, even the reckless parts, especially the reckless parts. And might I add, you did cut a dashing figure with the sabre." She giggled.

"Mmm. You say the sweetest things, my perfect duchess." He touched her cheek with bruised knuckles.

"No need to be perfect," she said. "I only want to be yours."

"Good, because I love you as you are." Drake traced her lower lip with his thumb, her cheek cradled in his palm.

He took a moment to admire her, smiling until she returned the expression. His eyes drifted lower, settling on her petite frame outlined by the breeches. Heavens, her legs were amazing. His moan of appreciation turned to a groan, his torso burning.

It wouldn't take much effort to play up the wound, he thought, given how much it really did pain him. What a perfect opportunity to be pampered by his wife, nursed back to health by her affectionate ministrations. Would she believe him if he said he needed her to hand bathe him? She wouldn't think him a tasteless rogue if he were injured, would she?

Charlotte ignored his roaming gaze. "Now, we must make something perfectly clear. Don't defend against insults again, not even if the insults are about me. I'll slay my own dragons, and I don't mind slaying yours, as well, if it comes to it. Repeat after me — we don't care what others think. We love ourselves and each other, and that's enough."

"Mmm. Slaying dragons. Will you do it wearing the groom's attire? Your legs look — "

The swift, playful kick to his shin took him by surprise.

"Oh my goodness!" Charlotte shrieked. "I didn't mean to kick you when you're down. I only meant — "

He drew her against him with a chuckle, but before he could kiss her, his wound protested. He grimaced and said instead, "Back to what you were saying about slaying dragons in breeches, my fetching heroine."

"Do be serious. This isn't a laughing matter. You could have died!"

"Against Stroud? Nonsense. Give me more credit than that. The only reason he touched me was my own arrogance. Are you certain you wouldn't rather have a happy ever after with your composer?"

"I want my happy ever after with *you*, arrogant fool that you are. Oh, Drake, you don't even know how much I love you, all of you, the rogue and the tender composer. I worried you'd die before I could tell you." Charlotte placed her hand to his bandaged chest, then cringed when he winced.

"So, how much?" he asked. When she looked at him in confusion, he smirked. "Well? Tell me how much you love me."

"You're incorrigible." She huffed. "It doesn't matter now because you're not going to die."

"My wound could fester. I could be at death's door. Once infection sets in, I'm a goner. You had better count the ways while you have a chance. Start at reason number one hundred and work your way from there."

She blushed, looking at him beneath sooty eyelashes. "Let's leave it at this. I love you enough to wear breeches to stop a duel."

"Convincing. Now for reason number ninety-nine. What if this leaves a scar? You know how vain I am. Think I could still be lovable with a scar?"

"It'll make you more dashing." She kissed the hollow of his neck, exposed above the bandage.

"Mmm. Reason ninety-eight next. Love me enough for a romp in the carriage on the way home?" he teased.

"Drake!" she exclaimed. "Didn't you say you could be at death's door?"

Drake waggled his eyebrows. "Then we better make it quick. Just in case."

Epilogue

April 1791

The curtain fell for intermission.

Rising from their seats in the duke's box at King's Theatre in London, Charlotte and Drake followed their family into the crowded corridor. A din of voices greeted the couple.

A few doors down, one gentleman said to his companion, "Incredible first act. Breathtaking."

"I hope the composer will consider conducting the next showing himself," a lady nearby said as she joined her friends in the adjacent box.

Elsewhere, a nasal tone rebuked, "It's too sentimental to be considered tasteful."

"Yes, we will see it every night if you wish, darling," assured a husky voice to his wife in the next box.

"And you say it is his first opera? I do hope we see more of his work," commented someone else.

Mixed accolades and criticisms greeted Charlotte and Drake as they stood with their family, celebrating the opening night of Drake's first opera.

The crowning glory of the evening was that Charlotte and Drake had arranged for all proceeds to be donated to the Foundling Hospital. Drake had wanted to do something for the people, and

Charlotte had the idea for the hospital in honor of Sebastian's sister, once an orphan herself. The Foundling Hospital wouldn't be the only place to benefit, as they'd collaborated with the Annick steward to set up multiple charitable accounts. With each performance, profits would be distributed across the country. Drake's hope was not solely about the redistribution of profits but more pointedly about bringing the music to the people, taking it out of the drawing rooms and theatres to make it accessible to all, performed for the public. But one step at a time, as it was only opening night of his operatic debut. It would take time for word to spread, if indeed his style was accepted.

Tonight was only the beginning.

Not long after they stepped out from their box were they accosted by members of the *beau monde*, all wishing to bask in the couple's success, for both received compliments on this most auspicious evening, Charlotte for hosting the squeeze of the Season the night before and Drake for shocking them all with an opera that defied musical conventions.

Giving him a moment to enjoy the adoration of the crowd, Charlotte stepped away to join her sister, who was standing with Aunt Hazel, Sebastian, Cousin Walter, and Papa Cuthbert.

Slipping her arm through Lizbeth's, she asked, "Is the corridor too hot? Should we return to the box?"

"Oh no, that's not necessary. I feel superb," Lizbeth reassured Charlotte.

"I'm surprised you came to London. I was confident you'd stay home for your confinement." Charlotte patted her sister's arm.

"And miss seeing family and the opening night of the opera? No, I'm only five months *enceinte*, hardly ready for confinement. Everyone is too busy ogling over Sebastian's marriage to notice his wife is in a delicate state, not that I feel remotely delicate. Besides, Sebastian said he couldn't possibly face the Season without me." Lizbeth's eyes twinkled, her smile warm.

Being in the family way suited Lizbeth. As difficult as it was for Charlotte to believe the moody Sebastian could bring her sister happiness, she recognized far more than contentment in her sister's face. Lizbeth radiated the joy Charlotte herself felt, as deeply in love with her own husband.

Charlotte said, "I'm so pleased Aunt Hazel, Papa, and Walter will be spending the summer in Northumberland. Are they staying until baby's arrival?"

"Yes, of course. It will be good to have them with us, especially when Sebastian forbids me to leave home. My midwife is already conspiring with him to hold me hostage inside the castle. I must enjoy these lively times while I can, Charlotte!" Lizbeth laughed, touching a hand to her increasing waistline. "I've been meaning to tell you, you're positively glowing."

"Am I?" Charlotte blushed. "It comes from being happy, I suppose."

"And are you? Happy, that is?" Lizbeth asked, lacing her fingers with Charlotte's to offer an affectionate squeeze.

"Oh, I am, Lizbeth. I truly am. My life is a dream come true. It's difficult to believe Drake and I will have been married a full year at the end of this Season."

Before Lizbeth could reply, Drake joined them.

"May I steal my wife?" he asked Lizbeth with a roguish wink.

Lizbeth slipped her arm from Charlotte's so Drake could take her place, but not before she leaned closer to him, a hand on his elbow. "Thank you, Drake," Lizbeth whispered. "Thank you for bringing my sister happiness."

Though Charlotte didn't hear all Lizbeth whispered to him, she caught enough to know that Liz bestowed the highest compliment of the evening, that of familial love.

As soon as Lizbeth was safely returned to Sebastian's side, Drake escorted his wife back to the box before the chimes sounded. Drawing the curtains on one side, he pulled her to him with a kiss.

Charlotte pushed him away with fervor. "Someone will see!" she rebuked.

"Good," he replied, brushing his lips against her cheek. "Let's cause a scandal, Charlotte."

She relaxed against him and returned his affections, willing the world to see what happiness looked like. When he loosened his hold, Charlotte placed both hands on his cheeks and fell into his blue eyes, darkened by the shadows of their box.

"I never expected my life to turn out like this," she said.

"That sounds ominous."

"Happy ever after, silly. You've shown me a part of life I never dreamt possible."

"On second thought, I like where this is going." He chuckled. "Now, tell me what part of life you never thought possible."

"Love, of course." She kissed the tip of his nose, as he so often did to her.

Only when the box door opened did he release her from his embrace, whispering as he did so, "You are love itself, my duchess, but please don't kick my shin when I kiss you during the third act."

And thus, this tale ends with a new beginning. The duke and duchess found their happy ever after, and in their eyes, their imperfections were nothing short of perfection. Even in the darkest of times — or the darkest of opera boxes — the light of love would guide them.

A Note from the Author

Dear Reader,

Thank you for reading this book. Supporting indie writers who brave self-publishing is important and appreciated. I hope you'll continue reading my novels, as I have many more titles to come. To learn more about the era, traditions, etiquette, and more, consider visiting my research blog, a new post added every one to three months: www.paullettgolden.com/bookresearch.

I humbly request you review this book with an honest opinion in as many venues as possible, be it Goodreads, Amazon, or otherwise.

One way to support writers you've enjoyed reading, indie or otherwise, is to share their work with friends, family, book clubs, etc. Lend books, share books, exchange books, recommend books, and gift books, be it personally, to a library, in a Free Little Library, or to a secondhand bookstore. If you especially enjoyed a writer's book, lend it to someone to read in case they might find a new favorite author in the book you've shared.

Connect with me online:
www.paullettgolden.com
www.facebook.com/paullettgolden
www.instagram.com/paullettgolden
www.twitter.com/paullettgolden

You'll also find me at such places as Goodreads, Bookbub, Amazon's Author Central, and LibraryThing.

All the best,
Paullett Golden

If you enjoyed *The Duke and The Enchantress*, read on for a sneak peek of the next book in The Enchantresses.

The Baron and
The Enchantress

Miss Lilith Chambers stepped onto the stone bridge with renewed determination. She swallowed against the brewing anxiety. They would not best her today, she resolved, nor best her again.

She strode across the bridge that separated the parish from Sir Graham's property, chin held high, spine rigid, and bag braced against her chest, marching more confidently than she felt.

And then she saw them approach. They saw her. Her grip tightened around the bag.

Two ladies on horseback cantered down the path ahead. The bobbing of the plumes on their cylindrical hats would be comical in any other situation, but Lilith didn't laugh. One of the ladies smirked and flicked her reins, urging the mount to pick up the pace.

Lilith hastened her steps. The quickening of her stride spurred them to match theirs.

Just as she reached the dirt path after the bridge, the two riders veered towards her. One woman with bouncing blonde ringlets tittered as her mare darted forward, nearly knocking Lilith off her feet. Lilith wobbled backwards onto the muddy river bank to avoid being trampled.

"I can't imagine what could have startled my horse," said the woman, laughing to her companion.

"Must have been a distasteful horsefly," the other woman added.

The two ladies continued towards the estate without a backward glance. As usual, they did not acknowledge Lilith with their eyes or words, rather loudly declared their feelings with actions.

Lilith stepped back onto the dirt path, wiping her muddy boots against the stones of the bridge and surveying the damage to her dress. Could be worse, she concluded. Only her dress and shoes were muddied. At least she held her own and hadn't careened into the river again, and best yet, her bag of midwifery herbs and tools remained clean and safe.

A smug smile tugged at the corners of her mouth. She hadn't given them a wide berth, rather stood her ground, challenging them to push her off the path, which they did, but she smiled proudly that only the horses had forced her movement. Orphan or not, Lilith would bow to no one, least of all those leeches who called themselves aristocrats.

She resumed her trek back into town with a confident spring in her step, despite the mud-drenched hem of her dress clinging to her half-boots. All in all, a successful morning, the quiet victory at the bridge, and before that, the visit to Arbor House, the home of Lady Graham.

That morning, Lilith had seen to the health of the twins, nearly one-year of age, and to Lady Graham's growing belly, ripe with her third child. Lady Graham was the only peer of the realm in Allshire parish who did not treat Lilith as a pariah. Despite Lady Graham's blue-blood lineage, she respected Lilith, and Lilith esteemed her in return. Since Lilith succeeded where several doctors had previously failed — aiding Lady Graham in carrying a child to term — the woman showed Lilith the utmost deference as the parish's midwife.

The remaining walk through town could only be described as pleasant, the sun drying the previous three days' worth of rain. The milliner and her husband waved from their shop window as she rounded the bend into town. Other familiar faces smiled greetings. Even a group of farmers walking out of the Black Bull Inn nodded to her.

Through a lifetime of effort, she had earned her place in the parish, a trusted member of the community.

Just past the church, her cottage stood, a welcoming sight for tired eyes. She loved the cottage with its walled terrace and herb garden in front, hilly paddock in the back, and wisteria climbing the stone façade of the one and a half story building. True, it was small inside with only a single parlor and kitchen down, and a set of curved wooden stairs from the kitchen leading to the bedchamber upstairs, but it was all she needed. It was home.

Her first order of business was to change into a fresh dress and wash the caked mud from her dress before it hardened. At least that was her plan until she saw her visitor.

The Reverend Harold Sands, fourteenth rector of Allshire parish, paced in the terrace. She knew at the agitated sight of him that he had likely waited for some time, as he always did. His brows furrowed over a frown twitching with impatience.

With a sigh, she approached.

"Miss Chambers!" exclaimed the rector, wiping away all evidence of agitation. "What a lucky coincidence that you should arrive just as I decided to pay you a visit." He scurried to greet her at the gate, his youthful face lighting with exaggerated, and feigned, exuberance.

"Yes, a lucky coincidence, I'm sure," Lilith replied, shifting her bag under one arm so she could reach for his outstretched hand. "How are you, Harry? Would you like a cuppa?"

"Your kindness knows no bounds! I would love tea," he released her hand and tugged at his forelock before following her to the front stable-door of her cottage.

Lilith opened the door and invited the rector inside, feeling more obligated than cordial. Closing only the bottom half of the stable-door, she left the top open for the breeze and the welcome view of the deep purple wisteria trailing up the terrace wall. Setting her bag next to the door, she invited the Reverend Sands to sit at the table while she went to the kitchen to setup a tea tray.

With a hardy stoking of the dying embers in the kitchen grate, she managed to rouse the remnants enough to heat the kettle. A quick glance to the parlor won her the view of Harold's expectant and watchful visage.

Harold's visits weren't quite daily occurrences, but they felt that way, especially when Lilith had plans and little time for his flirtations. While he appeared to believe their union inevitable, she resented his determination to wed her and his abuse of power.

"Packed for your grand adventure?" he asked, raising his voice more than necessary given the short distance from the parlor to the kitchen.

She replied, her eyes trained on the kettle, "I will this evening. I leave at first light, so I can no longer procrastinate."

Stealing a handful of currant cakes from the basket she made for the orphanage, she set up the tray.

"I do wish you would reconsider my offer before parting. Think how grand to arrive at your brother's home an engaged woman!" Harold exclaimed.

Lilith inhaled through her nose and exhaled through her teeth as she poured the boiling water into the teapot. The tea leaves steeped while she gripped the edge of the counter, answering him with silence.

He didn't act the least perturbed by her silence. On the contrary, his eyes twinkled malevolently when she carried the tray to the table. After a dash of milk in his cup, she poured the tea, focusing her eyes on her task rather than his stare.

He had always been her spiritual advisor, the single person to whom she confessed her troubles, but her confessions over the past year had been twisted from spiritual to personal confidences, which was never how she intended them to be taken. Everything she had told him about the recent discoveries of her identity had led to persistent presses for marriage on his part, all in the guise of helping her.

While he may turn out to be a devoted husband, and while she may become content as his wife, she resented his pity and questioned his motives.

"Now, Harry," she admonished lightheartedly, "Let's not revisit that now."

Sitting across from him, she hid her displeasure behind a steaming cup.

"You can't possibly be happy at the prospect of spending time with *him*. I know how you feel about aristocracy." He cast her a knowing glance. "And I cannot imagine his wife's family being kind to you." His hand slid across the table to take hers.

She ignored the outstretched hand, averting her eyes back to the contents of her cup. "I'm afraid I can't see that," she said, returning her cup to its saucer with a clink. "I'm positive they'll welcome me. I believe they want me there as a family member, not a servant."

At least that's what she hoped.

It had been a shock earlier that year to learn she had a half-brother, the legitimate heir of her father. While she had the privilege many orphans didn't of learning her family identity, that privilege came with the rude discovery that not only had her father been an earl, but she had been the by-blow of a premarital affair with a groom's daughter. The only person unperturbed by the details was her brother who was determined to treat her as a legitimate sister regardless of the facts.

"But what of *her* family?" Harold huffed, pulling his hand back to his side of the table. "They're members of the peerage! Has your brother been truthful with them about your lineage? I cannot believe they would accept an invitation to stay in the same house with you if they knew. Your visit will be a lie, and that is hardly Christian behavior."

Leaning forward in his chair, he tapped his cup with a dirty fingernail.

With another huff, he altered his plea. "Be sensible, Miss Chambers, Lilith, oh, my dearest Lilith," he implored. "Be sensible and marry me so we can remove the impediments to your happiness. If you delayed your departure, we could marry before your visit. You would go as a respectable woman."

"Stop pressing me," she snapped, exasperated. "You're my closest confidante so I appreciate your offer, but *no*."

He shook his head. "You're not being sensible. Who will ever offer you what I'm willing to provide? There is not an honorable soul who would offer you marriage, not once they find out you've spent your life in an orphanage." Lowering his voice, he said conspiratorially, "Not once they learn you're illegitimate."

About the Author

Celebrated for her complex characters, realistic conflicts, and sensual portrayal of love, Paullett Golden
writes historical romance for intellectuals. Her novels,
set primarily in Georgian England, challenge the
genre's norm by starring characters loved for their
imperfections and idiosyncrasies. The writing aims
for historical immersion into the social mores and
nuances of Georgian England. Her plots explore
human psyche, mental and physical trauma, and personal convictions. Her stories show love overcoming
adversity. Whatever our self-doubts, *love will out*.

Paullett Golden completed her post-graduate
work at King's College London, studying Classic
British Literature. Her Ph.D. is in Composition and
Rhetoric, her M.A. in British Literature from the

Enlightenment through the Victorian era, and her B.A. in English. Her specializations include creative writing and professional writing. She has served as a University Professor for nearly three decades and is a seasoned keynote speaker, commencement speaker, conference presenter, workshop facilitator, and writing retreat facilitator.

As an ovarian cancer survivor, she makes each day count, enjoying an active lifestyle of Spartan racing, powerlifting, hiking, antique car restoration, drag racing, butterfly gardening, competitive shooting, and gaming. Her greatest writing inspirations, and the reasons she chose to write in the clean historical romance genre, are Jane Austen and Charlotte Brontë.

Connect online
paullettgolden.com
Facebook.com/paullettgolden
Twitter.com/paullettgolden
Instagram.com/paullettgolden

Printed in Great Britain
by Amazon